Born in England in 1970, Santa Montefiore grew up in Hampshire. She is married to historian Simon Sebag-Montefiore. They live with their two children, Lily and Sasha, in London. Visit her at www.santamontefiore. co.uk and sign up for her newsletter.

Praise for *Last Voyage of the Valentina*:

'Santa Montefiore brilliantly captures the intrigue and skulduggery of a country at war in a very absorbing romance' *Red Magazine*

'Santa Montefiore's world of Italian peasants and partisans, Nazis and aristocrats is flamboyant and suspenseful. Anyone who likes Joanne Harris or Mary Wesley will love Montefiore's atmospheric sixth romance' *Mail on Sunday*

Praise for Santa Montefiore:

'Santa Montefiore is the new Rosamunde Pilcher'
Daily Mail

'A superb storyteller of love and death in romantic places in fascinating times – her passionate novels are already bestsellers across Europe and I can see why. Her plots are sensual, sensitive and complex, her characters are unforgettable life forces, her love stories are desperate yet uplifting – and one laughs as much as one cries'
Plum Sykes, *Vogue*

'A gripping romance ...  g is beautiful' *Daily Telegraph*

Last Voyage
of the Valentina

Last Voyage of the Valentina

Santa Montefiore

SIMON &
SCHUSTER

London · New York · Sydney · Toronto · New Delhi

A CBS COMPANY

First published in Great Britain in 2005 by Hodder & Stoughton
An Hachette Livre Company

This paperback edition first published in 2014 by Simon & Schuster UK Ltd
A CBS COMPANY

7 9 10 8

Simon & Schuster UK Ltd
1st Floor
222 Gray's Inn Road
London WC1X 8HB

www.simonandschuster.co.uk

Simon & Schuster Australia, Sydney
Simon & Schuster India, New Delhi

A CIP catalogue record for this book is available from the British Library

Paperback ISBN 978-1-47113-200-1
Ebook ISBN 978-1-47113-201-8

Typeset by Hewer Text UK Ltd, Edinburgh
Printed and bound in Great Britain by
CPI Group (UK) Ltd, Croydon CR0 4YY

To my aunt, Naomi Dawson

Acknowledgements

Thank you to Ian Chapman, Suzanne Baboneau and their brilliant team at Simon & Schuster for republishing this book with a beautiful new cover, and to my agent, Sheila Crowley for her wise counsel.

Prologue

Italy 1945

It was almost dark when they reached the palazzo. The sky was a turquoise blue, fading into pale orange just above the tree line where the sun was setting. The stone walls rose up, sheer and impenetrable, to quixotic towers, and a tattered flag drooped on its pole. Once, when the winds of Fate had blown more favorably, it had danced on the breeze with vitality, dominating all around it. Now ivy was gradually choking those walls to death, like the slow poisoning of an old *principessa,* whose breath now rattled up from her belly in fits and starts. Memories of her celebrated past, that lay within the fabric of the ramparts, were evaporating beyond recognition and recovery, and a foul smell emanated from her bowels where decay had set in, along with the putrefying foliage of the wild gardens. The stench was overpowering. There was a sharp edge to the wind, as if winter resisted the call of spring and clung on with icy fingers. Or perhaps winter lingered there, in that house alone, and those icy fingers belonged to death, who now came calling.

They did not speak. They knew what they had to do. Bound together by anger, pain, and a deep regret, they had vowed to seek revenge. A golden light glowed from a window at the back of the palazzo, but the thickness of the encroaching forest, the overgrown bushes and shrubs, prevented their reaching it. They had to risk entering from the front.

It was silent but for the wind in the trees. Not even the crickets braved the malevolence that surrounded the place, choosing to chirrup further down the hill where it was warm.

The two assassins were used to creeping about. They had both fought in the war. Now they were united again against a very different evil, one that had touched them personally, beyond all reason, and they had come to eliminate it.

Without making a sound they climbed in through a window left carelessly ajar. They made their way across the shadows. Silently like cats. Their black clothes allowing them to blend with the night. When they reached the room where the light melted through the crack beneath the door, they paused and stared at each other. Their eyes shone like marbles; their expressions grave, resolute. Neither felt fear, just anticipation and a grim inevitability.

When the door opened their victim looked up and smiled. He knew why they had come. He had been expecting them. He was ready and he wasn't afraid to die. They would see that killing him would do nothing to ease their pain. They didn't know that, of course; otherwise they would not have come. He wanted to offer them a drink. He wanted to enjoy the moment. To prolong it. But they were eager to get on with it and get away. His cool affability was sickening, his smile that of an old friend. They wanted to slice it off his face with a knife. He sensed their offense and it made him grin all the more. Even in death he'd smile. They'd never be rid of him and of what he had done. What he had taken from them he could never give back. He had won at their loss, and the guilt that would eat away at them would be his final victory.

The blade of the knife glinted in the golden light of the lamp. They wanted him to see it. They wanted him to anticipate it and fear it, but he did not. He would die willingly, joyfully. He would take pleasure from his pain as he took pleasure now from theirs. They looked at each other and nodded. He closed his eyes and lifted his chin, exposing his white neck like that of an innocent lamb.

'Kill me, but don't forget that I killed you first!' he gloated, his voice resonating with triumph.

When the blade sliced through his throat, a gush of blood spurted over the floor and walls, turning them a rich, glistening crimson. He slumped forward.

The one with the knife stood back while the other kicked the lifeless body to the ground so that he lay face up, his neck a crude, gaping gash of flesh. Still he smiled. Even in death he smiled.

'Enough!' the knifeman shouted, turning to leave. 'We have done enough. It was a matter of honour.'

'It was more than honour to me.'

The First Portrait

1

London 1971

'She's enjoying the attentions of that young man again,' said Viv, standing on the deck of her house boat. Although it was a balmy spring evening, she pulled her tasseled shawl about her shoulders and took a long drag of her cigarette.

'Not spying again, darling!' said Fitz with a wry smile.

'One can't help noticing the comings and goings of that girl's lovers.' Viv narrowed her hooded eyes and inhaled through dilated nostrils.

'Anyone would think you were jealous,' Fitz commented, grimacing as he took a sip of cheap French wine. In all the years he had been Viv's friend and agent she had never once bought a bottle of good wine.

'I'm a writer. It's my business to be curious about people. Alba's engaging. She's a very selfish creature, but one can't help being drawn to her. The ubiquitous moth to the flame. Though, in my case, not a moth at all but a rather beautifully dressed butterfly.' She wandered across the deck and draped herself over a chair, spreading her blue and pink caftan about her like silken wings. 'Still, I enjoy her life. It'll do for a book one day, when we're no longer friends. I think Alba's like that. She enjoys people, then moves on. In our case, it shall be I who moves on. By then, the dramas of her life will no longer entertain me and, besides, I'll have grown bored of the Thames too. My old bones will ache from the damp, and the creaking and bumping will keep me up at night. Then I shall buy a small château in France and retire to obscurity, fame having become a bore too.' She sucked in her cheeks and grinned at Fitz. But Fitz was no longer listening, although it was his job to.

'Do you think they pay for it?' he said, putting his hands on the railing and looking down into the muddy water of the Thames. Beside him, Sprout, his old springer spaniel, lay sleeping on a blanket.

'Certainly not!' she retorted. 'Her father owns the boat. She's not having to fork out twelve pounds a week in rent, I assure you.'

'Then she's simply liberated.'

'Just like everyone else of her generation. Following the herd. It bores me. I was before my time, Fitzroy. I took lovers and smoked cannabis long before the Albas of this world knew of the existence of either. Now I prefer bog standard Silva Thins and celibacy. I'm fifty, too old to be a slave to fashion. It's all so frivolous and childish. Better to set my mind on higher things. You may be a good ten years younger than me, Fitzroy, but I can tell the world of fashion bores you too.'

'I don't think Alba would bore me.'

'But you, my dear, would bore her, eventually. You might think you're a swaggering Lothario, Fitzroy, but you'd meet your match in Alba. She isn't like other girls. I'm not saying you'd have trouble bedding her, but keeping her, now that's a very different story. She likes variety. Her lovers don't last long. I've seen them come and go. It's always the same, they skip up the gangplank; then, when it's all over, they plod off like ill-treated mongrels. She'd have you for dinner then spit you out like a chicken bone, and that would be a shock, wouldn't it, darling? I bet no one's ever done that to you before. It's called karma. What goes around, comes around. Pay you back for breaking so many hearts. Anyway, at your age, you should be looking for your third wife, not a transitory thrill. You should be settling down. Set your heart on one woman and keep it there. She's fiery because she's half Italian.'

'Ah, that explains the dark hair and honey skin.'

Viv looked at him askance and her thin lips extended into an even thinner smile.

'But those very pale eyes, strange . . .' He sighed, no longer noticing the taste of cheap wine.

'Her mother was Italian. She died when Alba was born. In a car crash, I think. Has a horrid stepmother and a bore for a father. Navy, you know. Still there, the old fossil. Has had the same desk job since the war, I suspect. Commutes every day, very dreary. Captain Thomas Arbuckle, and he's definitely a Thomas and not a Tommy. Not like you, who are more of a Fitz than a Fitzroy, though I do love the name Fitzroy and shall continue to use it regardless. No wonder Alba rebelled.'

'Her father might be a bore, but he's a rich bore.' Fitz ran his eyes over the shiny wooden houseboat that gently rocked from the motion of the tide. Or from Alba's lovemaking. The thought made his stomach cramp competitively.

'Money doesn't bring happiness. You should know that, Fitzroy.'

Fitz stared into his glass a moment, reflecting on his own fortune that had brought him only avaricious wives and expensive divorces.

'Does she live alone?'

'She used to live with one of her half sisters, but it

didn't work out. I can't imagine the girl's easy to live with, God bless her. The trouble with you, Fitzroy, is that you fall in love much too easily. If you could keep control of your heart, life would be a lot simpler for you. You could just bed her and get her out of your system. Ah, about time too! You're late!' she exclaimed as her nephew Wilfrid hurried down the pontoon with his girlfriend Georgia in tow, full of apologies. Viv could be quite fearsome when they showed up late for bridge.

The *Valentina* was a houseboat unlike any other on Cheyne Walk. The curve of the prow was pretty, upturned, coy as if she were trying to contain a knowing smile. The house itself was painted blue and white with round windows and a balcony where pots spilled over with flowers in springtime and leaks let in the rain during the winter months. Like a face that betrays the life it has lived, so the eccentric dip in the line of the roof and the charming slope of the bow, like a rather imperious nose, revealed that perhaps she had lived many lives. The overriding characteristic of the *Valentina,* therefore, was her mystery. Like a grande dame who would never be seen without her makeup, the *Valentina* would not reveal what lay beneath her paint. Her mistress, however, loved her not for her unusual features, or her charm or indeed her uniqueness. Alba Arbuckle loved her boat for a very different reason.

'God, Alba, you're beautiful!' Rupert sighed, burying his face in her softly perfumed neck. 'You taste of sugared almonds.' Alba giggled, thinking him absurd, but unable to resist the sensation of his bristles that scratched and tickled and his hand that had already found its way past her blue suede clog boots and up her Mary Quant skirt. She wriggled with pleasure and lifted her chin.

'Don't talk, you fool. Kiss me.'

This he did, determined to please her. He was heartened that she had suddenly come alive in his arms after a sulky supper in Chelsea. He pressed his lips to hers, relieved that as long as he entertained her tongue she couldn't use it to abuse him. Alba had a way of saying the most hurtful things through the sweetest, most beguiling, smile. And yet, those pale grey eyes of hers, like a moor on a misty winter morning, aroused a strange kind of pity that was disarming. Drew a man in. Made him yearn to protect her. To love her was easy, to keep her unlikely. But along with the other hopefuls who walked the well-trodden deck of the *Valentina*, he couldn't help but try.

Alba opened her eyes as he unbuttoned her blouse and took a nipple in his mouth. She looked up through the skylight to wispy pink clouds and the first twinkle of a star. Overwhelmed by the unexpected beauty of the dying day she momentarily let down her guard and her spirit was at once filled with sadness. It flooded her being and brought tears to those pale grey eyes, tears that stung. Her loneliness gnawed and ached, and nothing seemed to cure it. Appalled by the ill timing of such weakness she wound her legs around her lover and rolled over so that she sat on top, kissing and biting and clawing him like a wild cat. Rupert was stunned but more excited than ever. He eagerly ran his hands up her naked thighs to discover she wore no pants. Her buttocks lay smooth and exposed for him to caress with impatient fingers. Then he was inside her and she was riding him vigorously, as if aware only of the pleasure and not of the man who was providing it. Rupert gazed upon her in awe, longing to put his mouth to her lips that were slightly parted and bruised. She looked wanton and yet, in spite of her lack of inhibition, she possessed a vulnerability that made him yearn to hold her close.

Soon Rupert's thoughts were lost in the excitement of their lovemaking. He closed his eyes and surrendered to his desire, no longer lucid enough to contemplate her lovely face. They writhed and rolled over the piles of discarded clothes on the bed until they exploded onto the floor with a thud, out of breath and laughing. She looked at his surprised face with eyes that shone and said with a throaty chuckle, 'What did you expect? The Virgin Mary?'

'That was wonderful. You're an angel,' he sighed, kissing her forehead. She raised her eyebrows and laughed at him.

'I do think you're absurd, Rupert. God would throw me out of Heaven for misbehaving.'

'Then that is not the Heaven for me.'

Suddenly her attention was diverted by a brown scroll of paper that had been dislodged from between the wooden slats under the bed. She couldn't reach from where she was lying, so she pushed Rupert away and crawled around to the other side. She stretched her arm beneath the bed.

'What is it?' he asked, blinking at her through a post-coital daze.

'I don't know,' she replied. As she stood up, she grabbed her cigarette packet and lighter from the bedside table and threw them at him. 'Light me one, will you?' Then she sat on the edge of the bed and slowly unfurled the scroll of paper.

Rupert didn't smoke. In fact, he loathed cigarettes, but not wanting to appear gauche, he did as she asked, throwing himself onto the bed beside her and running an appreciative hand down her back. She stiffened. Without looking at him she said, 'I've enjoyed you, Rupert. But now I want to be alone.'

'What is it?' he asked, astounded that she could suddenly turn so cold.

'I said, I want to be alone.' For a moment he was unsure how to react. No woman had ever treated him like that. He felt humiliated. When he saw that she wasn't going to change her mind, he reluctantly began to dress, clutching at the intimacy they had shared only moments before.

'Will I see you again?' He was aware that he sounded desperate.

She shook her head, irritated. 'Just go!'

He did up his shoelaces. She still hadn't looked at him. Her attention was entirely captivated by the scroll. It was as if he had already gone.

'Well, I'll just let myself out then,' he mumbled.

She lifted her eyes to the glass doors that gave on to the upper deck and stared at the pink evening sky, now dissolving into night. She did not hear the door slam or Rupert's heavy footsteps as he trod gloomily up the gangplank, only the whisper of a voice she thought she had forgotten.

'Oh dear! Someone doesn't look very happy,' commented Fitz as Rupert made his way to Chelsea Embankment and disappeared beneath the street lamps. His comment suspended their game of bridge for a moment. Sprout cocked his ears and raised his drooping eyes before closing them again with a sigh.

'Well, she does get through them, darling,' said Viv, curling a stray wisp of blond hair behind her ear. 'She's like a black widow.'

'I thought they ate their mates,' said Wilfrid. Fitz

contemplated that delicious thought before placing a card on the table with a snap.

'Who are we talking about?' asked Georgia, crinkling her nose at Wilfrid.

'Viv's neighbor,' he replied.

'She's a tart,' added Viv caustically, winning the trick and swiping it over to her side of the table.

'I thought you were friends.'

'We are, Fitzroy. I love her in spite of her faults. After all, we all have them, don't we?' She grinned and flicked ash into a fluorescent green dish.

'Not you, Viv. You're perfect.'

'Thank you, Fitzroy,' she replied, then turned to Georgia and added with a wink, 'I pay him to say that.'

Fitz glanced out of the little round window. The deck of the *Valentina* was still and quiet. He imagined the beautiful Alba lying naked on her bed, flushed and smiling, with curves and mounds in all the right places, and was momentarily distracted from the game.

'Wake up, Fitz!' said Wilfrid, snapping his fingers. 'What planet are you on?'

Viv placed her cards on the table and sat back. She took a drag of her cigarette and exhaled with a loud puff. Gazing upon him with eyes made heavy from drink and the excesses of life, she said, 'Oh, the same sad planet as so many other foolish men!'

Alba stared at the portrait sketched in pastels on the scroll of brown paper and felt a rush of emotion. It was as if she were looking into a mirror, but one that increased the loveliness of her image. The face was oval, like hers, with fine cheekbones and a strong, determined jaw, but the eyes weren't hers at all. They were almond-shaped, mossy brown in colour, a mixture of laughter and a deep, unfathomable sadness. They held her attention, stared right back at her and through her and, when she moved, they followed her. She gazed into them for a long while, swallowed up in hopes and dreams that never bore fruit. Although the mouth only hinted at a smile, the whole face seemed to open with happiness like a sunflower. Alba's stomach twisted with longing. For the first time in as long as she could remember, she was staring into the face of her mother. At the bottom of the picture, written in Latin, were the words *Valentina 1943, dum spiro, ti amo*. It was signed in ink *Thomas Arbuckle*. Alba reread those words a dozen times until they blurred with her tears. *'While I breathe, I love you.'*

Alba had learned Italian as a child. In an unusual moment of charity her stepmother, the Buffalo, had suggested she take lessons in order to maintain some contact with her Mediterranean roots, roots that in every other way the woman had tried to eradicate. After all, Alba's mother had been the love of her father's life. And what a great love it had been. Her stepmother was all too aware of the shadow Valentina cast over her marriage. Unable to erase so powerful a memory, all she could do was attempt to smother it. So Valentina's name was simply never mentioned. They had never travelled to Italy. Alba knew none of her mother's relatives, and her father avoided her questions, so she had long since given up asking. As a child she had shrunk into an isolated world of patchwork facts that she had managed to sew together by devious means. She would retreat into that world and derive comfort from the invented images of her beautiful mother on the shores of the sleepy Italian town where she had met and fallen in love with her father during the war.

Thomas Arbuckle had been handsome then; Alba

had seen photographs. In his naval uniform he had cut quite a dash. Sandy hair and pale eyes and a cheeky, confident grin that the Buffalo had managed, with the sheer weight of her forceful personality, to reduce to a disgruntled scowl. Jealous of the houseboat he had bought and named after Valentina, the Buffalo had never set foot on its deck, referring to it as 'that boat' and not by its name. *The Valentina* conjured up memories of cypress trees and crickets, olive groves and lemons, and a love so great that no amount of stamping and snorting could denigrate it.

Alba had never felt she truly belonged in her father's house. Her half siblings were physical reflections of their parents but she was dark and alien, like her mother. Her half siblings rode horses, picked blackberries, and played bridge, but she dreamed of the Mediterranean and olive groves. No amount of shouting at her stepmother and father had extracted the truth or compelled them to take her to Italy where she might get to know her real family. So she had moved into the houseboat that carried her mother's sacred name. There she felt Valentina's ethereal presence, heard her voice in the rise and fall of the tides a mere whisper away, and cocooned herself in her love.

She lay on the bed, beneath the skylight through which the stars now glimmered in their hundreds and the moon had replaced the sun. Rupert might just as well have never been there. Alba was alone with her mother, her soft voice speaking through the portrait, caressing her daughter with those soft, sorrowful eyes. Surely this picture would melt the layers of ice that had built up over the years and her father would remember and talk about her.

Alba did not waste any time. She rummaged around the untidy cupboards for suitable clothes, placed the scroll carefully into her bag, and hurried down the narrow staircase and out of the boat. A couple of squirrels were playing tag on the roof and she shooed them away irritably before setting off up the gangplank.

At that moment Fitz, having lost at bridge, was leaving Viv's houseboat, light-headed with wine and startled by the coincidence that set his path and Alba's in tandem. He didn't notice that she had been crying and she didn't notice Sprout. 'Good evening,' he said cheerfully, determined to ignite a conversation as they walked up the gangway toward the Embankment. Alba did not reply. 'I'm Fitzroy Davenport, a friend of your neighbor, Viv.'

'Oh,' she replied in a flat tone. Her eyes were fixed on the ground, partly obscured behind her hair. She crossed her arms and dug her chin into her chest.

'Can I give you a lift somewhere? My car's parked around the corner.'

'So is mine.'

'Ah.'

Fitz was surprised she didn't even raise her eyes. He was used to being looked at by women and was well aware that he was handsome, especially when he smiled, and he was tall, which was an advantage; girls always fancied tall men. Her lack of interest unbalanced him. He watched her long legs striding out, clad in blue suede boots, and felt the anxiety tighten about his throat. Her loveliness debilitated him completely.

'I've just lost at bridge,' he persevered frantically. 'Do you play?'

'Not if I can help it,' she replied.

He felt foolish. 'Very wise. Dull game.'

'Like the players,' she retorted, then gave a small smile before climbing into a two-seater MGB and disappearing down the road. Fitz was left alone under the street lamp, scratching his head, unsure whether to be offended or amused.

Alone in the car where no one could see her, Alba sobbed. She could fool everyone else with her bravado, but there was no point trying to fool herself. The sense of loss that had overwhelmed her earlier now resurfaced and this time with greater intensity. Her isolated world of cypress trees and olive groves was no longer sufficient. She had a right to know about her mother. Now she had the picture, the Buffalo would be forced to step back and let her father talk. How it had got there, she didn't know. Maybe he had put it there so the Buffalo wouldn't find it. Now she would know because Alba would tell her. It would be a pleasure. She changed gear and turned into the Talgarth Road.

It was late. They wouldn't be expecting her. It would take her a good hour and a half to get to Hampshire in spite of the clear roads. Not a cat on them. She turned on the radio to hear Cliff Richard singing *'Those miss-you nights are the longest,'* and her tears cascaded all the more. Out of the darkness and into her headlights her mother's face loomed. With long dark hair and soft, mossy brown eyes, she gazed upon her daughter with enough love and understanding to heal the entire world. Alba imagined she would have smelled of lemons. She had not a single memory, a single recollection of her scent. She had only her imagination and who knows what falsehoods that conjured up.

It was easy to see why the Buffalo hated Valentina. Margo Arbuckle wasn't beautiful. She was a big lady with sturdy legs better suited to Wellington boots than stilettos, a large bottom that molded well into the saddle of a horse and freckly English skin bare of makeup and washed with Imperial Leather soap. Her style of dress was appalling, tweed skirts and billowing blouses. Her bosom was substantial and she had lost any waist she once had. Alba wondered what her father had seen in her. Perhaps the pain of losing Valentina had driven him to choose a wife who was the opposite of her. But wouldn't it have been better to live with her memory than to compromise in such a pitiful way?

As for the children they had had together, well, they had wasted no time in that department. Alba had been born in 1945, the year her mother died, and Caroline only three years later in 1948. It was shameful. Her father had barely had time to mourn. He had certainly not had time to get to know her child, the one he should have loved more than anyone else in the world as the living part of the woman he had lost. After Caroline came Henry and then Miranda; with each child Alba was pushed a little further into her world of pine and olive groves and her father was too busy making another family to notice how she cried. But it wasn't her family. *God,* she thought unhappily, *does he ever sit down and think what he's done to me?* Now she had the portrait, she was determined to tell him.

She turned off the A30 and headed down narrow winding lanes. Her headlights illuminated the hedgerows bursting with cow parsley and the odd rabbit that darted hastily back into the bushes. She rolled down the window and sniffed the air like a dog, taking pleasure from the sweet scents of spring that swept in with the rattling sound of the motor. She imagined her father smoking his after-dinner cigar and swirling brandy in one of those large, swollen-bellied glasses he was so fond of. Margo would be rabbiting on about Caroline's thrilling new job in a Mayfair art gallery owned by a family friend and Henry's latest news from Sandhurst. Miranda was still at boarding school – little to report there except top grades and fawning teachers. *How dreadfully dull and conventional,* Alba thought. *Predictable.* Their lives would all run accordingly, along tracks laid down at their birth like perfect little trains. 'The runaway train came down the track and she blew, she blew ...,' sang Alba, her misery lifting as she contemplated her unconventional, independent existence that ran along a track entirely of her own making.

Finally she turned into the driveway that swept up for about a quarter of a mile beneath tall copper beech trees. She could just make out a couple of horses in the field to her right, their eyes shining like silver as they caught the lights of her car. Hideous beasts, she thought sourly. Amazing they weren't all buckling at the knees considering the weight of the Buffalo. She wondered whether the woman rode her father like she rode her horses. She couldn't help but giggle at the thought, then swiftly dismissed it. Old people weren't into that sort of thing.

The wheels of the car scrunched up the gravel in front of the house. The lights blazed invitingly but Alba knew they didn't blaze for her. How Margo must resent her, she thought. It would be easier to wipe away Valentina's memory if she weren't around as a constant reminder. She parked her car beneath the imposing walls of the house that had once been her home. With its tall chimneys and old, weathered brick and flint it had withstood gales and storms for well over 300 years. Her great-great-grandfather had apparently won it at the gambling table, but not before he had lost his wife as a consequence of his addiction. She had swiftly become mistress to some duke who had an addiction of similar proportions but a much deeper pocket with which to indulge it. Alba rather liked the idea of the mistress; her stepmother had forever tainted her concept of marriage.

She sat in the car, contemplating the picture while three

small dogs scurried out of the darkness to sniff the wheels and wag their stumpy tails. When her stepmother's face appeared around the door she had no option but to climb out and greet her. Margo looked pleased to see her though her smile didn't quite reach her eyes. 'Alba, what a lovely surprise! You should have telephoned,' she said, holding the door so that the orange light flooded the steps leading up to the porch. Alba went through the ritual of kissing her. She smelled of talcum powder and Yardley's Lily of the Valley. Around her neck hung a fat golden locket that rose up and down on the ledge of her breasts. Alba blinked away the image she had conjured up in the car of Margo riding her father like one of her horses.

She walked into the hall where the walls were wood-panelled and hung with austere portraits of deceased relatives. At once she smelled the sweet scent of her father's cigar and her courage flagged. He emerged from the drawing room in a green smoking jacket and slippers. His hair, although thinning, was still sandy and brushed back off his forehead, accentuating pale eyes that appraised her steadily. For a fleeting moment Alba was able to see beyond the heavy build and extended belly, past the ruddy skin and disgruntled twist of his mouth, to the handsome young man he had been in the war. Before he had sought comfort and oblivion in convention and routine. When he had still loved her mother.

'Ah, Alba, my dear. To what do we owe this pleasure?' He kissed her temple, as he always did, and his voice was thick and grainy like the gravel outside. Jovial, inscrutable; the young man had gone.

'I was just passing,' she lied.

'Good,' he replied. 'Come on in for a tipple and tell us what you've been up to.'

Alba clutched her bag. She could feel the bulge of the scroll tied up by a short piece of string. It demanded to be acknowledged, but she had to await her moment. And she needed a drink for courage.

'What would you like, Alba, my dear?'

'A glass of wine would be nice,' she replied, flopping onto the sofa. One of her stepmother's dogs was curled up asleep at the other end. *They look sweeter asleep than awake,* she thought to herself, *less like scruffy little rodents.* She looked around the room where she had so often sat as a child, while her half siblings played Racing Demon and Scrabble, and felt more keenly than ever the sense of being an outsider. There were photographs in frames on tables laden with little enamel boxes and other trinkets, pictures of her smiling with her arms around Caroline, as if they had a true, unbreakable friendship. If one didn't know better it would appear that she belonged to a large, united family. She sniffed her contempt, sat back, and draped one long leg over the other, admiring the blue suede clog boots she had recently bought at Biba. Margo sunk her large bottom into an armchair and picked up her brandy.

'So, how is it all going in London?' she asked. It was a deliberately vague question, because neither she nor Thomas knew what she got up to there.

'Oh, you know, same old thing,' Alba responded, equally vague, because she didn't really know either. She had almost become Terry Donovan's muse but had turned up late and he had already left. She had been too embarrassed to telephone to apologize, so she had simply let it go. Her attempts at modelling for fashion magazines had suffered from the same lack of motivation. People were full of promises: she could be the next Jean Shrimpton, they insisted, she could be famous, but she never quite managed to see anything through. As Viv said, 'God helps those who help themselves.' Well, until she got around to helping herself, her father's small allowance would keep her in Ace dresses. The Ruperts and Tims and Jameses would see to the rest.

'Surely you do more than sit about in that boat all day long?' said Margo with a smile. Alba decided to take offense. Margo was always tactless. Her manner was strident, insensitive. She would have made a good headmistress. Alba thought her deep, plummy voice was ideal for bossing schoolgirls about and telling them to pull themselves together when they dissolved into tears, missing their mothers. She had often told Alba to 'turn off the waterworks' when she had cried for something deemed trivial and not worth the fuss. Alba felt the resentment rise at all the humiliation she had suffered at the hands of her stepmother. Then she remembered the scroll and its very presence gave her a burst of confidence.

'The *Valentina* is lovelier than ever,' she replied, emphasizing the name. 'Speaking of which, as I was tidying up under the bed, I discovered, quite to my amazement . . .'

Just as she was about to launch her missile, her father stood over her and handed her a glass of red wine.

'It's a Bordeaux. Terribly good. Had it in the cellar for years.'

She thanked him and tried to resume, but once more she was interrupted. This time by a thick, reedy voice, wavering like the strings of a badly played violin. She recognized it at once as belonging to her grandmother.

'Am I missing a party?'

They all looked up in surprise to see Lavender Arbuckle in the doorway in her frilly nightcap and dressing gown, leaning heavily on a walking stick.

'Mother,' said Thomas, appalled at the sight. During the daytime, in her clothes, she passed for normal. In her nightcap and dressing gown she looked frail and tremulous as if she had stepped straight out of a coffin.

'Well, I don't like to miss a party.'

Margo put down her glass and pushed herself up with a weary huff.

'Lavender, it's only Alba. She's popped in for a drink,' she explained.

Lavender frowned, her small face resembling that of a bird with shiny eyes and a tiny beak.

'Alba? Do I know an Alba?' Her voice rose in tone and volume as she peered down her powdered nose at her granddaughter.

'Hello, Grandma!' Alba said with a smile, not bothering to stand.

'Do I know you?' she repeated, shaking her head so that the trims on her nightcap waved about her ears. 'I do not believe that I do.'

'Mother . . .' Thomas began weakly, but Margo stalked past him.

'Lavender, it's jolly late. Wouldn't you be happier in bed?' She took the older woman by the elbow and began to usher her out of the room.

'Not if there's a party. I don't like to miss a good party.'
She resisted the attempts to shift her and hobbled into the
room. Thomas dithered, puffing on his cigar while Margo
stood, hands on hips, shaking her head in disapproval.

Lavender sat down on the upright reading chair that
Thomas used for browsing through the Sunday papers.
It was large and comfortable and positioned under a
bright standing lamp. 'Well, is no one going to offer me a
drink?' she barked.

'What about a brandy?' suggested Margo, leaving her
husband hovering in the middle of the room and making
her way to the drinks table.

'Goodness, no. It's a party. A Sticky Green would hit
the spot. What do you think?' She turned to Alba. 'A
Sticky Green!' Her cheeks glowed pink.

'What's a Sticky Green?'

'Crème de Menthe,' muttered Thomas, frowning.

'A very *common* drink,' Margo huffed, and poured the
old lady a brandy.

Alba, although vaguely amused by her grandmother,
was anxious to tell her father about the picture. The wine
had made her head light and suitably numbed her nerves.
She was ready to face them, to demand the truth, and she
expected to be indulged. Glancing at the large silver clock
on the mantelpiece she realized that she didn't have much
time before her father and the Buffalo would wish to
retire to bed.

'How long are you staying?' she asked her grandmother, not bothering to disguise her impatience.

'And who are you again?' was the icy response.

'Alba, Mother!' interjected Thomas in exasperation.
Margo handed Lavender the brandy and returned to her
own chair and her own drink. One of her little dogs
trotted in and jumped onto her knee, where she stroked

him with her large, capable hands. Lavender leaned toward Alba.

'They think I'm on my last legs, you see, so they've brought me home.' She heaved a sigh, contemplating The End. 'This is the final station. I'll go soon and they'll bury me next to Hubert. Never thought I'd grow old. One never does. Nothing terribly wrong with me, though. My mind's going a bit, but apart from that there's fight in the old girl yet!' She knocked back her brandy. She suddenly looked shrunken and sad. 'This room used to buzz with parties when Hubert and I were young. Used to fill it with friends. Of course, in those days, one had plenty of friends. They're all dead now, or too old. No energy left for parties. When one is young one fully expects to live forever. One imagines one can conquer everything, but one cannot conquer the Grim Reaper. No, he comes and takes us all, kings and tramps alike. Still, we all go when our time is up, don't we? Every dog has his day, Hubert used to say, and I've had mine. Are you married? What was your name?'

'Alba.' Alba stifled a yawn. It was sometimes hard to understand what her grandmother said; her mouth seemed to contain the entire fruit bowl, never mind the odd plum. She sounded like a grand old duchess from another century.

'A woman is nothing without a man by her side. Nothing without children. One gains a certain wisdom when one is old. I am old and wise and thankfully my children will live on after I am gone. There's a great sense of satisfaction in that, which one can only appreciate when one is old.'

'One must also get one's beauty sleep, don't you think?' said Alba, draining her glass.

'Quite, my girl, quite. Though at my great age I don't see much point in sleeping. After all, it won't be long before I'm sleeping for eternity and goodness, I'll grow bored of that. Too much sleep is a bad thing. Good gracious, is that the time?' She sat up abruptly, fixing her eyes on the clock. 'I might not wish to sleep but my body's a creature of habit and I no longer have the strength to fight it. It was a pleasure,' she added, extending her hand to Alba.

'I'm your granddaughter,' Alba reminded her, not unkindly but her tone was impatient.

'Good gracious, are you? You don't look like one of us at all. Arbuckles are all fair and you're very dark and foreign-looking, aren't you.' Once again she peered down her nose.

'My mother was Italian,' she reminded her grandmother, and to her horror, her voice came out high-pitched and emotional. She looked up at her father, who remained in the middle of the room, puffing madly, his face flushed. The Buffalo showed nothing of her true feelings and stood up to escort her mother-in-law out of the room.

When Margo returned she dropped her shoulders and sighed heavily. 'Oh dear, she really is losing her marbles. Would you like to stay the night, Alba?' Alba seethed. Margo was treating her like a guest in her own home. Unable to contain her frustration any longer, she opened her handbag and pulled out the scroll.

'I found this under my bed. It must have been hidden there for years,' she said, waving it in the air. 'It's a drawing of Valentina by Daddy.' She held her father with those strange pale eyes of hers. She noticed the Buffalo's shoulders hunch with tension as she exchanged nervous glances with her husband. Alba was furious.

'Yes, Daddy, it's beautiful. Let me remind you when you drew it. In 1943, in the war, when you loved her. Do you *ever* remember her?' Then turning to Margo she added icily, 'Do you let him remember her?'

'Now Alba,' Margo began but Alba's voice rose above hers as she continued to put into words thoughts that had for years fermented in her head. Like wine left too long, they now tasted bitter.

'It's as if she never existed. You never talk about her.' She coughed to clear her throat and to loosen her vocal cords, but they simply ached with despair. 'How can you let another woman obliterate your memory of her? Why such cowardice, Daddy? You fought in the war, you killed men far stronger than you and yet you ... you ... you deny me my own mother for fear of upsetting Margo.'

Margo and Thomas both stood rooted to the ground in silence. Neither knew how to respond. They were used to Alba's outbursts but this was unexpectedly vitriolic. Only the smoke from the remains of Thomas's cigar disturbed the absolute stillness of the room. Even the dogs were too afraid to move. Alba looked from one to the other, knowing that she had let her feelings spiral out of control, but there was no going back now. The words had been fired and couldn't be retracted, even if she had wanted them to be. At last Margo spoke. Clenching her jaw in order to remain composed, she suggested that this was something best discussed between father and daughter. Without saying good night she left the room. Alba was pleased to see her go.

Alba walked over to her father and handed him the scroll. He took it and looked at her for a long moment. She stared back defiantly. But there was no fight in his expression, just an immeasurable sadness. Such sadness that Alba had to turn away. Without a word he placed his cigar in the ashtray and sat down in the reading chair his mother had vacated moments before. He didn't open the scroll. He just looked at it, stroking the paper with his thumb, the sweet smell of figs reaching him from the distant past, from a chapter of his life closed long ago.

Alba watched him closely. She saw the young man in naval uniform, like the photograph in his dressing room, with the white scarf, heavy coat, and crested hat. She saw him slimmer, more handsome, happier. There was no deep, unsettling sadness in his eyes, only the optimism that dominates the spirit of the young and the most valiant. There was no disillusion either, for his heart vibrated with love for her mother at a time when their future spread out before them like a sumptuous banquet.

Finally he spoke in a very quiet voice. 'You have pushed us too far this time.' Alba was stung. 'There is an enormous amount you don't even begin to understand. If you did, you wouldn't talk to Margo like that. You were unforgivably rude, Alba, and I won't tolerate it.' His words were like a slap on the face.

'No, *you* don't understand,' she whimpered. 'I simply want to know about my mother. I deserve to know. You haven't the slightest idea what it's like not to belong. To feel rootless.' He looked at her wearily then shook his head in resignation.

'*This* is your home.' His forehead creased into deep furrows. 'Aren't I enough? No, obviously not. You have pushed and pushed all your life. Nothing is ever enough, is it?' He sighed and turned his attention once again to the scroll. 'Yes, I loved your mother and she loved you. But she died, Alba, and I can't bring her back. There is nothing else for me to tell you. As for belonging, you never belonged in Italy. I brought you to England at the end of the war. You belong here and you always have. If there's an obstacle, it's not Margo, Alba, it's you. Look around you. You've just taken and taken all your life, without gratitude. I don't know what more you want and I'm tired of trying to give it to you.'

'So you're not going to tell me about Valentina?' She fought angry tears as, once again, she felt he was pushing her away, shutting her out along with her mother. But she knew the demon on his shoulder was not his conscience, but Margo. 'I don't even know how you met,' she said in a small voice. She saw the muscle in his jaw throb with discomfort. 'You've never shared her with me. Once it was you and me, Daddy. Then Margo came along and there was no longer any room for me.'

'That's not true,' he growled. 'Margo held it all together.'

'She's still jealous of my mother.'

'You're quite wrong.'

Alba chuckled cynically. 'It takes a woman to understand a woman.'

'And Alba, my dear, you are not yet a woman. You have a tremendous amount of growing up to do.' He raised his eyes, now bloodshot and watery. His desolation would have aroused her pity had she not harbored so great a resentment in her heart. 'Don't make me choose between you and my wife,' he said and his voice was so quiet and grave that her skin bristled and she felt the sudden chill of a cold draft.

'I don't need to ask you, Father, because I know who you would choose.'

As the car disappeared down the drive, Margo, who had heard everything, hovered by the drawing room door. She could see Thomas through the crack. His face was long and grey, and heavy with sorrow. He looked much older than his years. He fingered the scroll pensively. He did not open it. He simply nodded to himself before getting up and wandering into his study, where she heard the opening and closing of a drawer.

He had no wish to resurrect the past.

That night as Thomas climbed into bed, Margo took off her reading glasses and put down her book. 'I think it's time you got rid of that ghastly boat,' she said.

Thomas shuffled down the mattress and placed his head on the pillow. 'The boat's got nothing to do with Alba's bad behavior,' he replied. They had discussed this countless times before.

'You know that's not what I mean. It's bad luck.'

'Since when have you been superstitious?'

'I don't know why she can't rent a flat like Caroline.'

'Are you suggesting they live together again?'

'God, no, that was a disaster. No, I don't think that's fair to Caroline. Poor girl, Alba did nothing but argue with her and she's such a mess to live with. Caroline spent most evenings tidying up after her. Cigarette butts stubbed out in wine glasses and the like. No, I would not want to put Caroline through that again; she doesn't deserve it.'

'Alba is perfectly happy on her boat.' He closed his eyes, very weary.

'It would be fine if it wasn't *that* boat.'

'I'm not getting rid of the boat. Besides, how do you think Alba would interpret that? Another move to eradicate the memory of her mother?' He sighed.

Margo placed her glasses in their case and leaned over to put her book on the bedside table. She switched off the light and lay down, drawing the covers up to her chin.

'I'm not going to ask you about the picture, Thomas. It's none of my business. However, I think it a pity that Alba found it. It does her no good to dwell so much on the past.'

'The past,' he repeated quietly, considering the picture.

He blinked into the darkness, where he was sure he could see Valentina's face: vibrant with youth and that irrepressible energy. He was even sure that he could smell the sweet scent of figs, wafting down the years with that long-forgotten sense of what it had been like to love so intensely. His eyes misted and he inhaled. *After all these years*, he thought. *That the picture should turn up now, when I had almost managed to put it all behind me.*

'What are you going to do?' she asked. Thomas pulled himself back from his memories.

'About what?'

'About the boat.'

'Nothing.'

'Nothing? But . . .'

'I said nothing. Now I'm going to sleep. I don't wish to discuss this anymore, Margo. The boat remains, and Alba remains in it.'

Alba was barely able to see the road for the tears that welled and tumbled in an unceasing flow. It was past midnight when she parked her car beneath the street lamp on Cheyne Walk. She was furious that she had given him the picture. She could have kept it. It could have been her secret. Now she was left with nothing.

Slowly she walked down the pontoon to her boat, snivelling as she went, feeling extremely sorry for herself. She wished she had someone waiting for her, a nice man to snuggle up to. Not a Rupert or a Tim or a James, but someone special. She didn't want to be alone tonight. Knowing that Viv often wrote her novels well into the early hours of the morning, she knocked on her door. She waited for a sound, but only the creaking of the boat and the gentle lapping of the river against the pontoon accompanied the benign roar of the city.

As she turned away, downhearted, the door opened and Viv's pale face appeared in the crack. 'Oh, it's you,' she said, then added on closer inspection, 'Dear me, you'd better come in.' Alba followed the billowing caftan up the narrow corridor to the kitchen. Like her own boat Viv's smelled of damp, but it had a unique scent of something exotic and foreign. Viv was fond of burning joss-sticks from India and lighting scented candles she bought in Carnaby Street. Alba sat at the round table in the richly painted purple room and hunched over the cup of coffee that Viv poured her. 'I'm in the middle of a dreadfully difficult chapter so it'll be nice to take a break and talk to you. I don't imagine for a moment your tears are for a man.' She pulled out a chair and lit up. 'Take one, darling, it'll make you feel better.' Alba took a Silva Thin and leaned over as Viv flicked open her lighter. 'So, what are they for, then?'

'I found a sketch that my father did of my mother under the bed.'

'Goodness gracious, what were you doing under the bed?' Viv was only too aware that Alba never cleaned her boat.

'It's beautiful, Viv, really beautiful and my father won't even discuss it with me.'

'I see,' she replied, inhaling through her mouth and exhaling through her nostrils like a dragon. 'You drove all the way down to Hampshire at this time of night?'

'I couldn't wait. Thought he'd be pleased I found it.'

'What was it doing under the bed, of all the places?' The story of Alba's mother intrigued her.

'Oh, he put it there to hide it from the Buffalo. She's eaten up with jealousy and won't even set foot on the boat because Daddy named it after my mother. Silly woman!'

'What did he say when you told him you had found it?'

Alba took a gulp of coffee, wincing because it was too hot. 'He was furious with me.'

'No!' Viv gasped, appalled.

'He was. I told him in front of the Buffalo.'

'Well, that explains it.'

'I wanted her to know that he had hidden it from her.' She chuckled mischievously, revealing the crooked eye-tooth that Rupert, or was it Tim, said gave her mouth such charm. 'I bet they had one hell of a row after I left. I bet the Buffalo listened to every word we said. I can just imagine her heavy breathing down the keyhole!'

'Did he look at it?'

'No. He just went very red and looked sad. He still loves her, Viv. I think he always will. Probably regrets ever having married the Buffalo. I just wish he'd share her with me, you know. But he won't because of the Buffalo.'

'She's very cruel and stupid,' Viv said venomously, patting Alba's hand, 'to be jealous of a dead woman.' Alba's strange pale eyes welled with tears again and Viv felt the gentle tug of the mother in her. Alba was twenty-six, but a large part of her had never grown up. Beneath the self-confidence was a child just wanting to be loved. Viv handed her a tissue. 'Now, darling, what are you going to do about it?'

'There's nothing I can do,' Alba replied miserably.

'Oh, there's always something one can do. Remember, God only helps those who help themselves. I have a friend who might be able to help you,' she continued, narrowing her eyes. 'If there's a man capable of charming his way into someone else's business, it's Fitzroy Davenport.'

3

Fitz spent a fitful night dreaming of Alba, and when he woke in the morning her face was emblazoned on his memory. He lay in bed, heartened by the white beam of sunlight that streamed in through the gap in the curtains, enjoying her features all over again. Her oval face and large sensual mouth. He hated to think of the men who had kissed those lips and swiftly moved on to her unusually pale eyes. They were deep set, framed by black feathery lashes and rather heavy eyebrows but the shadows around them, not on the skin but somehow there, in the hollow, gave her a haunted look. The way she walked had aroused him too. Those long legs in boots. The smooth length of thigh before the little skirt only just protected her modesty. The confident manner in which she walked. The 'young colt' cliché that Viv thankfully avoided in her novels. Then she had been so unforgivably rude. But her smile, with that crooked tooth, had been so beguiling it was as if she had poured warm honey onto his skin and licked it off with one delicious flick of her tongue.

He heard Sprout downstairs in the kitchen and sighed. He did not want to get up. He tried to think of an excuse to visit Viv's houseboat again, just on the off chance that he might encounter Alba. Perhaps he could telephone her on the pretext of discussing an up-and-coming foreign deal, a possible publicity tour in France – the French loved her books – or recent sales figures. Viv was easy to please, as long as she talked about herself, and today he was very much in the mood for listening. He leaned over to pick up the telephone just as it rang. 'Bugger!' he muttered and lifted the receiver.

'Good morning, darling,' came Viv's cheerful voice. Fitz's spirits rose and soared to the ceiling.

'Darling,' he breathed. 'I was just going to telephone you myself!'

'Oh? What about? Something good, I hope.'

'Of course, Viv. You're my star client, you know that.'

'Well, don't keep me guessing.'

'The French want you to do a tour. Your public demand to see you,' he lied, biting his cheek. *It doesn't matter,* he thought, *I'll swing it later.*

Viv's voice rose in tone and she clipped her consonants with even more emphasis than usual. 'Oh, darling, that's tremendous. Of course, one must do one's duty. One mustn't keep one's public waiting. After all, I need them as much as they need me.'

'Great, I'll get on to them this morning.' He paused as Viv took a sharp intake of breath; he imagined her dragging on a Silva Thin in her purple kitchen. 'What did you want to talk to me about?' he asked, hopeful of an invitation.

'Oh, I nearly forgot.' In the shadow of Fitz's news Alba had paled into insignificance. 'Come for supper tonight. I have a job for you. I think you'll enjoy it. A certain damsel in distress needs a knight in shining armor to rescue her from a ghoul of a stepmother and a walrus of a father. It's right up your street and besides, you fancy her, don't you? Just don't fall in love, Fitzroy.'

'I'll be there,' he said, his voice hoarse with excitement.

Viv rolled her heavily made-up eyes and put down the receiver. She didn't think she was doing him any favours in the long run. It was all going to end in tears.

Alba awoke to a terrible emptiness. She rose and made a cup of tea. There was nothing to eat in the fridge, only half a pint of milk, a couple of bottles of wine, and rows of nail varnishes. It was a chilly morning and she was cold in spite of the paraffin stoves. She wrapped her dressing gown about her and rubbed her eyes, yawning loudly. She'd do a bit of shopping to cheer herself up and perhaps lunch with Rupert, who worked for an estate agent in Mayfair. Maybe he could take the afternoon off and they could roll around in bed until dusk. He was just what she required to lift her depression and make her feel good about herself. He had made love with great tenderness as well as enthusiasm and was exceptionally good at it. No fumbling and heavy breathing; she hated that, and she hated grabbers too. Rupert didn't grab and so far he hadn't pestered her with telephone calls either. He was simply there when she needed him and she felt better for his company.

She was about to telephone him when there was a heavy knock on the door. She recognized it immediately and smiled. It was Harry Reed, also known as 'Reed of the River.' In his stiff blue uniform and cap he patrolled the Thames as part of the River Police. Besides stopping off every now and then for a cup of coffee, he had warmed her bed on more than one occasion. However, his rough loving was not what she needed today. 'Hello,' she said, poking her head around the door. Harry was tall and willowy, like a bulrush, with soft brown eyes and a wide, cheeky smile on a handsome, though slightly coarse, face.

'I'd forgotten what you look like in the morning,' he said longingly, taking his cap off and holding it in his large, calloused hands.

'Is that why you've come knocking on my door?'

'Do you have time for a cup of coffee with a cold policeman? At least you know you'll be safe!' He had said that before and laughed at it, too heartily.

'I'm afraid I don't, Harry. Sorry. I'm in a bit of a hurry. I have an appointment,' she lied. 'Why don't you pass by tonight, before dinner?' Harry's eyes shone in the cold and he put his cap back on, rubbing his hands together happily.

'I'll pop in for a drink at the end of the day. I'll be meeting the boys in the Star and Garter after my shift, perhaps you'd like to come along?'

Alba remembered Viv's invitation to dinner with Fitzroy what's-his-name and had to decline, although she rather enjoyed sitting in the fug with the off-duty police in their blue pullovers.

'Not tonight, Harry.'

'I'll take you for a ride sometime. Do you remember when I had to drop you off at Chelsea Reach? The sergeant would have had my guts for garters if I'd been caught.'

'That was fun,' she agreed, recalling the exhilarating feeling of the wind raking through her hair. 'I'll try to keep out of sight, though I might like your sergeant.'

'He'd certainly like you, Alba.' *They all do*, she thought. Sometimes it was wearisome being so adored.

'A drink then?' he confirmed, not wanting her to forget.

'If you're lucky and I feel like it.' She smiled at him, revealing her crooked tooth. He seemed to wilt with pleasure.

'You're one in a million, Alba.'

'As you keep reminding me, Harry.'

'See you tonight, then.' And he climbed back into his launch and sped off up the Thames, waving his cap at her with gusto.

Alba went shopping. She bought a shirt and flares at Escapade on the Brompton Road for £14 and a pair of shoes at the Chelsea Cobbler for £5 before making her way by taxi up to Mayfair for lunch with Rupert. Rupert was barely able to conceal his delight, having worried that he had bored her. He hadn't expected to hear from her again. To his frustration he had a client to see in the afternoon, so they parted at two and Alba was left to brood in the park while Rupert showed people around houses in Bayswater, imagining a honey-coloured Alba lying in every bed he looked at.

Bored of the park and tired of traipsing around shops, Alba went home on the bus for entertainment. She no longer noticed people staring at her loveliness and glowered at men who tried to chat her up, but it was more amusing than taking a cab and it took up more time. She enjoyed watching people, listening to their conversations, imagining how they lived. She looked forward to dinner at Viv's and to Reed of the River dropping by for a drink. It didn't occur to her that her life was empty. She had friends and she took lovers whenever she needed company at night. She didn't analyse her existence or try to fill her days with something worthwhile, she just muddled through. Besides, nothing inspired her. Not like Viv, who had a hunger for life, eating away the time with hours at her typewriter producing books that reflected her enthusiasm (some would say cynicism) for people and their foibles. Alba didn't yearn for marriage and children, although she was twenty-six and 'getting on' as Viv was apt to remind her. She didn't think about the future. She didn't realize that she avoided it out of fear, because it was empty.

Alba was wrapped in a towel, having had a bath and washed her hair, and was painting flowers on her toenails when Reed of the River's launch motored up. In his keenness he was early. He smelled heavily of aftershave and had slicked his hair back with a wet comb. He looked handsome and Alba was pleased to see him. She didn't need to show him where the drinks were and he went straight ahead and poured them both a glass of wine. She noticed his eyes creeping up beneath her towel and shifted her position defensively. She wasn't in the mood and, besides, she had a dinner date. Having painted the last nail, she sat back on the sofa to let them dry.

'Revel found an arm in the river this afternoon,' said Harry, settling comfortably into a chair, stretching his long legs in front of him, making himself at home.

'How disgusting,' Alba gasped, scrunching up her pretty nose. 'What happened to the rest of him?'

'That's the mystery, isn't it,' he replied importantly. 'It's our job to find out.'

'Was it an old arm or a new one?'

'Old, I think. Pretty rotten I can tell you. The stench! I don't want to give you nightmares, though of course there's a cure for that!' He raised an eyebrow which Alba ignored.

'Perhaps it's the remains of a tortured Elizabethan courtier. You'll find the head next,' she said with a laugh.

'Have you been to Tower Bridge? It's quite a thing to have a piece of history like that bang in the center of the city!' Alba hadn't been to Tower Bridge and, as for history, well, she didn't care for it. What was the point of discussing dead people one had never known? The only history she was interested in was her own.

'About the head, it'll pop up when you least expect it,' she said.

'Or when *you* least expect it,' he added with a chuckle, running his eyes up her legs again. Alba wondered how Viv would react to an old dismembered head bobbing off the side of her boat and smiled as she contemplated sending it to the Buffalo in a cardboard box.

'If you find it, let me know,' she said with a smirk.

They continued to chat while Alba wandered upstairs to change for dinner. There was no door to close on him, for the bedroom and bathroom were built on a landing where one side was a balustrade overlooking the stairwell and corridor that led into the sitting room. It was getting late and Harry had been there for some time. She chose a pair of Zandra Rhodes hot pants, which she wore with boots and a cashmere sweater patched in calico. When Harry appeared at the top of the stairs, glass in hand and a lascivious glint in his eye, Alba was carefully applying black eyeliner in the mirror.

'Don't creep up on me like that,' she complained grumpily.

'I want you,' he said, his voice hoarse.

'Oh, Harry, please. I'm going out for dinner. Besides, I've put my clothes on. You don't expect me to take them all off again, do you?'

'Oh, go on, Alba,' he encouraged, coming up behind her and kissing her neck where her hair was still wet and tangled.

'All I can think of is that arm in the water, Harry. It's the least romantic thought I've had for some time.'

Harry wished he hadn't mentioned it. She finished the

eyeliner and turned on the hair drier, blowing Harry onto the bed, where he draped himself mournfully.

'Just a quickie, lovely. Keep me going in the cold.' He grinned mischievously and Alba couldn't help but smile. It wasn't their fault she was so desirable.

She finished drying her hair and walked over to the bed, where she lay with him a while, kissing. It felt nice to be held. Reed of the River was another shelter where she could take refuge. When he ran his hands over her thighs she moved away.

'I think you had better go now, Harry.'

'Who are you having dinner with tonight?' he asked, not bothering to hide his jealousy. 'I hope it's not a man.'

'My neighbor, Viv.'

'The writer?'

'The writer.'

'Well, that's all right, then. Don't want you to get into trouble. It's my job to protect you.'

'And the rest of London – from floating limbs,' she said with a laugh, kissing him again and pushing him out of the door.

To Harry's horror, while he had been enjoying an illicit glass of wine while still on duty, the tide had gone out leaving him marooned. He gazed in disbelief as his launch shuffled about like a beached whale, unable to break free, while a couple of ducks swam by, quacking in amusement.

'Shit!' he exclaimed, suddenly losing his sense of humor. 'I'm garters.'

At that moment, Fitz walked down the pontoon. This time he had brought his own wine. Two bottles of good Italian red. He wore a jacket over a green and white patterned shirt and his sandy hair bounced about in the wind. The moment he saw Alba and the policeman standing on the deck of her boat, he felt his gut knot with jealousy. Her hand on his arm suggested their intimacy and Fitz wondered whether they had just climbed out of bed. Viv had said she had tons of lovers. As his mouth twisted into a grimace she turned and waved, flashing him the most charming smile. Did she remember him from the evening before? To his annoyance he found himself beaming back and raised the wine.

'Don't be long,' he shouted, 'or it'll all be gone!'

'My friend's got himself into a bit of bother,' she replied, beckoning him over. She explained that Harry was stuck in the mud. 'He's like a dear old walrus, heaving on the beach,' she said, throwing her chin up and laughing. Fitz recalled Viv's having described her father in a similar fashion and dropped his shoulders with relief. Surely no woman would refer to a lover like that. Harry was not amused. He felt humiliated and irritated because Alba hadn't said a man was also coming to dinner.

As the three of them discussed what to do, another patrol launch motored up containing a very severe-looking man scowling beneath his navy cap. Harry visibly shrank.

'Well, well, well, what's going on here then?'

'I'm grounded,' Harry replied and was on the point of trying to explain why he'd been there in the first place, when Alba interrupted.

'Sergeant, how fortunate that you should arrive at this very moment.' The sergeant straightened up at the sight of Alba's hotpants and boots and his face softened into an expression of concern. 'My husband and I are so grateful to PC Reed.' She placed her arm around Fitz's waist. Fitz suddenly felt very hot. 'You see, I'm sure I saw a head, yes, a head, I swear it. Without a body. Bobbing about just there.' She pointed into the brown water. She raised her eyes to the sergeant and did her best to look frightened. 'It was most distressing, as you can imagine. A head without a body.'

'I'll have the team come and check it out, Mrs. . . .' Alba realized she did not know Fitzroy's surname.

'Davenport,' interjected Fitz, unprompted. 'Mr. Davenport. I'll be most grateful if you would. I don't wish my wife to come across it again.'

'Of course, Mr. Davenport.' He cast his eyes to Harry's pitiful launch. 'I'll take PC Reed with me in my launch and send him back when the tide's in. Leave it to me.'

'I most certainly will, and with the greatest confidence. Now I wish to take my wife out for dinner. Very nice to meet you, Sergeant and PC . . .' He stammered on purpose.

'Reed,' said Harry grudgingly.

'Of course, and thank you.' With that he drew Alba away, leaving Reed of the River to the mercy of his sergeant.

As they motored off, the sergeant turned to Harry and said with a knowing nod, 'Beautiful girl. Damn lucky she's married to a strong man or she'd get into an awful lot of trouble.' Harry watched helplessly as she disappeared into her neighbour's boat with Fitz.

Viv had donned a turban of old, Indian silk for the occasion. She sat wearing a sky blue caftan, smoking through an elegant ebony holder, her red nails so long it was a wonder they managed the keys of her typewriter. With her blond hair hidden from sight, her face looked much older, the makeup dry and caked into the wrinkles around her eyes and mouth. However, her features came alive when Fitz and Alba walked through the door and her cheeks glowed a natural pink.

'Come on in, darlings,' she said languorously, waving

at them and indicating that they should make themselves at home. 'What a rumpus you two were making out there. I see old Reedy's stuck in the mud. I'd like to have watched him squirm his way out of that one.' She cackled and took a slow drag of her cigarette.

Fitz was nervous, being in the company of the woman he had watched and dreamed about. He perched on the orange velvet sofa as if he were at a job interview, and fiddled with his fingers. Alba flopped onto the pile of brightly coloured silk cushions piled on the floor, curling her legs under her, and lit up. She watched Fitz with her strange pale eyes, wondering how he was going to solve her problem. The boat smelled heavily of incense. Viv had lit candles and placed them in vibrant glass cups around the small sitting room. The lights were dimmed and music played softly. Alba watched him through the smoke. He was attractive in a very aristocratic way: intelligent eyes that sparkled with humor; a wide, infectious smile; a strong chin and jaw line; scruffy, with curly hair the colour of hay that obviously hadn't seen a brush for a long time. She liked his eyes immediately. They were honest, and soft like Demerara sugar but with a generous sprinkling of pepper. She hated men whose kindness made them dull. He obviously wasn't one of those. Now he just looked anxious and she felt sorry for him. In her company men fell into two categories: the ones who pounced and the ones who were too decent to pounce. Fitz clearly fell into the latter, which she much preferred. So far she had never met a man who fell into the third: the indifferent.

'So, Fritz,' she began in an imperious voice. 'Where do you fit into Viv's life and why haven't I met you before?'

'It's Fitz,' he corrected earnestly. 'Short for Fitzroy. I'm her literary agent.'

Viv swept into the room with one of Fitz's bottles of wine and three glasses.

'Darling, you're much more than my agent. He's my friend too,' she added to Alba. 'I've kept him hidden away on purpose. I want him all to myself. I'm only sharing him with you tonight out of kindness, though don't be fooled, I'll bear a heavy grudge if you steal him, my dear. You see, one can always rely on Fitzroy to put a smile on one's face even when there's very little to smile about. That's why I invited him. I thought you needed cheering up.'

Fitz cringed; he didn't feel very amusing. His throat was dry for a start. Perhaps a little wine would loosen things up. Thank God he'd brought his own.

'Oh, Reed of the River has already done that,' she said, without considering the way it sounded. Fitz felt deflated. 'I hooted with laughter when I saw his silly boat had run aground.' Then she smiled her large, mischievous grin at Fitz and he felt inflated again. 'We saved the day, didn't we? Without our cunning he would have certainly lost his job. No more rides up to Wapping. I should miss that.'

'What was all that about the floating head?'

'Oh, Revel, one of the boys who works with him, found an arm floating in the Thames. Disgusting!' She lifted her chin and laughed heartily. 'I said that if he came across the head he should let me know. I'd adore to send it to the Buffalo in a box.'

'Ah, the Buffalo,' said Viv with a sigh, sinking into the armchair. 'That's the ghastly stepmother I was telling you about.'

Alba didn't concern herself with Viv's gossiping; it was perfectly natural that people should talk about her.

'I think I know the type. Capable but totally insensitive.'

'Exactly,' Alba agreed, flicking ash into one of Viv's lime green dishes. 'What are we going to do about her?'

'Like a good book, we need a plot,' said Viv importantly. 'Being the writer among us I have taken the liberty of coming up with one.'

'You never fail your public,' said Fitz jovially, remembering guiltily that he had forgotten to call the French.

'If it's anything like your books,' said Alba, who had never read one, 'it'll be spellbinding!'

Viv paused for dramatic effect, took a long sip of wine, then began very slowly, clipping her consonants.

'You're never going to get rid of the Buffalo. Neither can you win your father's affection if you fight with him all the time. No, it's really very simple. You are going to go down to Hampshire for the weekend with Fitzroy.'

'With Fitz?'

'With me?' said Fitz with a gulp, thrilled to be included.

'Yes. You are going to present to your parents your perfect new boyfriend.' Fitz took a deep breath to control his excitement. He liked this plot better than anything else she'd written. 'You see, darling,' she said, turning to Alba. 'You have always been the unconventional, rebellious child. Now you are going to turn up with the most conventional, charming, suitable man. Fitzroy will be everything they consider fitting and proper. He'll play bridge and tennis, pat the dogs, enjoy an after-dinner port with your father, talk about art, literature, politics, and his opinions will all mirror theirs. What a coincidence! His father also fought in the war, in Italy of all places. Did they know one another? Where was he stationed? Fitzroy will endear himself to Thomas Arbuckle, who will be so grateful to him for taking on his difficult daughter that he will let down his guard. Perhaps they will discuss the war over an after-dinner cigar, man to man, once the women have retired to bed. He'll confide in Fitzroy the story of his past. Yes, I can see it all happening.' She spread her fingers and moved her hand slowly for added effect. 'It is late. A crisp, starry night. Thomas feels wistful and there's nothing more effective than flattery at arousing the desire in a man for intimacy. If anyone can draw an old duffer out of his shell and into his confidence it is you, Fitzroy. Sir Fitzroy Can-Do.' She put her cigarette between her lips before exhaling the smoke in a long thin trail, clearly thrilled with her presentation.

Now Fitz sat forward, placing his elbows on his knees. 'Let me take this one step further, Viv,' he said, getting into the spirit of it.

'By all means, darling.'

'Once I have found out the details, there is one thing left to do,' he stated seriously.

Alba, who had remained quiet and watchful throughout, now spoke. 'What is that, Fitz?'

'If you really are serious about learning the truth about your mother, then you must go to Italy.'

Alba narrowed her eyes. Although that very thought had often crossed her mind she had never imagined doing it on her own. She had never done anything on her own. She considered Fitz. He was handsome, charming, and kind and obviously in love with her. *Let me take this one step further, Fitz,* she thought to herself. *You're coming with me.*

4

After dinner and a third bottle of wine, they moved out on to the deck to lie under the stars that peeped out every now and then from behind heavy black clouds. It was cold, so they lay close together beneath a blanket, staring above rather than at each other. After so much laughter it was inevitable that the wine, combined with the beauty of the tempestuous night, would arouse in them a certain melancholy. Viv thought of her ex-husband and wondered whether her books had replaced the children she had never had. Fitz was unable to think of anything other than Alba's warm body pressed up against his and the idea of playing such a large role in her salvation, while Alba filled the emptiness in her spirit with the image of her mother's gentle face.

'I have never known a mother's unconditional love,' she said suddenly.

'And I have never given it,' said Viv.

'I have had it,' said Fitz. 'And it's the most wonderful thing in the world.'

'Tell me about it, Fitz,' Alba asked. 'How is it so wonderful?' She felt as if her chest were being compressed by an invisible object that was solid and heavy.

Fitz sighed. He had always taken it for granted. Now his mind conjured up pictures of those times when, as a small boy, he had run into his mother's arms for comfort, and he felt desperately sad for Alba, who had never known that.

'As a child you know that you are the center of your mother's world,' he began. 'Nothing comes before you in importance. She'll sacrifice everything for you and often does, because your health and happiness are so much more important than hers. As a man, you know that whatever you do, however badly you behave, she will always love you. To your mother, you are brilliant, clever, handsome, and special. I cannot speak for everyone, only myself, but I believe that is the way it should be. My mother is my dearest friend. My love for her is unconditional too. But children are selfish. They don't put their mothers first. Perhaps we should.'

'I should have liked to have had a child,' said Viv in a quiet voice.

'Really, Viv? Would you?' Fitz had never heard her talk about a yearning for children.

'It's a very deep longing, Fitzroy, and most of the time I do not listen to it. However, when the night is so beautiful and I'm with friends, I start to think about the value of life and my own mortality. It is then that I feel I have somehow missed out on a very important aspect of it. But I am old and those useless thoughts do nothing but corrode one's spirit.'

'You would have been a good mother,' said Alba truthfully. 'I wish you'd married my father instead of the Buffalo.'

'I don't think I'd like your father,' Viv replied with a gentle cackle.

'No, I don't suppose you would.'

'Have you met him?' Fitz asked.

'No, but let's just say that I don't like the sound of him or his wife.'

'I shall reserve judgment until I meet them,' said Fitz.

'So, you will come?' asked Alba.

He wanted to reply that he'd do anything for her, but she must have heard countless men say those words so he just said that he wouldn't miss it for the world.

They lay on the deck until the stars retreated and the sky clouded over, giving way to a light, persistent drizzle. The boat began to rock as the river flowed faster, and the creaking and bumping intensified so that Viv decided she wouldn't even try to sleep but would sit at her desk and write another chapter. Alba had unwittingly opened an old wound. It was no use trying to close it tonight; only daylight could do that and she had no desire to lie in bed chewing over old regrets.

She bade them good night and returned inside where the candles had burned out and the gramophone ground to a halt. Incense still lingered in the air and there was another bottle of wine in the fridge. She took off her turban and caftan and wrapped herself in a cozy dressing gown. Taking off her makeup was always a sobering experience. Without it she looked old. She glanced in the mirror only when she had to and massaged her tired skin with a thick cream that promised to work miracles and turn back the clock. She would have liked to turn back the clock. Done it all again, but differently.

Love was a precarious business. Far better to write about it, she figured, than live it. She was too old for children now and too intolerant to live with someone. She might find a man with children of his own, God forbid, and have a stepdaughter like Alba. Secretly she felt some sympathy for the Buffalo. Alba was a handful and a self-centered one at that.

She hoped Fitzroy would be able to control his tender heart. He deserved better than Alba. *What he needs is a sure thing,* she thought. *A woman of substance who'll look after him, not an Alba who only thinks of herself.*

Fitz escorted Alba to her boat. He wished it was the other end of the Embankment, so they could walk together in the drizzle and talk. There were so many things he wanted to ask her. Her arrogance was beguiling but it was her fragility that attracted him. He wanted to be her knight in shining armor. He wanted to be different from all the others. He wanted to be the one she held on to.

When they reached her door she turned to him and smiled, not her usual charming grin but the sad smile of a lonely little girl. 'Will you stay?' she asked. 'I don't want to be alone tonight.'

Fitz was about to embrace her, kiss those plummy lips, and assure her that he would stay forever if she wanted, but he felt an insistent pull at his gut that he could not ignore. If he stayed he'd just be like all the others.

'I can't,' he replied.

Alba's eyes widened. No one had ever declined such an offer.

'Just to sleep,' she explained, wondering why she of all people was being reduced to begging in such a humiliating fashion.

'I've an early appointment in the morning and my briefcase is at home. I'm sorry,' he said lamely, also remembering Sprout shut up in the kitchen. 'It's not that I don't want to,' he added when her lips pursed in fury.

'Well, good night then,' she stated, coldly flinging him a withering look before disappearing inside her boat and locking the door behind her.

Fitz walked back onto the Embankment and tried to remember where he had parked his car. He felt miserable. She had opened up to him on Viv's deck. They had been intimate. Now they had parted as strangers. He longed to return and knock on her door and rehearsed the lines he would say. *'I've had second thoughts ... I've changed my mind ... I'm a fool to have put my work before you ... I want to share your bed and your life ... I love you madly ...'* He was drunk and emotional and couldn't find his car.

The evening had started off with such promise, he thought unhappily. She probably wouldn't want him to pose as her boyfriend now that he had turned her down in such an ungallant manner. He felt cold and dizzy and still couldn't find his car. He usually parked it just around the corner, there on that yellow line. He strode up and down in bewilderment, scanning the streets in the hope that it might magically appear. Finally, after a good while standing in the same spot, staring blankly into the road, he hailed a cab. He couldn't face walking home.

He flopped onto the leather seat and threw his head back. 'Clarendon Mews, please,' he stated. The cabbie started the meter and pulled out into the road.

'You're a bit wet,' he said, hopeful of a conversation. It had been a long night.

'I don't care,' Fitz mumbled. 'I'd do anything for her.'

'Ah, a lady friend,' said the cabbie with a knowing nod. He was used to the broken-hearted unloading their troubles on his back seat.

'The power they have to break us. One glance, one bat of the eyes, and we're pulp. Pulp. That's what I feel like, a bit of pulp.'

'Don't be hard on yourself, gov. She's not worth it.'

'Oh, but she is,' Fitz sighed melodramatically. The cab swung to the left and Fitz swung with it, his head rolling loosely on the back seat like a melon. 'She's not just anyone. She's different from all the others.'

'That's what they all say.' The cabbie chuckled. 'I

thought that about my missus. Now I can see that she nags me same as everyone else's missus. Whoever invented love had a wicked sense of humor. The trouble is, by the time the scales fall from your eyes it's too late, you're married and she's on your back whining about the rotten lot she's been given. If it wasn't for that trick of love no man would walk down the aisle. Bloody con, that's what I say and I fell for it, like a right sucker.'

'You don't understand. This is Alba Arbuckle I'm talking about.'

'Nice name, Alba.'

'It's Italian.'

'I wouldn't trust those wops, if I were you. Couldn't be trusted during the war. Hung about to see who was winning and then sided with the Germans. Bloody fools. We showed 'em, though, didn't we! Teach 'em to disrespect the English.'

'She's too young to know about the war.' Fitz rolled the other way as the cab turned into Clarendon Mews.

'Which number?' the cabbie asked, slowing to a crawl, leaning forward to peer through the windscreen, across which the wipers squeaked hypnotically.

'The second war, of course,' he replied with irritation.

'No, which number do you live in?' repeated the cabbie, shaking his head. It was always at this time of night that he picked up drunks. This one was posh and didn't seem violent, just melancholy.

Fitz opened his eyes. He leaned forward to see his car parked directly outside number eight.

'Damn it!' he said, frowning. 'How the hell did that get there?'

In his inebriated state, Fitz couldn't tell the difference between the coins and paid far too much, to the delight of the cabbie. He fumbled the key in the lock and stumbled inside. He was too tired to undress so he thought he'd lie down on the bed for a few minutes, just to steady his head. When he next opened his eyes it was ten o'clock in the morning and the telephone was ringing.

He dragged himself up onto one elbow and reached for the receiver. He coughed to clear his throat.

'Fitzroy Davenport speaking.' There was a pause. 'Hello?'

'Hi.' Alba's voice was thick and smoky.

Fitz sat up abruptly, unable to contain his joy. 'Hi,' he said happily. 'How are you feeling?'

'Sleepy,' she purred. She sounded as if she were still in bed.

'Me too.' Then he remembered he had told her he had an early appointment. 'I've been up since dawn. I enjoyed last night, though the wine has taken its toll. I think it was that last bottle that's done my head in.'

'I've got the most terrible hangover,' she sighed. 'In fact, I remember very little about the evening.' Which was a lie. But Alba did not wish to remember Fitz's rejection. Fitz felt a wave of disappointment. 'However,' she continued with a sleepy sigh. 'I do recall Viv's plot. It was a very good one. If you're still on?' Fitz now rode the crest of the wave rather than floundering beneath it.

'I'm most certainly on,' he said.

'Good. I'll call the Buffalo and book in for this weekend. It'll be a bore, believe me. We had better get together beforehand to discuss our plan of action.'

'I agree.'

'Say, Thursday evening?'

'I'll take you out for dinner,' he suggested, attempting to make up for having let her down the night before.

'No, I'll rustle something up. Come at eight.'

★   ★   ★

Alba was still furious with Fitz, but she needed him. Besides, Viv's plot really was tremendous. Once Fitz had learned about Valentina he would then accompany her to Italy where she would meet her family. She pictured the scene. The tears, the embraces, and then the stories of her mother's life for which she thirsted. There would be photographs. Brothers and sisters perhaps, nephews and nieces, uncles and aunts. Each would have memories that they would share with her. She would fill in the missing pieces and return complete. She would visit the grave, put flowers there, and all would finally be right in her world.

When Thursday arrived Alba made sure that Rupert came for a drink first. He arrived early with a large bouquet of red roses, the scent of which was carried on the breeze before him. Alba welcomed him at the door in a dusty pink silk dressing gown that barely reached her thighs. Her long glistening legs culminated in a pair of pink fluffy mules that revealed perfect pink toenails, carefully pedicured that afternoon in Chelsea. She breathed in the smell of the roses along with Rupert's familiar cologne, took him by his tie, and closed the door with a slam. Then she placed her lips on his and kissed him. Rupert dropped the flowers. She took him by the hand and led him upstairs to her small bedroom beneath the skylight. It had rained heavily the night before and for most of the day, but now the sky was a pale blue, with only the odd pink and grey clouds floating by.

She lay down on the bed and Rupert scrambled out of his clothes. She watched him with heavy eyelids, her long brown hair spread in a halo around her face. Her cheeks were pink: her lips parted, expectant, lascivious. Once undressed he fell upon her, devouring her flesh as a lion devours his prey. She closed her eyes and calmly stroked his hair as he traveled down her body, his tongue licking her skin as he went.

At a quarter to eight they lay entwined, flushed and tousled, smiling with contentment.

'It's such a shame you have to go,' she said with a sigh.

'Next time, don't arrange dinner. Then we can have the whole night together,' said Rupert.

'I know. Silly of me. We'd better get dressed. I don't want Fitz to see me like this.'

'Who did you say this Fitz character is?' Rupert asked, trying not to sound jealous. After all, he shared her bed, Fitz didn't.

'Viv's literary agent,' she replied casually, getting up with a yawn. 'It's a bore but I'm doing Viv a favor.'

'I see,' he said, reassured.

'He'll come on time and leave early, then I can get a good night's rest. I'm exhausted. You're such a beast, Rupert!' Rupert pulled on his trousers, feeling the tingling of arousal strain his pants.

'Shame I have to put him away,' he replied with a smile. 'He's ready to go again.'

'But I'm not.' She looked at the clock on her bedside table. It was five to eight. Knowing Fitz, he would be on the doorstep in about three minutes, at which point, she thought triumphantly, Rupert will be leaving.

Fitz had bought flowers, long-stemmed arum lilies, and a bottle of wine. Italian wine in preparation for their weekend, which he had termed 'Italy reconquered.' He had splashed his face with cologne and put on a brand-new shirt that his colleague, who was very fond of fashion, had recommended. He felt attractive. He felt optimistic. The very fact that Alba had telephoned him indicated that she had forgiven him. If she offered again, which he very much doubted, he would accept.

He walked down the pontoon, heart suspended, his breathing fast and excited. A moment later he stood outside her door. He had just lifted his hand to knock when it opened and Rupert strode out, flashing him a supercilious smirk, before whistling up the pontoon to the Embankment. When he turned back, Alba was grinning at him. As angry and humiliated as he was, his heart warmed in the radiance of her smile. He was intelligent enough to know that she had planned this moment to put him in his place. To show him that she didn't care. It had worked. He felt suitably humbled. When he smiled back he did so with diffidence, handing her the flowers.

'Oh, they're lovely,' she beamed happily. 'Come on in.' As he walked through the door he had to step over the roses on the floor. 'It's my lucky day,' she said with a giggle, picking them up. 'How many girls get two bouquets in one evening?' The word 'tart' leaped to Fitz's mind and he blushed, appalled that he was capable of thinking such a thing about Alba.

'You deserve them both,' he said, determined not to show her he minded. He followed her down the corridor into the kitchen. It didn't matter who had turned down whom, he thought with a sigh, watching her neat bottom in tight jeans; she had the attitude that would always win.

Her small houseboat was a mess. He caught a glimpse of the bedroom upstairs. Clothes were strewn over the antique French bed, overflowing onto the balustrade and down the stairs in a trail. A large cupboard was open, the drawers pulled out, lace knickers and shimmering silk petticoats tumbling out like hastily opened presents. A pair of pink platform shoes lay discarded on the floor in the corridor, as if she had just stepped out of them. In the sitting room, glossy magazines were tossed in disarray over the ivory-coloured sofas. The place hadn't been dusted for weeks. The kitchen sink was piled high with plates and cups. The rooms were small, decorated in pale pinks and blues, with low ceilings. The place smelled of perfume and paraffin combined with the pleasant scent of polished wood. However, in spite of the chaos, the boat, like Alba, had an enormous amount of charm.

In the kitchen Alba searched the cupboards for vases. Finding none, she placed one bunch of flowers in a jug and the other in the coffee pot, chatting all the time about the things Reed of the River had found in the Thames, sadly not the head, she said, not even the other arm, then poured them both a glass of Fitz's Italian wine.

'How very sweet of you to go to the trouble,' she said. 'Very appropriate.'

'It's to celebrate the start of "Italy reconquered,"' he said, raising his glass. Alba's pale eyes darkened and she suddenly looked moved.

'That's the nicest thing anyone has ever done for me. You have total faith and you're celebrating my decision to open old wounds. More than my father and stepmother would do. We're going to charm them both, together. Daddy will open up to you. He'll love you. Everyone loves you, Viv tells me. You're that sort of man.'

'I don't know whether it's a good thing to be that sort of man,' he said with a shrug. 'I've had two marriages and I'm only forty. I once had a fortune but it's all gone to the women I lost my heart to. I still feel guilty about breaking their hearts and ruining their lives.'

'You're too good,' she said truthfully. 'I don't have a conscience.'

'You don't look like you could hurt anyone.'

'Oh Fitz!'

'Well, your smile would heal any hurt inflicted, I'm sure.'

She laughed throatily and lit a cigarette. 'Are you terribly romantic? Is that your problem?' She sat down at the table, brushing aside small bottles of nail varnish. Fitz followed suit.

'I'm hopelessly romantic, Alba. When I lose my heart there's no getting it back. I believe in love and marriage. I'm just not very good at either.'

'I certainly don't believe in marriage. I'd be very bad at it, and love, well, there are lots of different kinds of love, aren't there?'

Fitz sipped his wine and felt better. 'Have you ever been in love, Alba? Really in love. Blown away?'

She considered his question, cocking her head to one side and glancing sidelong from beneath thick black lashes. 'No.' She spoke confidently. 'No, I don't think I have.'

'Well, you're young.'

'Twenty-six. Viv tells me I should get on with it if I want to have children.'

'Do you want children?'

She screwed up her nose. 'I don't know. Not yet. I don't much like children on the whole. They're sweet and all that, but they're demanding and tiring. Nice to look at but only for a minute or so.' She laughed again and Fitz laughed with her. Her nonchalance was alluring. She was incredibly at ease with herself. He envied her effortlessness. It must be so easy being Alba, he thought.

'You'll feel differently about them when they're your own,' he said, repeating what he had heard other people say.

'Oh, I do hope so. I'd like to be good mother.' Her voice trailed off and she lowered her eyes, looking forlornly into her glass. 'I think my mother would have been a good example.' She raised her eyes and smiled sadly. 'But I'll never know.'

'You will know,' Fitz said emphatically, reaching out and holding her hand. 'Because we're going to find out about her.'

'Do you really think we will?'

'When we've finished we'll know her very well, darling.'

'Oh, Fitz. I hope you're right. I've longed to know her all my life.'

She did not withdraw her hand but gazed at him longingly. 'I trust you, Fitz. I know you won't disappoint me.'

And Fitz prayed silently to whoever was listening, that he wouldn't.

5

Early Saturday morning Fitz picked up Alba in his Volvo with Sprout lying contentedly in the back, watching seagulls through the glass. He had to wait downstairs while she dressed. He could hear her above him, wandering back and forth while she deliberated what outfit to wear. He had noticed her clothes. They were carefully chosen and highly fashionable. He didn't know why she bothered. She'd look just as enticing in an old sack.

He peered through one of the windows in the sitting room to where Viv's boat lay quiet and still. He could imagine her typing away in a long flowing gown, cigarette smoking in one of those lime green dishes. He reflected too on how often he had sat on her deck trying to look into Alba's boat, hoping to catch a glimpse of her, a hint of her, *anything*. He remembered Viv's warning. 'Don't fall in love, Fitzroy,' she had said. *Too late,* he thought with a sigh.

He hadn't been disappointed the night they had dined together. He had fully expected to leave afterward and drive home. At least he didn't get drunk and lose his car. They had talked until long after midnight, their stomachs full of the risotto he had cooked; Alba wasn't capable of rustling anything up, in spite of her enthusiasm. She had told him about her childhood, her horrid stepmother, and the sense of isolation she had suffered all her life.

He had tried to explain that it was natural for her father to try to move on after the loss of his first wife. The tragedy of her death must have nearly broken him. Then to be left with a small baby. It would have been impossible for him to bring her up on his own. He had needed Margo. Alba was simply an innocent casualty in the wake of his determination to build a new life and to forget the past. 'I'm looking at it from a man's point of view,' he had explained. 'It doesn't mean that he loves you less, just that he doesn't want to be dragged back into the past and probably wants to protect you from it too.' Alba had gone very quiet.

'Maybe you're right,' she had conceded finally. 'But that doesn't change the way I feel about the Buffalo. I just feel deeply sorry for my father. He hides his unhappiness behind a superficial jolliness. Good-natured and gung-ho, that's Daddy. A tipple at six, dinner at eight thirty, glass of whisky and a cigar in his study at ten. He never wastes a cigar but smokes it right until the very end. Until it nearly burns his fingers. He protects himself in the structure of routine. Always the same three-piece tweed suit during the day, smoking jacket and slippers at night. Sunday lunch in the dining room, Sunday dinner in the hall by the fire. Cook makes the same roast every Sunday, though it's always something special when the vicar comes for lunch. Leg of lamb or beef, steamed pudding or apple crumble. He goes for a walk in the evening after arriving on the six thirty train from London, takes a stick and surveys his estate. Chats to the manager, discusses pheasants and tree planting. Everything is always the same, nothing changes. Nothing to scare the horses. Then I found the picture he never expected to see again. I dragged him back into his past. Poor man, he doesn't know what to do with me. He'll talk to you, though, I'm sure. He's a man's man and you're his sort.'

Fitz hadn't known whether that was a good thing to be. In Alba's eyes it probably wasn't. Viv had described Thomas Arbuckle as an 'old duffer,' but if he had been a young man in the war he'd only be in his fifties. Hardly the twilight years.

Fitz withdrew from the window and his thoughts when Alba appeared in the doorway. She wore a simple pair of slacks and a beige corduroy jacket over a white cashmere turtleneck. She had pulled her hair into a ponytail, leaving the long fringe to brush her forehead and cheekbones. She didn't bother to excuse the mess. 'I'm ready. I've put on my most conservative clothes so I match you.' Fitz could have taken offense had he not already considered himself conservative. However, once again her comment only emphasized the stark differences between them and the fact that she could not possibly fancy him. But he wasn't disappointed, for they were friends, at least, and that was better than being shut out in the drizzle.

'You look lovely,' he said, running his eyes up and down her body in appreciation.

She grinned broadly. 'I like it when you do that,' she said, turning and walking toward the door.

'Do what?'

'Look me up and down like that. I can feel your eyes like a pair of hands. They tickle.'

It was warm outside. The spring breeze danced up the river, causing it to ripple and roll. Gulls floated on the air, their cries punctuating the dull drone of traffic.

'Now, I hope you have a car to match your image. Not a sports car. Daddy is suspicious of men in sports cars.'

'I have a rather old, dilapidated Volvo.'

'Sounds good to me,' she said, linking her arm through ⸺ have to present ourselves as a couple,' she added ⸺ at her quizzically.

Alba climbed into the passenger seat, throwing a few books and a manuscript into the back to make room. Besides the literary chaos, it smelled of dogs.

'I didn't know you had a dog,' she said when he got in and started up the engine.

'Sprout. He's in the back.'

Alba's eyes widened. 'I hope he's not a scruffy little rat like Margo's.'

'He's a cross between a springer and a pointer.'

'Whatever that means,' she sighed, turning around to take a look. 'Oh yes, he'll do. Thank God he's a boisterous dog. I do hate yappers.'

'Sprout's bark is very manly, I assure you.'

'Thank heaven for that, otherwise he'd have to stay behind, unless, of course, he's willing to eat Margo's rats for tea.'

'Don't listen to her, Sprout. She's not really so hard-hearted.' Sprout could be heard sighing patiently in the back.

'You wait, you'll understand when you see them. The Buffalo likes things she can carry around under her arm.'

'Not your father, I hope!'

Alba giggled and nudged him playfully. 'You fool! She's strong but not Hercules!'

They chatted all the way down the A30. When they turned off the main road and began to thread their way down narrow winding lanes, the countryside revealed itself in all its glory. The woods were bursting into life with the warmer weather, vibrating with a bright, phosphorescent green that reminded Fitz of Viv's little dishes. The air was sweet and sugar-scented and birds flew overhead or perched on telephone wires, taking breaks from the rigorous task of building nests. They stopped talking and looked about them. The gentle stillness of the land was a refreshing antidote to the busy, bustling city. It calmed the soul. Made one breathe deeply, from the bottom of one's chest. Fitz felt his shoulders relax and his head empty of all the irksome things he had to do at work. Even Alba looked calmer. With the green land as a backdrop she looked younger, as if they had left not only the city behind but her urbane sophistication as well.

Fitz slowed down and they turned into the driveway. The drive itself was about a quarter of a mile long, lined with majestic copper beeches whose buds were beginning to open and reveal tender red leaves. On the right a field extended out to a dark wood. A few horses were grazing, hardly bothering to raise their eyes to see what the disturbance was, and a couple of large rabbits, their shoulders hunched and ears twitching, huddled together as if in deep discussion. Fitz was enchanted. But nothing could have prepared him for the beauty of the house.

Beechfield Park was a large, red-brick and flint mansion with immense character and charm. Wisteria and clematis climbed the walls with complete freedom to go where they chose. The lead windows were small but, like eyes, they were alert and watchful and full of humor. The roofs were uneven, curved, as if the spirit of the house had rebelled against the architect's stringent lines and had stretched and flexed its limbs to make itself comfortable. The result was a building with great warmth. 'It's glorious,' Fitz exclaimed as the car scrunched up the gravel and drew to a halt outside the front door.

'It belonged to my great-great-grandfather,' Alba explained. 'He won it at the gambling table. Sadly he lost his wife there before she could enjoy it.' Alba never let the truth interfere with a good story.

'He lost his wife gambling?'

'Yes, to a rich duke.'

'Perhaps she was a fright.'

'Well, she can't have been that great if he was prepared to gamble her away. Oh, the rats!' she said with a laugh as Margo's yapping terriers scuttled out of the door. 'They're Margo's loves. For God's sake, don't sit on one! Great-uncle Hennie once sat on Grandma's dog and killed it.'

'A slight faux pas!'

'They didn't discover it for a week. He hid it under the cushion for the housekeeper to find.'

At that moment Margo and Thomas emerged from the porch, smiling broadly. Margo called the dogs in her low, commanding voice, slapping her thighs. Her hair was grey and pinned up roughly at the back. She wore no makeup and her skin was lined and ruddy, as one would expect of a woman who spent a great deal of her time out riding horses. 'Hedge, do come here!' she barked. 'So nice to meet you, Fitzroy,' she added, extending her hand. Fitz shook it. She had a firm, confident grip.

'What a charming home you have, Captain Arbuckle,' said Fitz, shaking Thomas's hand.

'Call me Thomas,' he replied, chuckling good-naturedly. 'I hope you didn't encounter too much traffic. The roads can be rather dreadful on a Saturday morning.'

'No trouble at all,' Fitz replied. 'We flew down without a hitch.'

Thomas kissed Alba's temple as he always did and she found herself enormously relieved that he bore no grudge after their last meeting. Margo smiled tightly. She found it harder to hide her feelings.

'Would you mind if I let Sprout out for a run?' said Fitz. 'He's old and particularly kind to those smaller than himself.'

'Don't underestimate small dogs,' replied Margo. 'They're more than capable of standing up for themselves.'

Fitz lifted the trunk and a rather stiff, crumpled Sprout lumbered out. The dogs all sniffed each other curiously, though Margo's terriers showed a greater interest in Sprout than the old dog showed in them. He was keener to cock his leg on the tire and sniff the gravel than play with the scruffy little creatures who pressed their noses to his bottom. Fitz left the trunk open so Sprout could seek refuge there when the terriers became too much, and followed Margo and Thomas into the house.

'Caroline's coming down after lunch and Miranda's home from school. Poor Henry's at Sandhurst. They keep him busy there,' said Margo as they walked through the hall into the drawing room. Fitz was pleasantly surprised by Alba's parents. They weren't the ogres she had portrayed but conventional, country types. The drawing room was decorated simply in pale yellows and beiges. He sank into the sofa and, to his surprise, Alba positioned herself beside him and took his hand and squeezed it. He noticed Thomas catch Margo's eye. It was clear that Alba had never brought a boyfriend home before.

'A drink, Fitzroy?' Thomas asked. Fitz wondered what they would expect him to have, then asked for a whiskey on the rocks. Thomas looked pleased and walked over to the drinks table. Margo sat on the club fender and pulled one of the dogs onto her lap.

'So, Fitzroy, what do you do?' she asked, running a large hand down the dog's back.

'I'm a literary agent.'

'Ah,' she replied, impressed.

'Among others, I represent Vivien Armitage.'

She raised her eyebrows in recognition. Margo Arbuckle epitomized Viv's readership.

'Now, she's jolly good,' she said. 'I don't get much time to read. Running this house and my horses swallows up the days but when I get the chance I do enjoy her novels. Thomas likes Wilbur Smith, don't you, Thomas?'

'I like a good read. Mind you, I'm rather more inclined to read biographies these days.' He handed Fitz his drink. 'Nothing like a true story, is there?'

'Now, Fitzroy,' Margo began, 'are you one of the Norfolk Davenports?'

'Yes,' Fitz lied. If one was going to lie one should do so with the utmost confidence. He squeezed Alba's hand and she squeezed his back. She was enjoying this.

'Do you know Harold and Elizabeth?'

'Harold is my father's cousin,' said Fitz. He had never heard of Harold and Elizabeth.

'Ah, so your father is ...?'

'Geoffrey.' *Another lie, but why quit now,* he thought. Margo narrowed her eyes and frowned.

She shook her head. 'I don't know Geoffrey.'

'Do you know . . . George?'

'No.'

'David?' It was a gamble.

'Yes.' Her small brown eyes lit up. 'Yes, I do know David. Married to Penelope.'

'Absolutely,' said Fitz. 'Charming woman, Penelope.'

'Isn't she? Shame they had no children.' She sighed and pulled a sympathetic smile. 'So your parents live near Kings Lynn too?'

'No, my father moved down south, to Dorset. He has a grouse moor in Scotland though. When I was a child we divided our time between the two houses and of course the chalet in Switzerland.'

'You ski?' interjected Thomas, who loved all sports. He didn't know which impressed him more, the grouse moor in Scotland or the chalet in Switzerland.

Thomas sat down in the armchair and took a swig of

martini. 'I hope you'll stay the whole weekend, Fitzroy. We have the Reverend coming for lunch tomorrow, after the service. Do you play squash?'

'Absolutely,' said Fitz, which was the truth. 'I'd love a game, but preferably not with the Reverend. I daren't play a man with God on his side.'

Margo laughed. Alba was amazed. Her father was pink with pleasure. They really liked him. Viv had been right. She wasn't a best seller for nothing.

And as if Fitz hadn't charmed them enough, he bent down and picked up one of Margo's little dogs. 'My mother had terriers,' he said, stroking its fur. 'She stopped going on holidays simply because she couldn't bear to leave them behind.' Margo tilted her head to one side and gave the most understanding of smiles. 'And yours, Mrs. Arbuckle, are delightful.'

'Oh, Fitzroy, you make me feel so old. Call me Margo.'

'Only if you call me Fitz.'

At that moment Miranda hurried into the room. She was tall and slim with straight blond hair tied into a pony-tail. She wore jodhpurs and riding boots and an irritated expression on a round, flushed face. 'Summer's bolted again, Mummy!' she said, huffing and puffing in the doorway.

Margo stood up. 'Darling, let me introduce you to Fitz Davenport, Alba's friend.'

'Oh, sorry,' she said breezily, extending her hand. 'I'm afraid my horse is a bolter.'

Fitz was about to make a joke about the Bolter in Nancy Mitford's *Love in a Cold Climate* but changed his mind; such a reference would probably be lost on one so young.

'Do you want help getting her back?' he said instead. 'Sprout could do with a run.'

'Would you?' interrupted Margo. 'Gosh, Fitz, you are kind. You've only just arrived from London.'

'Let me go and change out of these clothes into something I don't mind getting mud on. Then we can all muck in together, can't we, Alba?'

'He's in the yellow room,' interjected Margo as they stepped out into the hall.

Alba looked horrified. She hoped that she could hold the gate open or something. As a child she had been forced into riding and cleaning tack, but when she grew old enough to express her opinions she kicked up such a fuss that Margo let her off, so long as she helped in the garden, podding and peeling beans all summer, which was the lesser of two evils. Picking vegetables wasn't so much an arduous task as a boring one and besides, there were other things she'd much rather be doing, like reading magazines and playing with Cook's makeup. At least, though, it was a solitary occupation that left her alone with her thoughts. She would hear the others shouting in the field above the house, their hearty voices echoing across the valley, grateful that she wasn't among them. She had always had an aversion to group activities – especially family ones. She led Fitz up the stairs and when they were alone she burst into commentary.

'You're first-class, Fitz!' she exclaimed, embracing him. 'You've already won them over and you know what? They think better of me because of you. Suddenly I'm being treated like a grown-up.' Fitz savored the sensation of her body against his, her arms wrapped around his waist, before she pulled away.

'You *are* a grown-up,' he said, watching her saunter over to the window. He peered into his empty suitcase, surprised that it had already been unpacked.

'That's Mrs. Bromley. She's the housekeeper. A

shadowy figure one rarely sees, like a little field mouse,' Alba added when she saw the puzzled look on his face.

'Does she always unpack?'

'Of course, for guests. Sadly not for me though, and I need it more than you do, because I'm chaotic.' She laughed huskily. 'No field mouse to scurry about in my room.'

'Will I find anything?' He opened a drawer to discover one pair of pants and one pair of socks neatly placed together like an old married couple in bed.

'That's a tough question. I don't know the way her mind works, assuming that she has one, of course. She's a fossil.'

'At least I know where my pants are!' he said with a chuckle, then opened the wardrobe to find his jeans draped over a hanger.

'Wouldn't it be awful if we really did end up together? They'd discover you'd lied.'

'I hadn't thought of that,' said Fitz seriously but Alba was giggling as if the mere idea was preposterous.

'I'll see you downstairs,' she said, tossing her ponytail. 'I'm not changing and I'm not chasing a bloody horse around a muddy field, either. Really, Fitz, that was beyond the call of duty. You know she has bloody pigs in the woods?'

'Pigs?'

'Yes, wild boars. Six sows and two boars in a pen that takes up about an acre. She thinks they'll make her money. They're always breaking free and believe me, you don't want to encounter Boris on a dark night. He's fearsome. He also has the biggest balls you've ever seen.' She raised her eyebrows playfully.

'Don't make me feel inadequate,' Fitz replied with a chuckle.

'Then don't make me run around after a bloody horse. I think you're enjoying this role-play much too much.'

Alba swept out of the room. Fitz changed into his jeans and a grey sweater. Alba was right, he was enjoying the act enormously. It wasn't hard. Thomas and Margo were easy to please. It wasn't difficult either to hold Alba's hand and pretend that her heart belonged to him. Sadly, though, it was only an act and, at the end of the weekend, he would drop her off in Cheyne Walk and return alone to Clarendon Mews. Hopefully he would find out enough about her mother for her to travel to Italy and discover more for herself. He would have served his purpose and she'd have no further use for him. He'd have to continue his bridge fours with Viv and endure the sight of Rupert whistling down the pontoon in anticipation of Alba's unique brand of hospitality, any intimacy with him having evaporated like the mists that hang over the Thames. He pushed that thought to the back of his mind and left the room. As long as he was in this house he was Alba's boyfriend and he would do his best not to let reality ruin it for him. He had no intention of turning into a pumpkin before it was absolutely necessary.

Margo and Miranda waited in the hall with Alba. Margo had tied a scarf around her head and put on a pair of brown corduroy trousers. Alba lingered by the window while her stepmother and half sister discussed the problem fence and Summer's extraordinary intelligence.

'It's becoming a pain,' said Margo stridently. 'Peter will simply have to go through every inch of it and mend the weak spots. We can't have her running off like this. One day she'll run into the road and cause an accident! Ah, Fitz,' she said, her ruddy face breaking into a large smile. 'You really are a sport!'

'It's a pleasure,' he replied. 'Besides, it's such a

beautiful day. It's a shame to waste it inside.' Miranda's cheeks flushed when he settled his eyes on her.

'I hope she hasn't gone far,' she mumbled, then turned and followed her mother out of the house. Alba rolled her eyes at Fitz.

'You're mad,' she said affectionately. 'I said they'd love you, didn't I? You're their sort of person.' Fitz knew she didn't mean it as a compliment.

Catching Summer was no easy task. She had headed off up the drive and was almost in the lane, chewing the cow parsley greedily. At first Margo gave the orders. Even Alba had to make up the circle in their attempts to corner her. No hanging around gates for Alba. She shot Fitz a furious look; if he hadn't suggested they help she would still be sipping wine in the drawing room. Sprout and the terriers raced around barking at Summer, but she simply tossed her head and cantered off triumphantly. When Margo's strategy failed, Fitz took over. His prime concern was not Summer but Alba, whom he wanted desperately to please. He ordered her to go back to the field and hold the gate wide open. Then he, Miranda, and Margo, instead of trying to catch the stubborn mare, encouraged her to trot back to the field on her own by simply walking toward her in a line with their arms outspread. Her natural instinct was to move away from them. Little by little, with patience, they managed to usher her back. To Miranda's amazement, Summer cantered into the field and Alba closed the gate behind her gleefully. It had taken time, but there was a large grin on Alba's face. It had been worth it.

When Margo congratulated Fitz, he explained that he had grown up with horses. 'I'd get that fence looked at, though,' he said, doing his best to sound like a man of vast experience. 'We had a mare once that bolted. Cut her leg on barbed wire. It got infected. Nasty business.'

'Oh dear. One wants to avoid that at all costs. Shame Alba doesn't ride; otherwise you could both have a good hack before lunch.'

Alba linked arms with Fitz. Miranda's admiration for him had not escaped her notice.

'I'd like to show him around the estate,' she said.

'Miranda will take you, if you'd like a ride,' Margo persisted in her usual tactless manner. Alba was furious. *She wants Fitz for Miranda,* she thought angrily. Fitz sensed Alba bristling at his side and declined politely.

'That's very sweet of you. Another time, perhaps.' Then he shouted at Sprout. 'Come on, old boy. Let's go and check out happy Boris.'

'Happy?' said Alba, crinkling her nose.

'Well, of course,' he replied, raising his eyebrows suggestively.

'Oh,' she said with a smile. 'Of course.'

Margo watched Alba and Fitz walk off in the direction of the orchard and turned toward the house. 'What a charming young man,' she said to her daughter.

'Lucky Alba,' Miranda replied with a sigh. 'He's attractive, isn't he?'

'Yes, he is,' Margo agreed. 'Not her type, though. She usually goes for pretty boys and fashionable ones too, according to Caroline.'

'He's ruggedly handsome, I'd say.'

'I hope he knows what he's in for.' Margo laughed and shook her head. 'She's a headstrong girl. Though, he's no shrinking violet, is he? He's tall and broad and strong. I'm sure he can manage her.'

'I'm glad she's found someone nice.'

'Oh, so am I. A *proper* person.'

'He's quite a bit older than her, though, isn't he?'

'Thank the Lord! No man her own age would cope.'

'Do you think he'll marry her?'

'One never knows with Alba.'

'Well, I think I'll ride out on my own then,' said Miranda, moving away.

'I'll come with you,' said her mother. 'Alba doesn't need me.'

Margo turned to look back up the garden but they had gone. She heaved a sigh and strode into the house to change.

Alba and Fitz returned at lunchtime. Their faces were flushed and their eyes shone. Alba had shown him around the estate. The gardens and the tennis court, the squash court and stables. She had showed him the swimming pool that was empty of water and filled with leaves, and the pond where ducks and moorhens swam among water-cress and bulrushes. Then they had wandered up to the woods, where Boris had been only too happy to show off his assets and how well he used them. They had even spotted a couple of fawns in the woods and heard the rasping cough of a muntjac. The bluebells were nearly out and the fertile scents of nature had filled the air and their spirits. Thomas was impressed. Alba never went on walks on her own. He was pleased that she took pride in her home and was keen to show it off. *Fitz is a good influence,* he thought happily.

Fitz had charmed the Arbuckle family with ease. Miranda watched him while her adolescent body stirred with something dark and primitive and deliciously confusing. Margo was overjoyed that Alba had found a normal man with a normal job. A man she could place. A man from her world. Thomas looked forward to an after-dinner cigar in the company of a man of education. It gave him pleasure to see his daughter so happy and calm, for calm was a stranger to Alba. Gone was the raging child who had turned up that night with a fistful of abuse. But there was one member of the family that Alba and Fitz had not considered.

6

Lavender Arbuckle hobbled into the drawing room. Margo looked on in horror while Thomas rose to his feet to allow his mother prime position in his comfortable reading chair. Lavender spent most days hidden upstairs in her suite of rooms, but she had smelled the excitement in the air like a dog smells dinner and had come down to find out what was going on. She wore an elegant tweed suit that dated from the twenties. It hung off her body; she had shrunk with the years and ate so little that her bones stuck out. It was a wonder they didn't penetrate her old flesh.

'Mother, let me present Fitzroy Davenport,' said Thomas. Fitz jumped to his feet. He bowed and shook her hand. Next to him she looked like a tiny sparrow.

'And who are you?' she asked in a slow, haughty voice, fixing him with her formidable gaze.

At this point Margo interjected, 'Lavender, he's Alba's friend.'

'Ah,' she said, raising her chin. 'Alba's friend.' She turned to Alba. 'You're back again! How nice.' Alba remained seated. No one spoke. They all waited for the old woman to settle into the reading chair. 'Are you married, Fitzroy?' Margo tried once again to intervene. It was most embarrassing.

'No,' Fitz replied coolly.

'Jolly good! You can marry Caroline, or Miranda. You look like a good sort.'

Alba took his hand in hers and inhaled sharply. 'If he marries anyone it shall be *me*,' she stated emphatically, clipping her consonants like Viv did.

'And who are you?' Lavender repeated, this time to Alba.

'For goodness' sake, Grandma, I'm Alba and I need a cigarette!' She got up and marched out of the room.

'I'd like a cigarette too,' said Fitz and hurried after Alba.

Once they had left the room the old woman blinked in bewilderment. 'Was it something I said?'

'Mother, it's really not on that you fail to recognize your own granddaughter,' Thomas complained, handing her a brandy.

'Oh yes, the dark one,' she said quietly and her voice trailed off as she tried to work out why the girl was so dark when all the Arbuckles were fair. 'I'm most confused.' She turned to Margo. 'Is she yours?'

'She's *ours*. Lavender, really!' Margo replied, now in a fluster. It had all been going so well before Thomas's dotty old mother appeared.

'Beautiful girl,' she said, oblivious that she had offended her daughter-in-law.

Then Thomas spoke, barely audibly. 'Her mother died when she was born. Surely you remember?'

Lavender's jaw dropped and she let out a deep groan. 'Oh, yes. Valentina,' she whispered as if afraid to mention the name. As if it were somehow sacred. 'I quite forgot. What a fool I am.' Her eyes suddenly glistened and her grey cheeks took on a purple hue. 'You must forgive me. Dear girl,' Lavender shook her head. 'What a business. A ghastly, ghastly business.'

'I think we should eat,' said Thomas, straightening up.
'Miranda, go and tell Cook that we are ready. If you can
find Alba, tell her too. Let's go into the dining room.'

Miranda left the room and Margo gave Lavender her
hand. Like most old people who refuse to accept that
they are fading, she shrugged it off and pushed herself up
with a great deal of effort. 'Nothing wrong with me, I
assure you,' she mumbled and hobbled into the hall. As
she made her way to the dining room she was enveloped
by a most delicious smell, warm, succulent, and foreign.
She let it fill her senses with pleasure. 'Figs,' she gasped
with a sigh. 'I haven't had a fig in years!'

'She's getting worse,' Margo muttered to her husband.
Thomas shrugged. 'It's most embarrassing. What will
Fitz think? Of all the questions to ask!'

'Alba's very keen on him, isn't she?' said Thomas. 'It's
a good thing.'

'It's a tremendously good thing, Thomas. I hope
Lavender hasn't frightened him off.'

'He's made of stronger stuff than you give him credit
for, Margo. Mark my words. He's keen on Alba too.'
Margo crossed her fingers, showing them to her
husband.

'Let's just pray,' she said and walked out into the hall,
her little dogs trotting after her.

Margo made sure that Lavender was placed between
Thomas and Miranda, putting Fitz and Alba next to herself. Cook served delicious lamb with roast potatoes and
beans as a special treat because Alba had brought her
new boyfriend. Lavender was chastened and picked at
her food in silence but barely took her eyes off Alba. She
didn't stare in the same way that people on the bus stared,
but with a mixture of curiosity and sympathy. Alba tried
not to mind; after all, her grandmother was old. Once she

had been lucid and had told wonderful stories of the people who had come into her life. Rainbows, she had called them. 'If it weren't for my friends, my life would be like a dull, empty sky,' she had often said. Then exclaimed heartily, 'God forbid!' Alba wondered whether there were any rainbows left or whether she now existed in the empty sky that she had so dreaded.

Fitz continued to charm her father and stepmother with his elaborate lies and boyish smile. Once or twice he forgot himself and the odd truth escaped to contradict the lies he had sown earlier, but he smoothed it over by stammering in that very English way and feigning vagueness, which was charming in itself. No one was any the wiser. Alba watched him with growing affection. He had followed her out onto the porch after her grandmother's tactless remarks and they had shared a cigarette. If it hadn't been for him she might very well have jumped into the car and driven back up to London. She never bothered to stick around when a situation upset her. Fitz had talked it over, made it into a joke. She had agreed to double-blink at him each time Lavender said something outrageous and rude. Now she waited, but Lavender said nothing.

Cook bustled in with a large, steaming treacle pudding. Lavender raised her head expectantly then dropped her narrow shoulders in disappointment. 'I thought we were having figs,' she said indignantly.

'Figs?' said Margo with a frown.

'Figs,' came the reply.

'It's steamed pudding,' Margo explained. 'Why doesn't everyone help themselves?' She nodded at Cook who put the plate on the sideboard.

'I definitely smelled figs in the hall. Didn't you?' She turned to her son.

'No, I didn't,' Thomas replied. But he knitted his eyebrows in bewilderment because in the last couple of weeks he could have sworn he had smelled that desperately familiar, fruity scent. It brought back memories he had shelved long ago. Of the war, of Italy, of a beautiful young woman and a terrible tragedy.

'I'm most disappointed,' she wailed. 'I haven't had a fig in years!'

'I'm terribly sorry, Lavender,' said Margo, her chest expanding in a deep breath. 'I'll find you a fig next time I'm at Fortnum's. I promise.'

Lavender placed her thin hand on her son's but stared down at the table. 'I did smell figs. I'm not losing my mind!'

Alba double-blinked at Fitz and smirked. However, Fitz was no longer amused. The old woman's confusion aroused nothing but pity.

After lunch they settled into the drawing room, where coffee was served with little shortbread squares. Margo's dogs lay down at her feet, but Hedge took his usual place of privilege on her lap. Lavender retired for a rest, and laughter once more returned to the group. Thomas suggested a rubber of bridge. Alba sat on the sofa smoking while Fitz settled down with her family. It was all part of the plan and, as much as she wanted to draw him away, she knew it would be unwise; after all, he was an excellent player and it was one of her father's favorite games.

Caroline arrived once the game was over. Margo and Fitz were enjoying a detailed postmortem, analysing where they had gone wrong and what they should have done. She hurried in with a large grin. 'Oh, it's so lovely to be home,' she enthused, kissing her parents and patting the little dogs excitedly. She hugged Miranda and Alba and extended her hand to the stranger.

'I'm in love!' she beamed, flopping into a chair and crossing her legs beneath her long skirt. 'He's called Michael Hudson-Hume. You'll love him,' she gushed to her mother. 'He went to Eton and then Oxford. He's very bright. Now works in the City.'

Margo looked pleased. 'Darling, how lovely. When are we going to meet him?'

'Very soon,' she replied, flicking the hair off her shoulder with a pale hand. 'His parents live in Kent. He goes there most weekends. He's a terrific tennis player, Daddy, and is going to teach me to play golf. He says he can already tell that I'll have a good swing.'

'Good,' said Thomas, chuckling good-naturedly.

'Is his mother Daphne?' Margo asked, narrowing her eyes and mentally placing Michael Hudson-Hume in a nice tidy box with *Proper Person* written on it.

Caroline's eyes widened, as did her smile. 'Yes!' she enthused. 'And his father's William.'

Margo lifted her chin and nodded. 'Daphne was at school with me. We did pony club camp together. She was a terrific horsewoman.'

'Oh yes, she still is. She's an eventer,' said Caroline with pride. Margo didn't feel it appropriate to mention that Daphne had also been very keen on the boys and had acquired the nickname 'Lapin' because, as they crudely put it, 'she went like a rabbit.'

'I do look forward to seeing her again.'

'Oh, you will,' said Caroline. '*Very* soon!'

Alba sensed that Michael was about to propose. Knowing the Hudson-Hume type he would drive down to ask her father for Caroline's hand. He would do the right thing as he had no doubt done all his life. Just like Caroline and Miranda. She inhaled her cigarette and blew the smoke out in a long puff, while her eyelids grew heavy with boredom. She was jolted back to wakefulness by Fitz squeezing her hand.

'Let's go for a walk,' he suggested in a low voice. *Before they ask me if I know the Hudson-Humes,* he thought, knowing that he'd find it irresistible to lie and say that he did, brewing up all sorts of trouble for the future. Then he frowned. If he succeeded in giving Alba what she wanted they wouldn't have a future, not together at any rate.

That evening while he changed for dinner Fitz realized, as he tried to subdue his windblown hair, that he wasn't charming the Arbuckles solely in order to dupe them, but because he sincerely wanted them to like him. It wasn't an act at all. So he had lied, which had been fun, and played with the Buffalo's weakness for surrounding herself with people from her own world. But he genuinely wanted them to think well of him. He wanted Alba to think well of him too. A part of him hoped that by helping her discover her mother he would make it all right with her father and that she would reward him with love.

He was hopelessly smitten. He was unable to withdraw his gaze without a great deal of effort, so compelling was she. Her sisters only confirmed what he had always suspected – that she was unique. Their veins shared Arbuckle blood and yet they possessed none of Alba's beauty or her mystery. God had broken the mold after creating Alba. He stared at his reflection. Could she ever grow to love him? Didn't she know how much she tormented him? Would his heart ever recover? Would he be left analysing his moves like he did after a rubber of bridge? Wondering that perhaps if he had played a little better, with a little more cunning, he might have won?

At dinner he was seated between Miranda and Caroline.

As he listened to them he was reminded of bread sauce and how bland it was without salt. Miranda and Caroline needed a good deal more salt. But as he and Alba had discussed on their walk, the likes of Michael Hudson-Hume didn't want spunky women. Spunky women frightened them. They lacked salt themselves. He gazed across the table at Alba. She looked tired, or bored, her strange eyes paler in the light of the candles and more shadowy than ever. She sat beside her father and yet they barely talked. It was imperative that he succeed tonight.

After dinner his moment came. Thomas put his hand on Fitz's back and suggested they go into his study for a glass of port and a cigar. Fitz managed to double-blink at Alba, but although she blinked back, her expression was one of defeat.

'I've had enough of the company of women,' Thomas said, pouring them both a glass of port. 'This is rather good,' he added, handing the glass to Fitz. 'A cigar?' He opened the humidor and pulled one out, passing it under his nose and sniffing it. 'Ah, the sweet smell of a cigar.' Fitz thought it would be rude not to smoke. Besides, this was his one chance to befriend him.

They both spent a good few minutes preparing their cigars. 'I smoked so many cigarettes in the war,' said Thomas, 'that afterward, when the beastly business was over, I took to cigars instead. Didn't want to be reminded of it. You know.'

He sat down in a worn leather chair. Fitz did the same. The lights were dim. He looked about the room, at all the books in their glass bookcases, most of them old, beautifully bound, inherited no doubt. After a good ten minutes of chat Fitz cut to the chase.

'My father was in the war. It changed him. He was never the same after that.'

'Where was he?'

'Italy.' Fitz noticed Thomas's forehead crease into deep furrows. He paused for a long moment, swirling the port around in his glass.

'Where?'

'Naples.'

Thomas nodded grimly. 'Terrible business, Naples.'

'He says he'll never forget the poverty. The despair. Human beings sunk so far, such depravity. The indignity of it. He's still haunted by what he saw, even now.'

'I never got as far as Naples.' Thomas took a swig of port and swallowed loudly. 'I was in the navy.'

'Ah,' said Fitz.

'I captained an MTB.' Fitz nodded. He had once read an article about the motor torpedo boats. They had harassed enemy coastal convoys in the Channel, the North Sea, the Mediterranean, and the Adriatic. 'It was quite a unique feeling to cut through waves at forty knots. We'd be in and out in seconds before our targets knew what had hit them. Bloody marvelous,' he continued, then drained his glass. 'I don't like to think of it these days. Haven't been back. It's a closed chapter. A man should suffer his pain in private, don't you think?'

'I disagree, Thomas,' said Fitz boldly. 'I believe a man should suffer his pain only in the company of other men. We fight together and we smoke together. There's a good reason why women leave the dining table at the end of a meal. Leaves the men free to show their vulnerability. There's nothing shameful about that.'

Thomas puffed away, watching with dewy eyes the man who seemed to have tamed his daughter. 'I never thought I'd see Alba with a man like you.'

'No?' Fitz chuckled good-naturedly. 'Why not?' He wasn't acting now.

'You're a sensible fellow. You have a good head on your shoulders. You're intelligent and driven. Have a proper occupation. Come from a good family. Why would Alba go for someone like you?'

'I don't know the sort of man she usually goes for,' said Fitz, trying not to take offense.

'Men who can satisfy her in the short term, not a runner like you.'

'She's a lively girl,' said Fitz, surprised that her own father should allude to her promiscuity, however obliquely. 'Not only is she beautiful, Thomas, but she's colourful, vibrant, mysterious. She intrigues me.' He sighed heavily and drew on his cigar. 'She's unfathomable.'

Thomas nodded knowingly and chuckled. 'Like her mother,' he said and it was as if Fitz was no longer there. 'She was mysterious too. That's what I first noticed about her, her mystery.' He poured himself another port. It was clear that he was drunk. Fitz felt a momentary stab of guilt. It wasn't fair to pry into the man's past, to take advantage of his vulnerability. But Thomas continued. It was as if he needed to talk about it. As if the drink had facilitated a deep and aching desire.

'Every time I look at Alba I see Valentina.' His mouth twitched and his face sagged and turned grey. 'Valentina,' he repeated. 'The mere mention of her name still has the power to debilitate me. After all these years. Why now the scent of figs? My mother isn't mad, you know. I smelled it too. Sweet and warm and fruity. Figs. Yes, Alba is her mother's daughter. I try to protect her . . .' He raised his eyes, now watery with tears. 'She was legendary. For miles around everyone knew her name. Her beauty had spread much further than that small bay of sorcery. Valentina Fiorelli, *la bella donna d'Incantellaria*. Strange little cove, Incantellaria. *Incanto* means 'charm,' you know.

It was charmed, bewitched, like someone had cast some sort of spell. We all felt it, but mine was the only heart that suffered. Oh, that it had been otherwise ... War does funny things to people. That sense of transience, of opportunity, of suspended reality, it gripped me too. I had always been reckless but Valentina made me forget myself entirely. I was a different man, Fitz.'

'Time doesn't heal pain, Thomas. It only makes it easier to live with.'

'One would hope. There are things that will haunt me for as long as I live. Dark things, Fitz. I can't expect you to understand.' He puffed a moment on his cigar before continuing. 'A man is the sum of his experience, you see. I can't shake off the war. It plagues the subconscious mind. I dream about it.' His voice dropped to a whisper. 'I hadn't dreamed of Valentina for years. Then the other night ... it's that picture, you see. I dreamed about her and it was as if she were alive.'

'You still have Alba,' said Fitz.

'Alba,' Thomas said with a sigh. 'Alba, Alba, Alba ... You'll look after Alba, won't you? One mustn't live in the past.'

'I'll look after her,' said Fitz, longing for the chance.

'She's not an easy girl. She's lost, you see. Always has been.' His eyes began to close. He willed them open, fighting sleep. 'You're a good man, Fitz. I thoroughly approve of you. Don't know about this Hamilton-Home or HarbaldHume ...' He cleared his throat. 'But I'm sure about you, Fitz.'

'I think I'll go to bed, if you don't mind,' said Fitz tactfully, pushing himself to his feet.

'Please. Don't let me keep you up.'

'Good night, Thomas.'

'Good night, m'boy. Pleasant dreams.'

Fitz returned to the drawing room to find the women had gone to bed and the lights had been switched off. He looked at the clock on the mantelpiece: the silver hands shone in the moonlight that spilled in through the windows. It was one in the morning. He hadn't noticed the time. It had gone so fast. He was sorry that he had lost precious moments with Alba. However, he had accomplished his mission. He now knew where Valentina came from. It wouldn't be hard to find Incantellaria on a map. With a little tenacity he could very easily find out the rest.

He went outside to check on Sprout. The sky was black, studded with stars and a bright, phosphorescent moon. When he opened the trunk Sprout raised his ears and wagged his tail, but he was too tired to lift his head. Fitz patted him fondly. 'Good dog,' he said softly, in the voice he reserved for his old friend. 'If only you knew what it was like to lose your heart, then you could give me a few words of advice. But you don't, do you, Sprout?' Sprout let out a loud and contented sigh. Fitz covered him with a warm blanket and, with a long and affectionate look, closed the trunk.

He walked slowly up the stairs, his heart growing heavier with each step. Soon the weekend would be over and Alba would no longer need him.

He made his way down the corridor. He would have liked to have knocked on Alba's door. To tell her what he had discovered. But he didn't know which room was hers and the house was so big, he couldn't begin to guess. He opened the door to his room and turned on the light. Alba stirred in the bed. 'Turn it off,' she murmured without opening her eyes.

'Alba,' Fitz gasped, switching it off. His initial thought was that he had blundered into her room by mistake. Perhaps he was as drunk as her father. 'I'm so sorry!'

'Don't be silly,' she said sleepily. 'Come to bed.' Then she giggled into the pillow. 'It is *your* bed after all. The Buffalo would be appalled.'

'Ah,' said Fitz, puzzled.

'You're not going to turn me down again, are you?'

'Of course not, I just thought . . .'

'Don't think, for God's sake. Thinking never got a man anywhere. Least of all into my bed. Do be quick, I'm cold. Your pajamas are under the pillow.' She yawned loudly.

Fitz slipped hastily out of his clothes and, when his eyes had adjusted to the darkness, he pulled his pajamas out from under the pillow, put them on, and got into bed. He was just deliberating his next move when Alba spoke.

'If you hold me, Fitz, I promise I won't bite.' He shuffled over and pulled her toward him. Her body was slim and warm beneath a brushed cotton nightshirt that had ridden up her legs. He felt his blood grow hot, but he controlled his impulses and wrapped his arms around her. She sighed happily. 'What did you find out, darling?' She had never called him 'darling' before.

'That your mother was the legendary beauty of Incantellaria. That you are just like her.' Alba turned over and tucked her head under his chin. 'Your father thinks of her every time he looks at you.'

'What else did he say?'

'That the mention of her name still hurts him.'

'Is that why he won't talk about her?'

'It's not that he wants to exclude you, Alba, but that it's too painful. You should have seen his face. It was grey with sadness.'

'Poor Daddy.' She yawned.

'You, my darling, long for someone you never knew. Your father longs for a woman he knew and loved. His pain is far greater than yours and if he wants to keep that pain to himself, you must let him.'

'Oh, I will, Fitz. Because now I can do the rest.' She kissed his cheek. 'Thank you.' She closed her eyes and after a while her breathing became regular and heavy.

Fitz lay awake, wondering where they would go from here. It didn't occur to him that he was already different from all the rest. Alba had never shared her bed with a man without making love. For the first time she derived comfort without feeling the need to offer her body as recompense. Alba didn't even know it herself; she was too deeply wrapped in his arms to ponder her actions.

When Fitz had gone Thomas walked unsteadily to his desk. He put down his glass and stubbed out his cigar, then he opened the drawer where he had placed the scroll. He picked it up and ran his thumb over the paper, deliberating what to do next. So many years had gone by and, little by little, those years had changed him, so that now he barely remembered the young man he had been when he had first lost his heart: carefree, insouciant, audacious. Like a caterpillar he had shed his skin but emerged a moth, when once, if things had been different, he might have emerged a butterfly. He was aware of what he had become and yet he had been powerless, or perhaps unwilling, to change. It was easier to build a shell and hide in it.

He sank back into the chair and opened the scroll. The sight of Valentina's face caused his heart to stumble and he took a sharp intake of breath. He could feel her. His eyes began to mist and he blinked to clear them. What unrestrained beauty. What mystery. His head swam as the recollections burst forth after such a long incarceration. He closed his eyes and pictured her smiling face. How beguiling that smile had been. And those dark eyes that hid so much. Eyes that drew a man in with an enchantment not of this world. As the tears ran down his face he knew that she still hadn't let him go. Alba's torch had illuminated the dark space in his heart that he had shut down and, yes, it was still as devoted as it had been. Then that familiar scent wafted in again. At first it was barely perceptible but, as he traced the sketch with his eyes, he began to discern that sweet smell of figs, now enveloping him in a miasma of memories. Then a light shone through the mist and there she stood, on the quayside dark, beguiling and achingly beautiful . . . Valentina Fiorelli, *la bella donna d'Incantellaria* . . .

7

Italy, Spring 1944

Lieutenant Thomas Arbuckle steered the motor torpedo boat into the quiet Italian harbor of Incantellaria, an unexpected jewel hidden within the red cliffs and caves of the Amalfi coast. The sea was clear, the colour of sapphires. Gentle ripples caught the pale morning light and twinkled like diamonds. His eyes swept across the horseshoe bay that was port to this quaint, medieval town where gleaming white and sandy pink houses basked in the sunshine, their open windows and wrought-iron balconies adorned with red geraniums and carnations. The mosaic dome of a church rose up to Heaven and beyond, the hills soared steeply into the distance, from where the scent of pine now reached him. Sky blue fishing boats were pulled up onto the sand, like beached whales waiting for the tide to come in and wash them out to sea. He squinted and adjusted his cap. There was a small group of people on the quayside, waving.

'What do you make of this place, sir?' asked Lieutenant Jack Harvey, standing beside him on the bridge.

On Jack's shoulder perched the little red squirrel that had accompanied him everywhere – from North Africa, where the acrid smell of death and mutilation had been tempered by the cheap whorehouses of Cairo and Alexandria, to Sicily, where even the bombings from

German Messerschmitts had not dampened his enthusiasm for adventure. Brendan, named after Churchill's
redheaded crony Brendan Bracken, lived in Jack's pocket,
having defied authority for the duration of the war. He
had earned his place in this family of eight battle-weary
men with his indomitable spirit and strong instinct for
survival. He was now a symbol of hope as well as a
reminder of home.

'Beautiful, Jack,' Thomas replied. 'As if time has stood
still for about three hundred years.' After the darkness of
war it was surreal to be blinking in the light of such tran-
quillity. 'Are we in Heaven?'

'I'd say if I didn't know better. It's so green and vibrant!
What about we hang around for a bit?'

'Take a holiday, you mean? There'll be more action in
this sleepy town than in the entire Med, I suspect. Still
waters run deep,' said Thomas with a chuckle, raising an
eyebrow suggestively. 'I could do with a bath and a decent
meal.'

'And a woman. I could do with a woman,' added Jack,
running a tongue over his dry lips, recalling the nubile
girls he had tasted on leave in Cairo. When he wasn't in
action he could think of little but Brendan and his cock,
not necessarily in that order.

'Now you're talking,' agreed Thomas, whose mind often
wandered to Shirley, who sent him perfumed love letters
and food parcels. Shirley, who in a fit of postcoital delusion
he had promised to marry if he survived. Shirley, who
would be intolerable to his parents as a daughter-inlaw by
virtue of the fact that her father was the local builder. 'We
could all do with that!' he said, remembering Shirley.

Since the Allied forces had moved north there was relatively little action at sea. His job now was to patrol the

Italian coastline, keeping the Allied supply lines open. Thomas had commanded the 70-foot Vosper, nicknamed *Marilyn*, for over three years now, based first in Alexandria, then Malta, Bône on the North African coast, and finally Augusta after the invasion of Italy. He – and she – had been in the thick of it: from aiding the landings in North Africa to nightly patrols of the Straits of Messina during the Sicily landings of July 1943. After that he had been used for clandestine operations by Special Services, which involved landing secret agents and supplies on Crete and Sardinia. Thomas was known for his daring and courage, especially during the dark days of 1942 when the devastating offensive against Malta peaked, nearly destroying the entire dockyard as well as practically all the Malta-based aircraft. MTBs were small and swift, capable of moving unseen over moonlit waters, penetrating minefields and harbor defenses, and sneaking up close to fire torpedoes at enemy vessels before speeding off into the night. The adrenaline rush was enormous. Since the death of his elder brother, Freddie, Thomas barely felt alive unless he was on the very edge of life's blade. He felt more comfortable when he didn't have time to feel guilty that while Freddie had died, he lived.

He had lost friends – everyone had – but no loss had been as devastating as that of Freddie, whom he had always looked up to, yearned to be like, and loved with the devotion of a dog. He had had a mountainous personality, Freddie, unbounded drive and ambition. He had been destined for greatness, not a gloomy grave at the bottom of the sea, entangled in the twisted wreckage of a Hurricane. No, Freddie had seemed immortal. If death had claimed Freddie, then death could claim anyone at any time. This left a deep and nagging scar on Thomas's soul.

Thomas would have followed Freddie into the air force had his mother not intervened, arguing tearfully that two sons in the air was like sending both to God 'and I'm not ready to hand you back, yet.' She would not have it. So Thomas had left Cambridge and signed up for the navy. He had been envious of Freddie; he was not envious now. Somewhere beneath his boat, in this vast, unforgiving sea, Freddie's body was swept about on the eternal current.

The boat motored into the harbor. The early morning mists hung over the hills and Thomas breathed in the woody scents of pine and eucalyptus, a welcome antidote to the saline smell of the sea. The crowd of townspeople stood waving, attracting more people who gathered around like a herd of curious sheep. He noticed a small boy raise his hand in the fascist salute before his mother hastily slapped it down and gathered him into her arms. *Il sindacco,* the town mayor, stood polished and preening on the quayside beside the local carabiniere, who wore a grubby khaki uniform with large brown sweat patches beneath his armpits. He puffed out his chest like a fat turkey bristling for prime position, and adjusted his hat importantly. In spite of the war, his belly was fat and drooped over his trousers. Neither man had seen any action since the Allies had landed, sending the Germans scurrying up north. Now was their moment to assert their authority and reclaim their sense of value.

Brendan curled up inside Jack's pocket, burying himself at the bottom as he had been taught. Suddenly Thomas noticed a beautiful girl with long black hair and large, timid eyes. In her arms she held a wicker basket. He couldn't help being drawn to the brown swell of her breasts, exposed by the low décolletage of her dress. She stood in the crowd yet seemed to have a space of her very own, as if she remained a little apart. Her loveliness was such that her image seemed more pronounced than the rest. The faces around her merged into one, but hers was clear and perfect like the evening star in the night sky. She was smiling, not the broad, bovine smile of the townsfolk, but a gentle curling of the lips that reached her eyes and caused them to narrow slightly. A mere whisper of a smile. So subtle that it made her beauty almost hard to swallow, as if she were a figment of his imagination and not real at all. It was then that Thomas Arbuckle lost his heart. There on the quayside of the small fishing town of Incantellaria he let it go willingly. He turned to greet the mayor. When he searched for the girl again, she was gone.

The *sindacco* shook hands formally and welcomed them in Italian. He did not notice Brendan pop his little red head out of Jack's pocket as if sensing that they were in Allied territory and free from superior officers who would object to his presence. Without taking his eyes off the mayor, who was excusing his poor English, Jack pushed the squirrel back into the dark. Thomas tried not to search the crowd for that beautiful girl. He reminded himself that he had business to do and, if he were cunning, he could extend that business until he found her again.

The mayor was a handsome man with black hair and skin the colour of toffee. He was short in stature and held himself erect in order to appear taller. His slim physique belied his age, which must have been around fifty, and he wore a pair of round spectacles on a slightly aquiline nose above a neat mustache. His uniform was clean and pressed and Thomas noticed his nails were pink and manicured as if he spent more time in the salon than on the streets or behind a desk. He was clearly a fastidious man and full of pomposity; now that the Germans had gone, he was the most important man in town.

The carabiniere raised his hand in imitation of the naval salute and his mouth twisted into a self-satisfied smirk. 'Lattarullo at your service,' he said, aware that he was upstaging the mayor. Thomas saluted back. His Italian wasn't perfect but he had had a good grounding at school and plenty of practice in the last couple of years, although his use of verbs relied heavily on the infinitive. Lattarullo already irritated him. He was a stereotype. Fat, lethargic, and most probably incompetent. They were all open to bribes, as corrupt as the mafia itself, and there was little that could be done about it considering the pittance that was their wages. In times of war, when civilians were barely surviving, it wasn't a surprise that the black market flourished, mostly on stolen Allied supplies, and that the local civil services were gaining from it. It was a losing battle the advancing armies didn't have time to fight.

Thomas explained why he was there. They had information of an arms dump left by the retreating German army. He had been sent to investigate, to make sure it didn't fall into the wrong hands. He asked to be escorted to a disused farm called La Marmella. The mayor nodded in acknowledgment. 'Lattarullo will take you into the hills. We have a car,' he said proudly, referring to the only one in town. Everyone else, besides the marchese, traveled by horse and cart, bicycle or on foot. The marchese, who lived in splendid isolation in the palazzo on the hill, had a grand old Lagonda, in which he would send his servant into town to buy supplies whenever he needed them. The marchese himself was a very rare sight. He didn't even attend church; instead, he had his own private chapel on his estate at which Padre Dino, the local priest, would administer communion once a month for a small fee. 'I hand you over to Lattarullo,' continued the mayor.

'If there is anything else you require, please don't hesitate to ask. It is my duty as well as my personal pleasure to make your stay as enjoyable as possible. Good day to you.'

'It really does sound like a holiday,' hissed Thomas to Jack as the mayor turned on his well-polished heel. Lattarullo scratched his groin and shouted into the crowd to let the officers through. The two tall men in their naval uniforms cut more than a dash in that small town. Jack strode behind, his eyes searching the faces for beautiful young women, of which there were one or two whose inviting eyes caught his attention and held it for a moment, before he was whisked off in the official car that gurgled and coughed like an asthmatic geriatric.

They bumped over the narrow cobbled streets, avoiding the odd cat that leaped back into the shadows again, unused to such a noisy vehicle. The road began to rise and wind as they left the quiet cove for the hills. Thomas wanted to ask about the girl he had seen on the quayside. Lattarullo was sure to know who she was. She had stopped time with her loveliness and held it there, quite still, so that nothing had moved around her, only the breeze wafting her long hair like threads of fine silk.

Lattarullo chatted all the way up the narrow, dusty track. He took great pleasure in his own importance, relating stories of his heroism against marauding bandits. 'I have seen Lupo Bianco,' he said in a low voice. 'I looked him straight in the eye, long and hard. He could see that I am a fearless man. Lattarullo is afraid of no one. Then, you know what he did? He nodded at me with respect. With *respect*! You have nothing to fear of Lupo Bianco while you are under my protection.'

Thomas and Jack knew all about Lupo Bianco, 'White Wolf': it was thanks to him and other powerful men that the Allies had successfully landed in Sicily. However, they were playing with the fire of hell, for Lupo Bianco was a murderous criminal. Both feared and admired, he was discussed in hushed voices, as if the very walls had ears and could inform against them. Of course, Lattarullo claimed he had never supported the Germans. Mussolini had been a big fool to take Germany's side. 'If Mazzini and Garibaldi could see their country now, they'd turn in their graves,' he said with a heavy sigh and Thomas knew that Lattarullo would scamper just as quickly to the other side if the war turned to favor the fascists.

They passed fields of olive groves and trellises of vines where the soil was arid, parched in the heat of the Italian sun, a small farm where skinny goats stood in the shade, sniffing the ground for blades of grass, and the odd, starving mongrel. Ragged children played with sticks and stones, and a haggard-looking mother washed clothes in a tub with her sleeves rolled up to her elbows, her face red and sweating with exertion. Thomas resolved to bring his pastels and paper next time he came ashore to record with his artist's hand what he saw as charming pastoral scenes. He had kept a pictorial record of his experiences. But his heart ached for the people whose innocent lives were blighted by war and his thoughts turned once again to the mysterious girl. He'd draw her too. So beautiful was she against the ugliness of war.

They found the munitions dump. It wasn't as big as Thomas had expected. Most of it stolen by the local Mafia, no doubt. Only hand grenades, machine guns, and other small arms hidden in an abandoned barn. Hardly worth the bother. With the enthusiastic help of Lattarullo, they loaded some of them into the back of the car.

While they stood, hats off, wiping their wet brows, Lattarullo suggested they stay. 'Have a wash, something to eat, a glass of Marsala. I can bring you women too, if that's what you want. Trattoria Fiorelli is the best restaurant in town.' He did not mention that it was the *only* restaurant in town.

'Something to eat would be nice,' Thomas replied, ignoring Jack, who was indicating with the frantic widening of his eyes that the women would be nice too.

'Do you want to catch the clap?' he hissed when Lattarullo was out of earshot. 'How many soldiers do you think have been there before?'

'There must be some clean ones, surely,' he pleaded.

'It's up to you, but I'm staying well clear.'

'My hand needs a break,' Jack chuckled, waving it in an unmistakable gesture. 'I saw a couple of girls on the quayside when we arrived. They were panting for it, I could tell. Probably on the game. Might try my luck. I always scored in the Four Hundred.' For a moment he could taste the smoke and perfume of the Four Hundred club he had patronized in London before the war. Thomas thought of those dark, mysterious eyes and his heart twisted with anxiety. He hoped she wasn't on the game. He'd rather she was married and out of reach than pursuing that shameful degradation. Brendan popped his head out of Jack's pocket again, as if in protest at the suggestion of whores.

'As you wish. We could stay a while. Why not? We all need to stretch our sea legs.'

'And these women need a bit of sea cock!' Jack added with a grin, squeezing his groin.

Lattarullo drove down the dusty track, the arms rattling in the back like a tool box every time the car hit bumps and stones. Suddenly there was a loud hooting, the screech of brakes, the flash of white and glint of metal, and Lattarullo shouting *'Madonna!'* in panic as he swerved off the road. A white Lagonda purred sedately to a halt. The skinny driver stepped out and dusted himself down, his face twisted with disgust. His immaculate grey uniform and cap did nothing to hide his emaciated, aged body, which would have looked less incongruous had it been laid out in a coffin. Lattarullo staggered on to the track, his face red with fury. He let out a round of profanities. The chauffeur simply looked at him as if he were an irritating beetle that had scuttled into his way. He sniffed, closed his eyes, and shook his head. Then he turned, climbed back into his car, and drove away. His nose barely reached over the steering wheel. It was clear from the way he squinted that the sun had momentarily blinded him, causing him to stray into the middle of the road.

'Who is he?' asked Thomas, once Lattarullo had managed to maneuver the car out of the ditch.

'The marchese's lackey,' he replied, then snorted and spat into the road. 'That is what I think of him!' he added, grinning as if the filthy gesture had won him a small victory. 'He thinks he's important because he works for a marquis. Once the Montelimone was the most powerful family in the region, a charitable family too, but the marchese has all but destroyed their good name. You know what they say about the marchese?' He narrowed his eyes, then shook his head. 'You don't want to know!' Although Thomas and Jack were mildly curious, they were drowsy and their bellies groaned with hunger. Lattarullo snorted and spat again before driving on, mumbling to himself the string of abuse he would have liked to have inflicted on the chauffeur.

They returned to the quay and, with the help of the rest of the crew, they unloaded the arms onto the boat. Joe Cracker, the fattest of the eight-strong team, opened his large mouth and began to sing his favorite aria from

Rigoletto, hence his nickname 'Rigs.' He was coarse to look at with ruddy skin and thinning ginger hair, yet he sang with the voice of a professional baritone. 'He thinks he'll get the girls like that,' said Jack, allowing Brendan to scamper up his arm and perch on his shoulder.

'It's his only chance,' commented another. 'He'll be singing under their balconies next.' They laughed heartily but Rigs continued to sing. He had seen their eyes mist on those lonesome nights when their survival had been nothing short of miraculous, when music had been the only escape from their fears.

Leaving a couple of crew on deck to keep watch over the boat, the rest walked the short distance to Trattoria Fiorelli. Wooden tables spilled out onto the road where a bony donkey stood with a couple of baskets over its back, blinking wearily in the sunshine. Two old men sat at a table playing a game with counters, drinking tumblers of local gin that smelled of turps, and ragged-looking children with grubby faces ran about with sticks, their shrill cries ricocheting through the still afternoon air. The menu was displayed by the open door. Inside a couple of waiters sat listening to a wireless in the cool, ready for business. When the two officers appeared with Lattarullo, followed by four crew members, one singing loudly, they leaped to their feet and showed them to tables outside with more enthusiasm than they had mustered since the Germans left.

Lattarullo sat with Thomas and Jack, amazed at the sight of Brendan, who in these hard times would make a tasty meal. 'You'd better keep your eye on him,' he commented, finding to his shame that his mouth was beginning to water. Squirrel prosciutto would be very tasty indeed. 'There is always food at Immacolata's. When the rest of the country is suffering from starvation,

Immacolata produces meat and fish in a sumptuous banquet. You will see! Jesus turned water into wine and fed the five thousand with nothing more than a few loaves of bread and some fish. Immacolata is blessed.'

Suddenly a voice bellowed from within. 'That is Immacolata Fiorelli,' hissed Lattarullo confidentially, taking off his hat and wiping his sweating forehead. 'This restaurant is the engine that makes the town turn. And she's in the driving seat. I know that, the mayor knows that, Padre Dino knows that. Even the Germans knew better than to mess with her. She's descended from a saint, you know.'

Thomas pulled back his shoulders. After all, he was a commanding officer in the British navy; what could possibly be so terrifying about a loud-voiced Italian woman berating her lazy staff?

'Signora Fiorelli,' said Lattarullo with the greatest respect, jumping to his feet. 'May I present to you two fine officers of the British navy.' He stepped aside and the tiny woman lifted her chin to reveal deep-set, intelligent eyes of chestnut brown. She narrowed them thoughtfully and studied their faces, as if calculating their reliability and character. Thomas and Jack rose to their feet, dwarfing her in size but noting that her personality was more formidable than the two of them put together.

'You are very handsome,' she said to Thomas in a quiet voice, quite unlike the bellow of earlier. Her beady eyes traced him from top to toe as if she were a seamstress assessing which suit would fit him best. 'I will prepare you *spaghetti con zucchini* and *treccia di mozzarella*.' She turned to Jack. 'And the good people of Incantellaria must lock up their daughters,' she said, sniffing through dilated nostrils. Jack gulped and Brendan scurried back into his pocket. 'For you, *frittelle*,' she added, nodding with satisfaction. 'Once this place vibrated with life. The war has choked the life out of it. People can barely afford to eat, let alone dine in a restaurant. I pray for better times. For a swift ending to the bloodshed. For the lion to lie down with the lamb. I invite you both to dinner at my house. A small corner of this country where civilization still exists as it has for generations. Where old-fashioned standards are upheld. I will cook for you myself and we can raise our glasses to peace. Lattarullo will bring you. You can bathe in the river and forget the war.'

'You are a generous woman,' said Thomas.

'I am just a humble hostess and you are in my town.' Thomas didn't think she looked at all humble; her face was etched with arrogance. 'Besides, your presence here will help the community. Your spending will add much needed fuel to the economy. What little economy we have. These are hard times, signore. If you are as rich as you are handsome we will all rejoice.'

'Do you have daughters?' Jack asked cheekily. She narrowed her eyes and looked at him down her imperious nose, although she was at least three feet shorter than him.

'And if I do, I would be unwise to introduce her to you and your squirrel.'

'Why Brendan?' he asked, putting his hand in his pocket to stroke the animal's fur. 'Brendan has an eye for the ladies.'

'Because my daughter has an eye for squirrels,' she laughed, but her laughter was heavy and doleful like the melancholy sound of bells. *Ah*, thought Lattarullo, *squirrel prosciutto*, and he licked his lips and salivated like a dog.

It wasn't long before the restaurant was full of pretty girls, their faces painted like dolls with the little makeup they could scrounge, wearing their best dresses and hairdos.

Their breasts swelled over the low décolletages of their dresses like creamy cappuccinos. They did nothing to hide their flagrant desire to hook an Englishman. These sailors were their tickets out of the poor, claustrophobic town. They eyed them flirtatiously, giggling and whispering behind brown hands, shamelessly displaying their calves and ankles by crossing their legs and raising their skirts immodestly.

Jack's eyes bulged and Brendan hurried up onto his shoulder for a better look. The pretty squirrel was irresistible to them and soon Jack was surrounded by perfume and brown limbs as they reached out to stroke the animal. 'Ah, Brendan, my lucky charm,' he chuckled, endeavoring to chat them up in broken Italian. Not to be outdone, Rigs climbed onto a chair and opened his tremendous lungs to everyone's delight. He gesticulated dramatically as though on the stage in Covent Garden.

Slowly the townspeople emerged from behind their shutters, drawn to Trattoria Fiorelli by the heartrending music of *Rigoletto* that resounded through the still afternoon air. The girls quieted down, returning to their chairs, their heads now resting on their hands, their eyes full of melancholy. Thomas lit a cigarette and watched the scene through a veil of smoke. He thought once more of the beautiful girl he had seen on the quay and wondered why she had not come. The others were nice enough to look at – Jack was barely able to keep himself contained within his trousers – but they weren't for him. As the crowd grew thicker his eyes searched their faces, ever hopeful that she might appear. But he was disappointed.

An old man with no teeth began to play the concertina.

Rigs sang with ever more drama, his eyes filling with tears as he lost himself within the words and the music, for they gave him the means to vent his desolation without shame.

The war now seemed very far away although its imprint burned upon all their souls. They would never be free from the horrors they had witnessed. Branded for life, they would carry the scars until their spirits outgrew their bodies and they joined those, like Freddie Arbuckle, who had gone before.

When Rigs finished, Thomas demanded a happy song, one with which they could all sing along. Rigs dabbed his damp face with a napkin, took a large gulp of water, and with great gusto launched into *La donna é mobile* ... and soon the trattoria was vibrating with voices, clapping hands and stamping feet.

8

Thomas and Jack didn't want to dine with Immacolata Fiorelli, and Brendan was more nervous than either of them. They would have preferred to have eaten again at the trattoria, where there was a dance floor. With Rigs and the toothless concertina player, there would surely be dancing. There would be women too, eager for love and excitement. Jack was furious that Thomas had accepted her invitation. 'Why couldn't you have just said "no"?'

'It would have been rude,' Thomas explained weakly. 'After all, she apparently runs the town while the mayor is at the beautician's.'

'She doesn't even have daughters!'

'The one she has eats squirrels.' Thomas snapped his teeth at Brendan, who stared back at him in a superior fashion.

Rigs and the boys waved them off with glee, amused by their reluctance. Lattarullo had slept all afternoon in his office with the door locked, his hat pulled over his eyes and his feet up on the desk, and was now perkier than ever.

They drove up the winding lanes in silence. Lattarullo tried to ignite a conversation but both men were alone with their thoughts: Jack of the women he would fuck when he got back to the trattoria, and Thomas of the lovely stranger who had taken off with his heart. Lattarullo persevered, not minding whether or not they were listening.

Finally he parked the truck beside a twisted olive tree. There was no road down to the house, only a well-trodden path. 'Immacolata Fiorelli will show you the river,' said Lattarullo, already out of breath. 'Besides, she has soap!' he chortled. Thomas knew that soap was only available on the black market and that most Italian women washed with pumice, ashes, and olive oil.

Thomas cast his eyes down to the sea that stretched calmly out on to the misty horizon before disappearing into the beyond. If it weren't for his naval uniform and the experiences that had left their indelible mark on his soul he could almost have forgotten the world was at war. Forgotten that, out there, the sea reached Africa's shore red with the blood of those who, like himself, had fought for freedom from tyranny, for peace. It was an enchanting view and his fingers twitched with the longing to capture it in pastels; he would have liked to set up an easel right there on the hillside, among the grey olive trees. If it wasn't for the war he would search for that girl and set her in front of that vast sky. He would draw her and he would take his time. The sighing of the sea and the chattering of cicadas would add their own unique melody to the easy languor of the fading day and they would lie down and make love. But it was wartime and he had a job to do.

After a while the modest farmhouse, sandy-coloured with a simple grey tiled roof, came into view. Thick branches of wisteria scaled the walls, their lilac flowers falling in heavy clusters like grapes, and small birds flew in and out in a game that only they understood. Sheltered by cypress trees and half-hidden behind pots of plumbago, tall arum lilies, bushes of lavender, and nasturtiums in great heaps, the house gave the impression of peeping out shyly. As they approached, they suddenly seemed to walk into an invisible cloud of perfume. It was warm and sweet and irresistible.

'What is that smell, sir?' Jack asked, sniffing the air with flared nostrils.

'I don't know, but it's like Heaven,' Thomas replied, stopping in his tracks. He put his hands on his hips and inhaled. 'It's so strong, it's making my head dizzy.' He turned to Lattarullo and asked him in Italian.

Lattarullo shook his head. 'I don't know what you're talking about. I can't smell anything.'

'Of course you can!' Thomas retorted.

'Niente, Signor Arbuckle.' He pulled an ugly face and shrugged. *'Bo!'*

'My dear fellow, you must have lost your sense of smell. Why, surely you can *taste* it?'

The expression on the Englishman's face was one of such incredulity that Lattarullo thought it better to agree. After all, he could detect a faint scent, though nothing unusual. The hills were full of smells; if one lived here one ceased to notice.

'I can smell figs,' he said grudgingly. Then he pulled his ugly fish face and shrugged, this time turning the palms of his hands to the sky.

'By God, that's it!' enthused Thomas. 'It *is* figs, isn't it?' he asked Jack.

Jack nodded and took off his hat to rub his sweating forehead. 'It's figs,' he repeated. 'Straight from God's garden.'

Lattarullo watched them with growing curiosity and shook his head. *Immacolata Fiorelli will know what to do,* he thought, taking off his hat and walking up to the door.

Immacolata Fiorelli never locked her door, even in these dangerous times of war. Being a formidable woman, she considered herself a match for any man, even one with a bayonet. Lattarullo poked his head inside and called her name. '*Siamo arrivati,*' he announced, then waited, turning his hat around and around in his hands like a diffident schoolboy. Thomas rolled his eyes at Jack. After a long moment Immacolata appeared, still draped in black as if in a permanent state of mourning. Around her neck hung a large silver cross, elaborately decorated with semiprecious stones.

'Come,' she beckoned them with a wave of her hand.

Inside, the house was cool and dark. The shutters were closed, allowing only the minimum light to enter in thin beams. The *salotto* was small and austere, with worn sofas, a heavy wooden table, and a simple flagstone floor. However, in spite of its austerity, it was cozy, a home used to the wear and tear of people. What immediately struck Thomas were the little shrines, crosses, and religious iconography that punctuated the bare walls and corners. In the dimness the silver and sparsely used gold leaf glittered and shone in a ghostly fashion.

'Valentina!' Immacolata's voice no longer bellowed, but called out in a low, gentle tone as one does to a loved one. 'We have guests.'

'La signora's husband died fighting in Libya,' said Lattarullo in a hushed voice. 'Her four sons are also fighting, though two are being held by the British and the other two, well, who knows where they are. Valentina is the youngest and most precious of all her children. You will see.'

Thomas listened as Valentina's soft singing could be heard outside. The strong scent of figs now preceded her and Thomas felt his head swim with the pleasure of it. He knew before he set eyes on her. He felt it. Nothing stirred except the silken breeze that slipped in through the door, a prelude to something magical. And then she was there, in a white dress that turned semitransparent with the sun behind it. With a suspended heart he took in her small waist, the gentle curve of her hips, the feminine shape of her legs and ankles, her feet in simple sandals. Her beauty was even more breathtaking than it had been when he had disembarked. He barely dared blink in case she disappeared again. But she was smiling and extending her hand. The sensation of his skin against hers sharpened his senses, and he heard himself stammer in Italian, '*È un piacere.*' Her smile, though slight, was full of confidence and knowing, as if she were used to men losing their tongues as well as their hearts in her presence. Immacolata's voice broke the spell and suddenly the room was moving once again at the normal pace and Thomas was left wondering if he was the only one who had noticed the change.

'Valentina will show you the river where you can bathe,' Immacolata said, bustling over to the chest of drawers upon which stood a framed photograph of a man, surrounded by small burning candles and a worn black Bible. Thomas presumed the man was her late husband. She pulled out a small object wrapped in brown paper and handed it to her daughter before closing the drawer. 'Even in times of war one must be civilized,' she said gravely, indicating with a nod that they go down to the river. *It must be the famous soap,* thought Thomas.

Valentina turned and walked out of the house. Thomas noticed that she had an unusual walk: her feet turning outward, she held her stomach in, pushed her bottom out, and swung her hips. It was a lively walk, unique, and Thomas thought it the most charming walk he had ever seen. He wished he were alone with her and not with Jack, who seemed as awestruck as he. Both men followed her down a steep path that was only wide enough to walk in single file.

The air was hot and sticky and full of mosquitoes. The scent of figs lingered, yet Thomas couldn't see one fig tree, only eucalyptus, lemons, pines, and cypresses. The hillside rang with crickets, their rhythmic, incessant chattering loud to those unfamiliar with it. The path was well trodden, the earth pale and dry and scattered with stones and small pine needles and cones. Every now and then wooden steps had been built into it to prevent slipping. Finally, Thomas saw the river through the trees. It was more of a stream than a river, but wide enough to swim in. It trickled down the hill, bubbling around rocks and smooth stones, resting for a while in a limpid pool before flowing out to sea. It was there that they were to bathe.

Valentina turned and smiled. This time her smile was wide and full of humor. 'Mamma must think very highly of you,' she said. 'She doesn't give her precious soap away to just anyone.' Thomas was shocked that her mother allowed her to walk alone with two strange men. She must indeed think very highly of them. Valentina held out the little parcel. 'Take it and enjoy it. Make it last.' Thomas took it, once again irritated that Jack was standing by, about to spoil the moment with a bad joke, no doubt.

'Will you join us?' Jack asked, grinning mischievously.

Valentina blushed and shook her head. 'I will leave you to bathe in private,' she replied gracefully.

'Don't go!' Thomas gasped, aware that he sounded desperate. He cleared his throat. 'Wait until we're in, then stay and talk to us. We know nothing of Incantellaria. Perhaps you can tell us a little about it.'

'I used to sit and watch my brothers,' she said, pointing

to the bank that lay in a large sun trap. 'They splashed so much.'

'Then sit there for us,' Thomas insisted.

'We haven't had the company of a woman for a long time. Certainly not one so lovely to look at,' Jack added, used to charming the girls. Under normal circumstances Thomas would have stood aside and let him woo her with his irreverent wit and raffish charm. After all, it was Jack to whom the girls were always drawn, not him. But this time, he had no intention of letting him dominate.

'Mamma wouldn't like to think of me alone in the company of bathing men.'

'We are British officers,' said Thomas, trying his best to look the part by standing tall and nodding his head formally. It was what Freddie would have done. 'You are in very safe hands, signorina.'

She smiled coyly and walked over to sit on the bank, averting her face while they undressed. When she heard their splashes she turned around.

'It's splendid!' Jack enthused, gasping as the cold water shrank his ardor. 'Just what I needed, I suppose!'

Thomas rubbed the soap between his hands and washed his arms. He was aware that her eyes were upon him. They were brown, but in the sunlight they appeared almost yellowy green, the colour of honey. When he looked up, she smiled at him. He was sure it was flirtatious. When he turned, he saw that Jack had ducked under the water. He knew then that she had smiled for him alone.

Once bathed, they sat in their underwear drying off. Thomas would have liked to have drawn Valentina there, with the sun in her hair and on her face, her head tilting forward, looking up at them from under her brow so that she didn't have to squint. She seemed shy. Thomas and Jack talked for her. They asked her questions about the town. She had grown up there. 'It's the sort of town where everyone knows everyone else,' she said, and Thomas was sure that even if it were the size of London, everyone would know who she was.

Once dry, they dressed and returned up the narrow path, refreshed after their swim. Valentina fired them both and gave them the feeling of having boundless energy and enthusiasm for life.

When they entered the house, the smell of cooking filled their nostrils and roused their hunger. Immacolata led them through the rooms to a vine-covered terrace fragrant with jasmine. On the grass beyond, a few chickens pecked at the ground and a couple of goats were tethered to a tree. The table was laid. A basket of bread sat in the middle, beside a brass *agliara* of olive oil. Lattarullo had returned to town, promising to collect them after dinner. He had suggested they return to La Marmella the following morning with a team of men to retrieve the rest of the haul. Thomas doubted there would be much to collect; he didn't trust Lattarullo any more than he would trust a greedy dog to guard a bone. It didn't bother him. He was fed up patrolling the coast. The action was up north now, in Monte Cassino. How could he, in his small boat, with only a handful of men, compete with the bandits? Corruption was as ingrained into the culture as machismo. He glanced across at Valentina's profile and decided that, whatever happened, he would contrive reasons to stay for as long as possible.

Immacolata instructed them to take their places for grace. She spoke in a low, solemn tone and wound her fingers around the cross that hung about her neck. '*Padre nostro, figlio di Dio ...*' Once she had finished, Thomas pulled out Valentina's chair for her. She turned her soft brown eyes to him and smiled her thanks. He wanted to hear her speak again but her mother presided at the table and it would have been impolite to have ignored her.

'My son Falco was a partisan, Signor Arbuckle,' she said. 'Now there is no fighting to be done here. With four sons it is not surprising that my family almost represents every faction of this war. Thankfully, I do not have a communist. I could not tolerate that!' She filled their glasses with Marsala, a sweet fortified wine, then raised hers in a toast. 'To your good health, gentlemen, and to peace. May the good Lord grant us peace.' Thomas and Jack raised their glasses and Thomas added,

'To peace and your good health, Signora Fiorelli. Thank you for this fine meal and for your kind hospitality.'

'I don't have much, but I do see life,' she replied. 'I am old now and have seen more than you will ever see, I am sure. What is your business here?'

'Nothing serious. Some armaments left behind by the retreating German army. Although there is not much of it left.'

Immacolata nodded gravely. 'Bandits,' she said. 'They are everywhere. But they know better than to rob me. Even the all-powerful Lupo Bianco would have trouble penetrating my small fortress. Even him.'

'I hope you are safe, signora. You have a beautiful daughter.' Thomas felt himself flush as he referred to Valentina. Suddenly her well-being was more important to him than anything else in the world. Valentina lowered her eyes. Immacolata seemed pleased with his comment and her face creased into the first smile she had deigned to give.

'God has been kind, Signor Arbuckle. But beauty can be a curse in times of war. I do what I can to protect her. While we are in the company of British officers we need not fear for our safety.' She lifted the basket of bread. 'Eat. You never know when you will eat again.' Thomas helped himself to a piece of coarse bread and dipped it in olive oil. Although chewy it tasted good. Immacolata ate with gusto. She had obviously gone to great pains to cook the pasta, which she had prepared with a fish sauce. There was very little food around and yet, as at the trattoria that morning, she had managed to give them the kind of feast they might have expected before the war. As if inspired by the banquet, her conversation turned to the golden days her family enjoyed under Imperial Rome.

'They were civilized times. I try to bring a little of that civilization into my house regardless of what is going on in the rest of the country, for my daughter.' She then proceeded to tell them about her ancestor who was a count: 'He fought with Caracciolo in the war against Nelson and the Bourbons, you know.' Thomas listened with half an ear; the rest of his senses were focused on the silent Valentina.

'How long will you be staying?' she asked when dinner was over and they sat feeling drowsy with wine and full bellies.

'As long as it takes to shift the arms,' Thomas replied.

'There are many more, you know. The hills are full of guns and grenades. It is your job to make sure that they don't fall into the wrong hands, is it not?'

'Of course,' Thomas replied, frowning.

'Then you must stay. This place may look enchanting, but there is evil in every shadow. People have nothing, you see. Nothing. They will kill for a morsel of food. Life has little value nowadays.'

'We will stay as long as we are needed,' he said confidently, although he knew that there was very little he could do against the sort of evil of which she spoke.

While the setting sun singed the sky pink, they sat chatting beneath the vine. Immacolata lit candles, around which moths and mosquitoes fluttered, their tiny wings ever closer to the lethal flame. Thomas and Jack smoked, both acutely aware of Valentina. When she spoke, they listened. Even Jack, who understood little of what was said, sat back to let her soft, beautifully articulated voice run over him like a delicious trickle of syrup. Jack had to let Thomas dominate the conversation; his Italian was far more fluent. However, he did have his lucky charm and, when he felt that he was disappearing with the sun, he let Brendan scamper up his sleeve to sit on his shoulder. As he predicted, the squirrel caught her attention and to the little creature's relief she didn't show the slightest intention of eating him. '*Ah, che bello!*' she sighed, stretching out her hand. Thomas watched her slender brown fingers caress the ginger fur and couldn't help imagining those same fingers caressing him. He didn't catch Jack's eye in case his friend raised a suggestive eyebrow. But Jack was also taken with her loveliness and was well aware that his lewd jokes had no place at that table.

At about ten thirty the car arrived in a cloud of dust. 'That will be Lattarullo,' said Thomas. He wished he had had the opportunity to talk to Valentina, but Immacolata had dominated the conversation. Valentina hadn't seemed to mind. Perhaps with so many brothers she was used to being in the shade.

Lattarullo appeared on the terrace, his brow glistening and his beige shirt stained with sweat. His belly had swollen in the heat like a dead pig and mosquitoes buzzed around his head. He was an unpleasant sight. He informed Thomas and Jack that the rest of the crew had danced all evening in the trattoria. 'The singer has entertained the whole town!' he enthused. Judging by the sweat on his shirt the fat carabiniere had been dancing too.

Thomas felt a wave of panic. When would he see Valentina again? He thanked Immacolata for her hospitality, then turned to her daughter. Valentina's dark eyes looked at him with intensity, as if she could read his thoughts. The corners of her mouth curled into a small, shy smile and her cheeks flushed. Thomas searched for words, any words, but none came. He lost his train of thought in her gaze. The sun had disappeared behind the sea and the light from the candles seemed to turn the brown of her eyes to gold. 'Perhaps we will have the pleasure of seeing you again,' he said finally and his voice was a rasp. Valentina was about to reply when her mother interrupted.

'Why don't you come for the *festa di Santa Benedetta* tomorrow night?' she suggested. 'In the little chapel of San Pasquale. You will witness a miracle and perhaps God will grant you luck.' She toyed with the cross about her neck with rough hands. 'Valentina will accompany you,' she added.

'Mamma has a role to play; I will be alone,' Valentina said, lowering her eyes as if embarrassed to ask. 'I would very much like you to come.'

'It will be a pleasure to accompany you,' said Thomas, enchanted by her diffidence. This was one excursion he would take alone.

Once in the car Jack burst into commentary. 'That Valentina is a real smasher!' he said. 'Even Brendan was impressed and he's very hard to please!'

'I've lost my heart, Jack,' Thomas announced gravely.

'Then you had better find it,' he replied with a chuckle. 'We won't be hanging around for long.'

'But I must see her again.'

'Then what?' Jack now pulled the same fish face as Lattarullo and raised his hands to the heavens. 'Nothing will come of it, sir.'

'Perhaps not. But I have to know.'

'Now isn't the moment to fall in love. Certainly not with an Italian. Besides, her mother gives me the creeps.'

'It's not the mother I'm interested in.'

'They say one should always look at the mother before making a play for the daughter.'

'Valentina's beauty will never fade, Jack. It's made to last. Even you can see that.'

'She is extraordinarily beautiful,' he conceded. 'Do what you must, but don't come crying on my shoulder when it all ends in tears. I have far more important things to think about. If I don't get laid tonight I'm going to bugger Brendan!'

But when they arrived back in town neither felt like dancing. Instead they wandered along the sea front. A couple of old men sat in their boats mending sails, their wrinkled, toothless faces lit up by hurricane lamps. On closer inspection it was clear that they were using stolen tapestries for their purpose. Someone sang *'Torna a Sorrento'* to the accompaniment of a concertina, his doleful voice echoing eerily through the streets. The sky blue shutters were all closed and Thomas couldn't help but wonder what went on behind them, whether the occupants were asleep or peeping through the cracks. Reluctant to return to the boat, they ambled up one of the narrow alleyways. A young woman appeared. Jack's face lit up. She was one of the girls he had admired that morning. With long curly hair and brown skin she was comely with a loose, dreamy smile.

'Come and see what Claretta can do for you. You look weary,' she purred as they approached. 'Italian women are famous for our hospitality. Let me show you. Come.'

Jack turned to his friend. 'I'll be five minutes,' he said.

'You're mad.'

'You're the madman. At least I'll come out with my heart intact.'

'But your cock might not be.'

'I'll be careful.'

'I don't want a sick number one. I can't replace you.'

'A man needs a fuck. I'm sure I'm going blind. A blind 'Jimmy' is no use to you either! Besides, I'll be helping the economy. Everyone needs to earn a living.'

Thomas watched as Jack disappeared into the house. He leaned against the wall and lit a cigarette. Alone in the empty street he thought once again of Valentina. He would see her the following evening for the ceremony of Santa Benedetta. He couldn't bring himself to think further than that. If he could sketch her then he would have something to remember her by. To take away with him. He felt sick in the stomach with longing. He had read love poems and the works of Shakespeare but never believed that such intensity of feeling really existed. Now he knew better.

A few minutes later Jack emerged with a large grin, still doing up his fly. Thomas dropped the butt of his cigarette onto the ground and scrunched it into the stones with his foot. 'Come on,' he said. 'Let's go back to the boat.'

In the morning they awoke to a magical sight. The MTB was adorned with flowers. Red and pink geraniums, irises, carnations, and lilies. They were carefully woven around the railings and scattered like confetti on the deck. Rigs, who had been on watch, had fallen asleep. He had seen nothing but the large audience in Covent Garden which had applauded his dream rendition of *Rigoletto*. Thomas should have been furious. To fall asleep on watch was a serious offense and one which could cost them all their lives. But the sight of those flowers, bright, vibrant, and innocent, softened his anger. He thought of Valentina, of the evening ahead, and he slapped the offending sailor on his back and said, 'If you catch the criminals who did this, sleep with them at once.'

9

That morning, as predicted, they reached the barn to find the arms were gone. Lattarullo groaned and shrugged. 'Bandits! We should have come earlier,' he said, shaking his head. Then, in a bid to win their favor, for he knew he was the major suspect, he told them of more dumps he had just been informed of. Thomas laughed. It was what he had expected. After all, this was Italy. What's more, he needed an excuse to stay another day and Lattarullo had given him that excuse. He patted the carabiniere on the back. 'Then we will have to find the others before Lupo's men do, shan't we?'

Once Lattarullo had gone, the two men ambled off to the trattoria for a drink. They found Rigs and the others sitting in the sunshine surrounded by girls. Rigs only knew opera Italian but this seemed to satisfy the girls, who were all laughing with him, caressing his cheeks and stroking his hair, much to the chagrin of the more hand-some of the crew members.

'Who said he'd never win a woman with his singing?' said Thomas with a chuckle. 'I'd wager he could have any one of those girls he wanted.'

'If he hasn't already,' added Jack. 'Here I come to break up the party with my lucky charm.' Brendan was now permanently perched on his shoulder.

'This could be interesting,' mused Thomas. 'The voice versus the rat!'

'How many times do I have to tell you, he's not a rat!' snapped Jack.

'A rat with a tail.'

'Ah, but what he can do with that tail is nobody's business,' he said with a leer.

Thomas screwed up his nose. 'I don't wish to know what you put that poor animal through.'

'Let's just say he's definitely a breast man!'

'Christ, there's no end to your perversions!'

Immacolata didn't appear for lunch. According to the waiter she was preparing herself for the *festa di Santa Benedetta,* a highly religious ceremony that required all her energies. However, she had suggested they eat *ricci di mare.* Thomas and Jack had never eaten sea urchins, and the thought of swallowing those shiny innards made their own innards churn. When the dish was put before them, one of the girls showed them how it was done. With expert hands she cut one in half, squeezed lemon onto the still quivering insides, then scooped them out with a spoon, straight into her wide, open mouth. *'Che buono!'* she enthused, licking the lipstick off her lips.

'I'll tell her what else she can put in that mouth of hers,' quipped Jack with a smirk. The sailors guffawed uproariously and the bewildered girl, not understanding what he had said, laughed too.

Soon they were the town entertainment once again. It made Thomas uncomfortable to eat in front of a herd of salivating onlookers. After a while *il sindacco* appeared, starched and smelling of cologne, to herd them away as a farmer would his cows. Flicking his fingers importantly he summoned a waiter. *'Ricci di mare,'* he said, swallowing the saliva that had gathered in his mouth at the sight of the Englishmen's plates.

As the *sindacco* carefully spooned his first mouthful, Lattarullo appeared with a stiff envelope of crisp white paper. Thomas took it and frowned. His name was written in ink in the most exquisite handwriting. He spent a few minutes staring at it, trying to guess whom it was from. Lattarullo knew, but he didn't say. He didn't want to spoil the Englishman's surprise. He stood in the heat, dabbing his grubby brow with a rag, longing for a nap. 'For God's sake, sir, open it!' said Jack impatiently, as curious as he. Thomas tore the envelope and pulled out an elegant card with the name Marchese Ovidio di Montelimone engraved on the top in navy blue. Beneath, in that exquisite hand, was an invitation to tea at his home, Palazzo Montelimone.

'So this is the famous marchese?' he said, raising his eyebrows at Lattarullo.

'Yes, the aristocrat who lives up there on the hill. The one whose chauffeur tried to kill us yesterday.'

'What does he want from me?'

Lattarullo shrugged and pulled his fish face. *'Bo!'* he replied unhelpfully. Thomas turned to Jack. Jack imitated the carabiniere.

'Bo! Let's go and find out. Perhaps he wants to apologize for his chauffeur.'

'Then we should accept,' Thomas replied, slipping the card back into the envelope. 'It's only polite. However, I imagine it's just an excuse to introduce himself. I know the type. Love to tell you a bit about themselves and how important they are.'

'They say he has a wine cellar the size of a house. That the Germans didn't find it. It's worth the visit just for that,' said Lattarullo, passing a dry tongue over scaly lips.

'I had better accompany you. Besides, you don't know the way.'

That afternoon the three of them set off along the dusty track. After a short drive, Lattarullo turned up a steep hill where the track curved around a sharp bend. The trees encroached further and further into the road until it was almost impossible to get the car through. It struggled on, choking and retching like a sick old man, until finally a pair of imposing black gates indicated the entrance to Palazzo Montelimone. They were rusting and peeling and overgrown with years of neglect. It was as if the forest were slowly invading the grounds, winding its green tentacles around those gates until one day they and the house would disappear completely, swallowed up by the superior force of nature.

They drove in, silenced by the scene. The building itself was beautiful yet corroded by lack of care and the ruthless abuse of time. Wisteria was tumbling over itself in glorious abundance as if the palazzo were trying to mask the rot with luxurious garments. The gardens were wild. Flowers had valiantly seeded themselves everywhere, but nothing could prevent the gradual choking by evil-intentioned weeds.

Lattarullo parked the car in front of the elaborate façade of pediments and moldings that rose up to towers and turrets and a tattered flag flying weakly in the breeze. Immediately the vast door opened in a silent yawn. A bent old man in black stood solemnly waiting for them. Thomas and Jack recognized him immediately as the marchese's chauffeur.

'He's as loyal as a dog,' said Lattarullo, not bothering to hide his loathing. 'He's worked for the marchese for decades. He'd sell his gold teeth for him if he had to. What he knows is nobody's business and he'll take it all to the grave. Shouldn't be long!'

'He's not going to pop off while there's all that wine hidden in the cellars,' said Thomas to Jack with a laugh. 'That wine is keeping him alive.' Then Lattarullo, who hadn't understood their English, said exactly the same thing in Italian.

They climbed out of the car and Alberto greeted them stiffly, without even the smallest hint of a smile. He looked as if he hadn't smiled in years. Or perhaps ever. They followed him into the dark hallway, through a shady courtyard where grass grew up between the paving stones and beyond, to the main body of the house. As they walked through the rooms, each more enchanting than the last in the intricate moldings and pale pinks and blues painted on the walls, the tapping of their shoes echoed about the high ceilings: there was no furniture to absorb the sound and the tapestries had long since disappeared. Marble fireplaces framed cold, empty grates and the glass on the tall windows was stained with mold. An eeriness pervaded the building, as if they were walking among ghosts.

Finally they reached one of the few rooms in the house that was occupied. There in an armchair sat a dignified gentleman of about seventy, surrounded by a vast library of beautifully bound books, a large globe, and two giant paintings. His grey hair was brushed back off his face, still handsome with a straight Roman nose and deep aquamarine eyes. He was impeccably dressed in a pressed shirt and tweed jacket with a silk scarf tied neatly about his neck. His origins were most certainly northern, for he was fair-skinned, and he held himself with the poise of a prince.

'Welcome,' he said in perfect English, rising from his

chair. He walked toward them, emerging from the gloom to shake their hands. He nodded at Lattarullo, then, much to the carabiniere's disappointment, told Alberto to take him to the kitchen for bread and cheese. He then gestured for them to sit down. 'How do you find my town, Lieutenant Arbuckle?' he asked, pouring them tea that had been carefully laid out on a silver tray. The china was thin and elegant and painted with delicate vines. Such a tea set seemed quite out of place in that shabby room.

'It is charming, marchese,' Thomas replied with equal formality.

'I hope you have taken time to look around. The hills are especially beautiful at this time of year.'

'Indeed they are,' agreed Thomas.

'It is a town full of simple people with little education. I was fortunate. My mother gave me an English tutor, after which I was sent to Oxford. Those were the happiest days of my life.' He tapped his long fingers on the arm of his chair. His hands reminded Thomas of a lady concert pianist's. He then heaved a wheezy sigh. Asthmatic perhaps, or some other lung complaint. 'These folk are full of superstitions,' he continued. 'Despite living in the twentieth century, they are obsessed with relics of medievalism. I keep my distance, living up here on the hill. I have a good view of the ocean and the harbor. I see who comes in and who goes out. I have a telescope, you see, out there on the terrace. I do not get involved in their rituals. However, rituals keep the people's minds occupied and therefore out of trouble, and the people of the south are very religious. I grew up here with my brothers and sisters, though where they are now I do not know, or if indeed they are still living. A bitter feud drove a splinter through the heart of our family. I was left with this palazzo. Perhaps if I had married, it might have benefited from the attentions of a woman, but sadly I did not and now never will. The house is falling about my ears, pushing me further and further into its core until there will be nothing left but this room. It survived the Germans but it won't survive the years. They are unforgiving. Are you married, Lieutenant Arbuckle?'

'No, I am not,' he replied.

'War is no time for love, is it?'

On the contrary, thought Thomas, but he said instead, 'I am happy I haven't left a woman behind in England. If I get killed only my mother will mourn me.' He thought of Freddie and his stomach twisted with pain. At least Freddie hadn't had a wife either, or children for that matter. He suddenly felt depressed and wished the man would get to the point of their meeting. It was dark in that room and the air was stale. It smelled like an old crypt.

'And you,' the marchese said, turning to Jack. 'I see you still have your little furry friend.' Jack's mouth fell open in surprise. Slowly Brendan crept out of his pocket like a naughty schoolboy discovered in the pantry. 'If you travel inland, which I don't presume you will, you had better hide him. There is great hunger. People are selling their own daughters for food.'

'Brendan has survived worse than hungry Italians, marchese,' said Jack, unusually respectful. The marchese had an aura of quiet importance.

'I imagine that you two were friends before the war,' he said.

'We were at Cambridge together,' Thomas replied.

'Ah, Cambridge. Then you are my rival!' He laughed, looking directly at Thomas. But the laugh didn't reach his eyes.

The marchese did not want to talk about the war. He didn't ask why Thomas and Jack were in Incantellaria;

with his telescope and apparent omniscience he must have known. He talked about his childhood in the palace, rarely making visits to the town, certainly never mixing with the other children there. It was as if they lived behind a pane of glass, he said. They could watch what went on but never be part of it.

'How long will you be our guests?' he asked suddenly. Thomas thought that now would be an appropriate moment to shrug like Lattarullo and pull a fish face, but he replied that they'd probably be summoned back to base in the morning. 'War is a dreadful business,' the marchese continued, getting to his feet. 'Now they're stuck in Monte Cassino. Do you really think the Allies will win? They'll trip up. What a waste of magnificent young men. People never learn from history, do they? We blunder on, making the same mistakes our fathers and grandfathers made. We think we'll make the world a better place and yet, little by little, we destroy it. Come, let me show you my telescope.'

They walked through the moldy French doors out onto the terrace, squinting in the sunlight. Thomas felt the fresh air like a wave of cool water that revitalized his senses. He looked about him. Once a manicured garden must have extended down the slope to an ornamental lake that now lay stagnant like a shallow wadi. He could imagine women in beautiful dresses wandering around the willow trees in pairs, chatting beneath their parasols, gazing at their pretty reflections in the water. It must have been breathtaking then, before time and abandon had robbed it of its glory. But now no one cared. It lay dying before him, like the house. Like the coughing old marchese in his airless room, clinging to the last of the family traditions.

The marchese walked over to the instrument that stood

pointing down into the harbor. He looked through it, turned a dial here, pressed a button there, and then stepped aside for Thomas. 'What do you make of that?' he said, his face lighting up with pleasure. 'Ingenious, isn't it?' Thomas could see the village clearly. The streets were quiet. He focused on his boat. Trusty old *Marilyn*. The boys were just hanging around, mobbing about, discipline all but gone. He wouldn't be able to keep them here for much longer. His heart lurched at the thought of leaving. He had only just met Valentina. He now scanned the quayside for her, but she was not there.

'Ingenious,' he repeated flatly. He would trade places now with the marchese, just to be near her. Jack took a turn.

'Do you stargaze?' he asked. The marchese was thrilled to be asked and embarked on a lengthy description of the constellations, shooting stars, and planets, his Italian accent becoming more pronounced as he no longer concentrated on how he sounded.

Thomas stood with his hands on the balustrade, gazing down at the sea that glittered in the afternoon sun. He was relieved when Lattarullo appeared, his belly bursting over his trousers from the bread and cheese. Alberto seemed even more skeletal; he looked as if he hadn't eaten for centuries.

'We had better be going,' said Thomas, still bewildered as to the purpose of their invitation.

'It has been a pleasure,' said the marchese with a smile, shaking his hand.

As they were on the point of leaving, a young boy wandered up a well-trodden snake path that wound its way to the terrace from some unseen place behind overgrown cypress trees and shrubbery. He was immensely pretty with a wide face, white-blond curls, and dark brown eyes as shiny as pearls. He looked surprised to see them but recognized Lattarullo, whom he greeted politely.

'This is Nero,' said the marchese. 'Isn't he beautiful?' Thomas and Jack exchanged glances but kept their expressions impassive. 'He runs errands for me. I try to help the community. I am fortunate. I am a rich man. I have no sons and daughters upon whom to lavish my wealth. These are hard times. The war is not only fought on the battlefield, but every day in every town, village, and city of Italy. It is a war of survival. Nero will not starve, will you, my dear!' He ruffled the boy's hair affectionately. When Nero grinned, they saw he was missing his two front teeth.

'What an odd fellow,' said Thomas as they drove away.

'Errands indeed!' scoffed Jack, in English so the carabiniere couldn't understand. He raised an eyebrow at Thomas. 'Nero is an extraordinary-looking boy. One doesn't expect to see that colouring down south.'

'There's something not quite right about that man,' said Thomas, scratching his head. 'I'd hate to think what he got up to at Oxford. The happiest days of his life indeed! What the devil were we there for? A cup of tea? To listen to him boring the pants off us about his family and the stars?'

Jack shook his head. 'I don't know. Baffles me.'

'I'll tell you one thing. He had a hell of a good reason for asking us up there today and, what's more, one way or another we have satisfied him.'

10

The shadows lengthened and the scent of pine thickened in the evening air. The people of Incantellaria emerged from their homes and gathered in front of the little chapel of San Pasquale. There was a sense of anticipation. Thomas stood outside the *farmacia* as instructed by Immacolata and waited with growing apprehension for Valentina. He noticed that many of the townspeople held small candles that flickered eerily in the fading light. A grubby hunchback weaved in and out of the crowd like a purposeful dung beetle as everyone touched his back for luck. Thomas had never witnessed such a scene before and he was intrigued. Finally the crowd seemed to part and Valentina floated toward him with her dancing walk. She wore a simple black dress imprinted with white flowers and she had put up her hair, decorating it with daisies. She smiled at him and his heart stumbled, for her expression was warm and intimate. It was as if they had already declared their feelings, as if they had been lovers for a long time.

'I'm glad you have come,' she said when she reached him. She held out her hand and he took it. Then he did something impulsive: he pressed her palm to his lips and kissed it. He gave her a long, intense stare as his mouth savored the feel of her skin and the now familiar scent of figs. She dug her chin into her chest and laughed. He had never heard her laugh. It made him laugh too, for it bubbled up from her belly and tickled her with delight.

'I'm glad I have come too,' he replied, not wanting to let go of her hand.

'Mamma is one of the *parenti di Santa Benedetta*,' she said.

'What is that?'

'One of the saint's descendants. That is why she sits by the altar to witness the miracle.'

'What is meant to happen?'

'Jesus weeps blood,' she told him, her voice turning solemn and the smile dissolving into an expression of the utmost reverence.

'Really?' Thomas was incredulous. 'And what if he doesn't?'

Her eyes widened with horror. 'Then we will have bad luck for the following year.'

'Until the miracle happens again?'

'Exactly. We light candles to show our respect.'

'And touch the hunchback for luck.'

'You know more than I thought,' she said, the laughter returning to her face.

'Just an educated guess.'

'Come, we want to get near the front.' She took him by the hand and led him through the crowd.

It was dark when the doors to the chapel opened. It was small and rustic, decorated with frescoes of the birth and crucifixion of Christ. He suspected that anything of any value had been stolen by the Germans, or looters, so there were only simple candlesticks on the altar and a plain white cloth. Behind, the marble statue of Christ on the cross remained intact.

A heavy silence, filled with fear, uncertainty, and expectation vibrated in the air like the muted sound of violins. Thomas didn't believe in miracles but the spirit of this one was infectious and he began to feel his heart accelerating with those of the believers. He sensed many pairs of eyes upon him, some of them hostile, for there were those in the congregation who thought his presence might prevent the miracle from taking place. Or perhaps they didn't like the fact that Valentina had caught the attention of an Englishman. He noticed an elderly woman glower at Valentina, then look away with a disapproving sniff. He hoped he hadn't compromised her by coming.

Although curious, he longed for the ceremony to be over, so he could take Valentina somewhere quiet where they could be alone. Just as he was envisaging their first kiss, the heavy wooden doors reopened and a gust of wind blew in three small women draped in long black dresses and diaphanous veils. Each held a candle which lit up her wizened face to eerie effect. Immacolata walked a little in front of the other two, who shuffled in behind her like maids of honour at a grim wedding. Their heads were bowed while Immacolata's chin was up and proud, her small eyes fixed on the altar with self-importance. Even the priest, Padre Dino, walked behind them, carrying rosary beads and mumbling prayers. A little choirboy accompanied him, gently waving a thurible, filling the air with frankincense. Everyone stood.

The procession reached the altar and the three *parenti di Santa Benedetta* took their places in the front pew. Padre Dino and the little boy stood to one side. No one spoke. There was no welcoming address, no song, no music, just eager silence and the invisible force of prayer. Thomas's eyes were drawn, like everyone else's, to the statue. He couldn't believe that a thing of marble would actually bleed. It would surely be a trick. He'd know. They wouldn't be able to fool him. Everyone watched. Nothing happened. The town clock chimed nine. The congregation held its breath. The heat in the chapel was now intense and Thomas began to sweat.

Then it happened. Thomas blinked a few times. Surely he was imagining it. He had willed too much along with everyone else and now he was hallucinating. He turned to Valentina who crossed herself and mumbled something inaudible. When he looked back, the blood was trickling down the impassive face of Christ, scarlet against the white marble, dropping off his chin on to the floor.

Immacolata rose to her feet and nodded solemnly. The chapel bell was rung in a doleful monotony and the priest, the little boy, and the three *parenti di Santa Benedetta* filed out.

The town erupted into jubilation. Musicians played and a large circle was formed in the middle of the throng. Suddenly the young women, before so modest, now danced the tarantella with the exuberance of the possessed. The crowd clapped and cheered. Thomas stood enthralled, clapping too. Valentina appeared in the midst of the revelry to great applause and wolf whistles from the men and surprisingly spiteful looks from the women. Thomas thought how ugly their jealousy made them. It deformed their normally pretty features into grotesque parodies, like reflections in distorting fairground mirrors. Valentina moved center stage until she was dancing alone. She danced with grace, her hair now loose and flying about her head as she twisted and turned to the lively beat of the music. Thomas was astounded: no longer in her mother's shadow, she showed herself to be surprisingly gregarious. There was no inhibition in the way in which she moved her body, her skirt rising up her legs as she danced, exposing her shiny brown calves and thighs. The tops of her breasts, revealed in the low décolletage of her dress, rose like milk chocolate soufflé, and Thomas was gripped with longing. Her virginal charm fused with a bursting sexuality that Thomas found irresistible.

He watched transfixed; she looked directly at him. Her dark, laughing eyes seemed to read his mind for she danced up to him and took his hand. 'Come,' she whispered into his ear and he let her lead him out of the square and down the little streets to the sea. They walked hand in hand along the beach, then further, around the rocks until they reached a small, isolated cove where the light of the moon and the gentle lapping of waves revealed an empty pebble beach where they could, at last, be alone.

Thomas didn't waste time talking. He wound his hand around her neck, still hot and damp from her dancing, and kissed her. She responded willingly, parting her lips and closing her eyes, letting out a deep and contented sigh. The music could still be heard in the town, now far away, a distant hum like the merry buzz of bees. The war might as well have been on another planet, so dislocated were they from reality. He wrapped his arms around her, pulling her against him so that he could feel the softness of her flesh and the easy relinquishing of her body. She didn't pull away when he buried his rough face in her neck, tasting the salt of her sweat on his tongue and smelling the now muted scent of figs. She tipped her head back, exposing it willingly so that his lips could kiss the line of her jaw and the tender surface of her throat. He felt excitement strain his trousers. But she didn't pull away. He ran his fingers over the velvet skin where her breasts swelled out of her dress. Then he cupped them, stroking the nub of her nipple with his thumb and she let out a low moan, like a whispering sigh of wind.

'*Facciamo l'amore,*' she murmured. He didn't question whether it was wrong or right to make love, or whether he was ungallant to take her like that, on the beach, having known her only a couple of days. It was wartime. People behaved irrationally. They were in love. They might never meet again. Her innocence was something that he would take away with him. He hoped that if he claimed her now, she would wait for him. He'd return for her at the end of the war and marry her. He prayed that God would protect her until he could protect her for himself.

'Are you sure?' he asked. She didn't reply, simply brushed his lips with hers. She wanted him. In a swift movement he lifted her into his arms and up the beach to a sheltered spot where he laid her down on the pebbles. In the phosphorescent light of the moon he made love to her.

They lay entwined until the red rays of dawn stained the sky on the horizon. Thomas told her about his life in England. The beautiful house they would one day live in and the children they would have together. He told her how he loved her. That it was possible after all to lose one's heart in a moment, to surrender it joyously.

They walked back across the rocks. The celebrations had finished and the town was still and eerie. Only a stray cat crept along the wall searching for mice. Before he escorted her home he collected his painting case from his boat.

'Let me draw you, Valentina. I don't ever want to forget your face.'

She laughed and shook her head. *'Che carino!'* she said tenderly, taking his hand. 'If you want to. Follow me, I know a nice spot.'

They climbed a little path up the rocks, then down a dusty track that cut through a forest. The scent of thyme hung in the air with eucalyptus and pine, and crickets rattled among the leaves. The odd salamander darted off the track to hide in the undergrowth as they walked past, and the song of birds heralded morning. After a while the trees gave way to a field of lemon groves. From there they could see the sea, flat like molten silver, sparkling behind clusters of cypress trees.

At the top of a slight hill there stood a derelict lookout point, the bricks crumbling from centuries of sea wind and salt. It was a breathtaking position. From there they could see for miles around. Valentina pointed out her home, laughing at the thought of her mother tucked up in bed, oblivious of the adventure on which her daughter was embarking. She sat down against the lookout tower, her hair blowing in the gentle wind, and let him draw her. He sketched in oil pastels, enjoying analysing her face, translating it as best he could onto paper. He wanted to portray her mystery, that quality that made her different from everyone else. As if she had a delicious secret. It was a great challenge and he wanted to get it right so that when they parted, he could gaze upon the drawing and remember her as she was now.

'One day we will tell our children about this morning,' he said finally, holding the paper out in front of him and narrowing his eyes. 'They'll look at this picture and see for themselves how beautiful their mother was as a young woman, when their father fell in love with her.'

She laughed softly and her face glowed with affection. 'How silly you are,' she said, but he knew from the way she was gazing at him that she didn't think him silly at all.

He held it up for her to see. Her cheeks flamed with astonishment and her face turned very serious. 'You're a maestro,' she gasped, tracing her lips with her fingers. 'It's beautiful, Signor Arbuckle.' Thomas laughed. She had never said his name before. After such intimacy 'Signor Arbuckle' sounded formal and clumsy.

'Call me Tommy,' he said.

'Tommy,' she replied.

'Everyone at home calls me Tommy.'

'Tommy,' she said again. 'I like it. Tommy.' She raised her dark eyes and stared at him as if for the first time. She gently pushed him back onto the grass and lay on top of him. *'Ti voglio bene, Tommy,'* she said. When she pulled away, her eyes shone golden like amber. She ran her hand over his forehead and through his hair, then planted a lingering kiss on the bridge of his nose. *'Ti amo,'* she whispered. Over and over again she whispered it, *'Ti amo, ti amo,'* pressing her lips against every part of his face, like an animal marking her territory, willing herself to remember it.

He did not want to take her home. He feared the agonizing moment when he would lose sight of her. When he'd have to walk away. They remained as long as they could on the hillside by the lookout tower, both afraid of the sea and the terrible divide it would impose upon them. They held each other tightly.

'How is it possible to love you so deeply, Valentina, when I have known you so little?'

'God has brought you to me,' she replied.

'I know nothing about you.'

'What do you want to know?' She chuckled sadly, tracing his face with her fingers. 'I like lemons and arum lilies, the smell of the dawn and the mystery of the night. I like to dance. I wanted to be a dancer as a little girl. I'm frightened of being alone. I'm frightened of being no one. Of not mattering. The moon fascinates me; I could sit all night just staring up at it and wondering. She makes me feel safe. I hate this war, but I love it for having brought you to me. I'm afraid of loving too much. Of being hurt. Of living my life in pain and suffering for loving someone I am unable to have. I'm frightened too of death, of nothingness. Of dying, and finding that there isn't a God. Of my soul wandering in a terrible limbo that is neither life nor death. My favorite colour is purple. My favorite stone a diamond. I would like to wear a necklace of the finest diamonds just to sparkle for a night, to know what it feels like to be a lady. My favorite part of the world is the sea. My favorite man is you.'

Thomas laughed. 'That's quite a summary. I like the last part best.'

'Is there anything else you want to know?'

'You'll wait for me, won't you?' he said seriously. 'I will come back for you, I promise.'

'If there is a God, He will know what is in my heart and bring you back to me.'

'Christ, Valentina,' he sighed in English. 'What have you done to me?'

They walked back to her house in silence and he kissed her for the last time. 'This is not goodbye,' he said. 'It's farewell. It won't be long.'

'I know,' she whispered. 'I trust you, Tommy.'

'I'll write.'

'And I'll kiss the paper you write upon.'

To prolong the moment would have been torturous, so she ran down the path and hurried into her house without a parting glance. Thomas understood and turned around. The morning suddenly looked less fresh, as if dark clouds had now obscured the sun. The countryside had lost its sparkle. The song of birds ceased to sound so melodious, and the rattling of crickets pounded against his eardrums like cymbals. Only the scent of figs lingered on his skin to remind him of her, and the picture he had drawn. With a heaviness of heart such as he had only ever felt once before in his life, when his beloved brother had been killed, he walked slowly back to the harbor. Back to his boat. Back to the war.

11

Beechfield Park 1971

Thomas awoke to the sound of the clock in the hall. His neck was stiff and aching and he blinked about him in bewilderment. For a moment he was confused. Where was he? He expected to be on the boat but the ground beneath him was solid. Slowly the study came into focus. It was cold. It was dark, except for the lamp on his desk. God, what time was it? He looked at his watch. Three in the morning. He glanced down at the portrait in his hand. Valentina's face gazed out at him as she had done that day on the hill. He had captured all that was unique about her, all that he couldn't possibly ever put into words. Even the one quality that he hadn't even known she possessed. Even that. How could he have missed it?

He noticed he had been crying. Tears had dampened his cheeks while he slept. While he dreamed. He rolled up the scroll and stood up stiffly. He'd lock up the picture in the safe and never look at it again. She was dead. What was the point of remembering it all? Of crying in one's sleep like a child? It was all in the past and that's where it belonged. He painstakingly took down the portrait of his father that concealed the safe Margo had had built after they got married. She thought of everything, Margo. He retrieved the key and opened it. Boxes of jewelry and papers lay in the velvet-lined cavity. For a second he held on to the portrait. Part of him didn't want to relegate that lovely face to the back of a dark box. It was like placing her in a coffin all over again. However, he knew he had to. It was right. Without looking at it for one more time he put it at the very back of the safe. Once it was out of sight he felt better. It didn't pull at him so. He replaced the portrait of his father, took a step back, and rubbed his chin as he gazed up at it. No one would know. Perhaps even he would forget.

When Fitz awoke, Alba was in the bathroom. He lay blinking in the dim light, and although the curtains were heavy he sensed that the day was bright and sunny. He stretched and placed his hands behind his head. Although disappointed that he hadn't awoken with Alba's warm body pressed against his, he realized that it was probably for the best. They hadn't made love. They had done nothing more than sleep together, as friends. He heard her brushing her teeth, humming to herself as she did so. He felt awkward. What was he meant to do?

When Alba came out of the bathroom she was still in her nightshirt, her hair knotted and falling across her face and her long brown legs tantalizingly naked. She grinned at him lazily before climbing back into bed. 'I used your toothbrush,' she said. 'Hope you don't mind.' Fitz was confused. She was back in the bed again, having shared his toothbrush, which was pretty intimate for a couple not sleeping together. He got up and used the bathroom himself.

When he emerged he wasn't sure whether she expected him to get back into bed or to get dressed but it was a dilemma he had to solve in a split second. Alba lay with her head on the pillow smiling up at him. She was amused by his hesitation.

'Men don't usually hover by the bed when I'm in it,' she said with a laugh. 'You do like girls, don't you, Fitz?'

Fitz climbed into bed, annoyed at her teasing. Without waiting for an invitation he took her neck in his hand and pressed his lips fervently to hers. She did not resist but kissed him back enthusiastically. She let out a low moan and wound her arms around him. It was that moan that redressed the balance and made him feel like a man again. When he traced his hand up her leg, beneath her nightshirt, he found that she was wearing no knickers.

'Have you been naked all night?' he asked, stroking her bottom.

'I never wear pants,' she replied. 'They just get in the way.'

'Never?' *God, I'm so conventional,* he thought to himself.

'Never, Grandpa!' She giggled into his neck.

'I can assure you I make love like a boy lover!' he laughed.

'Don't assure me, boy lover, show me.'

Fitz tried not to think of the many men who had slept with Alba. He tried to imagine her pure and untarnished. This was hard, for Alba had indeed enjoyed the attentions of many men, too many to count. She had learned along the way from the sheer enjoyment of sex. Her innovation was born out of enthusiasm and a natural earthiness about which she was completely unabashed. As much as Fitz tried to take the lead and will her to be innocent, she wriggled and moaned like the *femme du monde* that she was.

'Darling, kiss me a little higher, yes . . . there . . . with your tongue . . . softer . . . softer . . . slower, much *much* slower. *There.* Yes!'

She was quite happy to tell him what she wanted and

sighed with pleasure when he got it right. He couldn't deny that she was wonderful in bed. Technically, she was tremendous. But afterward, as they lay spent and panting, their heartbeats racing in chests damp with sweat, Fitz couldn't help but feel that something was missing. Oh, it was all there, the skill, the know-how, the technique. But technique was of little value to him without feeling. It was passion that made lovemaking special. Fitz loved Alba but she clearly did not love him.

After a while, Alba tiptoed down the corridor to her room, half hoping to bump into the Buffalo, simply for the pleasure of seeing her face. Fitz was left feeling empty. Dissatisfied. As if he had eaten his way through a delicious doughnut to find the center entirely without jam. He had given Alba his soul and she had simply lent him her body with a playful laugh. He thought of Viv and what she would say if he told her. 'You silly fool!' she would snap. 'I told you not to lose your heart. Alba will chew it all up and spit it out when she's done.' That is how she had treated every man before him. But he was different. Even her father had admitted that: 'Why would Alba go for someone like you?' Why indeed? Because he was a runner.

He dressed smartly, anticipating church and the reverend who was invited back for Sunday lunch. Fitz wondered how things would go when they returned to London. Was she simply enjoying the role-play? Or did he mean more to her than that? 'I'm behaving like a woman!' he snapped at his reflection as he tried to tidy his hair. He resigned himself to the fact that, however much he brushed, combed, or wet his hair, it remained a mass of unruly curls. The reverend would have to accept him as he was.

On his way back from letting Sprout out of the car to

run around the gardens, he heard voices from the dining room. He entered, and Margo greeted him warmly. 'Did you sleep well, Fitz? I hope the bed was comfortable. Were you warm enough?'

'It was most comfortable and certainly warm. Very warm indeed,' he replied, glad that Alba wasn't there to catch his eye and make him smile.

'Good. Now there's tea and coffee over there,' she said pointing to the sideboard. 'Eggs and bacon, toast. If you'd like a boiled egg, Cook will do it for you. Just ask.'

'No, fried eggs are perfect. What a feast.' He sniffed the salty bacon and his mouth watered.

'Cook is a little wonder. I don't know what I'd do without her. She's been with us for years. She was Lavender and Hubert's cook when Thomas was little, wasn't she, Thomas?' Thomas, who was sitting at the large round table reading the newspapers and sipping coffee, trying to ignore the frivolous chitchat of his wife and daughters, raised his bloodshot eyes and nodded. Fitz noticed at once how tired and ill he looked. His face was grey, as if all the blood had drained into his red socks.

'Morning, Fitz,' he said. 'I trust you slept well.'

'Yes, thank you,' Fitz replied, sensing that he did not wish to engage in conversation. He turned to Margo, leaving Thomas to disappear once again behind his paper.

After a while, during which Caroline talked incessantly about the man she was in love with, Alba walked in. She was dressed in the shortest skirt possible, patterned tights, and suede boots to her knees. Fitz immediately thought how gorgeous she looked, then remembered that she never wore pants and felt an erection stir in his trousers. There was no way he could leave the table now. As well as the outrageous outfit, she wore an expression of triumph.

It didn't take long to work out why. He shifted his eyes to her stepmother. Margo stood with her jaw slack, uncharacteristically dumb. Alba strode over to Fitz and took his face in her hands, planting on his mouth a passionate and lingering kiss. Now he was as mute as Margo. Only Thomas was untouched by her, reading the paper oblivious of the change in the air.

Finally, as Alba poured herself a cup of coffee, Margo voiced her fury. 'My dear girl,' she said in a tone that suggested to Fitz that she might have once been in the army, or police force at the very least. 'You are not thinking of going to church dressed like that.'

'Oh, I am,' Alba replied, unflustered. Fitz's eggs and bacon suddenly lost their appeal. He took a sip of coffee instead and waited for the row that was about to ensue.

'No, you are not,' retorted Margo, articulating each word slowly to be as frightening as possible. But Alba was no longer a child and that sort of manner only encouraged her to behave worse.

'Why?' she said, turning around with her cup of coffee and taking the place next to Fitz. 'Don't you like it?'

'It's irrelevant whether or not I like it. It's unsuitable for church.'

'I think God will love me as I am,' she said, buttering a piece of toast.

'Reverend Weatherbone won't.'

'What's he going to do? Throw me out?' she challenged. Fitz tried to mediate. A big mistake.

'Darling,' he began valiantly. 'Perhaps if you wear a coat you'll please yourself as well as Margo.' To him that seemed a satisfactory solution. Margo did not agree.

'I'm sorry, Fitz, but it's not dignified. We're the first family of this village and it's up to us to set an example to the rest of the community.'

'Oh, for goodness' sake,' exclaimed Alba. 'No one's interested in what I wear. I haven't been to church for years. They should just be grateful that I'm there.'

'While you're in my house, my girl, you'll abide by my rules. If you want to flounce about in next to nothing you may do so in London, in that boat of yours, but not here where we are respected.'

Fitz hunched his shoulders. He knew that the reference to her boat would have infuriated Alba. He held his breath. Alba pursed her lips and chewed on her toast a moment. There was silence. Caroline and Miranda tried to intervene on behalf of their mother.

'Do you have to come to church?' Caroline asked.

'You could take Summer out for a ride,' Miranda suggested.

'I'm coming to church and I'll wear whatever I want to wear. It's none of anyone else's business.'

Now Margo resorted to her husband, dragging him out from behind the paper like a reluctant tortoise from his shell.

'Do support me, Thomas!'

Thomas straightened up. 'What's the problem?'

'Well, have you seen what your daughter is wearing?' Alba hated it when Margo referred to her as Thomas's daughter, in spite of the battle she fought to distance herself from her stepmother.

'I think she looks charming,' said Thomas. Alba couldn't contain her delight. Her father's reaction was entirely unexpected. Rarely had he sided with her.

'Are you all right, Thomas?' said Margo. 'You've gone a jolly strange colour.'

'Perhaps a coat over the top would be appropriate for Reverend Weatherbone,' he said, without answering his wife, for he didn't feel at all well. He thought of the portrait locked up in the safe. Valentina still reached him from that dark place, in the face of his daughter.

'Oh, all right, I'll wear a coat,' Alba conceded happily. 'Perhaps you could lend me one, Margo. I'm afraid the one I brought with me will be as inappropriate as my skirt.' She placed the last piece of toast in her mouth. 'Delicious!' she exclaimed.

They congregated in the hall, Miranda and Caroline in plain brown coats and hats, and Margo in a tweed suit with a large brooch of flowers on her breast. Thomas wore a suit and Fitz, who had been brought up in the country, was highly appropriate in a jacket of muted greens, a sober tie, and fedora hat. Alba bounced down the stairs in the shapeless camel-hair coat that Margo had lent her. She had buttoned it up to placate the Buffalo, but once in church she intended to undo it. She strode up to Fitz and took his hand. Then she whispered into his ear, 'When you see me praying I'll be thinking of making love to you!' Fitz chuckled. Margo sniffed her disapproval; if there was one thing she abhorred it was whispering.

Thomas drove his car with his wife and their two daughters while Fitz drove Alba in his Volvo with Sprout hanging out of the rear window panting into the air.

'I hope Reverend Weatherbone is ready for Alba,' said Margo, trying to make light of the situation.

'She still manages to look indecent in your coat, Mummy,' Caroline chirped from the back seat.

'Fitz is so handsome,' Miranda gushed. 'He looks lovely in that hat.'

'What does he see in Alba?' Caroline asked. 'They're so different.'

'Let's just be thankful he's willing to take her on,' Margo said, glancing at her husband, then adding tactfully, 'She might be unconventional but she's lively. I bet life is never dull with her.'

'She might be lively, but no one has a temper like Alba,' said Caroline. 'I hope Fitz knows what he's got himself into.'

'I bet he hasn't seen her temper yet!' said Miranda.

'God help the poor man,' said Margo under her breath. She glanced again at her husband. But he was miles away.

Beechfield church was as one would expect: quaint, picturesque, and very old. It was built of brick and flint, with a wooden bell tower where Fred Timble, Hannah Galloway, and Verity Forthright had held the much-coveted positions of bell ringers for over thirty years. Margo took her duty as lady of the village with the utmost seriousness. She was on the list for doing the church flowers once a month and made sure that her creations were the most elaborate. That was quite a challenge, for Mabel Hancock cultivated a stunning garden and her arrangements were always adventurous. When it was Mabel's turn, Margo's stomach would churn all the way to church until she had satisfied herself that she hadn't been outdone by a woman of the village.

As they arrived the bells rang out, drawing the villagers, dressed in their finest, to worship. Socializing was left for afterward when prayers had been said and consciences cleared. Alba took Fitz's hand and followed her father and stepmother. When they weren't looking she unbuttoned her coat. 'What are you doing?' Fitz asked, concerned. He didn't want to have to listen to another row.

'Giving the vicar a lesson in fashion,' she replied.

'Don't you think you should . . .'

'No,' she answered brusquely. 'I don't care what the

Buffalo thinks. I'm twenty-six for God's sake.' He couldn't argue with her. 'This way you can look at my legs,' she added with a smirk. 'I want to feel you looking at them.'

She flashed him the most alluring smile and he couldn't help but smile back. She was irresistible. His heart buckled and he tried to forget that earlier feeling of emptiness. Perhaps if they made love again it would be different. Maybe she had been nervous and all that moaning and thrashing about was simply covering up.

'Don't worry. I'll be thinking of nothing but your legs,' he replied as they walked through the large wooden door and up the aisle.

The church was full. Only the front pew was empty, reserved for the Arbuckles as it was every Sunday. Thomas stood aside for his wife and two younger daughters, who filed past him and sat down. He nodded at Fitz, the kind of nod a man only gives to another man, a nod of silent complicity, and sat down, leaving the last two places free for him and Alba.

Alba sat with the coat falling apart at the thighs. She admired the patterns on her sugar-almond tights, bought for forty pence at the Army and Navy Store. She felt Fitz's eyes on them and relived their lovemaking. What she remembered most, though, was his kiss. It was somehow more tender than any kiss she had ever had before. She had felt embarrassed. It had been too intimate. It had frightened her. But she had liked it. Maybe he would kiss her like that again. If he did, perhaps she'd manage to control the unbearable sensation of losing her stomach, like she did every time she drove too fast over that bridge outside Kings Worthy.

Suddenly Reverend Weatherbone swept into the nave. He definitely swept, robes flying behind him as if a great wind blew up the aisle. His hair was a shock of grey, wild and long, dancing on an imaginary wind like his robes. His face was illuminated with enthusiasm, his eyes blazing, his mouth wide and smiling. Alba had grown up with the dour, self-important Reverend Bolt. She had not expected his replacement to resemble a mad scientist. His voice was mesmerizing, bouncing off the walls in vibrant echoes. Not a single person moved. It was as if he had enchanted them all with his awesome presence. Alba hastily threw the coat over her knees. He turned his eyes to her and she gasped beneath the weight of his gaze. 'Oh God!' she exclaimed.

'Thank you, Miss Arbuckle, for the promotion,' he said and a light, nervous titter rippled through the congregation. Alba blushed a deep scarlet and lowered her eyes. She gulped and glanced across at her stepmother.

Margo's expression was one of deep, unfailing admiration. *Here he stands before these good villagers,* she thought to herself smugly, *and he's lunching with us!* She must let Mabel know that the reverend was a guest at her table. *Totally harmless, of course,* she reassured herself, aware of where she was. *Childish rivalry is not a sin.*

Alba had only attended church to irritate the Buffalo in her short skirt and to show off her 'boyfriend.' She had not intended to listen. Not for a moment. God was not someone she welcomed into her life. If she thought about Him at all, it was out of guilt. She had grown up with Him, as they all had in that small, rural community of Beechfield. But then she had outgrown Him. Of course, she knew there was some sort of higher power. Her mother was up there somewhere. She certainly wasn't dead in a coffin buried in the ground for the worms to eat. There was some sort of spirit life but she never let herself wonder about it for too long, mainly because if her mother could see her she would no doubt disapprove of the promiscuous and decadent life she led, which left Alba, momentarily, very unhappy and riddled with self-loathing. No, better to live in the present. However, Reverend Weatherbone captured her attention. She didn't take her eyes off him for a second. He strode the nave, arms flapping, robes flying, hair waving about as if it had a life of its own, with such charisma that even she, the most skeptical of the congregation, believed that God must be speaking through him directly to her.

She didn't think about sex. She didn't dwell on Fitz's kiss. For once in her life, Alba Arbuckle thought about God.

12

When the service was over Reverend Weatherbone stood in the porch shaking the congregants' hands as they filed out. Margo found herself behind Mabel Hancock. She tensed competitively as the reverend congratulated Mabel on the flowers she had arranged the week before and felt compelled to interrupt, desperate for Mabel to know that the reverend was lunching at Beechfield Park. 'Oh yes, couldn't do without her.'

'Nor you, Mrs. Arbuckle,' said the reverend diplomatically.

'An invigorating service.' Margo returned the compliment.

'I'm glad to see Alba attending today.'

'Yes, she's down for the weekend with her new boyfriend. We're all rather hoping this one's for keeps. I'm glad you will meet her properly over lunch. Come whenever you are ready.' She smiled at Mabel in triumph.

'My mind boggles at the things young people wear these days,' said Mabel, as she walked away, shaking her head.

Margo turned to see Alba greeting the vicar, her coat open and flapping in the wind, revealing her small skirt and patterned tights. She stalked over to intervene. She would have to make a joke of it. Why hadn't the silly girl buttoned up her coat? To Margo's astonishment, as she approached, she realized that their entire conversation now revolved around that dreaded slip of material and that the vicar was voicing, very loudly and with great enthusiasm, his approval.

Alba's little skirt had also aroused the interest of the invisible bell ringers: Fred Timble, Hannah Galloway, and Verity Forthright. Once they had finished their highly skilled job, which, they lamented, went unnoticed by the majority of the community, they sat down on the wooden benches, high above the now dwindling congregants, to catch their breath and discuss the service. They didn't waste time dissecting the sermon or admiring the flowers, or indeed the village characters whose familiarity now bred a kind of affectionate contempt, but zoomed straight in on Alba Arbuckle.

'You could see the look of disapproval on Mrs. Arbuckle's face,' commented Verity, who never had a good word to say. 'Even with that long coat you couldn't miss that skirt and those boots. In church of all places!'

Fred had been infatuated with Margo for many years. He thought her a real lady. Gracious, capable, dignified, and very upper-class. He liked the way she spoke, that old-fashioned articulation of words that set her so far apart from everyone else in Beechfield. Once or twice she had deigned to speak to him. She had praised his bell ringing, told him he did a terrific job. 'It sets everyone's mind in the right frame for worship,' she had said. He had remembered that, word for word. But she thought less of him ever since she had discovered him having an illegal drink and cigarette with fourteen-year-old Alba, in the Hen's Legs pub. She had marched in, face pinched and angry, and hauled the teenager away. 'Mr. Timble, you disappoint me!' she had exclaimed. It still hurt to remember it. 'I would have thought you more honourable than this. She's a child and you are leading her astray.' She had dragged Alba out by the ear. A month or so later, when Alba had sneaked back in again, she had told him she had had every privilege withdrawn: no sweets, no outings, and a ride every day of the holidays on Miranda's skittish pony. She had added with a wicked grin that her legs had grown so sore she could barely close them. 'Serve the old Buffalo right if she raises me to be a tart!' she had said with a raucous laugh. They had taken care after that to hide around the corner.

'Alba's always pushed the limits,' he said in response to Verity's comment. 'Mrs. Arbuckle's long-suffering.'

'Oh, Alba's just young. She's enjoying herself, poor lamb,' said Hannah, who had the gift of seeing only the good in everyone. 'I thought she looked lovely. She's a beautiful girl and she has a nice new boyfriend.' She patted her grey bun to make sure it was all in place. She was a neatly dressed, full-bodied woman who liked to look her best on a Sunday. She was getting too old for bell ringing, she had decided; one or two more years and she'd be too doddery to climb the narrow staircase. 'She'll probably marry that nice young man and settle down. They all seem to in the end. My granddaughter . . .'

Verity wasn't interested in Hannah's granddaughter. She was bitter because she hadn't had children, just a cantankerous old husband who was more work than any baby would have been.

'Oh, he'll be out on his ear,' she said acerbically. 'I know Alba's type. She's had more lovers than I've had hot dinners!'

'Verity!' Hannah exclaimed, appalled.

'Verity!' Fred repeated. Sometimes they forgot they were in the company of a man.

'It's disrespectful to speak of her like that, in this place!' Hannah hissed in a whisper. 'You know nothing about it!'

'I do,' said Verity, standing up and straightening her pleated skirt. 'Edith hears everything that goes on up at the Park. Give her a little sherry and out it all comes. Not that I'd dream of asking.' She pursed her lips, irritated that she had been forced into betraying Edith, who had cooked at Beechfield Park for the last fifty-two years. Now, of course, she was unable to stop herself. 'They've had some terrible rows, you know. Edith says that Alba and Mrs. Arbuckle are at loggerheads all the time and that Captain Arbuckle just sticks his head in the sand like an ostrich. He feels guilty, she says, that she hasn't a real mother. It's not his fault, of course, but he carries it all on his shoulders. He looks much older than his years, don't you think? Mrs. Arbuckle is far more interested in her own daughters. After all, blood is blood, isn't it? And her daughters give her no trouble. Not like Alba.'

'Edith should keep her mouth shut if she knows what's good for her!' said Hannah in an unusually brisk tone of voice.

'She's very discreet. She only tells me.'

'And you tell everyone else!' said Hannah, putting her arms through her coat sleeves. 'Right, I'm off for lunch.'

'And I'm off to the Hen's Legs,' said Fred, shrugging on his old sheepskin.

'Rev Weatherbone is lunching at the Park today. I wonder what he'll make of Alba. I don't believe they've met before.'

'Well,' huffed Hannah, making for the door. 'If anyone will find out, Verity, it's you!'

Back at Beechfield Park Margo was seating everyone for lunch. Cook had spent all morning sweating over roast beef, Yorkshire pudding, roast potatoes, which were always especially crispy, and an array of vegetables cooked al dente. The gravy was thick and brown, her own recipe, which she refused to share with anyone, even Verity Forthright, who had begged for it on a number of occasions.

Cook was pretty unshockable. She had lived more than half her life with the Arbuckles and had seen everything, from Alba's tantrums to the boys she had kissed behind the hedges in the garden when as a teenager she had profited from the tennis tournaments and pony club camps that her stepmother had held for Caroline and Miranda. However, the scrap of cloth Alba had worn to breakfast *had* managed to shock her. Beneath that excuse for a skirt, Alba's legs were long and somehow awfully tarty in those boots. No wonder Mrs. Arbuckle refused to allow her to attend church without covering up. Therefore it came as a terrible shock when the good vicar arrived for lunch, making jokes about her wardrobe. Wasn't he a man of God?

Indeed, as Cook was serving, pretending to mind her own business, she couldn't help but hear the odd snippet of conversation while they helped themselves to beans and potatoes. The vicar was seated between Mrs. Arbuckle and Alba, a dreadful mistake on the part of the hostess, Cook thought, for when she was sitting down, Alba's little skirt disappeared completely. She might as well have been sitting in her knickers. It wasn't right for a man of God to gaze at a girl's thighs. Let alone talk about them.

'When I was a young man one certainly didn't see a woman's thighs until one was married,' he said. Alba giggled that provocative laugh of hers. Low and husky like chimney smoke. Cook was appalled at her flirting.

'I would have hated to be so restricted. Besides, these

boots make me feel on top of the world. I stride about as if I own it,' she replied. 'They're Italian suede, you know.'

'I'd like a pair of boots like that. How do you think they'd look beneath my robes?'

'I don't think it matters what you wear underneath. You could be wearing nothing at all and no one would be any the wiser.' They both laughed.

Cook glanced across at Mrs. Arbuckle, who was talking to Fitz. Now, *he* was a charming man. Sensible, gentle, kind. He had even come into the kitchen after dinner the night before to thank her for such a 'sumptuous feast' as he had so sweetly put it. She noticed the reverend take four potatoes. Not only an eye for the ladies but a very healthy appetite to boot. In her day vicars were men of moderation and modesty. She sniffed her disapproval, drawing the dish away before he helped himself to a fifth.

Captain Arbuckle complimented Cook on the lunch. She was very fond of the captain, had known him most of his life. When he came back from the war with that tiny baby in his arms, it broke her heart. How could he possibly cope on his own with such a small creature? The grief had distorted his features. He looked like an old man, not the glossy young boy who had been the rebel of the family. A character he had been, always up to no good, but with the charm of a monkey. He could smile his way out of anything, that Tommy, as he was known in those days. Not when he returned from the war. He had changed. Despair had changed him. If it hadn't been for the little girl he held in his arms so possessively he might have lost the will to live and faded right away. That happened. Cook had heard. They had talked about Valentina in hushed voices, as if to mention her name at such a sad time was in some way to denigrate it. Beautiful, she had been. An angel, they said. Then the new Mrs. Arbuckle came on to the scene and

Valentina's blessed name was never again mentioned in the house. Not directly. It wasn't a surprise that Alba had rebelled. Cook snorted her displeasure and the captain, thinking it was on account of his having taken too many potatoes, discreetly put one back.

Cook moved on to Fitz. He smelled of sandalwood. She could smell it above the aroma of her cooking. She liked Fitz. Though they did make an odd couple, he and Alba. They were clearly fond of each other. Fitz made Alba laugh. That was the way to her heart, though Cook wasn't sure that he had got there. He knew where it was, he aimed straight at it, and yet, as with all the young men Alba entertained, he didn't quite penetrate it. She could see it in Alba's eyes. Fitz might get there in time, if he persevered. Though Alba didn't have a good track record. She wasn't a long-distance runner, as Captain Arbuckle had put it. She had heard him talking to his wife one evening, lamenting the lovers Alba took, her decadent lifestyle, longing for her to settle down. She was getting on, after all. As Fitz served himself the last potato, Cook didn't mind a bit.

It was later in the afternoon when Cook just happened to be wandering through the house to tell her employers she'd left cold meat and salad in the fridge for supper that she stumbled upon Alba rootling around in her father's study. Cook stood in the drinks room, spying on Alba through the crack in the door, unable to contain her curiosity. She knew it was wrong, but she couldn't restrain herself.

Alba carefully opened the drawers of his desk, lifted papers, sifted through them, scowling all the while. She obviously couldn't find what she was looking for. She kept glancing up from under her brow at the door to the hall, afraid someone might walk in and catch her.

Occasionally she'd pause and stiffen like a startled cat before relaxing with relief and resuming her search. Cook was fascinated. What could she be searching for?

Suddenly Cook stiffened too, as a shadow was thrown across the room. Mrs. Arbuckle stood in the doorway, her large frame obscuring the light that came in from the hall. Alba stood up abruptly and gasped. For a moment they simply stared at each other. Mrs. Arbuckle's face betrayed a seething yet controlled fury. Now Cook couldn't leave even if she had wanted to. The slightest movement would most certainly have given her away. Her skin bristled with apprehension.

Finally Mrs. Arbuckle spoke in a very quiet voice. 'Are you looking for something, Alba?' Cook, who could only see Alba's profile, was able to detect a sly grin across Alba's face. She leaned across her father's desk and lifted a pencil out of his pen holder.

'Found it,' she said flippantly. 'Silly me. It was in front of my nose all the time.'

Mrs. Arbuckle watched in disbelief as her stepdaughter flounced past her out of the room.

At last Mrs. Arbuckle moved. She walked calmly across to the desk and began tidying it. She closed the drawers that were left ajar and put her husband's letters back in a neat pile on the blotter. Her capable hands moved slowly and carefully, and she didn't stop until she was satisfied that all was as it should be. The captain was a fastidious man. His years in the navy meant that he liked his things to be orderly. Then her hand hovered over one of the drawers. She chewed the inside of her cheek as if deliberating what to do. It was as if something within pulled at her. Was she perhaps looking for the same thing as Alba? After a long moment she withdrew her hand and walked out, closing the door softly behind her.

When Cook found Mrs. Arbuckle in the sitting room, she was perched on the club fender talking to Caroline as if nothing had happened. She smiled at Cook, thanked her for lunch, and bade her good night. Cook was intrigued. The animosity between Alba and Mrs. Arbuckle was well known, but she now realized that no one really appreciated the full extent of it.

Cook walked home to find a message from Verity. Could she telephone her? Cook snorted self-importantly. *That Verity,* she thought intolerantly. *She's after my recipe again. I shan't give it to her. I absolutely shan't.*

Alba and Fitz left not long after Cook. Thomas kissed her temple and shook hands firmly with Fitz. 'I hope to see you again,' he said.

'So do I,' Fitz replied. 'I've enjoyed every minute of it. Now I've met Alba's parents I know where she gets all that charm from.'

Thomas chuckled. For a moment he felt the young lieutenant laughing inside the heavy skin of the old captain. He had forgotten how good it felt. He patted Fitz on the back and suddenly it was Jack's face that grinned back at him. He blinked the image away. He hadn't spoken to Jack since the war. He didn't know where he was, if indeed he *was* at all. He turned to the porch and remembered climbing those steps, holding little Alba, his world in shreds. Yet, hadn't that small bundle in his arms represented hope and light when all around him was hopeless and dark? He watched her climb into the car. They waved and then were gone.

In the car Alba vented her fury. 'He's hidden it!' she exclaimed. 'I looked in every drawer in that desk. He's either hidden it or destroyed it. I wish I had never given it to him. I'm a fool!'

'I don't think he'd destroy it, Alba. Not after the way he talked about her last night.' Fitz tried to soothe her. Besides, he genuinely liked her father. He wasn't an old duffer at all. He was a relatively young man. *Should* have been in his prime. Yet, like many who survived the war, his experiences had robbed him of his youth. 'Did you ask him for it?'

Alba looked surprised. 'No,' she replied. 'We don't talk about her. Every time I have brought her name up in the past we've had a terrible row, all because of the Buffalo. I suspect he's hidden it somewhere safe where he can take it out and look at it every once in a while in private. He's hardly going to leave it in his desk. Margo would find it in a second. It should be something that we can share,' she said in a quiet voice. 'She belongs to me and Daddy. Not to the Buffalo, Caroline, Miranda, or Henry. It should be something that we can talk about by the fire, over a glass of wine. It could have been so special. But because of the Buffalo it's a dirty secret and I feel unworthy because I'm the product of that secret.'

They drove on in silence, each trying to find a way through the terrible muddle that Valentina had unwittingly created by dying. The sun was setting behind them, turning the sky a brilliant gold, and pale pink clouds wafted across it like goose down. Sprout slept peacefully in the back.

'I'm going to go and find her myself,' Alba said, sliding down the seat and folding her arms. 'I'm going to find Incantellaria.'

'Good,' Fitz replied. 'I'll help you . . .'

'Will you?' she interrupted before he had finished his sentence. 'You mean, you'll come with me?' She sat up happily.

Fitz chuckled. 'I was going to offer to help you find it on a map!'

'Oh,' she said, disappointed.

When they arrived in Cheyne Walk Fitz pulled up beneath the street lamp. He didn't know what to expect. They no longer had a role to play. Normality could be resumed.

Would he go back to his bridge nights with Viv, only to gaze longingly through Alba's windows and suffer her suitors' walking up her gangplank with armfuls of roses and self-satisfied smirks?

'You'll get a ticket if you park it here,' she said.

'I'm not staying,' he replied.

She frowned. 'Why not?'

Fitz sighed. 'I don't want to share you, Alba.'

'Share me?'

'Yes, I don't want to share you with Rupert or Reed of the River or any of your other friends. If I'm with you I want to be with you exclusively.'

She laughed happily. 'Then you'll be exclusive, darling Fitz. You can have me all to yourself.'

Once again Fitz felt that uncomfortable emptiness. Her tone had been flippant. It was all too easy. 'You mean you'll stop seeing anyone else?'

'But of course. What do you think I am?' She looked hurt. 'Haven't you thought that I might not want to share you, either?'

'Well, no,' he replied, baffled.

'Then park the car in your clever little place and let's go and have a bath together. Sprout can watch if he's good. There's nothing I like better than a glass of wine in the bath and no, in case you're wondering, I haven't shared a bath with anyone before. It'll be a first with you and a first with Sprout.'

Fitz felt guilty. 'I'm sorry,' he said, kissing her cheek.

'Apology accepted.' Then she laughed that infectious laugh that bubbled up from her belly. 'To think that we've turned into the couple we've been pretending to be all weekend. Isn't life funny?'

13

Alba did as she had promised and told all the other men who enjoyed the warm excitement of her bed that she now had a boyfriend and would no longer be able to see them. Rupert was heartbroken. He turned up at her boat, with armfuls of flowers and a long, unhappy face, begging her to marry him. Tim shouted at her down the telephone, hung up, and then sent a gift from Tiffany by way of an apology, hoping that she'd accept it and marry him. James, usually so mild-mannered and gentle, came around one evening drunk and, with the rifle his father had given him, shot at the squirrels on the roof of her boat until the police, alerted by Viv, arrived to take him away. Alba shrugged it off nonchalantly, poured herself another glass of wine, and took Fitz upstairs to make love.

Fitz ignored Viv's warnings and blindly pursued the object of his love. He spent most nights on the *Valentina* for Alba hated to be alone. She relished the nights when they didn't make love, when she could curl up against him, his arms around her, his breathing brushing her skin and his voice murmuring into her ear. He was more than her lover; after all, lovers were two a penny. He was her friend. She had never had a friend like Fitz.

Alba took him shopping at Mr. Fish in Beauchamp Place and persuaded him to buy new shirts. 'Your clothes were in the Dark Ages,' she said when he wore one to lunch at Drones. 'Really, you fitted in much too well at Beechfield Park for my liking. I bet the Buffalo was sizing you up for Caroline. I won't burn the old shirts, just in case.' Fitz didn't like her teasing. Didn't she know she was going to marry him?

They went to Andy Warhol's exhibition of pop art at the Tate and, in an effort to be trendy, Fitz bought her Led Zeppelin's new LP which contained her favorite song, 'Stairway to Heaven.' In the evenings they went to Tramp or Annabel's and danced until dawn. The only thing that kept him dancing into the early hours was Alba's new pair of hot-pants. It was all right for her; she didn't have to get up in the mornings, although Reed of the River often came calling at dawn, remaining obediently downstairs. Fitz, on the other hand, had a job to do. Viv was pestering him about her book tour, which looked like it would encompass more than just France. He also had to get up early to take Sprout for a walk in Hyde Park.

'You look tired, Fitzroy,' Viv commented, dealing the cards.

'I'm shattered,' he replied. Viv couldn't help but notice his mouth curl up at the corners smugly.

'It won't last,' she said caustically, flicking ash into the green dish.

'What do you want to play?' asked Wilfrid. 'Weak or strong, no trump?'

'Weak,' said Viv with a sigh. 'I still see that Reed of the River dropping by in the mornings.'

'I trust her,' said Fitz confidently. 'She's perfectly entitled to have friends.' Fitz would have liked to explain that she had only slept with men out of loneliness. Now she had him, she didn't have to feel lonely anymore.

'I have plenty of female friends and Georgia doesn't mind, do you, darling?' interjected Wilfrid, sorting his cards and rubbing his chin.

'I bet none of them are like Alba,' said Viv. Georgia was offended; as much as she would have protested otherwise, she would secretly have loved to have friends like Alba.

'I'm not going to discuss her over the bridge table. It's not gallant,' said Fitz defensively. 'One diamond.'

'You've changed your tune.' Viv was put out. 'No bid.'

'One heart,' said Georgia.

'No bid,' said Wilfrid with a sigh.

'Three no trumps. I respect her,' said Fitz.

Viv snorted. 'People aren't always what they seem, Fitzroy. Being a writer I observe people all the time. Alba's used to being different things to different people. She's an actress. I'll bet she doesn't even know who she is underneath all that bravado.'

'Is she going to go to Italy to find her mother?' Georgia asked.

'Yes, I think so,' Fitz replied.

'What is she hoping to find?' asked Wilfrid, who, having only picked up the odd remark, was confused about Alba's mother.

'That's a very good question. I don't think Alba's really thought it through. We're talking thirty years ago. A lot can happen in thirty years. Her mother's family might have even moved away. But I suspect she's looking for memories, anecdotes, to be reassured that her mother loved her. She's never felt she's belonged in her stepmother's family. She wants that sense of fitting in, of looking at her relations and seeing her features reflected in theirs.'

'You're an incurable romantic, Fitzroy. Are you going

to go with her?' asked Viv, narrowing her eyes as Georgia won the trick.

'No,' he replied. 'It's something she has to do on her own.'

'I don't imagine she's ever done anything on her own,' added Viv.

'Where is this place?' asked Wilfrid, who flattered himself he knew Italy, having studied history of art at Oxford.

'About an hour or so south of Naples, on the Amalfi coast. We've already found it on the map. She's going to break it to her father this weekend.'

'So you still have a role to play in this drama?' said Viv.

'It's no longer a drama, Viv,' retorted Fitz. 'It's life.'

That night at Beechfield Park, Margo and Thomas were undressing for bed. Outside it was raining heavily, large icy drops that fell like stones against the window panes. 'Bloody cold for spring,' said Thomas, peering through the curtains of his dressing room. When he managed to see past his reflection to the dark garden below, wet and glistening in the light that escaped from the house, he suddenly recalled the night he had returned with little Alba. It had rained then too.

'I hope there's not a frost; it'll kill all the little buds that have just begun to sprout,' Margo replied. 'It's been so warm lately, and now this. One never can tell in this country.' She stepped out of her skirt and stood in her petticoat, undoing her necklace. 'Did you remember to tell Peter to have a look at Boris's foot? I notice he's limping.'

Thomas pulled himself away from the window and closed the curtains.

'He's probably done it chasing those sows around the pen all day,' he said, folding his trousers and placing them on the chair. Suddenly Jack's face appeared in his head, with Brendan alert and playful on his shoulder. Jack was laughing at his joke, his cheeky smile wide and infectious.

'What did you say?' Margo let her petticoat drop to the floor.

'Nothing, darling,' he replied, undoing the buttons of his shirt.

'Do you know Mabel telephoned to remind me to do the church flowers this Sunday? As if I'd forget!' She took off her pants and bra and slipped into her white nightie. Then she sat in front of the mirror and combed her hair, now almost totally grey. Margo didn't seem to care. She rubbed some Pond's cream into her hands, wiping the excess onto her face. 'Really, Mabel's such a busybody. She should run for mayor or something. Put that nosy talent of hers to good use. Alba's coming down with Fitz,' she added. 'That's three times this month,' she went on when he didn't respond. 'I think Fitz's a bridge over troubled water, don't you?'

When Thomas walked into the bedroom his face was flushed and his eyes burning. 'Are you all right, darling?' Margo asked, frowning. 'Are you unwell?' He hadn't been himself lately.

'I'm perfectly well,' he replied. 'Let's make love.'

Margo was surprised. They hadn't made love in, well, ages. She couldn't remember the last time. There was always so much on her mind: Summer, Boris, the children, Alba, the village fête, the church flowers, the Women's Institute, not to mention all the entertaining they did. There simply wasn't time for lovemaking.

They climbed beneath the sheets. Margo would have liked to read her book. She was past the difficult first chapters now and the characters were really beginning to live. With a sigh of resignation she switched off the light and lay down expectantly. Thomas turned off his light and rolled over to kiss her.

'Aren't we a bit old for this?' she said, embarrassed.

'It's only our bodies that have aged, Margo,' he breathed into her neck. 'Surely our spirits are still young.'

His voice sounded desperate, as if he needed her to agree. Margo sensed in his soul a terrible unrest. He hadn't been the same since Alba came down with the portrait of her mother. Those memories had been nicely stored away like silt at the bottom of a clear pond. Now Alba had gone and raked her fingers through it, leaving the water cloudy. As he made love to her, Margo couldn't help wondering whether Thomas was thinking of Valentina.

Alba listened to the rain tapping on the skylight. She was happy and satisfied. Fitz, however, was not. He was still unable to get close to her. 'How much closer can one possibly get?' she would argue, pressing her warm body against his. But that was not what he meant. He didn't expect Alba to understand. Perhaps it was just her nature, but he knew there was a part at the very core of her being that remained a stranger to him. He simply couldn't help feeling she was acting. He didn't believe she was superficial, he knew she had secret depths, he just didn't know how to get to them. *Give it time,* he reassured himself.

'Darling, please come with me?' she pleaded, running her hand across his chest.

'Of course,' he replied, assuming she was referring to the weekend.

'No, I mean to Italy.' There was a long pause.

Fitz took a deep breath, anticipating her reaction. 'You know I can't.'

'Is it Sprout?'

'No.'

'Is it work?'

'Not really.'

'Viv wouldn't mind. You could say you were setting up her book tour. I'm sure there's a bookshop in Incantellaria.'

'I wouldn't be so sure.'

'Don't you love me?' She sounded hurt.

'You know I love you. But Alba, this is something you have to do alone. I'll just get in the way.'

'Of course you won't get in the way. I need you,' she pleaded, a steely undertone to her voice.

Fitz sighed. 'Darling, I don't even speak Italian.'

'That's the lamest excuse I've ever heard. I had expected you, of all people, to be more loyal.' She sat up sulkily and lit a cigarette.

'It's got nothing to do with loyalty. I'm one hundred percent loyal to you. Look on it as an adventure.'

She looked at him as if he had done the most wicked thing. 'I'm so disappointed in you, Fitz. I thought you were different.'

Now it was his turn to be affronted. 'How can I drop everything to follow you around Italy? I have a life and, although you are very central to it, there are things I just can't leave for other people to do. I'd love to take a long holiday with you in a pretty place. But right now is not a good time.'

She got up and flounced into the bathroom and slammed the door. Fitz stared up at the skylight, where the rain was still splashing off the glass in a torrent. Since they had met he had been wary of upsetting her. He had witnessed the fire of her temper and made a conscious effort to avoid igniting it. He had been too afraid of losing her. He now realized, as she sulked in the bathroom, that his inability to get close to her might have something to do with that pretense. They hadn't been honest with each other. He wasn't doing her any favors pandering to her every whim; he was simply encouraging her to be manipulative and spoiled. If their relationship was going to work it had to get real.

When she came out she was in her pink dressing gown with fluffy pink mules on her feet. 'I'm not used to being treated like this,' she said, her mouth tight and petulant. She folded her arms in front of her and glowered at him. 'If you're not going to support me, why are you with me?'

'Just because I refuse to go to Italy with you doesn't mean that I don't love you,' he explained, but she wasn't listening. When Alba was cross she heard nothing but her own voice.

'This is the most important thing I will ever do in my life. I can't believe that a man who claims to love me doesn't want to share it with me. I don't think we should be together anymore,' she said tearfully.

'We can't split up because of a trivial argument,' he reasoned, his gut twisting with regret.

'That's just it. You think it's trivial. To me, my mother is the most important person in my life. Finding her is the biggest thing I've ever done. To me it's not trivial at all.'

'Splitting up over it is. Alba, you must understand the world doesn't revolve around you. You're beautiful and adorable but you're the most selfish human being I've ever met. If I give in to you I wouldn't be true to myself or to you. If splitting up is what you want, I'll leave right now, with enormous regret.'

Alba's lips quivered and she looked up at him from under her eyelashes. She had pushed but he had not budged. They *always* budged. 'Yes, I want you to leave.'

He shook his head sadly. 'I know you don't really want to do this. It's a matter of pride, isn't it?'

'Just leave!'

He dressed and packed up his belongings while she watched him. They didn't speak. The boat rocked and creaked in the choppy Thames, bumping every few seconds against the rubber tire that protected Viv's boat from the *Valentina*. Fitz suddenly felt seasick. He hoped that if he took his time she might reconsider. As much as he longed for her to change her mind, he was too proud to beg and too much a man of principle to bend to her will. The scent of paraffin from the stoves that heated the boat rose up on the damp as the rain continued to fall in sheets. He didn't like the idea of being out in such weather in the middle of the night. He hadn't brought his car and had no umbrella. Sprout would be miserable in the rain. He had made himself very comfortable downstairs in Alba's warm kitchen.

'Right, I suppose it's goodbye then,' he said, giving her a last chance to change her mind, but her mouth was firmly set into a thin line of resolve. 'I'll see myself out.'

Alba heard the door close behind him, then there was silence but for the forlorn creaking of the boat and the low moan of her own sobbing. She sank onto the bed and put her face in her hands.

Her attention was diverted by the sound of dripping. It was louder and slower than the rattling of the rain on the skylight. She lifted her face out of her hands to see a leak in the roof. The water was falling in large plops, like fat tears, onto the rug below. She heaved herself off the bed, her body weighed down as if by a suit of armour. She took the bin from the bathroom and put it under the drip. It made a loud metallic noise, then a wet plop as it filled up. She wished Fitz hadn't gone. He would know what to do. Usually Harry Reed or Rupert would do repairs for her, or even Les Pringle from the Chelsea Yacht and Boat Company, who came daily to fill up the water tank. But she didn't want Harry or Rupert anymore. She wanted Fitz.

Miserably she climbed into bed and curled up on the electric blanket that had begun to steam against the damp. She persuaded herself he might send her flowers in the morning, or a gift from Tiffany. She'd take him back and all would be right again. She wouldn't be alone. For the rest of the night she slept with the light on.

Fitz stepped onto the gangplank and felt the rain go straight down his back. He pulled his coat up to his chin and hunched his shoulders. Sprout cringed and whined miserably. The Embankment was quiet. The odd car came and went but there was no sign of a taxi. He couldn't walk home: it was miles away. He had no choice but to knock on Viv's door. There was a long wait until the lights were switched on. She had not been up writing that night. When she appeared at the door she looked surprised.

'Oh, I thought you were Alba,' she said sleepily. She looked very different without her makeup on. But before he could explain she added, swiftly ushering him through the door and shutting out the rain, 'I won't say I told you so, I'm not a gloater, and yes, you can stay the night. Sprout can sleep in the kitchen. Just one thing. For God's sake, don't send her flowers in the morning; it's terribly cliché and I know you are in the right.'

Alba was first disappointed, then furious, when she received nothing the following day from Fitz. No flowers, no gift, and no telephone call. She waited in her dressing gown, not bothering to get dressed. She wasn't going to see anyone and if Fitz did come by, there would be less to take off. She just lay on her bed painting her nails red for comfort. Finally, at the end of the third day she realized that he wasn't going to make contact, at least for the moment. She would have to go down to Beechfield Park on her own.

Her father and stepmother's reaction to her decision to travel to Italy was entirely as she had expected. This time she picked her moment during dinner. Lavender had appeared, dressed in a silk dress with the pearl choker Hubert had given her for one of their wedding anniversaries. Her short-term memory was terrible but she recalled everything from the distant past as if it had happened yesterday and took great pleasure in recounting to the entire table the story of its purchase. Cook had made a cottage pie which she served with peas and carrots and Thomas opened a bottle of wine. When asked about Fitz, Alba lied.

'He's had to go to France on business. He's organizing Viv's book tour. She's big in France.' Margo imagined they had had a row. Alba was not at all her usual imperious self.

During the pudding, without waiting for Cook to leave the room, Alba dropped her bombshell. 'I'm going to Italy to find my mother's family,' she said. Margo looked horrified. Henry, Caroline, and Miranda held their breath.

'I see,' said Thomas.

'I feel that since you won't tell me about her, I will have to find out for myself. As Viv says, 'God only helps those who help themselves,' so I'm counting on his guidance too. Reverend Weatherbone would approve, I'm sure.' Her tone was flippant.

'Darling,' Margo began, trying not to sound flustered. 'Are you sure you want to delve into the past?'

'Absolutely,' Alba replied.

'Surely it's better left where it is.'

'Why?' Her question was delivered with unexpected serenity and Margo felt a fool for having said it.

'Because,' she stammered.

'Because, my dear,' interjected her husband, 'it all happened a very long time ago. But if it is what you want then we cannot stop you. We can only advise you against it. For your own happiness.'

'I can't be happy unless I have gone back to my roots,' Alba explained, surprised at her own composure.

'Do you know where those roots are?' he asked.

'Incantellaria,' she responded. He suddenly felt dizzy.

'Incantellaria,' echoed Lavender. The whole table turned their eyes to the old lady. 'There is only death and unhappiness to be found in Incantellaria.'

'Would you like another slice of tart?' asked Margo, offering her the plate. Then, suddenly noticing that Cook was still in the room, she added, 'Cook, please could you bring us some more cream.' She was aware that the little silver jug was full, but she hadn't been able to think of anything else. 'I don't think we should discuss this in front of the staff,' she said to her husband. 'In fact, I don't think we should discuss this at all. Alba knows our feelings. Your family is here. Why go all the way to Italy to dig up a whole lot of ghosts?'

Alba was weary. 'I'm going to bed,' she said, getting up. 'I'm going to go with or without your support. I just thought it right that I should tell you. After all, Daddy, she was your wife!'

Thomas watched his daughter leave the room. Instead of feeling that terrible hopelessness, he felt a sense of release. It was no longer his responsibility. She was no longer a child. If she wanted to go, he could not stop her.

After dinner, Thomas retreated into his study to smoke

a cigar and drink a glass of brandy. He sat in his leather chair and stared up at the portrait of his father, until his vision blurred and his eyes began to glisten. Behind the dignified pose of Hubert Arbuckle lay the portrait of Valentina, a dark secret.

Yet she wasn't forgotten. Thomas had tried but failed to forget her. Now the scent of figs reached him once again as if she were bending over his chair to plant a kiss on his temple. The lookout tower loomed out of the nostalgic mists of his mind and he was finally returning to Incantellaria.

14

Italy, May 1945

Thomas felt a rush of emotion as the boat sped into the little harbor of Incantellaria. He looked up to the top of the hill where the old lookout tower was silhouetted against the sky. He remembered Valentina as she had been. Her hair blowing in the wind, her eyes full of sadness, her cheeks en-flamed with their lovemaking. She had appeared like that in his dreams too. Beguiling, mysterious, like a beam of light that was impossible to hold.

Once they had parted he had fought in the taking of the island of Elba, before being transferred to the Adriatic. On August 15, 1944, he had commanded his torpedo boat in the invasion of southern France, the lesser-known sequel to the more famous Normandy landings – D-day. Immediately after the death of his brother, Thomas hadn't cared whether he lived or died. He had engaged in combat with a recklessness seen only in those valiant men whose lives mean little to them. Then he had met Valentina and suddenly life was precious once more. Every skirmish had filled him with terror. Every time he had boarded enemy cargo ships, he had crossed himself and thanked God for preserving him another day, for each day inevitably brought him closer to her. His will to live was so strong that his courage was now greater than it had been before, for it was no longer flawed with recklessness.

Afterward, Thomas was sent to the Gulf of Genoa where he patrolled the coast. He wrote to Valentina whenever he could. His written Italian wasn't good, but he was able to communicate the longing in his heart in spite of his poor grammar and limited vocabulary. He told her how he gazed at the portrait he had drawn of her, up on the hill, beside the crumbling old watchtower, where the love they made had fused them together in an unbreakable bond. He wrote of their future. He would marry her in the pretty chapel of San Pasquale and take her back to England, where he would ensure that she lived like a queen with everything she could ever want. He received nothing from her. Only perfumed letters and food parcels from Shirley. Then one evening in September, after having successfully sunk an enemy merchant ship, he returned to base at Leghorn to find a letter waiting for him. The writing was curled and childish and foreign. The postmark was Italian.

He studied the envelope for a long moment, his heart suspended. He desperately hoped it was from Valentina. Who else would write from Italy? Then his optimism faded. What if the letter was one of rejection? How would his fragile heart bear such a heavy loss? He fingered the letter, his face contorted into a worried frown. Then he sat down, took a deep breath, and opened it.

It was only one side long, written on paper as diaphanous as butterfly wings, and dated August 1944. *My dearest Tommy. My heart longs for you too. Every day I stand and wait at the watchtower on the hill, hoping for the sight of your boat motoring in to our little harbour. Every day I am disappointed. I have news for you. I wanted to wait until I saw you, but I fear for you in this war. I fear that you will die not knowing. So I will tell you in this letter and hope that you receive it. I am pregnant. My heart is filled with joy for I am carrying the child we made together out of love. Mamma says he will be blessed for he was conceived at the* festa di Santa Benedetta *when our Lord demonstrated His love for us by shedding tears of blood. I pray for your safe deliverance from this war and that God will bring you back to me so that you may know your son or daughter. I wait for you, my love. Your devoted Valentina.*

Thomas read the letter several times, barely able to believe that a child of his was about to be born into the world. He pictured Valentina with her belly round and her eyes bright with the light of impending maternity. Then he was gripped with a shudder of alarm: she was vulnerable in that small cove. He stood up and strode across the room in agitation, envisaging all the terrible things that might happen to her without his protection. He yearned to go to her and yet he could not. His job was up in the north and the war was still raging like a forest fire. The Allies had contained it and the prospects were good, yet their fortunes could change in a moment.

Then he thought of all the innocence that war had destroyed, the horrors seen by eyes too young to understand, and his heart flooded with fear. His child was to be born into all this terror. Was it right to bring an innocent into so cruel a world?

'What are you looking so down about?' asked Jack, taking the seat beside him.

'I've had a letter from Valentina,' he replied, shaking his head in amazement.

'What's happened?'

'She's carrying my child, Jack.'

Jack gasped. 'Christ!' Then after a long moment of contemplation he added seriously, 'What the hell are you going to do?'

'Marry her,' he replied without hesitation.

Jack looked at him askance. 'That's a bit drastic, isn't it? You don't even know her!'

'I know all I need to know about her. She likes lemons, the sea, and the colour purple.' He smiled with tenderness as he recalled her childish soliloquy. 'Christ, I've been hit between the eyes, first by love and now this!'

'I can't see Lavender and Hubert taking to her!'

'Better than Shirley!'

'I don't know. Your father's an arch snob and he's wary of foreigners, especially Italians . . .'

'They'll have no choice.'

'Now Freddie's gone, you're the heir.'

Thomas shrugged. 'To what? A house? It's not as if my father has an earldom to pass down, is it!'

'But he takes Beechfield Park very seriously. It's no joke running an estate like that.'

'She'll learn. I'll teach her.'

'Bloody hell. You a father!' Jack shook his head in wonder. Then he looked at him with intensity, no longer as his subordinate but as his childhood friend. He spoke in a low voice, his eyes misty with emotion. 'The war's changed you, Tommy. You and I were once so similar. We flouted the rules at Eton, disrupted the classes, swanned around like we owned the place. Oxford wasn't much different, fewer rules to break, that's all. Then this bloody war. We've become men, haven't we? We never thought we would. Hubert would be damn proud of you, if he knew. When all this is over, I'm going to tell him.'

Thomas sighed heavily and took the cigarette that Jack offered him. 'But you were the one who got all the girls. I just got the crumbs from the rich man's table!'

'But you got the one that mattered, Tommy.'

'This time, I did.'

'And you deserve her,' Jack said, though he felt

apprehensive. Valentina spoke no English, had been brought up in a small, provincial harbor town with a population of no more than a few hundred people. How did Tommy think she was going to cope in a house the size of the marchese's palazzo? To find herself among the cool, snobby British who, when it came to class, were more formidable than ten Immacolatas. The fantasy was all very romantic, but the reality would throw up all sorts of problems that he hadn't considered. However, now wasn't the time to discuss them. He had got the girl pregnant and he was a man of honour. He would do the right thing. 'You're more like Freddie than I imagined, Tommy,' Jack said finally, his eyes suddenly betraying the strain of war that humor usually covered up. Thomas was too moved to speak: a thick lump of anguish had lodged itself inside his throat. He straightened up and cleared his throat.

'That's sir to you, Lieutenant Harvey,' he said to diffuse the emotion.

Jack blinked away the childhood memories that had suddenly found their way through his weakened defenses. 'Yes, sir,' he responded. But both men continued to look at each other with the eyes of boys.

Now, as Thomas sailed into the tiny port on a small motorboat, he was no longer commanding the MTB. The war was over. They had been demobbed and he had been given a desk job in the Ministry of Defense. Jack, Rigs, and the boys had gone home. Brendan had survived, miraculously, not only the war but Jack's deep pocket and Rigs's renditions of *Rigoletto*. Thomas planned to return to England with Valentina and their child, as soon as they were married.

He had fantasized about this moment for the last few months. He had received word from Valentina that she had been safely delivered of a little girl. She hadn't mentioned a name. He had celebrated quietly with Jack. A drink and a cigarette and tears he felt unashamed to shed in front of his friend. He had written back hastily. Pouring out his pride and love in bad Italian, confusing verbs and tenses in his emotion. Even his handwriting, usually so clear and neat, shot erratically up and down the page.

Now he pictured their daughter in her mother's arms and was gripped with longing to embrace them both. In his hand he held the few letters she had sent him, worn thin and frayed like a child's well-loved muslin. They smelled of figs – that indelible scent of hers that had managed to banish the acrid smell of death. Now he inhaled the pine and eucalyptus of Incantellaria and recalled with nostalgia the first time he had set eyes on this enchanting little town, with Jack and Brendan by his side, not knowing then how much it would settle in his heart. He was a changed man and it wasn't just the war that had altered his state of mind. Valentina had awoken his instincts to provide and protect. Now he had a child, he had a far greater responsibility than any he had ever had before.

The boat drew up against the quay and Thomas stepped out with his small bag of belongings, still dressed in his tired blue naval uniform. He peered out from under his cap at the sleepy harbor bathed in the warm springtime sun. At first no one noticed him. He was able to pass his eyes over the row of white houses, their iron balconies adorned as before with bright red geraniums, and on the little Trattoria Fiorelli. He was drawn out of his sentimental recollections as the fishermen put down their nets and women emerged out of the shadows, drawing their children to their aprons, looking at him through narrowed, suspicious eyes. Then the old man who played the concertina recognized him. He pointed his arthritic finger and his wizened face collapsed in on itself as his mouth opened into a toothless smile. *'C'è l'inglese!'* he exclaimed. Thomas's heart swelled with happiness. They remembered him.

The garbled words of the old man ricocheted down the sea front as the townspeople spread the news. *'È tornato, l'inglese!'* It wasn't long before the dusty street was crowded. They clapped their hands and waved. The little boy who that first time had given the fascist salute now put his hand to his brow as Lattarullo had done and Thomas smiled at him, saluting back. This time his mother did not slap him, but patted him proudly on the head. The little boy blushed crimson and clamped his legs together, for all the excitement had brought on a desire to pee.

Then Thomas's eyes were drawn back to the Trattoria Fiorelli. The waiters were standing outside, their mouths agape, trays in hands that had only recently held guns. The old ones, who had been there all along, smiled wistfully, remembering the singing and the little red squirrel. A stillness now surrounded the café while the crowd agitated and swelled around him like waves on the sea. It was as if the modest little building held its breath, awaiting something magical to happen. Then she appeared. Thomas's heart soared and there it remained, in suspended animation, neither rising nor falling but motionless, afraid that, if it stirred, the spell would break and she would disappear like a rainbow into the sunshine.

The waiters stepped aside. Not once did Valentina take her eyes off the man she loved, but walked toward him with her unique, lively walk. In her arms she held her threemonth-old baby, wrapped only in a thin white sheet, pressed tightly against her bosom. Her cheeks glowed with pride and her lips curled into a small smile. It was only when she came closer that he saw her eyes were glistening with tears.

Thomas took off his hat, and noticed his hands were trembling. Valentina stood before him. At the sight of the baby blinking up at him he was humbled. In the midst of all this horror and bloodshed here was a pure, innocent soul. It was as if God had shone a bright light into a very dark place. Her face was a miniature reflection of her mother's, except for her eyes, which were pale grey like his, a stark contrast to her dark hair and olive brown skin. She waved her tiny hand about. Thomas took it and let her wrap her fingers around one of his. He smiled. Then he raised his eyes to Valentina.

The townspeople continued to watch transfixed as Thomas bent his head and planted a kiss on Valentina's forehead. He rested his lips for a long moment, inhaling her unique scent and tasting the salt on her skin.

Suddenly a loud voice boomed out above the clapping and cheering of the townspeople. 'Move on. This is not a show! It is a private moment. Come on, everyone, enough. Move on. Move on.' Lattarullo's voice was unmistakable. Slowly the people began, reluctantly, to disperse. They had all watched Valentina's growing belly and witnessed her longing and often her despair. As they returned to their afternoon naps, the fishermen to their sails and nets, the children to their games, Lattarullo appeared, hot and sweating and scratching his groin.

'Signor Arbuckle,' he said as Thomas reluctantly withdrew his lips from Valentina's forehead. 'Many doubted you would ever return. I am happy to say that I was not one of those. No, I never once doubted you. That is not solely to compliment your character but the signorina's beauty. Helen of Troy was not as fair, and look what effect she had on men! I would have been astounded, not to mention a good deal poorer, had you not returned for la signorina Fiorelli.'

Thomas imagined them all sitting in the café placing their bets on whether or not he would come back for her.

They walked to the Trattoria Fiorelli. Inside the café, like a small and solemn bat, sat Immacolata. She was dressed in black, from the shawl on her head to the shoes on her feet, and was fanning herself with a wide black fan, embroidered with flowers.

When she saw Thomas she put the fan on the table and walked over to him with her hands outstretched, like a blind woman begging for alms. 'I knew God would spare you for Valentina,' she said and her small eyes brimmed with tears. 'Today is blessed.' He let her slap his cheeks affectionately, although when he withdrew they smarted and grew pink. 'Sit down, Tommasino. You must be tired. Have a drink and tell me everything. Three of my four sons have returned to my bosom. God saw fit to take my Ernesto. May his soul rest in peace. Now you have made my happiness complete.'

Thomas sat down. It was impossible not to do as Immacolata said. She was a formidable woman used to being obeyed. Besides, Thomas was in no position to disobey. She was a deeply religious woman and he had impregnated her daughter out of wedlock. He shuddered to think what she would say about that. To his surprise, she had welcomed him warmly. However, her first question revealed her true intention.

'So,' she said, watching the waiter pour two glasses of wine. 'You have returned to marry my daughter?'

Thomas looked shamefaced. 'I was going to ask your permission formally,' he replied.

Immacolata's face contorted with sympathy. 'When it

is God's will, you don't have to ask permission of any-body.' Her voice was soft, the voice of a young girl.

He took Valentina's hand in his. 'I knew we were des-tined to marry from the first moment I laid eyes on her.'

'I know,' she said, nodding gravely. 'My daughter is very beautiful and she has given you a daughter. Alba.'

'Alba? That's a lovely name,' he said, not wishing to dwell on the reactions of his parents. Perhaps she could have Lavender as a second name.

'Alba Immacolata,' Valentina added. *Perhaps not,* thought Thomas. He was relieved Jack was not there to witness their conversation.

'This child is very special to me,' said Immacolata, gripping her bosom. 'She holds a very special place in my heart.'

'She looks like her mother,' said Thomas.

'But her eyes are her father's. There is no doubt to whom she belongs.' Immacolata ran her fingers over the baby's face. 'See, her eyes are the palest blue-grey. Like the sea when it is shallow and calm. You must hold her,' she added, nodding at her daughter. Valentina held the baby out to him. He had never held such a small baby before and wasn't exactly sure how to do it. To his sur-prise it wasn't so difficult and little Alba did not cry. 'You see,' said Immacolata. 'She knows you are her father.'

Thomas stared into the features of his child, scarcely able to believe that she carried his genes and those of his entire family, including Freddie. She looked nothing like him. Certainly nothing like an Arbuckle, except for the eyes which were indeed just like his. She was so vulner-able. So defenseless. But what made him love her was the fact that she so resembled her mother. She was a part of Valentina and therefore more precious than anything else in the world.

'You will marry in the chapel of San Pasquale,' continued Immacolata. 'I will invite Padre Dino to lunch tomorrow so you can meet him. You are not Catholic?' Thomas shook his head. 'That is not a problem. When it is God's will, nothing is a problem. You are joined together by love and that is all that matters. You will stay here at the trattoria until the marriage. I have a comfortable room upstairs.' Thomas shifted his gaze from little Alba to Valentina and her soft, mossy brown eyes smiled back at him tenderly. In that moment of silent communication they said all they needed to say.

Lattarullo sat outside, as if he were a guard dog, ready to bite anyone who dared try to enter. It wouldn't be long before the Trattoria Fiorelli vibrated with the music of celebration, he mused. The whole town would be invited and there would be dancing. Valentina loved to dance. The small area within the café wouldn't be large enough to accommodate everyone so they would spill out onto the street and dance there, beneath the full moon. Immacolata would choose an auspicious day for the wedding, beside the sea that had brought them together.

Valentina placed Alba in her Moses basket and Thomas carried her out to the cart which awaited them in the shade of an acacia tree, attached to a large, docile horse. Lattarullo offered to drive them himself, proudly announcing that he was in possession of the town car, but Thomas declined politely. He didn't want to share Valentina with anyone else, least of all Lattarullo, who smelled strongly of his own unique brand of sweat. 'You can fetch me after dinner,' he said to the grubby carabiniere, who nodded in bewilderment.

They waved at him as the horse plodded off. There was no hurry. There was nothing pressing to get back to. They had all day if they so wished. The slow clip-clop of the horse's hooves bounced into the still, warm air and roused the sleepy town from its shameless ogling. Even the children suspended their games to watch the cart move off and disappear up the shady alleyway toward the hill. Lattarullo stuck out his bottom lip and dabbed his forehead with a damp hanky. He couldn't understand why they had refused the car.

He hoped no one had heard the Englishman decline his offer. *Che figura di merda!* It was a matter of pride, of *apparenza*.

Valentina took Thomas's hand and pressed it to her cheek, kissing it affectionately. 'At last, we are alone.'

After a long while the soft rattling sound of a motor reverberated out of the tranquil silence of the afternoon. Thomas immediately thought of Lattarullo and his heart sank. But then he realized that the car was coming down the hill toward them, not from the town they had just left. Valentina steered the horse to the side of the road and the cart ground to a halt. The rattling increased in volume until the marchese's shiny white Lagonda appeared sedately around the bend. The metal of the radiator shone brilliantly in the sunshine and the two round headlights twinkled like a pair of large frog's eyes. It was impossible not to be impressed by the fine craftsmanship of such an elegant vehicle. The memory of the near crash the year before was now distant and misty in the glare of Thomas's appreciation. The motor ticked over with such efficiency it sounded more like a song than a mechanical rattle: *tick-a-tick-a-tick-a-tick*. It slowed down. In the front seat, his face cast in the shade of his hat, sat the skeletal Alberto. The canvas roof of the car was down so that he could be seen clearly in all his glory. His grey uniform was as clean as the car itself and his white-gloved hands gripped the steering wheel as if it were the reins of a magnificent and powerful beast. His nose was so high in the air his chin had almost disappeared. He did not smile, nor did he wave, though it was clear from the sudden pallor that washed the colour from his already grim face that he recognized Thomas, and he almost lost control of the car. *L'inglese* was back.

15

Thomas was not ready to meet the rest of Valentina's family. He wanted to take her to the ancient lookout point where they had made love. So they steered the horse down the dusty track to the field of lemon groves. Having dozed half the way, allowing his hooves to plod automatically up the all too familiar hill, the beast now awoke and looked about him with uncharacteristic vigour. The smells of the cypress trees, rosemary, and thyme, seemed to enliven his senses too, and he suddenly began to walk with a spring in his step, snorting into the fragrant air with gusto. Thomas was unable to restrain his ardour. He kissed Valentina's neck and her chest where the low cut of her dress exposed the springy tops of her breasts and glowed a rich honey brown. He ran his fingers through her long wavy hair and inhaled the warm scent of figs. She laughed her soft, bubbly laugh and pretended to push him away in case someone chanced to see them.

'The only person who could possibly see us is the old marchese,' he said as he buried his face in the neat curve where her shoulder met her neck. He envisaged momentarily the effeminate marchese, with his greased-back hair and watery eyes, peering through his telescope, but dismissed the thought at once. He had left the decaying palazzo the year before feeling decidedly uneasy; the image of the old man's face was enough to bring back that unease. Valentina stiffened and grew serious.

'I don't want to be seen by anyone, Tommy,' she said, then cast her eyes behind her to check that their daughter was still asleep in the shade. 'You will take me away from here, won't you?' Her eyes suddenly filled with fear.

He caressed her cheek, shook his head, and frowned. 'Of course I will. Once we are married we will leave for England. What are you frightened of?'

'Of losing you again,' she replied hoarsely.

'I'll never leave you as long as I live,' he said gravely. 'The only reason I survived this war is because I had you to live for. Then I had you and Alba to live for and my life became more precious than it had ever been. I'm going to look after you, I promise.'

She smiled and the light returned to her eyes. 'I know you will. You don't know how much I love you. You don't know how much it hurts.'

'It hurts me too,' he said and before them the hill rose up to the ancient lookout point that was exactly as it had been that previous spring. *How much my life has changed,* Thomas thought to himself. *And how changed am I. Jack was right. I'm no longer like him. My life has purpose. I never chose to be responsible, responsibility chose me, and now I'm grateful for it.*

He carried little Alba in her basket up to the crumbling tower. She was still asleep, her hands beside her ears and her head on one side. She looked angelic, like one of Raphael's sleeping cherubs. She might just as well have been on a cloud and if she had turned over to reveal wings he wouldn't have been in the least bit surprised.

'She's just like you,' he said as they sat down in the shade. The aromatic scent of the hills was carried on the breeze with the fresh smell of the sea and Thomas felt that in all his life he had never been filled with such light-ness, such happiness.

'I hope she does not grow up to be like me,' she replied, but Thomas shook his head.

'How lucky she would be if she were to grow up like you, Valentina.'

'I don't want her to make the mistakes that I have made in my life.'

'But you're so young. What mistakes could you have possibly made?' He laughed at her and she grinned bashfully.

'We all make mistakes, don't we?'

'Yes, we do. But . . .'

'The best thing I ever did was meet you.' She wrapped her arms around him and they lay down on the grass and kissed. As much as he wanted to make love to her he didn't feel it was right while their baby slept beside them. He knew Valentina felt the same, for small beads of sweat had collected on her brow and nose and her breathing had grown heavy, but she did not encourage him to take it further.

They waited as long as they could before returning to Immacolata's house. They lay entwined as the day slowly drained away. Alba awoke and Valentina put her to the breast. Thomas was moved. He had never seen a child suckled before. Valentina looked luminescent, serene, unattainable somehow. As she fed her baby she no longer belonged to him, but to Alba. Once again he sensed her ethereal nature. That quality he had recognized the year before that placed her beyond his reach. He suffered a moment of possessiveness. It didn't matter how much she told him she loved him, or that the child she fed was his child. He felt as if a hand squeezed his heart.

'Christ, Valentina,' he said in English. 'You do the

strangest things to me!' She turned her head on one side and looked puzzled. 'You're so beautiful,' he continued in Italian. 'I just want to hold you forever.'

Now she laughed at him. 'You don't know me, Tommy.'

'You like lemons, the dark, the sea, and the colour purple. You wanted to be a dancer when you were a little girl. You see,' he chuckled wistfully, 'I remember everything about you.'

'But you don't know me.'

'We have the rest of our lives to get to know each other.' He swept her hair over her shoulder so that it did not obscure her face. 'It's going to be the greatest project of my life.'

'We will have more children,' she said, stroking Alba's forehead as she suckled. 'I want Alba to have brothers and sisters. I don't want her to be alone. I've been alone in this war. I hope she grows up in a peaceful world,' she said suddenly and her eyes filled with tears. 'War reduces men to animals and turns women into shameful creatures. I want her to see only the good in people. Not to be cynical. To be able to trust without that trust being broken. I want her to be sure of who she is. To be confident. Not to have to rely on anyone. To be independent and free. She will be all these things in England, won't she?'

Thomas was confused. 'Of course she will. That is what we fought for, Valentina. For peace. So that children like Alba can grow up unafraid, in a free, democratic society.'

'You are so brave, Tommy. I wish I was brave like you.'

'You don't have to be, because I'm here to protect you.' He traced his fingers down her cheek where the tears had left shiny wet trails. 'Alba will grow up not knowing the horrors of war. But we will tell her about how brave men lost their lives so that she appreciates her good fortune.'

Then he spoke in a quiet, sad voice, about Freddie, memories he had only ever shared with Jack. 'My brother died, Valentina. He was a fighter pilot. No one imagined he'd go down. Not Freddie. He was indomitable, larger than life. Yet so many were lost in Malta, in the end he was just another number. I never got to say goodbye. Death is a lonely business, Valentina. One always dies alone. I'd like to believe in Heaven. I'd like to believe he's with God now. The truth is, his body's at the bottom of the sea and I have no way of honouring him.'

Valentina reached out her hand and touched his. 'I understand, my darling Tommy. My father and Ernesto, one of my brothers, died too. So many lost and yet there is no comfort in numbers, is there? Mamma built a shrine for my father and now she has built one for Ernesto. The candles flicker day and night; like their spirits they never go out. They live on in our memory. It is all we can do. You honour your brother by remembering him, Tommy. You must tell me about him. You must tell me all that you remember because it is by remembering that we give them life.' Her face had taken on a maturity and wisdom he hadn't seen in her before. To his surprise her words comforted him; Jack's had never been able to.

Finally, Thomas grew hungry and Valentina was anxious to get home for Alba. They sat in the cart once again and the horse, who had been asleep in the shade of a gnarled eucalyptus tree, reluctantly set off up the dusty track.

Valentina warned Thomas that her brothers had returned from the war. Ludovico and Paolo, the two who had been imprisoned by the British, would be friendly enough now that the war was over and they had been well treated in captivity. Falco, however, would not. He had been a partisan, she explained, and was dark, mercurial, and troubled.

'He is a complicated man,' she said. 'He always has been, ever since childhood. Mamma says that because he came out first he expected to be loved more than the rest of us and was consequently disappointed and jealous. He has a wife, Beata, and a little boy of five called Toto. You would have thought that the love of a woman and an adoring child would soften his heart, but it has not. He is as cold and suspicious as ever.'

Thomas felt anxious about meeting Falco. He was the head of the family now their father was no longer alive. Yet, he reasoned, how difficult could he be? They had fought on the same side. If anyone was going to begrudge him it was the other two, who had sided with the Germans.

As they approached the house the scent of figs engulfed him again and he was reminded of his first visit the year before. Like a bat, Immacolata bustled out, blinking in the light, wringing her hands. She was clearly agitated. 'Where have you been? I've done nothing but worry.'

'Mamma!' Valentina scolded. 'We only took Alba to the lookout point.'

'Falco has been anxious. Filling my head with all sorts of rubbish.'

'I apologize, signora,' said Thomas, helping Valentina down from the cart. 'We wanted to spend the afternoon alone.'

At that moment Falco stepped out and stood beside his mother. He was a rough-looking man, coarse due to years of fighting, with deep-set eyes of the darkest brown and thick, weathered skin. He was undoubtedly hand-some with his long, curly hair and brooding brow. Thomas noticed at once that he was tall and broad in the shoul-ders; he also walked with a limp, an injury probably left over from his violent past as a partisan. He doubted he'd come off very well in a fight. He attempted a smile but the man, who looked older than his thirty years, simply scowled at him.

'You have to be careful,' he growled and his voice was deep and grainy, like sand. 'The war might be over but the hills are full of bandits. People are still starving. You don't appreciate how lucky we are in Incantellaria. Beyond is a dark and dangerous world.'

Thomas immediately felt irritated that Falco was implying he was naïve. 'We were quite safe, I assure you,' he replied coldly.

Falco laughed at him. 'You don't know these hills. I know them better than I know the lines on my own hands. I know my way around every rock and bush with my eyes shut. You'd be surprised at the demons that lurk there. Sometimes they do not appear like demons at all.'

Valentina placed her hand on Thomas's arm and said, 'Don't listen to him. There were no demons where we were. The only demons that haunt these parts are the ones in Falco's head.' Thomas leaned over the cart and pulled out the Moses basket. Valentina walked straight past her mother and brother and into the house.

'Valentina knows what I'm talking about although she's as stubborn as a mule.' Thomas wanted to leap to Valentina's defense but he saw the pain contort Immacolata's face and took the peaceful option instead. He extended his hand to Falco.

'The war is over,' he said. 'Let's not start a new one here.'

Falco's mouth tightened but he took his hand. Thomas felt his rough, calloused skin but there was something reassuring about his grasp which was the firm hold of a man in possession of himself. However, he did not smile and his eyes were dark and impenetrable so that Thomas was unable to decipher his thoughts. Immacolata, subdued by the presence of her son, was no longer the omnipotent matriarch she had been before. She was clearly in awe of him, if not a little afraid. However, she was pleased they had called a truce.

'God has brought you together through Valentina. Let us eat and be friends.'

It wasn't long before the rest of the family turned up. Ludovico and Paolo, who still lived with their mother, were the total opposites of their elder brother. Where the battle-weary partisan was as dark and cold as a winter's night they were warm rays of summer sunshine. It was difficult to tell them apart, for they were both short, wiry, and athletic with brown eyes like their sister's and crooked, mischievous grins. They did not possess their brother's magnetism or his good looks, but they were amusing and their laughter had worn through the youth on their faces and carved out deep, attractive lines. In spite of having fought against the Allies they shook Thomas's hand and slapped him on the back, making jokes about taking Valentina off their hands and saving her from the motley lineup of poor Italian suitors.

Beata arrived with Toto for dinner. She was a sweet-natured woman who clearly knew nothing of her husband's wartime activities. She was a simple peasant girl who thought little beyond her child and preparing the next meal. Fearful of the foreigner, she did not even shake his hand but lowered her eyes and took her seat at the long table beneath the vine where Immacolata had presided over dinner the year before. Her son sat beside her and rested his head against his mother's body, nestled beneath her protective arm. Like a docile, watchful animal, Beata blinked about her, listening to the conversation but contributing nothing. Falco rarely looked at her and certainly didn't talk to her. Beata had obviously been pummeled into the dust by this overbearing, overopinionated man. Thomas was thankful he had arrived in time to save Valentina from a similar fate.

Immacolata punctuated their discussion with religious references. She seemed to have God's ear for she knew exactly what His intentions were, why He had allowed the war to happen, even why He had taken her husband and son. God was the only way she could make sense of it all. Perhaps it hurt less to believe in the will of God, like a child who trusts without question the actions of its parents. Thomas was barely able to reconcile the woman who had bellowed at her staff in Trattoria Fiorelli with this soft-spoken, submissive mother who seemed to have shrunk in the shadow of her eldest son. *If Lattarullo was able to see her now,* he thought with amusement, *she would no longer frighten him so.*

At the end of the meal Valentina and Beata cleared away the plates, taking the dishes through to the kitchen. Toto followed, carrying the small things that weren't too heavy. He was a pretty child with wide brown eyes and a full, sensual mouth that curled up at the corners in quiet amusement. He clearly loved his grandmother, who stroked his face and kissed him with solemn affection.

It was dark. Moths fluttered around the hurricane lamps and the chorus of crickets rang out in the bushes and trees. Thomas lit a cigarette and watched the smoke float up on the cool air, twisting and turning as the breeze blew in from the sea. He could hear Beata and Valentina laughing in the kitchen. There had been no laughter at the table and Immacolata seemed to have lost her sense of humor a long time ago. It was heartening to hear their gaiety. He imagined they were talking about their children, sharing the day's stories or perhaps a joke at the expense of the men, he didn't know. He noticed that for some reason Valentina incensed Falco. He watched her through narrowed eyes and there was dislike in them bordering on hatred. Valentina, to her credit, ignored him. When he tried to put her down she retorted with amusement and rolled her eyes. Thomas was proud of her. He remembered her dancing at the *festa di Santa Benedetta;* she had shown surprising spirit then too. He gazed upon her through the smoke with sleepy eyes and realized that she was right; he barely knew her.

Finally the family retired to bed. Immacolata knelt before the shrines to her husband and son and mumbled an inaudible prayer. After crossing herself vigorously she bade them good night. Then she took Thomas's hand and thanked him for returning. 'You will take my Valentina to a better place,' she said solemnly, patting it with soft, doughy fingers. 'Tomorrow you shall meet Padre Dino. The sooner you are married the better.'

Valentina kissed her fiancé demurely on the cheek, but Thomas knew from the glint in her eyes that she longed to take him to her bed. 'Until tomorrow, my love,' she whispered, then disappeared into the shadows. He thought he heard Lattarullo arrive in the car he seemed to share with the rest of the town and wandered over to the window. Behind him, Falco smoked alone on the terrace, with only the night animals and crickets for company. He looked troubled as he sat hunched over the table, the last of the wax maintaining the flame in one of the hurricane lamps. Beata had returned to their house, a short walk through the olive grove and well lit by the moon. Thomas wondered why Falco had not accompanied his wife and son.

There was no sign of Lattarullo. He must have heard the roar of the sea in the distance, or the echo of bombs dropped months ago that still rang in his ears and in his dreams. He withdrew from the window. Not wanting to join Falco, he took a seat in the dark and lit a cigarette. He watched the flickering candles illuminate Immacolata's shrines to her husband and son, causing the gold leaf on the icons to glitter. It wasn't long before he heard voices coming from the terrace. They were muffled but staccato. There was obviously a heated discussion going on. He recognized Valentina's voice. Hidden in the shadows he looked out on to the terrace where she stood in front of her brother, her hands raised in protest, her voice an angry hiss. They spoke so fast and so low that Thomas was unable to understand a single word. He strained his ears until they ached, but still he was unable to make sense of it. Suddenly Falco leaped to his feet, leaned across the table, and fired a sentence at her in fury, his hands on the table like two large lion's paws. She retaliated like a fiend, her chin up, her face proud, her eyes lively and bright. Once again Thomas recalled her dance in the street the night of the *festa*. She had had the same light in her eyes then too.

The normally demure Valentina possessed a passion that she rarely revealed. She looked even more beautiful enraged and Thomas's blood grew hot in his veins at the sight of her blazing eyes and haughty smile, enhanced now by the eerie flicker of the dying candle. He caught his breath as he felt the dizzy sensation of falling in love again. He wondered whether they were fighting over him. Perhaps Falco was angry with her for falling in love with a foreigner. Thomas was wise enough to remain hidden, and anyway, it wouldn't be long before she was far from Incantellaria and her surly, resentful brother.

Finally the rattle of Lattarullo's car alerted him to the carabiniere's arrival. He leaped to his feet and hurried quietly out of the door. He did not want Falco and Valentina to know that he had witnessed their argument.

In the car Lattarullo took great pleasure in telling him all about his own wedding day. 'Though sadly,' he said without sounding sad, 'my wife left me. A personal tragedy of no consequence to anyone but myself.' Thomas wasn't listening. 'The war taught me that there are things of far greater importance and significance than women.'

Once back at the trattoria, Thomas undressed for bed. Immacolata had placed a large jug of water beside a wash bowl. He picked up the small bar of soap and remembered the bath he had enjoyed in the stream with Jack. He imagined Valentina as he had first seen her, dressed in that virginal white dress that clung so nicely to her slender young body. He remembered the way the sun had shone behind her, casting her legs in silhouette.

He lay awake, staring up at the ceiling, mulling over the scene he had just witnessed and its implications. Outside the breeze danced among the cypress trees, whispering playfully at his window with softly salted breath. Tormented by anxiety, he felt hot and uncomfortable and deeply protective of Valentina and their child. *No one is going to prevent my taking them both to England,* he thought angrily. *Even if I have to sneak off in the middle of the night like a criminal.*

16

Padre Dino had the deep, gritty voice of a bear. It echoed up from his round and cavernous belly. His face was almost entirely covered with bushy grey hair that fell from his chin and cheeks down to his chest, ending in knotted clumps that resembled tiny paws. When he spoke his beard twitched as if it were a mangy animal and not something he had grown out of choice. It didn't look clean, and Thomas had the distinct feeling that if he were unfortunate enough to get too close he would be struck by an extremely unpleasant odor. Surprisingly, above the beard the padre's eyes were long and sweeping and a rather beautiful shade of green: pale, iridescent, like a mossy pool bathed in sunshine.

The priest had arrived on a bicycle. It was a wonder his long black robe didn't get caught in the spokes and cause a terrible accident. He shuffled onto the terrace huffing and puffing after the exertion of pedaling up the hill. However, when Immacolata offered him wine he brightened and what little one could see of his cheeks flushed the colour of plums. 'Blessed be the Virgin and all the saints,' he said, tracing the sign of the cross in the air in front of him. Thomas caught Valentina's eyes but her expression was one of solemn reverence.

Thomas glanced at Falco, recalling his furious

argument with his sister the night before. In the presence of Padre Dino he was taciturn and acquiescent, though his face was still twisted into a scowl. Beata stood with Toto; Thomas imagined he would enjoy his thoughts on the old man's beard. Children were quick to see the grotesque and to laugh at it. Making fun of people was what they loved best, before their parents taught them it was rude to point and stare. Paolo and Ludovico were uncharacteristically serious. Padre Dino's arrival had changed them all. Thomas suddenly felt guilty for his irreverent thoughts. After all, the man was going to conduct their marriage ceremony.

'I remember you from the *festa di Santa Benedetta*,' said Padre Dino to Thomas, extending his hand.

'It was an extraordinary event,' Thomas replied, trying to respond in the right tone. 'I was honoured to take part.'

'It was nothing less than a miracle,' said Padre Dino, 'and through miracles we are reminded of God's omnipotence. In times of human conflict it is important to remember that God is more powerful than we are, however efficient our weapons, however strong our armies. God showed Himself in the blood of Christ's tears and will do so again when we celebrate, as we do every year, this sacred and most holy of miracles.'

'It's coming around again?' Thomas asked, turning to Valentina. Padre Dino answered for her, as he would continue to do in all matters that concerned the Lord.

'Next Tuesday. Perhaps God will see fit to bless your wedding and your future together,' he said solemnly. Then for a moment his forehead darkened. 'You have brought a child into the world.'

'All children are blessings, Padre Dino,' interjected Immacolata, lifting her chin. Because of Immacolata's lineage, her direct link to Santa Benedetta who first witnessed the miracle 254 years before, Padre Dino held her in the highest esteem.

'All children are indeed blessings. However,' he frowned again and he looked directly at Thomas. 'God must bless your union so that your child becomes the product of holy matrimony and not of unholy carelessness. But God forgives, does He not? In times of war it is sometimes impossible to follow God's path in that respect.' Then he laughed and the air vibrated around him. 'God's path is not always easy to follow. If it were we would all go directly to Heaven and I would not have a job to do.'

'Tommasino is a young man of honour, I knew that from the first moment I saw him. I did not think so of his friend.'

'The one with the squirrel?' said Valentina with a laugh. Padre Dino looked perplexed.

'The one with the squirrel,' said Immacolata. 'Let us eat and drink to celebrate their future and thank the Lord that she did not fall in love with *him*.'

After Padre Dino had said an unnecessarily long grace, Thomas sat down beside his fiancée, opposite the priest. He turned his thoughts to Jack and hoped that he had remembered to send his letter to his parents, informing them of his return to Italy and of his plans to bring his bride and child back to Beechfield Park as soon as they were married. It did not perturb him in the slightest that his parents might disapprove of his choice. The fact that he had survived the war was surely enough to excuse him any unsuitable choice of bride.

Thomas took Valentina's hand. At first she tried to wiggle it away, torn between respect for the priest and her newfound longing to collude with Thomas. After a while she gave in and let Thomas hold it tightly under the table where no one could see.

Suddenly a low rumble came up from the padre's belly. Padre Dino continued, unperturbed. But Immacolata's face softened as she tried to contain her amusement. Again came the whine. It began low, rose in the middle, then fell again before dissolving into bubbles. The priest shuffled uncomfortably in his chair. Immacolata offered him more wine. Normally he would have declined. The day was hot, the sun scorching, the languor of the afternoon already penetrating his mind and melting his concentration. But he held out his glass while Immacolata poured. When the moaning increased not only in frequency but in volume too, the poor priest downed the glass in one. Beads of sweat appeared on his brow and nose and glistened in the light. His voice rose and his beard began to twitch restlessly, the little paws clawing at his cassock as he moved his head from side to side. His conversation departed from God's mighty strength and purpose to more earthly things like prosciutto and plums. Again and again the whine rose up from his belly until finally Toto's innocent little voice stated what they had all been longing to say. 'Padre Dino?' he asked with a naughty smile.

'Yes, my child?' replied the priest through clenched teeth.

'Have you swallowed a dog?'

Thomas was surprised when Falco roared with laughter.

Padre Dino excused himself and disappeared inside, where he remained for a long time.

Immacolata gave deep sigh. 'Poor Padre Dino,' she said. 'He works too hard.'

'And eats too much,' said Ludovico.

'It's not a good idea to eat dog,' added Paolo. 'Indigestible!' The brothers began to laugh. Falco knocked back his glass of wine with a loud gulp, then wiped his mouth with the back of his hand.

'I pity the poor soul who uses the bathroom after him,' he said, and his brothers erupted into laughter again.

'Enough!' said Immacolata and her tone was more reminiscent of the strident old woman Thomas had met in the Trattoria Fiorelli the year before. 'He is a man of God. Have respect!' But nothing could stop the boys' laughter now that they had started.

After lunch Padre Dino departed rapidly on his bicycle, though Immacolata tactfully offered him a seat in the shade where he could spend the afternoon in quiet contemplation, overlooking the sea. He disappeared unsteadily down the dusty track and Thomas and Valentina hoped that he would arrive in town safely so that he'd be fit to wed them the coming week, following the *festa di Santa Benedetta*.

Later, while Valentina fed Alba, Thomas took out his paper and pastels and drew them. The afternoon heat was no longer so intense and the light was soft and mellow as the day slowly died away and evening drew in. A whisper of a breeze swept up from the sea, carrying with it fresh smells from the hills and the promise of a future far away on another shore. Alba, clothed in a thin white dress, lay against her mother's belly, sucking milk from her swollen breast. Valentina held her close and every now and then inclined her head to watch her beloved child. Her expression was gentle and full of love for the tiny being she had brought into the world. Her eyes brimmed with pride, and the sadness that Thomas had depicted in his last picture was no longer there. With her spirit bursting with optimism her beauty was all the more unearthly and she ever more remote; the pedestal upon which he had placed her was so high her head disappeared into cloud.

Thomas talked about their future. He described the house where she would live and the village over which she would preside. 'They'll love you at Beechfield,' he said, imagining the looks of admiration and envy when he introduced her to his friends and family. 'I don't think the people of Beechfield have ever seen a real Italian. They'll think they're all as beautiful as you. But they'll be wrong. You're unique.'

'Oh, I long to be far away from here,' she replied with a sigh. 'It's grown too small for me. I'm barely able to stretch my legs anymore.'

'You won't miss your family?' he asked, drawing the line of her jaw that was surprisingly strong and angular for such a gentle face.

'I won't miss Falco!' she laughed gaily. 'Silly Falco. I wonder what will become of him. I don't think he's finding it easy to adjust to life after war. I think he was happier fighting his own people and hiding in bushes than eating with his family in peacetime.'

'He's troubled. Perhaps you should try to understand him,' he suggested diplomatically, colouring in the shadow her chin cast upon her neck.

'Why should I?' she replied petulantly. 'He doesn't try to understand me.' Her expression suddenly darkened. Thomas imagined it had something to do with her argument with Falco the night before.

'He fought bravely. He fought for all the right things. There's no shame in fighting against one's own countrymen if it's in aid of peace.'

'He thinks he's better than everyone else. He thinks he has a right to interfere in my life. Well, he knows nothing about me anymore. The war changes people and it changed me too. Just because I wasn't on the front line doesn't mean that it passed me by. I have struggled to survive in my own way. I'm not proud of myself. But I survived and looked after Mamma as best I could. No, he knows nothing of what I've been through.' Her forehead crinkled as she knitted her eyebrows. 'He's been away hiding in bushes. How can he expect to waltz back in and take our father's place as head of the family? He wasn't around when we needed him.'

Thomas didn't really understand what she was talking about. He felt as if he had arrived in the middle of a conversation, having missed the most important part. 'Don't worry,' he said, concentrating now on Alba's pretty head. 'Soon you'll be far away and no one will tell you what to do anymore.'

'Not even you?' she said with a smile.

'I wouldn't dare!' He laughed and was pleased that her face was no longer dark and anxious.

Once he had finished the picture, he held it up for her to see. Beneath the portrait he had written *Valentina and Alba 1945. Thomas Arbuckle. Now my love is twofold.* Her expression unfolded like a sunflower that has just seen the sun, and she put her fingertips to her lips in wonder. 'It's beautiful,' she gasped. 'You're so talented, Tommy.'

'No, you're the inspiration, Valentina. You and Alba. I don't believe I ever drew Jack so well, or Brendan!'

'It's perfect. I'll keep it forever. The pastels won't fade, will they?'

'I hope not.'

'I want Alba to see it one day. It's important for her to know how much she is loved.'

She placed Alba against her shoulder and gently patted her back. Thomas bent down to kiss her and she raised her chin to give him her lips. He rested his mouth on hers for a long moment, wishing that they could spend the rest of the evening in bed, wrapped in each other. He withdrew with a sigh.

'We'll be married soon,' she said, reading his thoughts. 'Then we'll have the rest of our lives to lie together.'

'God willing,' Thomas added, not wanting to tempt the fates.

'God will bless us. You will see. He will cry tears of blood at the *festa di Santa Benedetta* and then we will begin the rest of our life far away from here.' She cast her eyes around her home. 'I won't miss it,' she said. 'But perhaps it will miss me.'

Only once were they able to lie naked together, in the lemon grove at dawn, while the town slept below them. There, in the pale light of the rising sun, Thomas drew her a third time, the last time. And that portrait was so intimate he knew he would never show a soul. When he gave it to her she blushed, but he could tell from the sparkle in her eyes that she liked it. 'This is *my* Valentina,' he said proudly. 'My secret Valentina.' And Valentina rolled it up so that it should remain so.

Thomas spent every moment he could with Valentina and their daughter. However, there were empty hours that he had to fill on his own while Valentina made her wedding dress with her mother and Signora Ciprezzo. During those long, hot hours he would sit outside the trattoria and watch the children playing on the quayside, the fishermen mending their nets or sailing out to sea to cast them. They'd arrive back with barrelfuls of fish which they would sell in the local shop or farther inland, where there was still a great deal of hunger. The children would gather around and watch as they unloaded, and once or twice a small fish would slither out by mistake and they'd grab it and rush off to play before the fishermen noticed and stopped them. He would share a drink with Lattarullo or *il sindacco,* who'd cross his legs to reveal polished black shoes and perfectly pressed trousers.

When he was alone, Thomas watched the tide come in and go out in a gentle dance across the pebbles. He imagined the same shore thousands of years ago. For the first time he was aware of the constant changeability of human nature and of his own mortality. *One day,* he thought, *I will be nothing more than sand on a beach and yet the years will roll on, the tides will continue to come in and out, and there will be other people to watch them.*

Finally the day of the *festa di Santa Benedetta* dawned. It was an exquisite morning. The sky was bluer than Thomas had ever seen it and seemed to be full of tiny particles of fairy dust that glittered in the sun. He stood, marveling at such magnificence, sure that if there was a God, He was here. The air was fresh and sugar-scented and a heady smell of carnations was carried up from the sea on the breeze. When he looked down to the seafront, he saw a most extraordinary sight. The tide was far out, leaving the pebble beach wide and open and covered, by some strange miracle, in a sparkling gown of pink carnations. The flowers glittered and shimmered as the wind caught the petals, causing them to flutter like tiny wings. Boats that had been moored just offshore were now stranded in the midst of this delightful, fragrant pasture of flowers.

Thomas dressed hastily and with the rest of the town stood transfixed in the face of such unearthly splendor. No one spoke, they were all afraid to, in case the verbal acknowledgment of the magic might cause it to disappear. How the flowers had got there no one knew. When the tide swept in, the flowers would be washed away, leaving everyone wondering whether it had really happened or whether they had all been involved in some sort of hallucination.

Thomas put his hands behind his head and smiled a broad smile. *If you're watching this, Freddie, I hope it's filling you with as much joy as it's filling me,* he thought happily. *Today is the* festa di Santa Benedetta. *Surely this is a sign from God. Tomorrow we marry. After the bloodiness of war we can now build a lasting peace. Our future is written in flowers.*

But old Lorenzo scratched his chin and shook his head. 'The carnation is a symbol of death,' he said darkly for only Thomas to hear. 'If each flower symbolizes a person we will all die together.'

Thomas ignored the old man's gruesome prediction, preferring to remain with his own. It wasn't long before word had spread of the latest *miracolo*. Padre Dino arrived to witness it and categorize it along with the other minor miracles that had happened at Incantellaria. Lattarullo scratched his groin in bewilderment while *il sindacco* considered taking a few flowers home to his wife. Immacolata and her family came down from the hill as soon as they received the news. Valentina held Thomas's hand as they gazed upon the vision of their future, their hearts overflowing with joy. Then Thomas's attention was diverted by a sudden glint from the top of the hill, far off in the distance. He pondered it for a moment before realizing that it was the marchese, watching them from his terrace through his telescope. Was he watching *them* now, or was he simply marveling at the incredible display of carnations along with the rest of them?

That evening Thomas experienced a sharp sense of déjà vu as he sat with Valentina in the little chapel of San Pasquale. Together with the rest of her family they waited for the blood to seep from Christ's eyes. Immacolata, draped in the traditional black that she had worn since the death of her husband, stood proud and solemn but isolated from the rest of the town. She appeared shrunken, as if the weight of so much hope caused her body to stoop. Thomas felt a wave of compassion for this woman who had lost a husband and a son and was poised to lose her only daughter and granddaughter too. She had seemed so strong before, so formidable, but suddenly, alone in the aisle of that chapel, with the other two *parenti* standing obediently behind her, she seemed vulnerable and alone.

Thomas did not care whether or not Christ cried blood. He was convinced that it was a cunning trick played by Padre Dino or one of his cronies. He minded for Valentina and for her mother, who all placed far too much emphasis upon it, as if it had the power to decide the future. *They don't realize,* he thought to himself, *that they hold the future in their own hands. The miracle has nothing to do with it.* But he couldn't tell them, of course. All he could do was hope that the blood was as thick and crimson as cherry syrup. They waited, and the more they waited the hotter the chapel became and the more intoxicating the smell of incense. The silence grew deafening, as if it were the screech of a dog whistle they couldn't hear, penetrating their brains and causing them pain. Valentina's hand grew damp in his. He squeezed it to reassure her but she did not squeeze back. She simply stared at the statue of Christ, willing it to shed tears with all her strength. Because she cared so much, Thomas began to care too. *Surely the flowers on the beach had been a positive sign?* he thought hopefully. But not even the will of the entire population of Incantellaria could force those eyes to bleed. The clock struck the hour and Immacolata collapsed to her knees.

As they filed out in disappointment, Valentina smiled up at Thomas. 'Don't worry, my love,' she said. 'We're getting married tomorrow and then we leave any bad luck behind.'

'Doesn't the beach of carnations symbolize good luck for us?' he asked in a whisper.

'Yes, it does. But we need Christ's blessing. I know how to get it. I'll put it right, you'll see.'

Thomas thought her peasant superstitions charming and innocuous. But later he would regret with all his heart how little he had known her.

17

London 1971

Alba packed her bag. She didn't know what to take and she wasn't exactly sure how she was going to get there. She hadn't spoken to Fitz since he had left her houseboat over a month ago. When he hadn't called, she had been reduced to longing that they might bump into each other on the pontoon. Not a glimpse. Nothing. Now her bedroom echoed with an inconsolable loneliness. In spite of Rupert and Tim and James and Reed of the River, Fitz's scent lingered in the air and sometimes, when it caught her off guard, her eyes stung with tears. She missed his silly old dog too. There had been something very sweet about their friendship. Why couldn't he have accompanied her on her adventure? If he loved her, he would have come without question. Perhaps she demanded too much. That was her nature. If he couldn't take the pace, then it was right for him to get out of the race. Still, she missed him. Now there was only sex, and her soul ached for what it had briefly known.

Naturally Viv had taken his side. Alba had always suspected her to be a man's woman. She now imagined that Viv fancied Fitz for herself, even though she was way past it.

Initially, Alba had felt abandoned and alone. She had grown to rely on Viv. She had grown to love Fitz. They had turned into the family she felt she had never had. She looked back with nostalgia on that evening when they had lain under the stars. That evening had been perfect.

For the last few weeks Viv had been ignoring her. On the odd occasion that their paths had crossed on the pontoon, the older woman had pursed her lips and snorted, lifting her chin and striding by, as if it were all Alba's fault. Fitz had obviously been extremely economical with the truth. Well, if Viv was foolish enough to believe his word over hers, then they could both stew in their own juice. She was going to Italy and when she found her family there, she might just decide never to come back. They'd regret their behavior then, wouldn't they? Once they'd driven her away.

Rupert, Tim, and James had been only too happy to return to her bed, delighted that Fitz hadn't lasted the course. 'He's not a runner,' said Rupert happily, now confident that he was. Reed of the River came calling again and she allowed him to take her to Wapping, hiding on the floor of his launch when the sergeant cruised by. She hung out with the boys in the Star & Garter, drank beer and joined in their jokes, revelling in their attention.

Les Pringle from the Chelsea Yacht and Boat Company came by regularly to deliver the post and fill up the water tank. Although far too old to take her to bed, he sat at her kitchen table, drank coffee, and gossiped about the odd people he met, confessing, to her amusement, that no one was as eccentric as Vivien Armitage.

'Strange bunch, writers,' he mused. 'You know her Elsan is never full. I think it's because she makes her men friends pee off the side of the boat.'

'Jolly good idea,' said Alba. 'I wish I had thought of that myself. Mind you,' she added bitchily, 'she may be clever but have you seen her without makeup? I thought

Frankenstein was scary until I saw Viv at two in the morning with her curlers in!'

How could she possibly be lonely with so many friends? she thought, closing her bag and sitting on top to zip it shut. It was the beginning of June. The weather was warm in London so she presumed it would be even hotter in Naples. She had packed most of last summer's wardrobe and was sure that in a small, provincial seaside town she would cut quite a dash. Lonely indeed!

She sat on her deck, scowling at the squirrels and throwing the odd piece of bread into the water for the ducks. She looked over at Viv's houseboat. It was pristine. Pots of geraniums hung on the railings and their flowers trailed over the side in long red tentacles. There were also large black boxes of lemon trees and perfect spheres of topiary. Even the windows were polished until they shone. Alba looked about her own deck. She had pots of flowers too, lots of them, but they all needed dead-heading, not to mention watering; it hadn't rained for a good fortnight. She hadn't swept it for months. The squirrels loved to play there, leaving nuts and excrement which the wind blew away and the rain washed to some extent, but it wasn't clean like Viv's. Neither was it tidy inside and no one had mended the leak. She had left it for Fitz. But Fitz hadn't come back. There was a hole in her heart that leaked as well, but Fitz didn't care to mend that either. She looked across at Viv's perfect home again and was struck with an idea.

On top of the cabin Viv had grown grass. She had gone to the garden center and bought ready-made squares of it. Lush and green. Perfect. Over one weekend she had taken great trouble to treat the roof so that the water had a place to drain away and wouldn't corrode her ceiling and drip into her bedroom, then she had laid the sod out carefully so that the cabin now looked as if it had acquired an expensive haircut. Viv took great pride in it. She grew daisies and buttercups and was experimenting now with poppies. Alba stared at the grass roof and grinned. *I bet Viv hasn't the slightest idea what a good gardener I am,* she thought mischievously. *I think I'll show her just how innovative I can be.*

Alba had bought a pretty pink Vespa for riding about town. It was easier to park than her car. Her flight wasn't until the evening so she had plenty of time to kill. Lunch with Rupert in Mayfair sounded appealing. She had told him she was off to Italy, but not that she planned never to come back.

Before lunch she would make a telephone call to her old friend, Les Pringle. He'd do anything for her. And what she was about to ask him was something which, she was quite sure, he had never been asked before.

Viv sat with Fitz in the little café he regularly frequented just around the corner from his mews house. It was quiet, old-fashioned and made exceedingly good coffee. Sprout lay on the concrete, watching impassively the shoes of the people who wandered by. Viv smoked into the air, her eyes obscured by large black sunglasses that left only her small nose and chin exposed. When he had admired them, calling them fashionable, she had retorted crossly. 'I'm not fashionable, Fitzroy, you should know that. I'm above it all. Beyond it. Don't look at me like that. I told you I didn't want to see your lovely brown eyes brimming with tears.'

'She leaves tonight, doesn't she?' he said, heaving a sigh.

Viv exhaled the smoke out of the side of her mouth. 'Yes. Shame it's not on the earlier plane.'

'I should go and say goodbye.'

Viv was appalled. 'Goodbye?' she barked. 'Good riddance. She's brought you nothing but misery.'

'And a couple of rather smart shirts from Mr. Fish.'

'Don't be foolish, darling. If she chose to break up over something so trivial, she couldn't possibly have loved you. I always predicted it would end in tears and I was right. It didn't take her long to invite Rupert back into her bed, did it? I don't imagine she's shed a single tear. Silly tart. Sad though it is, I think you have to accept that it's well and truly over and move on. There are plenty of other girls about who would fall over themselves to look after you properly.'

'I don't want anyone else. I should have tried harder to understand her,' he said regretfully, lowering his eyes.

'Oh, for goodness' sake, Fitzroy. Snap out of it. She's hardly the Sphinx. In fact, she's very easy to understand. Spoiled, too pretty for her own good, and far too willing to share herself with any Tom, Dick, or Harry who bothers to compliment her. It's all very sad. She's looking for a father figure. One doesn't have to have a university degree to work that out. Maybe you were just *too* like her father.'

'I was *acting*!' he stressed.

'No you weren't,' she said with a knowing smile. 'Darling, you're not a bore and you're not an old duffer, but you're conventional, decent, sweet, funny, and without swagger. You don't cause ripples but neither do you set the world alight in an outrageous fashion. You're not a show-off. Alba wants a man made of fireworks. She'll find him in Italy, I'm sure. Italy's full of bottom-pinching fireworks.'

'You know, you're wrong. We were very happy together. We laughed a lot. We were great in bed and I was just beginning to flower as a fashion icon.' He grinned boyishly and Viv stubbed out her cigarette. She looked at him for a long moment and her face softened with tenderness. She patted his hand affectionately, as a mother might.

'That's right, darling. You make a joke of it. It might have been good, but it's over. Let her go off to Italy. If you're lucky she'll sleep with all the fireworks she can find and realize in the end that not one of them has made her happy. If you're right together she'll come back. If not, then you'll just have to marry me.'

'I could do a lot worse,' he said, taking her hand in his.

'And so could I.' She took off her glasses to reveal watery red eyes heavily made up with black mascara. 'You know, it's been hard ignoring her.'

'You shouldn't take sides.'

'I'll always take your side, Fitzroy. Even if you committed murder, I'd think the world of you.'

'Not just because I pull off the most wonderful deals for you?'

'That too, of course. But you're one in a million. She's a superficial girl. She's not going to see the value of you. I don't want to see you wasting your life away with a woman who thinks only of herself. Why settle for a woman who will only ever know the half of you, and not the better half either? The deeper one digs into your heart, Fitz, the more one appreciates your value.'

He laughed at her sadly. 'How very kind, Viv. I don't know that I deserve quite so much praise. However, I can't help loving her.'

'I love her too, silly. That's Alba's gift.'

Fitz spent the afternoon in the office. He took calls, did his paperwork, ran his eyes over a couple of new manuscripts but at the end of the day he couldn't remember whom he had spoken to, what letters he had written, and whether or not the new manuscripts were any good. He was due for bridge at Viv's at seven. The previous few weeks they had deliberately played at Wilfrid's or Georgia's so that he avoided a glimpse of Alba or her boat. But he had been distracted then too. Not even the postmortem, which usually had the power to rouse him from the heaviest thoughts, could coax him out of his daydreaming. Sprout now accompanied him everywhere, delighted not to be left at home in the kitchen or in the back of the car. In fact, he was upgraded again to the well in front of the passenger seat and sometimes, if there was room, he lay across the back seat like a Roman emperor, watching the tops of buildings whizz past the window. He was good company, of course, but it wasn't the same.

Fitz missed Alba. He missed everything about her and was happiest at night when he could lie in the dark remembering the good times. He had enjoyed making love to her, but there was something touching about the way she had lain against him on those nights when she simply wanted to be close. He knew that kind of intimacy was a novelty to her. She hadn't known how to handle having a man in bed without having sex. Then she had discovered it and quickly thought up a name. Alba was good at names. She called them 'pod evenings' because they lay like peas in a pod, so close they could almost have been one.

Sprout sensed that his friend was out of sorts and wagged his tail as if trying to compensate. Fitz wrapped his arms around his dog and buried his face in his fur. He didn't want to succumb to tears, not even in front of Sprout. It wasn't dignified; it certainly wasn't manly. But once or twice, after a couple of glasses of wine, beneath an exceptionally beautiful sky, he had let himself go.

After he left the office he took Sprout for a walk around

the Serpentine. It was too early to go to Viv's; she was having a drink at the Ritz with her new editor. It was a lovely evening. The sky was pale blue descending into pinks where the sun was low in the sky. The air was warm and balmy, smelling of cut grass. Squirrels scampered over the recently exposed earth, picking up pieces of food dropped by tourists. He thought of Alba, how she hated the little creatures, afraid that they'd find their way into her bedroom and hide beneath the sheets to nibble her toes. That's what he loved about her; her thought process was unlike anyone else's. She lived in a world all her own. The tragedy was that, as hard as he had tried, he had not been able to share it with her.

He looked at his watch. He didn't know what time her plane was due to leave but if he hurried he might just make it to Cheyne Walk before she left for the airport. He should have gone earlier. He should at least have telephoned her to find out how she was. What if she was as miserable as he was? What if she was just waiting for him to extend the olive branch? Had he been too hurt and furious to see beyond it? Viv had advised him not to call her, but he didn't have to take her advice. He loved Alba. It was as simple as that.

He hurried into the road and hailed a taxi. 'Cheyne Walk,' he said, closing the door behind him. 'As fast as you can, please.'

The taxi driver nodded glumly. 'No one ever says as slow as you like, gov, do they?'

Fitz frowned in irritation. 'I imagine not.'

'I always drive as fast as the law permits,' he said, trundling down Queensgate at a gentle pace.

'Most taxis I know take great pleasure in breaking the law,' said Fitz, wishing he'd step on it a bit. Alba might be leaving her boat at that very moment.

'Perhaps they do, but laws are put there for a reason and I abide by them.'

'What about the eleventh Commandment?' Fitz suggested.

'I thought there were only ten.' The taxi driver sniffed and wiped his nose on the back of his hand.

'No, there's one that's often forgotten. Thou shalt not get caught.' Even the taxi driver managed a chuckle.

'All right, mate, I'll do as best I can,' he said and Fitz watched the speedometer push for thirty.

Viv said goodbye to her editor, pleased that she liked the way the current book was going. Ros Holmes was a splendid woman, she thought. Direct, sensible, plain-talking, and warm in a truly British way. Viv couldn't abide gushers. Ros didn't gush and never would, however brilliant her work was, and in Viv's opinion, it was beginning to show flashes of brilliance. She hailed a cab on Piccadilly. It was five to seven, so she'd be a little late; they could wait on her terrace, admire her new roof garden and lemon trees. Then she thought of Alba and felt guilty. Perhaps it hadn't been right to cut her like that. After all, Alba had spent many evenings in her kitchen, pouring her little heart out over endless glasses of wine. Beneath her sharp talking there was a very lovable girl. Viv was too old to behave in such a childish manner. Alba couldn't talk to her parents and now she no longer had Fitz. *Shameful!* She hissed under her breath. *I should know better.*

'Do drive a little faster, taxi!' she shouted over the drone of the radio. 'I'm not a tourist so let's just hurry on, shall we?' The taxi driver was so taken aback he put his foot down out of sheer panic.

* * *

Viv thought it an incredible coincidence when Fitz and she arrived in Cheyne Walk at the same time. Neither spoke; they both knew that it was much more important to get to Alba than to explain why they were hurrying down the pontoon to the *Valentina*. Fitz knocked on the door. The houseboat looked desolate. Only a gang of squirrels played on the roof of the cabin.

'Bloody hell!' Viv swore. 'Are we too late?'

'I think so,' said Fitz.

'Try again!' she encouraged.

'What do you think I'm doing!' he exclaimed irritably, banging on the door with his fist. Still there was no reply and still the squirrels remained, scampering across the roof with their sharp little claws.

'Well, that's it then. She's gone.'

'I don't believe it. I'm such a fool!'

Viv put her hand on his shoulder. 'Darling, you weren't to know.'

'I could have come any day over the last month, but I didn't. I left her alone when she needed me. I didn't even telephone to wish her luck.'

'She'll be back,' she soothed.

Fitz turned to her with angry eyes. 'Will she?'

'Well, there's no point standing here banging. Let's go and have a drink.' She pulled him away from the door.

It was at that moment of utter despair that they both saw the incredible sight on Viv's beautifully manicured roof garden. Viv's hand shot to her mouth as she let out a strangled gasp. Fitz's face opened into a wide smile.

'Alba!' they both exclaimed in unison.

'How on earth . . . ,' began Viv but her voice trailed off and for once she was lost for words.

'Typical!' said Fitz, feeling a little better.

'Well, I suppose I deserve it,' Viv added with a sigh, shaking her head.

On top of her perfectly clipped grass was a goat, chomping through the buttercups and daisies and probably hoovering up the poppy seeds as well.

Alba was in the cab on her way to Heathrow. She thought of the goat on Viv's houseboat and hoped it had eaten all the grass by now. With any luck it had fallen into her bedroom and was working its way through her underwear. *Good old Les!* But, despite the joke, inside she felt miserable. Fitz hadn't bothered to telephone to wish her luck and now he never would, because even she wasn't sure where she was going. She knew she had to take the plane to Naples, the train to Sorrento, and then a boat to Incantellaria. The travel agent had said the roads were narrow and winding and she certainly wasn't going to risk her life with an Italian at the wheel. They drove on the wrong side of the road for a start. No, much better to take a boat. It was an adventure. Fitz had said she had to go it alone. She was on the brink of discovering her mother. It was both liberating and frightening.

The Second Portrait

18

The moment Alba sank into the seat on the airplane, her reserves of energy dried up and she yawned sleepily. She was weary. Weary of the same old emptiness and weary of hoping that Fitz was going to fill it. It would be good to get away. To leave it all behind. To start afresh in a new place with new people.

She had deliberately chosen the seat next to the window so that she only had one stranger to contend with. At least on a bus she could sit where she liked and move if an undesirable took the place beside her. In an airplane it was quite different. She was stuck with whomever Fate had chosen to put in 13B. The number thirteen did not augur well. A handsome Italian man entered the plane, clearly fed up with the slow line of people who shuffled up the aisle, pausing every few paces while someone placed their case in the overhead locker. He caught her eye. Alba was not surprised when he didn't look away. They rarely did. She stared back at him confidently until the sheer boldness of her gaze caused him to drop his eyes to the ticket he held in his hand. She hoped he had been dealt the unlucky number, which wouldn't be so unlucky, of course, if it belonged to him. As far as she could tell, he was the only vaguely decent man she had seen that evening and it would be nice to talk to someone, considering how nervous she felt about flying into the unknown.

She continued to watch him. Her pale eyes obviously disconcerted him. Judging by his sudden diffidence he clearly wasn't a pouncer, she thought, cheering up. She wasn't in the mood for a pouncer. He stole another quick glance at her before walking to the back of the plane. She huffed grumpily and folded her arms. Before she had a chance to size up the rest of the passengers, a large, swollen man, a pyramid of blubber, fell into the seat beside her.

'Do you mind,' she said haughtily.

The man apologized in a thin, reedy voice and tried unsuccessfully to squeeze himself into a small person.

Alba huffed. 'They should make special seats for people like you,' she said, without smiling.

'I suppose they should.'

He extracted a white hanky from his trouser pocket, with some difficulty, and wiped his forehead. *Sweaty too,* she thought in distaste. *Just my bloody luck.* He strapped himself in and Alba thought it miraculous that the airline made seat-belts big enough. *How very inconsiderate of him to be so fat,* she thought meanly. *He's obviously a very greedy man.* She wondered whether the handsome Italian was still thinking of her and wishing that he had been lucky enough to sit next to her. Anything would have been better than Fatman, she mused crossly. She turned to face the window in order to make it quite clear that she had no wish to engage in conversation. When he opened a book she felt it was safe to read *Vogue*.

She absorbed herself in the fashion pages of her favorite magazine, forgetting about Fitz and Italy for a while, focusing instead on the pictures of girls in hotpants and boots.

She lit a cigarette regardless that Fatman began to wheeze beside her like an old steam engine. When the trays of food were handed out she was appalled that he took one and tucked into the bread roll without so much as a thought for the pounds he was piling on.

'You know you shouldn't eat so much,' she said, tapping him on the hand. 'You'll just get bigger and then seats on airplanes will be the least of your worries.'

Fatman suddenly looked crestfallen and stared miserably down at the white roll and butter in his fingers, while Alba returned to her own food and *Vogue*. He put down the roll and swallowed the ball of anguish that had lodged itself in his throat.

Finally they touched down in Naples. It seemed a small airport, though it was too dark to see much of it. Alba's travel agent had booked her into a hotel in the city. The following morning she would take a train to Sorrento and then a boat to Incantellaria. She was relieved to stand up and stretch her legs. Fatman made way for her but she was too busy searching for the handsome Italian to thank him.

She saw him inside the airport while they both waited for their luggage. After catching his eye a couple of times she decided to be a little more encouraging. She smiled before lowering her gaze coyly. It didn't take long for him to get the message and stride up to talk to her. As he approached, she appraised him appreciatively. He was tall with broad shoulders and light brown hair that fell over a wide, angular face. His eyes were pale green and deep set. As he grinned, the crow's feet darkened into his temples giving him a humorous, insouciant air.

'I see that you are alone,' he said in English. She liked his accent; it sounded wonderfully exotic after a lifetime of English ones.

'Yes, I am,' she replied, grinning at him. 'I've never been to Italy before.'

'Then welcome to my country.'

'Thank you.' She tilted her head to one side. 'Do you live in Naples?'

'No, I'm here on business. I live in Milan.' He looked her up and down without trying to hide his admiration. 'You're staying in a hotel?'

'Yes, the Miramare.'

'What a coincidence. So am I.'

'Are you?'

'I always stay there. It's one of the nicest hotels in the city. We can share a taxi. As it's your first time in Italy you will allow me to be your host and take you out for dinner.'

Alba was scarcely able to believe her luck. 'I would love that. After all, what is a girl to do in Naples all on her own?'

'My name is Alessandro Favioli.' He extended his hand.

'Alba Arbuckle,' she replied. 'It doesn't have the same ring to it as yours. My parents obviously didn't think very hard about how the words would sound together. My mother was Italian.'

'She must have been very beautiful.'

Alba smiled, recalling the portrait. 'She was.'

'What are you here for? You don't look like a tourist.'

'Certainly not! I'm going to Incantellaria.'

'Oh?'

'Don't tell me. You're going there too!'

He laughed. 'No. But I know of it. A magical place, so I'm told. Full of ridiculous miracles and strange supernatural phenomena.'

'Really? Like what?'

'Well, apparently, one day just after the war, the

townspeople awoke to find the beach covered in pink carnations. Then the tide came in and washed them away.'

'Do you believe it?'

'Oh, I believe it happened. But I don't believe the sea
brought them all in. Some sly joker was probably having
a laugh. The funny thing is the local priest declared it a
miracle. That is Italy for you. Especially Naples. It is full
of saints who bleed. We are rather top-heavy with regards
to religion.'

'Well, I'm not at all religious so they'll probably cast
me into the sea.'

Once again he looked her up and down with his lazy
gaze. 'I don't think so, Alba. They'll probably sanctify you
and fashion you in marble.'

They shared a taxi to the hotel. Alba liked his good
manners in opening the door for her and helping her in
and out. She showered in her room and changed into a
simple black dress, before meeting him downstairs in the
lobby. She laughed as he kissed her hand. He smelled
strongly of lemon cologne and his hair was still wet.

'You look beautiful,' he said.

'Thank you,' she replied graciously, suddenly realizing
that she hadn't thought of Fitz since leaving England. *I
think I'm going to like Italy,* she mused. 'Are all Italians as
charming as you?' she said out loud.

'No, of course not. If they were, all the women of
Europe would live in Italy.'

'That's good. I like to feel I have something that is
unique.'

'So do I, which is why I noticed you on the plane.'

'Shame we weren't sitting together. I was squashed up
against the window by a big, greedy, fat man.'

'Thirteen is not a lucky number.'

'No, but I've been rather lucky since, haven't I?' She

grinned at him with her characteristic arrogance and he seemed to fall, as they all did, into her strange, pale eyes.

They dined in a small restaurant on the waterfront, overlooking the sea and the castle of Sant' Elmo. He didn't want to talk about himself. He asked her about her life in England.

'My father is rich and spoils me rotten,' she said. 'But I have a ghastly stepmother who raises pigs and rides horses. She has a big bottom and a big voice that she uses for bossing people about. My half brother and sisters are conventional and hearty, the result, I'm afraid, of an uninspiring union.'

He found her amusing and laughed at most of the things she said. She noticed, as he smoked over a cup of coffee, that he wore a simple gold wedding band on the third finger of his left hand. It didn't bother her; in fact, it delighted her. She liked to think that she had the power to lure a man away from his wife.

They chose to walk back to the hotel so that Alba could see a little of Naples. It was a hot, sticky night. The air was still and heavy. Alba admired the narrow streets, the pretty pale houses with iron balconies and shutters, the ornate moldings that gave them character and charm. The city had come alive with music, laughter, cars, horns, and the aroma of good Italian food. The sharp, staccato voice of a mother berating her child soared above the rise and fall of engines, like the cry of a bird against the roar of the sea. Dark-skinned men stood talking in the alleyways, their eyes on the women who walked by. Although they didn't wolf-whistle at her, she could feel their eyes undressing her, peeling her naked layer by layer. She knew she was protected by Alessandro and was thankful she wasn't having to walk through the city alone. She rode London like a docile pony; Naples, on the other hand, was like an uncontrollable rodeo horse and it unnerved her.

They arrived at the hotel and Alessandro didn't wait to be invited to her room. He followed her up in the lift and along the corridor. 'You're pretty sure of yourself,' she said. But her smile told him that he was right to be so.

'I want to make love to you,' he murmured. 'After all, I'm only a man.'

'I suppose you are.' She sighed in sympathy and turned the key in the lock.

Before she had time to switch on the light, he had swung her around and was kissing her ardently on her surprised mouth. For the first time since their breakup she was sufficiently distracted to fend off comparisons with Fitz. She didn't think about him at all. Alessandro, consumed with lust, pressed her against the wall and buried his face in her neck. She smelled his lemon cologne that had now mellowed with the natural scent of his skin, and felt his rough bristles against her flesh.

He ran his hands up her legs to her hips. His touch was strong and masterful, taking her breath with each stroke. He fell to his knees and lifted her dress to her waist so that he could kiss and lick her naked belly with his tongue. She was allowed no control. Every time she attempted to reclaim a little lost ground he withdrew her hands and buried his head further into her flesh, giving her such shivers of delight that she soon gave up the battle and succumbed.

They made love five times, finishing in a heap of exhaustion on the bed. They slept draped over one another, though the intimacy had gone. The excitement of the chase was over and Alba knew, even in her sleep, that she would have to dismiss him coldly in the morning.

She didn't dream of Fitz. She didn't dream of

anything. But when she woke, she was sure that she was still within the realm of fantasy, for she didn't recognize the room. Streams of light filtered in through the gaps in the shutters. The sound of the city outside penetrated the sleepy silence of her room, although it seemed very far away. She blinked and oriented herself. As usual, she had had too much to drink. Her head ached and her limbs felt as if they had been given the most strenuous workout. Then she remembered Alessandro and she smiled inwardly at the memory of the devilish Italian she had met at the airport. She turned, fully expecting to see him in her bed, but it was empty. She listened for a noise in the bathroom, but the door was ajar and the light was off. He was gone. *Just as well,* she thought. She hated it when they outstayed their welcome. She was a physical wreck. The last thing she needed was to make love again.

She looked at the clock beside the bed. It was still early. She didn't have to be at the station until ten. She had time for a shower and breakfast. On second thought, she'd order room service. She didn't want to bump into him in the dining room.

After her shower, during which she washed off the scent of lemon, she dressed and packed her bag. As she looked at her reflection in the mirror, she recalled the excitement of the night before. Alessandro had been good for her. He had at least put a plaster across her broken heart and mended it temporarily. He had taken her thoughts away from Fitz to a more exotic world of adventure, where she was free to be whoever she chose, in a place where no one knew her. In a moment of enthusiasm she decided she would telephone Alessandro's room and thank him. After all, he had given her an enormous amount of pleasure. Perhaps they could breakfast together; then, at least, she wouldn't have to eat alone.

She called reception. 'I would like to be connected with Alessandro Favioli,' she demanded in a haughty voice. There was a pause while the receptionist looked in the book.

'Alessandro Favioli,' repeated Alba. *God, they don't even understand their own language,* she thought irritably.

'I'm afraid there is no one by the name of Favioli in this hotel.'

'Well of course there is. I dined with him last night.'

'No Signore Favioli.'

'Look again. We arrived together yesterday evening, then returned together after dinner. Surely you saw him.'

'I was not on duty last night,' the receptionist informed her coldly.

'Well, ask your colleague. I didn't dream him up, you know.'

'Do you know which room he is in?' The receptionist was getting impatient.

'Of course not, that's why I'm calling you!' Alba retorted. 'Maybe he's checked out.'

The woman repeated herself with forced politeness. 'There was no one by the name of Favioli in this hotel. I'm sorry.'

Alba suddenly felt sick. On reflection, it did seem too much of a coincidence that he had booked into the same hotel. He hadn't invited her back to his room, either. At the time she hadn't thought it strange at all, but now it did seem a little odd. With a suspended heart, she opened her handbag and shuffled around for her wallet. *This has got to be a joke,* she thought, feeling as if she were swimming against a strong current. The wallet wasn't in her bag. She swallowed hard, desperately turning the bag upside down so that all the contents tumbled onto the bed. She was relieved to find her passport still there, but no money. He had taken her wallet containing all her travelers' cheques and lire. How the hell was she going to pay the hotel bill, train, let alone the boatman to take her to Incantellaria?

She sank onto the bed. *The bastard. He used me, then robbed me. He had it all worked out, the shit. And I fell for it like a fool.* She felt too angry to cry and too embarrassed to telephone anyone in England to admit her stupidity. She'd simply have to work it out for herself.

As she wasn't intending to pay the bill, she thought she'd at least go and enjoy a good breakfast. Besides, she'd need to eat as much as she could now for she had no money for food later. She'd steal a few bread rolls from the buffet.

Downstairs, she greeted the receptionist in the most friendly tone she could muster and strode confidently into the dining room. She sat down at a small table in the middle of the room, and ordered coffee, orange juice, croissants, toast, and fruit salad. While she watched the other guests, she began to feel increasingly alone. She had no friends in Italy. No one at all. What if her family had moved away from Incantellaria? What if she were chasing a rainbow? She had no money. It would take a few days to get it wired to the bank in Incantellaria. She wasn't prepared to hang around in Naples in case she bumped into Alessandro again. She remembered the sinister-looking men who had leered at her in the dark alleyways the night before and suddenly felt exposed and vulnerable. He might just as well have robbed her of her clothes, she felt so naked and lost.

Suddenly, to her enormous relief, she spotted Fatman sitting alone at the other end of the dining room. With a wave of affection for the person she had previously thought beneath contempt, she swept over to his table. She didn't notice the look of horror that crossed his features when he laid eyes on her. He looked down at his bread roll, already buttered and dripping with strawberry jam, and tried to hide it under his pudgy hand. She sat down and put her elbows on the table.

'I hope you don't mind if I join you,' she said in the sweetest voice she could manage. She looked up at him with big doe eyes. 'I've been robbed. An Italian man has stolen *everything*. My money, my clothes, my passport, my ticket home. *Everything*. You're the only person I know in the whole of Italy. In the whole of Europe, in fact. Could I be so bold as to ask you the hugest favor? Could I borrow some money off you? Just enough to get me to Incantellaria? I'll take your address and pay you back with interest. I'd be so grateful.' She smiled at him and added, 'Don't stop eating on my account.'

Fatman considered his position for a long moment. Suddenly, in a violent gesture that caused Alba to shrink in horror, he stuffed the entire roll into his mouth. She gasped, trying not to show her disgust, as he chewed it slowly and deliberately, butter seeping between his lips and dribbling on to the stairway of chins that descended from his mouth. Finally, he wiped his mouth with a napkin. 'Delicious!' he exclaimed. 'I must order more!'

Alba's hopes slowly began to deflate. She recalled with shame that she had not only been rude to him on the plane, but unforgivably offensive. Why should he do anything for her? 'It's okay,' she stammered, feeling tearful. 'I'm sorry to have bothered you.'

'You shouldn't pick up strange men at airports,' he said, gaining confidence. 'Being robbed is the least of your worries.'

Alba's mouth hung open. 'I'm sorry?'

'You heard me. What do you expect? Have you no sense of decorum or are you as easy with every man who offers to pay for your dinner? In fact,' he said, clearly enjoying humiliating her, 'if you suck my cock I'll pay for your flight home!' Alba recoiled, struggled to her feet and hurried out of the dining room as fast as her shaking legs could carry her.

Back in her room, she exploded in fury, kicking the bed and the cupboard and anything else she could attack with her foot. How rude! How ungallant! How *could* he?

Self-pity didn't suit her. She pulled herself up and dusted herself off. Fury and revenge were as always her best options. She couldn't pay the bill and she had no one to do it for her. There was only one thing to do. When in doubt, flee.

She dragged her bag down the corridor, took the lift to the first floor then searched for a suitable window. Finding one in a dark corner where the light bulb had expired, she threw her bag into the back street below, then jumped down after it. She didn't stop running until she reached the station.

19

Alba arrived at the station out of breath but unexpectedly triumphant. She felt as if she had committed murder and gotten away with it. She wondered what the manager of the hotel would do once he discovered the unpaid bill and the wrecked room. By the time they traced her she'd be miles away. An anonymous face among thousands. She looked about her. The Italian women were olive-skinned and brown-haired like she was. There wasn't a blonde in sight. She fitted in. No one stared at her as if she were alien. In fact, no one stared at her at all. The fear she had had of predatory men, hiding down alleyways and loitering outside bars, lifted. One or two smiled at her warmly, their eyes running admiringly up her long brown legs and over her yellow sundress. They weren't menacing. They were appreciative. She was used to that kind of benign interest and she enjoyed it. However, she had a huge practical problem. She intended to take a train to Sorrento, then a boat to Incantellaria, but she had no money. She was about to return one of the smiles in the hope of borrowing the money from one of those kind, appreciative men, but Fatman's harsh words were now branded upon her soul. 'If you suck my cock I'll pay for your flight home.' She blushed with shame and averted her eyes, hurrying on.

The next train to Sorrento departed in fourteen minutes. She found the platform, then watched the gate like a train robber. The official checking tickets was a small, skinny youth with a nervous twitch. Every few seconds his whole face disappeared into one monumental blink. Alba suddenly felt a wave of compassion. Unaccustomed to that particular emotion, her whole body bristled as if trying on a new skin. Like Fatman, the young official was too easy to intimidate. She wished he were tall, strong, and capable; then at least she wouldn't feel so bad making a fool of him. Passengers strode up to him, chatting to one another while he punched holes in their tickets. They recoiled in horror at his nervous tic or tittered behind their hands. They didn't care to return his polite greeting. Some didn't even mutter 'thank you.' Alba lit a cigarette and sat down on her suitcase. She knew what she'd do. Normally this kind of charade would have amused her. But today it didn't. Alessandro Favioli's mocking face rose up in her mind and Fatman's obscene suggestion echoed against the weakened walls of her conscience. Her spirit flooded with self-loathing.

Right, now's your moment, Alba. Seize these tears and make good use of them! She stubbed out her cigarette and strode toward the twitching official.

As Alba approached, the young official's face convulsed uncontrollably. He wasn't struck so much by her beauty as by the sheer scale of her grief. She was inconsolable. Her lovely face was red and blotchy, her shoulders hunched and shuddering with every sob.

'I'm so sorry,' she sniffed, dabbing her cheeks with a damp tissue. Then she lifted her eyes and he took a step back. They were the palest grey, like rare, bewitching crystals and so exquisite that his mind went blank. 'My lover has left me,' she wailed. The official looked appalled and his face suddenly stopped its violent twitching. 'He doesn't love me anymore, so I'm leaving Naples. I can't live in this city knowing that the one who has crushed my heart is living here too, breathing the same air, walking the same pavements. You do understand, don't you?' She reached out and placed a hand on his arm. Her ploy was working beautifully. His still face was frozen into an expression of the deepest compassion and for a moment she forgot herself. She stopped crying and smiled at him. 'You have a lovely face,' she said truthfully, for now that she could see it properly, she realized that he was still a boy, and surprisingly handsome. He blushed but did not turn away.

'*Grazie, signora,*' he said finally in a soft, shy voice.

She gripped his arm with her fingers. 'Thank *you*,' she said meaningfully, before hurrying down the platform, her spirit buoyant with the knowledge that she had got away without showing a ticket, but also that her scam hadn't humiliated him. She had made him happy. The surprising thing was that his obvious joy had infected her with happiness too.

Alba had learned a valuable lesson: people wore their bodies like coats. Whether ugly or beautiful, fat or thin, still or twitching, they were all vulnerable human beings beneath, deserving of respect. Then she remembered something Fitz had once said. 'If you look hard enough you'll find beauty and light in the ugliest and darkest places.' Alba realized she rarely looked at all.

She placed her bag in the luggage rack at the end of the carriage, then found a seat beside the window. When the ticket collector came through she would simply explain that she must have dropped hers on the platform. She wouldn't have been allowed through the gate without a ticket, obviously?

A couple of attractive young men took the seats opposite her and placed sandwiches and drinks on the table dividing them. She wished she had brought a book. The last time she had read an entire volume had been at school: Jane Austen's *Emma*, which had been such a struggle she was still getting over it a decade later. Reluctantly, she pulled out the well-handled *Vogue* she had read on the plane and flicked aimlessly through it.

It wasn't long before the young men attempted to ignite a conversation. Normally she would have been only too happy to talk to them, but today their attention offended her. Did she look that approachable? That easy?

'Would you like a biscuit?' asked the first one.

'No thank you,' she replied without smiling. The first looked at the second for encouragement. The second nodded.

'Where are you from?' he persevered.

She knew her accent gave her away. Then she was struck with an idea and a smile crept onto her face.

'I'm English, married to an Italian,' she said, leaning forward and looking up coyly from under her lashes. 'It is so nice to talk to a couple of handsome young men. You see, my husband is old. Oh, he's rich and powerful and gives me everything I want. I live in a vast palazzo. I have houses all over the world. Enough staff to sink a liner and countless pieces of jewelry. But when it comes to love, well, as I said, he's old.'

The daring one nudged the other excitedly. They both wriggled in their seats, barely able to restrain their lust as they contemplated this frisky young woman whose husband was too old to make love to her.

Then, remembering that she was seated in a second-class carriage, she added, 'Sometimes I like to be anonymous. I like to ride with normal people. So I leave the car and the chauffeur at the station and take the train. One meets fascinating people on trains and, of course, I am beyond my husband's reach.'

'What you need are a couple of young men to give you what your husband can't,' said the first, bolder now but speaking in a hushed voice, his eyes feverish with intent. She appraised them slowly through narrowed eyes, withdrew a cigarette from its packet, placed it between her lips, and lit it. As she blew out the smoke she leaned forward again, placing her elbows on the table.

'I'm more careful these days,' she said casually. 'The last lover I took had his balls chopped off.' The two men blanched. 'As I said, my husband is powerful – very powerful. With power comes possessiveness. He likes to keep all that he owns for himself. But I like to take risks. I like the challenge. I like to defy him. It gives me pleasure. Do you understand?'

They nodded, their mouths agape. Alba was relieved when they got off at the first stop, their throats too dry to bid her farewell.

When the ticket collector wandered through, she was at her most charming. 'I have to confess that I have lost my ticket,' she said, smiling sheepishly. 'I'm so sorry and so useless, but that young boy with the twitch,' the ticket collector nodded in recognition as she imitated the way he blinked, 'I was so distracted talking to him, he was so dear and I was so dreadfully sorry for him, that when he gave me back my ticket I must have dropped it onto the platform. Of course, I'm more than happy to buy another one.' She began to delve into her handbag, hoping he'd stop her before she had to make up another story about losing her wallet too, which might have stretched his sympathy beyond its limit.

'Please, signora,' he said kindly. 'Michele is a good lad

but a little simple. He probably forgot to give it back to you.' Then, in the manner of most men she encountered, he endeavored to take his generosity a step further. 'If you have a heavy bag please allow me to help you carry it down from the train.'

'Thank you,' she said, knowing that if she declined his offer she would dent his pride. 'That would be most kind. I do, as it happens, have a heavy bag and, as you can see, I'm not very strong.'

After lingering for longer than was necessary, the ticket collector wandered off, reassuring Alba that he would return at the end of the line to help her down. Once he had gone, she gazed out the window.

She thought of Fitz. She blushed as she remembered his kiss. The intimacy of it. It had been like slow dancing after a frenetic round of the twist. It had almost been too much, excruciatingly slow and tender. It had strained every nerve in her body, forced her to feel. To *really* feel. Not to pretend. It had come so naturally to him, this feeling thing. To her it had been embarrassing, then amusing, and finally almost painful.

The countryside glimmered in the haze of the late morning sun. Tall cypress trees rose up with the heat and sandy-coloured houses sheltered in the shade of pine and cedar. Alba wanted to stick her head out of the window and sniff the air like Sprout did in the back of Fitz's Volvo. She had imagined these smells all her life. She had seen Italy in films, but nothing could have prepared her for the aching beauty of the country. It was fitting that her mother had come from this earthly heaven, for in Alba's mind she embodied all those qualities; her spirit moved among the abundant bougainvillea, olive groves, and heavy vines.

The train screeched to a halt in Sorrento. As he had promised, the ticket collector returned to help Alba with her bag. Eager to please, he wheeled it all the way along the platform and out onto the street, then bade her goodbye. The town was busy. People walked by, their thoughts on themselves, oblivious of the young woman who stood in bewilderment, her stomach now twisting with hunger. The buildings were white, yellow, and red, their shutters closed to keep the rooms cool, the ground-floor windows protected by iron bars, the doors vast, shut, and inhospitable. Although pretty, there was something unwelcoming about the place.

Finally, the street opened onto the seafront. Boats bobbed up and down on the water or had been dragged up onto the beach. The wet sand was brown like gravel and people ambled up and down the quay, enjoying the sunshine. A couple of restaurants and shops spilled out onto the pavement and the smell of roasting tomatoes and onions wafted on the breeze. She felt her stomach rumble and her mouth salivate. She longed for a glass of water. In her fury she hadn't thought of stealing a few supplies from the hotel minibar. The more she thought about food and drink, the hungrier and thirstier she became.

She did not allow herself to wallow in self-pity, as she would have been tempted to do had her will weakened. Self-pity never got anyone anywhere and she despised those weeping women in the movies. She had got this far; with a little charm she could get to Incantellaria. Leaving her bag on the quay, she gathered her courage and marched up to a wizened old fisherman pottering about his boat. As she approached, the smell of fish invaded her nostrils and she was struck by a wave of nausea. 'Excuse me,' she said, smiling sweetly. The old man looked up. He didn't smile. In fact, he looked more than a little irritated to have been disturbed. 'I need to get to Incantellaria,' she stated. He looked at her blankly.

'I can't take you,' he replied, shaking his head as if she were an annoying fly he wanted to be rid of.

'Do you know anyone who can?'

He shrugged unhelpfully, raising the palms of his hands to the sky. 'Nanni Baroni will take you,' he said after a moment's thought.

'Where can I find him?'

'He won't be back until sunset.'

'But isn't it just around the bay? Aren't boats going there all the time?'

'Why would anyone want to go to Incantellaria?'

Alba was confused. 'Isn't it a big town, like this one?'

He laughed cynically. 'It's a small, forgotten little place. It's asleep. It's always been asleep. Why would anyone want to go to Incantellaria?' he repeated.

Alba's travel agent had specifically said that she should take a boat. She had implied that there were boats leaving all the time, like the trains from Basingstoke to London. Alba muttered crossly under her breath. For a second, she forgot her bearings. She was sure she had left her bag beside the bollard. Perplexed, she looked about her. It was nowhere to be seen. Once again, in the short space of twenty-four hours, she felt the sickening surge of blood to the head, the hot pounding in her ears, the giddy plummeting of her stomach, the anguish, as she realized to her utter disbelief and horror that she had been robbed again. Now she had nothing but her handbag containing lipstick, diary, a rather crumpled *Vogue*, and, thank God, her passport.

'Someone has fucking robbed me!' she shouted in English, screaming the words into the heavy afternoon air. She stamped her feet and flung her arms about her head. 'Arrrrrrgh! I hate this fucking country. I hate fucking Italians. You're not a nation, you're a profession.

Thieves. The whole bloody lot of you. Why the fuck did I come? It's been nothing but a fucking disaster, a fucking waste of time! Arrrrrgh!'

Suddenly she heard the gentle, patient voice of a man and felt a warm hand on her shoulder. 'I'm glad you're swearing in English,' he said with a smile. 'Otherwise they'd lock you up for the afternoon!' She stared at him furiously.

'I've just been robbed,' she fumed, fighting tears. 'Someone has just taken my bag. I was robbed of my money in Naples and now my bag in this godforsaken little backwater!'

'You have obviously never been here before,' he said kindly, turning serious so as not to offend her. 'You have to guard your possessions with your life. You're English?'

'Yes. In London you can leave the Crown Jewels in the middle of Piccadilly Circus, have lunch, do a bit of shopping in Bond Street, walk around Hyde Park, have tea at the Ritz, a drink at the fucking Connaught, and they'd still be there at six.' It wasn't strictly true, but it sounded good. 'Now I have no money, no clothes!' Her heart sank deeper at the thought of those beautiful clothes now lost. 'I need to get to Incantellaria and I can't find a single bloody person to take me. Nanni bloody Baroni is home shagging his mistress or something and won't be back until six. What am I supposed to do until six? Mm? I can't even buy myself a bloody sandwich!'

'Why on earth do you want to go to Incantellaria?'

She glared at him, pale grey eyes turning to stone. 'If one more person asks me that, I'm going to bloody well thump them!'

'Look,' he suggested with a smile. 'Why don't you let me buy you lunch, then I'll take you to Incantellaria myself. I have a boat.'

'Why should I trust you?'

'Because you've got nothing more to lose,' he replied with a shrug, putting his hand in the small of her back and guiding her to the restaurant.

Gabriele Ricci explained over a glass of rosé that he lived in Naples but summered on the coast with his family, who had a house there. 'I have spent every holiday here since I was a boy but never have I come across a woman as lovely as you.'

Alba rolled her eyes. 'I don't want to be told I'm beautiful, or lovely. I've had you Italians up to here!' she placed her hand on her neck.

'Don't Englishmen appreciate women?'

'They do. Quietly.'

'Or do those boarding schools they send their sons to encourage them to like boys instead?'

'Certainly not. Englishmen are gorgeous and respectful.' She thought of Fitz. She would never have gotten herself into such a mess had he had the decency to come with her.

'You've barely set foot in my country and yet you are already cynical.'

'I've been robbed by a handsome Italian just like you. Wherever I go, men try to chat me up. I'm sick of being seen as a sexual thing. I'm sick of being robbed!'

'At least you're in one piece,' he said reassuringly.

'You don't know the half of it.'

'So how did you get here without any money?'

'It's a long story.'

'We've got all afternoon.'

'Well, if you pour me another glass of wine, stop telling me I'm beautiful, and promise not to make a pass at me, rob me, or murder me on the way to Incantellaria, I'll tell you.'

He rubbed his chin playfully, considering her conditions. 'I can't deny your beauty, but you are very rude. You swear too much for a lady as well. I won't rob you because you have nothing left worth robbing. I'm not a murderer. However, I can't promise never to make a pass at you. I'm Italian!'

'Oh God!' she sighed melodramatically. 'Just allow me to get my strength back so I can decline with force.' Alba would have normally noticed the attractive lines around his mouth when he laughed and his pale green eyes that sparkled with mischief and a warm affability, but she was numb.

They shared a simple meal in the sunshine and the wine softened her anger and gave her a false sense of optimism. She recounted her adventure, omitting Fatman and his lewd suggestion as well as her night of passion with the stranger she had met at the airport, of which she was now deeply ashamed. Gabriele's obvious enjoyment encouraged her to elaborate even further until her story grew into a work of fiction of which Vivien Armitage would have been proud.

Finally, as they sipped glasses of limoncello, he asked her again why she was going to Incantellaria. 'Because my mother lived and died there,' she replied. 'I never met her, for she died just after I was born. I want to find her family.'

'I shouldn't think you'll have much trouble, if they're still there. It's a tiny place. Only a couple of thousand people, I suspect.'

'Why doesn't anyone go there?'

'Because there's nothing to do. It's sleepy. A forgotten little corner of Italy. It's very beautiful, though. Quite unlike the rest of the coast. It's meant to be enchanted.'

'Carnations,' she said with a smile. 'I've been told.'

'And weeping statues. I've been there many times. If I want to be alone, I go there. It soothes the soul. If I wanted to disappear, I'd go there too,' he added with a wry smile. 'I hope you don't disappear.'

'Remember your promise,' she said, her voice cold.

'Look, if once you get there you find you need money to tide you over, I'll lend you whatever you need. I'd give it to you, but I know you won't accept. Consider me a friend in a strange place. I promise you can trust me.' He touched her naked arm. His hand was warm and unexpectedly reassuring.

'Just take me to Incantellaria,' she said, getting up. His hand fell onto the table. Then she turned to him and her face softened. 'Friend.'

20

It felt good to be at the helm of a fast speedboat. The wind raked through her hair with cool, brisk fingers, taking her hopelessness with it. The boat jumped as it cut through the waves and Alba had to hold on to prevent herself from toppling over. There, with the sun on her face and an irrepressible sense of optimism burning through her chest, she had no cares in the world.

Gabriele grinned at her, taking pleasure from this lovely stranger who had lost everything on his shore. He pointed out the sheer rocks that rose from the sea like the walls of an impenetrable fortress and explained that Incantellaria was a place entirely on its own, as if God had taken a small slice of paradise and placed it in the midst of this unforgiving terrain. 'Its loveliness is quite unexpected,' he said as the boat passed cove after cove of hard grey rock.

It was farther than Alba had imagined. She had thought it was literally around the corner from Sorrento.

'If it doesn't work out,' Gabriele shouted against the roar of the wind, as if reading her thoughts, 'I'll come and get you. You only have to telephone.'

'Thank you,' she replied gratefully.

Her unease was returning. Incantellaria was obviously cut off not only from Italy but from the rest of the world.

The sun was obscured behind a solitary cloud and the sea darkened ominously, mirroring her own inner fears. What if her family had all died or moved away? She couldn't bear to go home with nothing resolved.

As Gabriele placed a reassuring hand on hers, the cloud moved on and the sun shone brilliantly again. The boat sped around a vast and solid wall of black rock behind which the coast opened up unexpectedly like the lid of a crude treasure chest, to reveal a glittering, verdant bay.

For Alba it was love at first sight. It sucked her in and filled her spirit. The very shape of the shoreline was as harmonious as the gentle curve of a cello. The white houses glimmered in the dazzling light, their wrought-iron balconies dripping with red and pink geraniums. The dome of the chapel rose above the grey-tiled roofs where doves settled to watch the coming and going of fishermen. Alba's body quivered with excitement. Surely there, in that little chapel, her parents had married. Without even setting foot on the shore she felt that their love affair was at last becoming tangible.

She raised her eyes to the emerald hills behind, where pine trees twitched their spiky green fingers and the ruins of an old lookout tower stood proud and dignified still, after centuries of abandonment. She breathed in the aromatic scents of rosemary and thyme that were carried on the wind with the whiff of mystery and adventure.

'Beautiful, isn't it?' said Gabriele, slowing down the boat to motor gently into the harbor.

'You're right. It's completely different from the rest of the coast. It's so green. So vibrant.'

'It's only when you see the place that you realize its inhabitants probably thought little of the carnation miracle. It would be odd anywhere else in the world, but here, one imagines such things happen all the time.'

'It's already home to me,' she said in a quiet voice. 'I feel it *here*,' she added, placing a hand on her heart.

'It's a wonder, really, that it hasn't become a tourist trap with restaurants and bars and clubs. Of course, there are some, but it's not exactly Saint Tropez.'

'I'm glad it isn't Saint Tropez, because it's going to be *my* secret place.' Her eyes blurred with tears. No wonder her father and the Buffalo had never brought her here; they knew they would lose her forever.

Gabriele steered the boat into the harbor. As it nestled against the walls of the quay, a little boy hurried up to secure the rope to the wharf, his round face bright with excitement. Gabriele threw him the rope, which he caught with a triumphant squeal, shouting to his friends to come and join in the fun.

'They obviously don't get many visitors,' said Gabriele. 'I think we're going to cause a bit of a stir.'

Alba disembarked and stood, hands on hips, gazing about her with pleasure. Up close it was even more charming, like stepping back in time to a slower, quainter age. Fishermen sat in their boats, chatting to one another as they mended their nets and emptied the day's haul into barrels. They cast wary glances in her direction from under furrowed brows. A group of young boys had now congregated around her, shuffling their feet, nudging one another, giggling behind grubby hands. Women stood gossiping outside the shops and a few people drank coffee beneath striped awnings that shaded the bars and restaurants from the sun. They all watched the young couple curiously.

Gabriele jumped onto the quay and put his hand in the small of her back. 'Let's go and get a drink. Then we'll find somewhere for you to stay. I can't leave you to sleep on the beach.'

'There must be a hotel, surely,' she said, gazing about her.

'A small *pensione*. That's all.'

One by one the faces of the fishermen froze at the sight of the chillingly familiar beauty of the young woman who had stepped onto their shore. Like old tortoises, they craned their necks and, one by one, their chins dropped to reveal toothless mouths gasping in wonder. It didn't take long for Alba to notice. Even Gabriele felt uneasy. A silent ripple seemed to reverberate through the town.

Suddenly an old man, as squat and fat as a toad, emerged from the dark interior of Trattoria Fiorelli and stood in the doorway, scratching his groin. His heavily lidded eyes fell on Alba and the dull wall of cataracts shone with unnatural brilliance. He let out a whispery wheeze, from deep down at the bottom of his chest, and stopped scratching. Alba, frightened now by the strange hush that had come over the town, took Gabriele's hand.

'Valentina!' the man exclaimed, fighting for air.

Alba turned and stood staring back at him as if he had just breathed life into a ghost. Then a man of about sixty with brooding looks and a formidable physique stepped out from behind him. He came down to where Alba stood, her legs trembling. He walked with a slight limp, but this did not slow him down. His expression was dark, as if the sun had been obscured by a cloud.

When he reached her, he seemed unsure of what to say, and it was Gabriele who spoke first. 'Where can we get a drink around here?' he asked. His eyes shifted from the man to the fishermen, who had all climbed out of their boats and were now forming a ring around them.

'My name is Falco Fiorelli,' said Falco in a low voice. 'You . . . you . . .' He didn't know how to say it. It sounded absurd. 'A drink, of course.' He shook his head, hoping to dispel the phantom that he was now sure only played with his mind and did not, as he had hoped, stand before him.

'My name is Alba,' said Alba, her face as white as the doves that sat on the grey-tiled roofs. 'Alba Arbuckle. My mother was Valentina.' Falco's weatherbeaten cheeks glowed and he heaved an almost painful sigh of relief and joy.

'Then I am your uncle,' he said. 'We thought we had lost you.'

'I thought I'd never find you,' she replied. A murmur rose up from the band of fishermen.

'They thought you were the ghost of your mother,' Falco explained. 'A drink for everyone,' he shouted heartily, raising his hand to a cheer from the crowd. 'Alba has come home.' Ignoring Gabriele, Falco took his niece's hand proudly and led her up the steps to the restaurant. 'Come, you must meet your grandmother.' Alba was overwhelmed. Her uncle was like a powerful lion, his hand so large that hers disappeared inside it. Gabriele shrugged helplessly and followed.

Immacolata Fiorelli was now old. Very old. The numbers had gotten confusing around eighty. Eighty-one? Eighty-two? She hadn't a clue. She could be one hundred for all she knew. Not that she cared. Her heart had died after losing her precious Valentina. Without a heart to keep her young she had slowly withered away, literally shriveling. But she was not yet dead, which was what she prayed for, so that she could be reunited with her daughter.

She emerged with the help of a stick, like a mangy little bat, unaccustomed to the light. Her grey hair was piled on top of her head, her face peering through a smoky black veil.

Alba stood before her, the image of Valentina, but for the unnaturally pale eyes that exposed the stranger within the unbearable likeness. Immacolata's own eyes filled with tears and she lifted her hand, trembling with age and emotion, to touch the young woman's soft brown skin. Wordlessly her fingers touched the living part of her daughter. The part she had left behind. The grand-daughter who had been taken across the seas, lost, as good as dead. Thomas had never brought her back as he had promised. They had hoped. They had nearly died hoping.

At the sight of the old woman's tears, Alba's eyes misted. The love on her grandmother's face was so intense, so painful, she wanted to wrap her arms around her, but Immacolata was too frail and small. 'God has blessed this day,' she said in a soft, childish voice. 'Valentina has returned in the form of her daughter. I am no longer alone. My heart is stirring with life. When I die, God will receive a happy, grateful soul and Heaven shall be a better place for it.'

'Let's go inside where it is cool,' Falco suggested. Remembering Alba's companion he turned and nodded. 'Forgive us,' he added.

'Gabriele Ricci,' he said. 'Alba has come a long way to find you. I won't stay. Just give her this.' He pulled a white card out of his pocket and handed it to Falco. 'She can call me if she needs anything, but I don't think she will need to.'

Although curious, Gabriele knew he was out of place in this family reunion. He slipped away without any fuss, longing to kiss Alba goodbye, to encourage her to get in touch so that they might see each other again. He turned, hoping she would run out to thank him, but the restau-rant was teeming with people and he was alone on the quay. Only the little boy skipped toward him to help him with the rope.

Inside the restaurant, drinks were poured and celebrations ensued. Lattarullo sat with Immacolata like a parody lady-in-waiting, pleased that it had been he and not *il sindacco* who had been there to welcome Alba home. *Il sindacco* was not long in arriving. He didn't look a day over fifty. His hair was neatly parted and combed, still jet black with only a few grey hairs around the temples. He was dapper in a pair of olive green trousers, belted high on the waist, and a pale blue shirt, perfectly pressed. When he entered the restaurant, his perfume filled the air so that everyone knew the most important man in town had arrived and they all parted to let him through.

When he saw Alba, seated with Immacolata, Lattarullo, and Falco, his closely shaven jaw dropped and he let out an audible gasp. *'Madonna!'* he exclaimed. 'The dead do indeed rise!' For a town used to miracles, the resurrection of Valentina was not beyond the realms of possibility. He pulled up a chair and Falco introduced them.

'Is this coincidence?' he asked. 'Did you just happen to wander into Incantellaria?'

'God has brought her to me,' said Immacolata.

'She came to find us,' Falco interjected.

'I've been longing to find you since I was a little girl,' said Alba, delighted by all the attention. She had now forgotten the humiliation she had suffered in Naples and her lost bag, even Gabriele.

'You see,' said Immacolata, her voice sweet and happy like her daughter's had been when Tommy returned at the end of the war. 'She didn't forget us. You even speak Italian! You see,' she turned to her son, 'Italy is in her blood.'

'You will stay with us,' Falco instructed in his deep,

gruff voice. He had moved back into his mother's house with his wife and son after Valentina's death. Now Toto lived there too, with his own six-year-old daughter, Cosima; they had moved in when Cosima's mother had run off with an Argentinean tango dancer.

'She can have Valentina's old room,' Immacolata stated gravely and the air seemed to be sucked out of the little group. It was well known that Immacolata kept Valentina's room as a shrine. For twenty-six years she had lovingly cleaned it and cared for it, but no one was allowed to use it. Not ever. Not even Cosima.

Alba sensed the significance of the gesture and thanked her grandmother. 'I will be honoured to have my mother's room,' she said sincerely. 'I feel I am beginning to know her through you. It is what I have longed for all my life.'

Immacolata, exhausted by the excitement, ordered Lattarullo to take her home. 'I have given the people of Incantellaria a public celebration; now I would like to celebrate alone with my family.' Alba was excited to be going to the very house where her mother had lived, to sleep in the bed she had slept in. If she had known it would be as magical as this she would have come years ago.

'Where is your suitcase?' Falco asked Alba as they walked out into the evening sunshine.

'Lost,' she said casually. 'It was stolen, but it doesn't matter.'

'Stolen?'

'Good gracious, where's Gabriele?' She turned to look about her, ashamed that she had forgotten him.

'Oh, he left.'

'He left? I never thanked him!' she exclaimed, disappointed. 'He didn't even say goodbye.' She turned to look at the harbour as if by some small chance he might still be there, waiting beside his boat.

'He gave me this to give to you.' Falco handed her the little white card. It was engraved with Gabriele's name and telephone number.

'How smart!' she said, slipping it into her handbag.

'So you have nothing?' Falco said incredulously.

'Nothing. If it hadn't been for Gabriele's generosity, oh, and the unwitting generosity of the Italian railway officials, I wouldn't have gotten here at all!' She climbed into the back of the car and leaned against the hot leather, warmed by the sun. Falco climbed in beside her. Immacolata sat in front, eager to get back to the quiet sanctuary of her home and the relics of the deceased. Lattarullo drove.

The ride up the hill was a bumpy one: the road was little more than a dusty track. 'They tried to tarmac it about ten years ago but ran out of money, so it's smooth for about half a mile out of town and then this!' Falco explained.

'I think it's charming,' Alba replied. To her, everything about Incantellaria was charming.

'You wouldn't think so if you had to drive up it every day!'

Alba had rolled down the car window in order to wave goodbye to the townsfolk celebrating her homecoming. Now as they neared the house she stuck her nose out to breathe in the woody scents of the countryside. From up here on the hill she could see the sea, shimmering blue in the soft evening light. She wondered how often her mother must have gazed upon that very same view. Perhaps she had seen her father motor into the bay in his MTB.

They climbed out of the car to walk down the grassy path to the house. The track had been extended in the last few years so that it now almost reached the front door.

Suddenly Alba was struck with a sweet, succulent smell. 'What is that?' she asked, sniffing the air like Sprout did. 'It's divine!'

Lattarullo looked at her. 'Your father asked me that very same question when he arrived here for the first time.'

'He did?' she asked brightly.

'Figs,' said Immacolata gravely. 'Though I defy you to find a fig tree!' Alba looked inquiringly at Falco.

Her uncle shrugged. 'She's right. It's always smelled of figs.'

'It's intoxicating,' she said, heaving a sigh. 'Magical.'

She followed them into the sand-coloured house, almost entirely obscured by heavy clusters of wisteria. Her grandmother led the way through the tiled hallway into the sitting room. There, in the corner, burned three shrines. One to Immacolata's husband, one to the son she had lost, and the third, which appeared to blaze brighter than the other two, to Valentina. As Alba walked nearer she saw the black-and-white photograph of her grandfather in uniform, standing proud and erect. His eyes were full of zeal for the cause he naturally thought to be just, and his mouth was set in a determined grimace, not unlike Falco's. The photograph of his son, Alba's uncle, was also in black and white and showed him in uniform. Handsome, with the cheeky face of a prankster, he smiled out from under his cap. When her eyes settled on her mother's shrine she caught her breath. There was no photograph. Just a portrait. Done in the same pastels as the one she had found beneath the bed in her houseboat. *Valentina and Alba 1945. Thomas Arbuckle. Now my love is twofold.*

She picked it up and walked over to the window so that she could see it better in the light. This one was even more extraordinary than the first, for it depicted her mother gazing adoringly upon the baby feeding from her breast. And that baby was herself, Alba, no more than a few months old. Valentina's expression was soft with tenderness and she radiated a fierce, protective love that seemed to extend beyond the paper and pastels and reach her now, where she sat alone by the window, twenty-six years later.

'She loved you intensely,' said Immacolata, hobbling over to sit beside her. 'You symbolized a new beginning. The war was over. She wanted to start again, be someone else. You were the anchor she needed, Alba.' Alba didn't understand, but it sounded nice.

'I've always wondered what kind of mother she was,' she said quietly.

'She was a good mother. God gave her a child to teach her compassion, selflessness, and pride. She put you first, above everything else, even herself. Perhaps that is why He took her back, because she had learned the lesson she came here to learn.'

'It's a beautiful picture.'

'I'll get Falco to make a copy. It's a wonder what things they can do nowadays.'

'I'd so adore one. My father has the only other one. I have nothing.' Immacolata took her hand.

'You have us now, Alba, and I will share my memories with you. I know that is what Valentina would want. You are so like her. So very like her.' Her voice was reduced to a whisper.

'No, I'm not,' Alba replied sadly, recalling with a bitter taste her promiscuous, empty life. 'I'm not like her at all. But I can be. I will be. I'll change and become a good person. I'll be everything she would want me to be.'

'Alba, my child, you are already everything she would want you to be.'

Suddenly the scent of figs blew in through the open window, even stronger than before. Immacolata took the picture and replaced it carefully behind the dancing flame so that Valentina's face was illuminated. 'Come,' she said. 'Let me show you to your room.'

21

Immacolata led Alba up a narrow stone staircase. The house was old, far older than Immacolata herself. It smelled of age, of time ingrained into the very fabric of the building. Immacolata climbed slowly and Alba had to restrain her impatience, for each step brought her closer to her mother.

Finally they crossed the landing to a bleached oak door. Immacolata reached underneath the black shawl she wore and pulled out a ring of heavy keys; they rattled metallically on a chain where her waist should have been, as if she were a medieval jailer. 'Here we are,' she said softly.

The room was small, with white walls and shutters that were closed. Soft beams of amber light filtered in through the gaps in the wooden slats, giving the room an eerie mistiness. The air vibrated with life, as if the spirit of Valentina still lingered there, clinging on possessively to her lost world. Immacolata lit the candle on the pine dressing table. It illuminated the embroidered linen cloth upon which Valentina's brush and comb, bottles of perfume, flasks of creamy lotions and stout crystal pot of face powder were placed neatly in front of a large Queen Anne mirror. Alba noticed her mother's hair was still entwined within the bristles of the brush. Immacolata shuffled over to the wardrobe that was bleached and carved with vines of grapes. She opened the doors to reveal a row of dresses.

'Valentina had simple tastes,' said her mother proudly. 'We didn't have much. It was wartime.' She pulled out a white dress and held it up for her granddaughter to see. 'She was wearing this when she first met your father.' Alba reached out and ran her fingers over the soft cotton. 'Your father fell in love with her when he saw her in this. She looked like an angel. So pretty. So very pretty, so innocent. I told her to take him down to the river to bathe. It was hot. They needed little encouragement. I knew they wouldn't have much time to get to know each other. I understood that they wanted to be alone.' She crossed herself. 'God forgive me.'

'It's so small. I always imagined she was tall.'

Immacolata shook her head. 'She was Italian. Of course she wasn't tall.' Her arthritic hands rifled through the other dresses until she came across a black one embroidered with white flowers. 'Ah,' she sighed wistfully. 'This she wore to the *festa di Santa Benedetta*. Your father accompanied her. I helped sew daisies into her hair and rub oil into her skin. She was radiant. She was in love. How could she have known how it would all end? Her future held such promise.'

'What is the *festa di Santa Benedetta*?' Alba asked, watching Immacolata replace the dress carefully in the cupboard.

'You are descended from Santa Benedetta, a simple peasant girl who witnessed a miracle. The marble statue of Christ that stands in the little chapel of San Pasquale shed tears of blood. It was a miracle, God's way of showing the people of Incantellaria that His power was total. Every year the statue wept. Sometimes the blood was a mere drop; then the fishermen would harvest few fish, or the water turned sour, or the grape *vendemmia* poor. If the blood was shed in abundance, the year that ensued was golden. Incantellaria produced juicy grapes and barrels of olives. The lemons grew heavy and succulent; the flowers blossomed more radiant than ever. They were good years. Then there was the year he shed not a drop, not a single drop. We waited, we watched, but he had written what was to come and He punished us by taking our most precious Valentina.' She crossed herself again. 'He has not bled for twenty-six years.'

Alba was slightly spooked by her grandmother's devoutness. Alba rarely mentioned God, except when she swore, so Immacolata's simple peasant beliefs seemed absurd to her. Her eyes shifted to the end of the bed where a wicker Moses basket stood on a stand. She sat on the bed and peered inside to the white sheet and woolen crocheted blanket.

'This was mine?' she asked in wonder, picking up the blanket and bringing it to her nose so that she could smell it.

Immacolata nodded. 'I kept everything,' she said. 'I needed something to hold on to after she was gone.' The two women looked at each other. 'You have made me very happy. My little Alba.' She stroked her granddaughter's cheek with her thumb. 'Let me show you where you can have a bath. You can borrow Valentina's nightdress tonight, then tomorrow we will buy you some clothes to wear, *va bene?*' Alba nodded. 'Come. We will eat.'

As they walked onto the terrace, the shrill sound of a child rang out to the accompaniment of a chorus of crickets. 'Ah, Cosima,' said Immacolata, and her expression softened like snow caught in a ray of sunshine. A little girl skipped out from behind a cluster of bushes, followed by a small red dog. She saw her great-grand-mother and hurried up to her, breathless with giggles, her dark, honey-coloured curls bouncing about a round, rosy face, her pale blue and white dress flapping around her knees. *'Nonnina! Nonnina!'* Instinctively she stopped before falling into the old woman's arms, knowing that her enthusiasm would unbalance her. Immacolata placed her hand on the child's head and bent to kiss it. She turned to Alba.

'God took my Valentina, but He blessed me with Cosima.' The little girl stared at Alba, her brown eyes wide and curious. 'Cosima, this is Alba. She is your . . .' Immacolata paused, unable to work out the relationship. 'Cousin. Alba is your cousin.'

Alba had never liked children. They never seemed to like her much either. But the vulnerable expression in Cosima's eyes, a blatant desire to be loved, like a puppy or a young calf, took her by surprise. She had a mischievous face with pretty curled lips. Her upper lip was plumper than the lower one and her nose was slightly upturned. Like Alba, she had charm. Unlike Alba, she was unaware of it. Cosima, noticing that she was being stared at, smiled shyly and blushed.

'Who's this?' Alba asked, bending down and patting the dog.

'Cucciolo,' the child replied, drawing close to her grandmother. 'He's a dragon.'

'He looks very frightening,' said Alba, playing along with the joke. Cosima giggled and looked up at her from under thick black eyelashes.

'Don't be frightened, he won't hurt you. He's a friendly dragon.'

'I'm so pleased. I was rather nervous. After all, I've never seen a real dragon before.'

'He frightens the hens, and Bruno.'

'Who's Bruno?'

'The donkey.'

'You have lots of animals.'

'I love animals,' she said, her little face beaming with pleasure. When she walked toward the tethered donkey, Alba noticed she bounced on the balls of her feet. The exuberant gait of a child without cares.

It wasn't long before Falco appeared with Beata and their son, Toto, whose wife had run off with the Argentinean tango dancer. He was a handsome young man, five years older than Alba, with brown curly hair and a wide, open face like his daughter. On seeing her father, Cosima threw her arms around his waist. 'Alba is frightened of the dragon!' she squealed, nestling her face excitedly into Toto's stomach so that her giggles were muffled against his shirt. He wrapped her in his arms and lifted her off the ground.

'Well, you had better tell him to behave, or she might run away.'

'Alba is not going anywhere,' said Immacolata, sitting down at the head of the table where she had sat for the best part of her eighty-odd years. 'She is home now.'

Toto shook her hand and smiled at her warmly. 'From what I remember of your mother, you look very like her,' he said. Alba was surprised that his voice didn't resonate with the same wretchedness as his father's and grand-mother's when they mentioned Valentina.

'Thank you,' she replied.

'I remember your father too, on account of his uni-form. He was the most glamorous man I had ever laid eyes on. I couldn't stop staring at him. I remember his humor too, because he was the only one to smile when old Padre Dino farted throughout an entire luncheon.'

'Really, Toto!' Beata protested. But Alba was delighted by her cousin. His earthy presence lifted the heavy atmosphere that Valentina's ghost had placed upon the house.

Immacolata was keen to speak of her daughter. Suddenly, she had the excuse to tell stories and reminisce. Wounds still stung at the mention of her name, like throwing salt water onto cuts that had never been allowed to heal. But Alba forced her to open up the past, and Immacolata succumbed willingly. All the while she told stories illustrating her daughter's virtue, her wisdom, her unparalleled goodness, Falco's face darkened and his mouth thinned into a scowl.

When the women retired to bed, Falco remained at the table, slumped over a glass of limoncello, smoking a cigarette and staring vaguely into the dying flame of the hurricane lamp. Alba's return had been an unexpected blessing. She brought with her joy that she couldn't begin to understand. However, she was also a piercing reminder of a part of his life too terrible to contemplate.

Alba bathed, washing away the emotions of possibly the longest day in her life. It had been heady, fascinating, and somehow dreadful too. If she had thought the ghost of her mother haunted her little houseboat, how much more did it haunt this house. Immacolata had given her matches so that she could light the candle on the dressing table and the one beside her bed, explaining that they hadn't had electricity during the war so she hadn't had it installed in Valentina's room when she renovated the rest of the house. She had wanted to keep it exactly as it was. So when Alba sat in front of the mirror, dressed in her mother's white nightdress, her hair falling over her shoulders, her face pale in the dancing light of the flame, she was almost as frightened by her own reflection as she was by the sense of death that pervaded the little room.

She picked up the hairbrush. It was silver and heavy. With slow, deliberate strokes, she began to brush her hair, watching herself in the mottled glass of the mirror. She knew she was staring at the truest likeness of her mother that she would ever see. More startling perhaps than the portraits, for it was alive and breathing. As she gazed upon it, her eyes grew heavy with sorrow, for she was aware that her mother possessed a virtue that she could never ever possess. If she were alive there was little doubt in Alba's mind that she would be disappointed. Valentina had touched everyone with an effortless, otherworldly grace. If Alba were to die suddenly, what would people remember her for?

That night she slept fitfully. She hadn't imagined that her expedition to find her mother would lead her to search deep within herself. She had hoped to be able to move on, but Valentina's ghost was now haunting her in a way that it had never done before.

When she finally slept, her dreams were strange, incomprehensible, unsettling. When she awoke she was relieved it was day, that the sky was clear and blue and that the sun was shining, throwing light into the shadowy corners of the room.

When Alba wandered out onto the terrace in the yellow sundress she had worn the day before, only Toto and Cosima were up and eating breakfast. The little girl's face expanded into an enormous grin, her pretty pouting mouth revealing pearly teeth.

'Alba!' she exclaimed, climbing down from her chair to embrace her. 'You didn't dream of dragons, did you?' she asked, wrapping her arms around Alba's waist as she had done with her father the previous night.

'No, I didn't.'

'You look tired,' said Toto, chewing on a piece of brioche.

'I didn't sleep very well. I think I was almost too tired to sleep.'

'Well, have some food and then Cosima and I will take you into town if you like. I gather your suitcase got stolen.'

'I need to go to the bank,' she said, sitting down next to Cosima, who had pulled out a chair for her.

'Sure. You can buy now and pay when the money comes through. Your credit is good here.'

It was good to be outside, with the eucalyptus-scented breeze wafting up from the sea. 'It's beautiful here,' she said. 'It pulls at the soul, doesn't it?'

'I would never live anywhere else. It's a quiet life, but I don't hanker after anything more.' He grinned at his daughter. 'It's a good place for a child to grow up. You have lots of friends, don't you, Cosima?'

'Costanza is my best friend,' she said in a serious voice. 'Eugenia wants to be my best friend, but I told her she couldn't be, because Costanza is.' She sighed heavily. 'Costanza doesn't like Eugenia.' She screwed up her nose then forgot her train of thought as Cucciolo trotted out of the house with Falco. Falco smiled, but his eyes remained as hard as stone; there was something about them that reminded Alba of her father.

'I'm going into town with Cosima and Toto,' she said as her uncle sat down and poured himself a cup of coffee. 'Perhaps you can show me the chapel of San Pasquale,' she said. 'It would be nice to see where my parents got married.' Falco put down the coffee pot and stared as if she had struck him on the face. 'Immacolata told me about the *festa di Santa Benedetta*. It all happened in the chapel, didn't it?' she continued, oblivious.

'That miracle ground to a halt years ago,' said Toto with a grin. It was clear that he didn't think much of the medieval ritual either.

'Is my mother buried there?' she asked, directing her question at Falco, who had turned pale.

'No,' he replied flatly. 'She is buried on the hill over-looking the sea. It is a secluded spot where she can rest in peace. There is no headstone.'

'No headstone?'

'We didn't want her disturbed,' he said. 'I'll take you there this afternoon.'

As Toto drove Alba and his daughter down the winding lane to the town, she couldn't help but reflect on the mystery that surrounded her mother's death. She wanted to ask Toto about it, but she felt it wasn't right to speak of such things in front of Cosima. Instead she asked the child about her animals, the real ones as well as the imaginary ones. Cosima leaned through the gap in the seats and chirped with the enthusiasm of a spring bird at dawn.

In town Toto took Alba to the bank and helped her set up an account with the manager, whom he had known since his school days. They were happy to give her credit, having gotten through to her manager in London. Cosima was thrilled to accompany her into the boutique to buy clothes. Having no mother, she was unaccustomed to watching a woman try on dresses and shoes; her great-grandmother only ever wore black. Inspired by the child's enthusiasm, Alba tried on everything, asking her to classify her opinion on each item with a number between one and ten. Cosima squealed with delight, gig-gling at the ones that looked awful, shouting out 'zero' with exuberance. Toto left them alone to browse while he had coffee in the trattoria. Everyone knew Cosima and there were few who hadn't heard of Alba's dramatic arrival the day before. Together they walked hand in hand up the pavement, stopping at each shop, laughing at their reflections in the glass. It hadn't escaped Alba that Cosima could be her daughter. They were very much alike.

'Now I'm going to introduce you to the dwarfs,' Cosima announced merrily.

'The dwarfs?' Alba repeated, not sure she had understood correctly.

'*Si, i nani!*' said Cosima, as if it were the most natural thing in the world. She led her cousin into the dark interior of a cavernous shop that seemed to contain everything, from mops and food to clothes and toys. The woman behind the counter smiled affectionately at Cosima. She didn't look like a dwarf at all. It was only when she stepped out that Alba realized she had been standing on a specially built box, so that she appeared higher. Without her pedestal she was no taller than four feet.

'I am Maria. You are Valentina's daughter,' said the woman eagerly. 'They say you look just like her.'

Before Alba could reply, the rest of Maria's family appeared like mice out of doors hidden among the goods. There must have been about six of them, all four feet tall, with shiny red faces and merry smiles. Alba thought they'd all look wonderful in a garden with fishing rods and funny hats, then curbed her wicked thought, remembering that she was trying to be a good person.

'Do you sell children's clothes?' she asked.

'Oooh! They do!' exclaimed Cosima, disappearing down one of the aisles, her lustrous curls bouncing about her head like springs. Alba, followed by an entire entourage of dwarfs, chased after her. The child was pulling out pretty dresses and holding them up for Alba to see. Her brown eyes were ablaze with hope.

'Okay, Cosima, one to ten. Which ones do you like?' she said, folding her arms and assuming a serious face. At first Cosima didn't know what to do with herself. She had never been offered more than one at a time. Feverish with excitement, she tore off her own dress and stood in her white pants, holding three at once, not sure which to try on first. Helped by Maria and her daughters, the child paraded the dresses like a princess, striding up and down the aisle, twirling around so that they billowed out like pretty flowers. None warranted a zero. Overcome with the pressure of the decision, Cosima was unable to decide.

'I don't know,' she wailed tearfully, her chest expanding as her breath quickened. 'I don't know which to choose!'

'Then we'll just have to buy them all,' Alba replied casually. The child stared at her with eyes as large as moons. Then she burst into tears. Maria wrapped her arms around her, but Cosima pulled away and sobbed against Alba.

'What's the matter?' Alba asked, stroking her hair.

'No one's ever bought me so many dresses before,' she said, swallowing hard. Alba thought of Cosima's mother who had deserted her child for a tango dancer, and her heart buckled.

'Wait until your father sees you in them. We can put on a fashion show this evening. We'll keep it a secret and surprise him.'

Cosima wiped her eyes with the back of her hand. 'Oh, yes, can we?'

'He'll think you've been turned into a princess.'

'Oh, he really will.'

'Now, can you do something for me?'

'Yes.'

'I want you to let me draw you.' Alba hadn't drawn since childhood. She wasn't even sure that she *could* still draw. 'We'll buy paper and pencils and you'll sit for me. Will you do that?' The child nodded enthusiastically. 'You can take me somewhere nice. We'll prepare a picnic and you can tell me all about Costanza and Eugenia and all your other friends at school.'

When they arrived at the trattoria with armfuls of bags Toto's jaw dropped. 'The shops have probably made more today than they make in a month,' he said. Cosima smiled and puffed out her chest. Her father narrowed his eyes. 'What's that face for?' he asked her, pulling her onto his knee.

'A surprise,' she said with a giggle. He looked at Alba and then down at the bags.

'Ah, I see.'

'I lost an entire wardrobe. A girl's got to have clothes,' Alba explained.

'She really does,' Cosima agreed, and her cherubic face glowed with happiness.

Before returning to the house for lunch, Toto and Cosima took Alba to the chapel of San Pasquale. It was in the center of town, up a narrow street that opened into a small yard. Painted white and blue, its symmetry and stoutness gave it a quaint charm. The mosaic dome soared into the fresh sea air, a serene lookout point for doves and gulls. Alba walked through the heavy wooden door where her mother had stood almost three decades before, dressed in white lace and daisies, to marry her father. She paused a moment and savored the sight of the aisle, imagining it festooned with flowers, the glittering icons and frescoes that decorated the walls, the shining gold candelabra that caught the light and twinkled. The altar stood at the foot of an elaborate altarpiece depicting scenes of the Crucifixion, its starched white cloth neatly laid with gold candlesticks and the highly crafted trappings of ceremony. After the simplicity of the town, the opulence of the chapel was remarkable. However, what drew her attention was the white marble statue of Jesus that had supposedly once wept tears of blood. She strode up to it, her espadrilles soft on the flagstones.

It was smaller than she had imagined, with no sign of tears, blood or otherwise. She craned her neck to look behind it, searching for some explanation, for some proof of trickery.

'There's nothing there,' said Toto, appearing beside her while Cosima sat at the back, guarding the shopping bags with her life.

'Did it really happen?' Alba asked.

'Oh, I don't doubt that something happened. I just doubt that it was inspired by God.'

'But it hasn't happened in years?'

'Not since Valentina's death.' His tone was matter-offact.

'Immacolata says that it was because of her that the miracle dried up.' Alba ran her fingers over the cold, lifeless stone face of Christ.

'Immacolata is a deeply religious woman. She lost a husband, a son, and then a daughter. It's not surprising that she tries to explain it all in those terms. To her, Valentina is a saint, but she was a human being. A fallible human being like the rest of us.'

'I had no idea how much she had affected Incantellaria.'

'She was beautiful and mysterious and died young. This is a small town, a superstitious town. Her story was a romantic and tragic one. There's nothing quite like the combination of romance and tragedy to touch people. Look at Romeo and Juliet. Then your father took Valentina's baby overseas. It's the stuff of novels.' Alba thought of Viv getting her hands on it and immortalizing it in words.

'And twenty-six years later she comes back,' Alba added.

Toto nodded. 'And the whole damn thing is opened up again.'

'Your father is very sad, isn't he?' she said.

'He's never gotten over her death. Neither has Immacolata. But Immacolata's sorrow is the natural sorrow of a mother bereft of her child. With my father it's like a torment.'

'Why?' she asked, recalling with a strange sense of déjà vu the inconsolable expression on her father's face the evening she had given him the portrait.

He shrugged. 'I don't know.'

22

There was much excitement as Alba helped Cosima into the first of her three new dresses. Immacolata sat at the head of the table with the rest of her family, speculating about the nature of the surprise.

'They're going to be amazed,' said Alba, tying the bow neatly at the back. 'You look like an angel.' She felt the urge to mention the girl's mother. Since she had arrived no one had uttered her name. Cosima acted as if she didn't exist, but Alba knew the truth because she recognized herself in the child's silence. There were questions that simmered inside that would one day boil over and cause everyone pain unless they were answered now, with honesty and sensitivity. 'Now go and show them all how beautiful you look.'

Cosima skipped out into the sunlight, dancing with the light feet of a garden fairy. Her entrance was welcomed with exuberant applause and cries of 'There's more . . .' from Cosima as she dived back into the house to slip into the next dress.

Alba shared Cosima's happiness. She watched the expressions of the child's family; none was more indulgent and delighted than her father's. Alba sighed heavily and cast her thoughts back to her own father. She didn't often dwell on memories; the present was more agreeable. However, she recalled with some surprise the time her father had taken her into the woods behind the house at Beechfield to shoot rabbits. They had walked up the hill hand in hand, his gun slung over his shoulder, his strides long and purposeful, then lain down on their stomachs, the damp grass tickling their chins. The scent of the recently harvested cornfields reached her now from the misty past and caused her head to swim with nostalgia. Her father had shot a rabbit, skinned it, gutted it, and they had built a fire and cooked it, while the sun flooded the countryside and turned it pink. Just the two of them. She remembered it now.

Cosima skipped in again for her third change and Alba was shaken from her thoughts. She helped her wriggle into the last dress. Alba found herself picking up the clothes that the child had left in a heap on the floor and folding them neatly over the back of the chair. She noticed her uncharacteristic tidiness, the almost motherly fussiness, and was surprised at how normal it felt. At the end of the show she came out of the shadows and joined in the applause. Toto thanked her and she knew what was contained within the pauses between his words; he felt his wife's absence ever more acutely now that she was there.

After lunch Immacolata disappeared inside for a nap. Falco offered to take Alba to Valentina's grave. Cosima leaped off her chair, wanting to go too. She looked up at Alba forlornly. But Alba wanted to talk to Falco alone. She suggested that they take a picnic somewhere nice later on in the day, just the two of them. This appeased the child, who watched them walk off through the olive grove, then turned on her heel to play with the donkey.

'She's adorable,' said Alba, hoping to distract him from thoughts of his dead sister.

Falco nodded. 'She's delightful. My son is a good father. It hasn't been easy.'

'He's a tremendous father. He gives her everything she needs.'

'He can't give her everything,' he said gruffly. 'He must remarry and give the child a mother.'

'No one can replace Cosima's mother,' she said a little too quickly, thinking of herself.

'No, of course not,' he replied, looking at her long and hard for a moment. 'But see how she has flourished since you arrived.'

'I've only bought her a few dresses,' she said with a shrug.

'It's more than that. You are young. She needs a young woman to look up to. To set an example.'

'She has Beata, her *nonna,*' Alba suggested, though she knew that the quiet woman's presence around the house was not enough.

'You know you are welcome to invite your friend, Gabriele, whenever you like,' he said and Alba smiled. She knew they all hoped she'd stay.

'Thank you. I might just do that,' she replied, recalling Gabriele's handsome face.

They walked down the hill along a dirt track that cut through the forest. The ringing of crickets resounded through the still, afternoon air that smelled pleasantly of rosemary and pine. Alba felt uncomfortable with Falco. It wasn't that he was disagreeable, although his manner was abrupt, but there was something dark and depressing about him, as if he walked in shadows. Walking beside him, she was cast in shadow too. She felt her spirit grow heavy with doom. She found conversation with him hard. At first, he had been pleased to see her, pleased beyond words. His joy had overflowed in tears, then transformed into raucous laughter. He could cry one moment and howl with amusement the next: wholly unpredictable. Now it was as if the very sight of her reminded him too much of Valentina. She wasn't Valentina. Her presence couldn't bring her back. She wasn't like her. Maybe that had been a disappointment. Perhaps he had hoped for not only a physical likeness but a characteristic one too. Judging from the stories Immacolata had told of her, Alba was a pale reflection. It was a relief they knew nothing about her.

Falco was the same age as her father, late fifties, more or less, and yet they both were old beyond their years. They both stooped in the same way, weighed down by an invisible force that leaned heavily on their shoulders. They both smiled, but their eyes contained an unfathomable disquiet.

The track left the forest and opened into a lemon grove. Up high to the left where the hill rose sharply, the crumbling old lookout point she had seen from the sea stood defiantly against the elements.

'She loved it here,' he said, putting his hands in his pockets. 'She loved the smell of lemons, and of course, the view of the sea is magnificent.' He led her through the grove to the end, by the cliff, where a solitary olive tree stood gnarled and twisted in the sunshine. 'We buried her here.' Beneath the tree was a simple wooden cross that bore her name. He looked out over the ocean, flat and shining like glass. 'She saw your father's boat come in long before anyone else did and ran down to the harbor. If you cut directly down the rock you can get there surprisingly quickly. When Valentina wanted something, she let nothing stand in her way.'

'I'm sure she's happy here. It's very peaceful.'

'The lookout point was a favorite spot too. She spent

many hours there, waiting for your father to return at the end of the war.'

'It's very romantic.' Alba wanted to feel her mother's presence there in the shade of that tree, but all she could sense was the heavy cloud that surrounded Falco. 'Show me the tower?' she asked, turning to walk up the hill. Falco followed her without saying a word.

'Wow! You can see for miles,' she exclaimed exuberantly, filling her lungs with the clean, sea air.

She looked at Falco's anguished features. 'Do I remind you of her?' she asked boldly, her head on one side, frowning. He stared at her, surprised. 'Do you see her every time you look at me? Is that why you're so unsettled?'

He shook his head and shrugged, raising his palms to the sky. 'Of course you look like her, you're her daughter.'

'But does it hurt, Falco? Does my presence here bring it all back?' Her question had caught him off guard.

'I suppose it does,' he replied quietly. She suddenly felt compassion for this big man and wanted to offer words of comfort.

'She's with God now,' she said lamely.

'Yes she is, but we are left in hell.'

The violence of his words struck her and she flinched. She blinked in confusion. There was something he wasn't telling her. Perhaps they had fought the day she was killed. Maybe she died before he could apologize. Wasn't that a common problem for the living?

She turned and looked around. Above them, obscured behind thick forest, were the distant towers and turrets of a palace. 'Who lives there?' she asked, changing the subject.

'No one. It's a ruin.'

'It must have been impressive once.'

'It was, but a feud splintered the family and the palazzo was left to rot.' His voice was flat.

'No hidden treasure then?'

'You couldn't even get there if you wanted to,' he added. 'The forest has taken over.'

'How sad.'

Falco shook his head. 'Come. Cosima will be waiting for you.'

'Thank you for bringing me here,' she said, smiling at him. 'I understand how hard all this must be for you. Loving someone and losing them, the pain never goes away, does it?' He nodded brusquely and walked back down the hill.

As Falco had said, Cosima was waiting for her in the olive grove, a basket of food in her hand. Alba's mood lightened when she saw the small figure, still some way off, standing patiently in the sunshine. The moment the child saw her, she waved her hand excitedly and Alba waved back and hurried on, happy to leave the brooding Falco to continue in shadow alone.

Alba suggested they return to the lookout point. Not only was it exceedingly beautiful but she wanted to be near the twisted olive tree where her mother was buried. Cosima waited for Alba to collect her paper and crayons from the house. When Alba returned she took her hand. 'What have you got in the basket?' Alba asked, peering inside.

'Apples, mozzarella and tomato *panini,* and biscuits.'

'Delicious,' she said. 'A feast!'

'Don't you eat as well in England?' Cosima asked innocently.

'Of course not. Italy is famous for its food as well as the beauty of its countryside, architecture, and language.'

'Really?' she screwed up her nose. 'Language?'

'Absolutely, you should hear some of the other languages. Horrible, like clashing chords. Italian is like music played beautifully.'

'I don't like to listen to Eugenia when she plays her recorder. It hurts my ears.'

'Then be thankful she speaks Italian when she's not playing!'

They settled down beside the lookout point and Cosima bit into an apple. Alba opened the sketchbook and placed a crayon between her thumb and fingers. She didn't know where to start: head, hair, or eyes. She sat and watched the child for a long moment. It wasn't so much her features she felt the need to capture but the expression within them. Cosima's expression was angelic and mischievous as well as slightly imperious. Though, with her mouth full of apple, her cheeks were puffed out like a squirrel's.

'Are you any good?' the child asked in a muffled voice, chewing happily.

'I don't know. I haven't ever drawn before. Not properly.'

'If it's good, can I keep it?'

'Only if it's good. If it's terrible it's going to the bottom of the sea.'

'Like this apple core,' said Cosima, throwing it as far as she could. It landed on rock.

'Nice try.'

'I don't like to stand close to the edge. I might fall off.'

'That would be a great shame.'

'Why do you speak Italian?' Cosima took a *panino* from the basket.

'Because my mother was Italian.'

'Your mother was my great-aunt. Daddy told me.'

'Yes, she was.'

'She was killed.'

'Yes, sadly she died before I could know her. My father married again.'

'Do you like your new mother?'

'Not really. No one matches up to one's real mother. She has always been kind to me, but I suppose I wanted my father all to myself.'

'I have my father all to myself,' Cosima said proudly, smoothing down her new pink dress.

'You're very lucky. He's a good man, your father. He loves you very much.'

As they talked, Alba's hand began to sketch. She didn't concentrate, she just let the crayon wander.

'You must miss your mother,' she said. Cosima's face suddenly turned serious.

'I don't think she's coming back,' she said with a sigh, then added brightly, 'It doesn't matter though, does it?'

'You know, when I was a child no one ever talked about my mother. This made me very sad because I wasn't allowed to remember her. The world of grown-ups can often seem confusing. At least, it was confusing to me. I wanted to be reassured that she loved me and that her dying had nothing to do with me. I didn't want to feel that she had left me. Your mother had good reason to leave, but it wasn't because she wanted to leave *you*. I imagine she knew that she couldn't take you with her. It was better for you to remain here with your family. She must miss you very much.'

Cosima thought about it, her face solemn. This expression wasn't good for the portrait.

Alba stopped drawing. 'What is she like, your mother?'

The child's face opened up again and Alba put her crayon to the paper once again.

'She's very pretty. She likes to wear her hair up. She

has long, shiny hair. I like to wear mine up too. I look like her, I think. At least, that's what everybody says. She used to tell me stories before I went to bed so I wouldn't be frightened. I didn't like it when she shouted at Papa. Papa didn't like it either. She never shouted at me, though.'

'Of course not. Grown-ups shout at each other for the silliest reasons, especially Italians,' said Alba, working on the eyes. Cosima had wide-set eyes like Toto's. They were the softest honey brown.

'She's a good cook,' Cosima continued. Then she laughed. 'Papa said she cooked the best mushroom risotto in Italy.' She paused a moment then added lightly, 'She never bought me three dresses.'

Alba looked up from her drawing. 'She'd be very impressed with those, wouldn't she?'

'She'd brush my hair and wash my face.'

'No point wearing lovely things if your face and hair are a mess.'

'Do you have children?'

Alba smiled and shook her head. 'I'm not married, Cosima.'

'You might marry Gabriele, though.' Cosima giggled mischievously.

Alba was taken aback. 'Who told you about Gabriele?'

'I heard my grandfather talking to Papa.'

'I don't really know Gabriele,' she said. 'I met him in Sorrento and he brought me here in his boat.'

'Papa said you might telephone him and invite him here.'

'He did, did he?'

'Is he handsome?'

'Very.'

'Do you love him?'

Alba chuckled at her innocent questions. 'No, I don't

love him.' Cosima looked disappointed. 'I love a man called Fitz,' she said. 'But he doesn't love me.'

'I'd forget Fitz then. I bet Gabriele loves you.'

'Love is something that grows, Cosima. He hardly knows me.' She shaded in the hair ponderously.

'He can come on one of our picnics if you like. Then you can marry him.'

'I wish life were that simple,' said Alba with a sigh, missing Fitz.

'You know, I'll be seven soon,' chirped Cosima, beginning to tire of sitting for the portrait.

'You're very grown-up!'

'I'll wear one of my new dresses,' she said happily. 'And I'll wear my hair up like Mamma.'

When Alba had finished she held the pad out in front of her to study it from a distance. It was really rather good. This surprised her, for Alba had never been good at anything – except shopping. Cosima stood behind her and breathed heavily over her shoulder. 'That's brilliant!' she exclaimed.

'It is brilliant, isn't it?'

'You won't throw it into the sea, will you?'

'No, I don't think so.'

'Can I have it?'

Alba was reluctant to part with it. 'Well, all right,' she conceded. 'If you bring me a *panino*?'

They walked down the hill to the olive tree. 'This is where my mother is buried,' she told Cosima. It was strange to think she was under her feet, the closest they had been for twenty-six years.

'She's not in there!' Cosima exclaimed. 'She's in Heaven.'

'I like to think of her there too,' she said, but privately she thought Valentina's spirit lingered in the house amid the candles and shrines and the memorial Immacolata had made of her room.

As Alba walked down the path toward the town, having left Cosima at the house with her animals and the portrait to show her family, she found her thoughts returning to Fitz. She considered telephoning him. Her spirits were high, having enjoyed a picnic with Cosima, of whom she was growing extraordinarily fond. The beauty of her surroundings was breathtaking. The evening light was pink and wistful and her heart yearned to love. She wished he were there to wrap his arms around her and kiss her in that intimate way of his. She didn't think she'd feel so embarrassed by it now. Perhaps she'd telephone him that evening after all, what was the worst that could happen?

When she got to the trattoria, she was greeted by Lattarullo, who sat on his own, drinking a cup of strong coffee. His shirt was stained with grease and his hair was unkempt, sticking up in grey tufts. He invited her to join him. 'Let me buy you a drink to welcome you to Incantellaria,' he said, beckoning the waiter. 'What will you have?' Although Alba wanted to be on her own to wander about the town where her mother had grown up, she was left no option but to accept his offer.

'I'll have a cup of tea,' she said, sitting down.

'Very English,' he chortled, sniffing and running the back of his hand across his nose.

'Well, I am English, after all,' she replied coolly.

'You don't look English, except for the eyes. They're very strange.' She didn't know whether to take that as a compliment. Lattarullo, who enjoyed the sound of his own voice, continued regardless. 'They're very pale. An odd colour of grey. Almost blue.' He leaned toward her and his coffee breath enveloped her in a malodorous cloud. 'I'd say they were violet. Your mother had brown eyes. You look just like your mother.'

'Did you know her well?' Alba asked, deciding that if she were going to suffer his coffee breath and intrusive observations she might at least get something back.

'I knew her when she was a little girl,' he said proudly.

'So, what was she like?'

'A little ray of sunshine.' *Most unhelpful,* Alba thought. He and Immacolata had the habit of speaking about Valentina in clichés.

'What was her wedding like?' she asked. That, at least, was one question she hadn't asked yet. Lattarullo frowned at her.

'Wedding?' he repeated, looking at her blankly.

'Yes, her wedding.' For a moment she thought she might have chosen the wrong word. 'You know, when she married my father?'

'There was no wedding,' he said in a whisper.

Alba's heart stopped. 'No wedding? Why not?'

He looked at her for a long moment, his face reminiscent of those stuffed fish stuck on the walls of English pubs. 'Because she was dead.'

Alba's face drained of colour. Valentina had never married her father? 'The car crash happened *before* the wedding?' she asked slowly. No wonder her father hadn't wanted her to come to Italy.

'There was no car crash, Alba,' he said. 'Valentina was murdered.'

23

Beechfield Park, 1971

After Valentina's murder, Thomas vowed to himself that he would put the memories of that dreadful time in a trunk, lock it up, and let it sink to the bottom of the sea, like the scuttling of a boat that contains the bodies of the dead. For years he had resisted the macabre temptation to find it, prise open the lock, and rifle through the rusty remains. Margo had rescued him from the dark shadows where he dwelled and brought him, blinking in bewilderment, into a world of light and love, albeit a different kind of love. He never forgot the locked chest, but the memory of it only tormented him in dreams. Then Margo was there to run a soothing hand across his brow, and the chest was willfully discarded in the ever-mounting silt at the bottom of the ocean. He had hoped that when he eventually died the chest would sink into the silt, never to be seen again.

He had not anticipated Alba's determination to dive into those waters. For years he had endeavored to keep her firmly on dry land. But she had found the portrait, the key to the chest, and she knew that somewhere was a lock that fitted it to perfection. He was proud of her intelligence and a part of him admired her resolve; it was the first time in her life that she had demonstrated purpose. But he feared for her. She hadn't the slightest idea of what lay in the chest. That, once opened, it could never be closed. She would learn the truth and have to live with it, even rewrite her own past.

Now Thomas was left with no choice but to drag the chest out of the sea, brush off the silt and coral that had grown up around it, and open it again. The mere thought of it caused his skin to bristle and turn cold. He lit a cigar and poured himself a glass of brandy. He wondered whether Alba had found Immacolata. Whether she was still alive. Perhaps Lattarullo was there too, retired maybe, chatting as he did without caring whether or not anyone was listening. He thought of Falco and Beata. Toto would be grown up now, perhaps with children of his own. After Valentina's death they might have decided that living on in that peculiar place would only bring them unhappiness. Alba might never find them. He hoped, for her sake, that she'd return with her imagination still fresh and innocent for, although he had never lied to her, he had never corrected her own childish version of the truth. He hadn't told her that he had never married her mother. That she had been murdered the night before the wedding. After all, he had done it for her. He was protecting the secure world he had built for her. If she discovered the truth, would she understand? Would she ever forgive him?

Puffing on his cigar, he sat back in his leather chair. Margo was out with the horses and he was alone, the chest at his feet, the key in his hands. All he had to do was turn the lock and lift the lid. He didn't need to look at the portrait, for her face was as clear now as if she were standing before him. Once again the warm scent of figs enveloped him, transporting him back to Incantellaria. It was evening.

*   *   *

He'd be married in the morning. His heart was full and bursting with happiness. He had forgotten the *festa di Santa Benedetta*. The disastrous moment when Christ had refused to bleed. He had ignored Valentina's strange words. Now he put the key in the lock, lifted the lid, and remembered them, pondering their significance.

'We need Christ's blessing. I know how to get it. I'll put it right, you'll see.'

Italy 1945

That night Thomas was restless with excitement. He was unable to sleep in the trattoria, for the air was hot and sticky, in spite of the breeze that swept in off the sea. He pulled on a pair of slacks and a shirt and walked up and down the beach, hands in pockets, contemplating his future. The town was silent. Only the odd cat crept silkily across the shadows in search of mice, belly to the ground. The blue boats dragged up onto the beach took on an inky colour in the semi-darkness. The moon was full, the sky deep and glittering with stars that reflected off the gentle waves like gemstones. He recalled his wartime adventures, now an age ago, and felt a moment of guilt that his family were excluded from his wedding. But he would take Valentina and Alba home and surprise everyone. He was sure they would love them as he did.

With a smile he thought of Valentina. He would show her off in town. Take her to church on Sunday, as was tradition, with little Alba in her arms, and everyone would admire her beauty and her poise. They would watch her glide down the aisle in that unique way she walked, as if she had all the time in the world. He would invite Jack for the weekend and they'd share a cigar and a glass of whiskey after dinner in the study. They'd laugh about the war. About the adventures they had. And they'd reminisce about the day Fate took them to the shores of Incantellaria. They would remember Rigs's rendition of *Rigoletto,* the wanton women of the night, and Valentina, as she had been then, standing in the doorway of Immacolata's house in her white dress, semitransparent in the sunlight. Jack would envy him and admire him. *Oh Jack,* he thought as he wandered up the beach, *oh that you were here to share this with me.*

Thomas had left the wedding plans and preparation to Immacolata and Valentina. He knew the little chapel of San Pasquale would be adorned with flowers, Valentina's favorite arum lilies. He knew her dress would be exquisitely made by the ancient but incomparable Signora Ciprezzo, whose fingernails were long and yellowed like old cheese. There would be dancing afterward at the trattoria. He imagined the whole town would be invited. Lorenzo would play the concertina, the children would sip wine, and laughter would resound, the war forgotten, a bright and optimistic future attainable to everyone. Immacolata, Beata, and Valentina had been cooking for days. Marinating, baking, icing, garnishing. There seemed no end to the preparations. So much so that Thomas had barely seen his fiancée. She had left him with Alba while she disappeared into town on an errand or for a dress fitting, skipping happily off down the rocks, waving to him as she went, shouting out instructions for Alba, who was fastidious and indulged.

He looked forward to nights alone with his wife, when he could taste again the salty pleasure of her skin. When he could kiss her mouth knowing that he could take his time, that he wouldn't be interrupted. He looked forward to making love to her. To holding her in his arms as his wife. He looked forward to their belonging to each other by law, as God would be their witness.

If Freddie were alive today, what would he make of her? Knowing Freddie, he would mistrust her beauty and her smile. He hadn't been a romantic, Freddie. He had been a realist. He would have married a woman he had known all his life. A cheerful, earthy woman who would have made a good wife and mother. He hadn't believed in the kind of love that Thomas and Valentina shared. He had thought it a dangerous thing, that ferocious, all-consuming love. Now, when Thomas thought of Freddie, he didn't wince with pain. He had grown to accept his brother's death and although no one could replace him, Thomas's love for Valentina had filled his heart where before it was desolate. But he believed Freddie would have come to love her in the end. It was impossible not to. Freddie would have patted his brother on the back and conceded that he was truly blessed, beyond the expectations of an ordinary man.

It was three in the morning. He didn't want to be tired on his wedding day. In Italy wedding celebrations went on for days, so he needed to muster all his strength. He wandered back up the beach toward the row of buildings that looked out across the sea. Soon it would be dawn and the blue shutters would be thrown open to allow the sun to tumble in. The pots of geraniums that adorned the balconies would be watered and dead-headed, and the cats would return from their night's hunting to sleep there in the warmth. As he walked back to the trattoria he heard the distant though unmistakable music of the concertina. Lorenzo's low, doleful voice rose into the sultry air as he sang words of sorrow and bereavement. His words of death were lost in the echo and Thomas was none the wiser.

Tonight I sleep as a bachelor for the last time, he thought happily. *Tomorrow I will be wed.* He placed his head on the pillow and drifted into a serene and contented sleep.

He awoke a few hours later to frantic knocking on the door. 'Tommy, Tommy!' The voice was Lattarullo's. He sat up in bed, gripped by icy fear. He opened the door to find the carabiniere grey-faced with desolation. 'It's Valentina,' he gasped. 'She is dead.'

Thomas stared at him for a long moment while he tried to make sense of what he had just heard. Perhaps he was trapped within a nightmare. He hadn't woken up properly. He narrowed his eyes and shook his head. 'What?'

Lattarullo repeated what he had just said, then added, 'You have to come with me.'

'Dead? Valentina dead? How?' Thomas felt the world falling away around him as his heart began to unravel, slowly at first and then with frightening speed. He held on to the door frame to steady himself. 'She can't be dead!'

'She's in a car on the road from Naples. We have to go now before ... before ...' He coughed.

'Before what?'

'Before the circus,' said Lattarullo.

'What are you talking about?'

'Just come with me. Then you will understand.' Lattarullo's voice was a plea.

Hastily Thomas pulled on the trousers and shirt he had worn the night before, slipped into his shoes, and followed Lattarullo outside to where Falco waited in the car. Falco's face was white and gaunt. Dark shadows circled his eyes and bore into the hollows of his cheeks. His eyes were raw and shifty. Thomas didn't trust him. The two men exchanged glances but neither spoke. Falco was the first to look away, as if Thomas's stare weighed too heavy with suspicion. Thomas climbed into the back seat and Lattarullo started the engine. The car coughed and wheezed and finally revved sufficiently to start. Dawn was breaking. The sun was pale and innocent as if it knew nothing of the brutal murder it now brought into the light of day.

Thomas had dozens of questions to ask, but he knew he had to wait. His head throbbed as if clamped in a cold metal frame. He wanted to abandon himself to tears as he had done when he heard of his brother's death, but he was unable to let go in the company of Lattarullo and Falco. Instead he clamped his jaw and tried to breathe evenly. What was Valentina doing on the road from Naples in the middle of the night? The night before her wedding? He remembered her words: *'We need Christ's blessing. I know how to get it. I'll put it right, you'll see.'* What had she meant? Where had she gone? He felt his stomach plummet with regret. He should have asked her. He should have paid more attention.

Finally, he could take the suspense no longer.

'How did it happen?'

Falco groaned and rubbed his forehead. 'I don't know.'

Thomas was irritated. 'For God's sake, this is my fiancée we're talking about,' he shouted. 'You must know something! Did the car fly off the road? There are no barriers to prevent an accident . . .'

'It wasn't an accident,' Falco said in a quiet voice. 'It was murder.'

When they arrived at the scene, the first thing Thomas noticed was the car. It was a convertible burgundy Alfa Romeo with an exquisite leather and walnut interior. It was parked neatly in a turnout overlooking the sea. When he saw the woman lying slumped in the passenger seat his heart momentarily inflated with joy. It wasn't Valentina. Of course it wasn't she. Here was a woman with her hair piled on top of her head, her wrists and fingers and ears sparkling with diamonds, her face painted like a whore's with black kohl and crimson lipstick. Her neck had been sliced with a knife and blood had stained the front of her sequined evening dress and the white fur stole that was draped over her shoulders like a slaughtered beast. Her cheeks were as white as the stole. Beside her was a man he did not recognize, elegant, with grey hair and a thin grey mustache. Blood dribbled out of his mouth. It had already dried on the ivory silk scarf that was tied around his neck. Thomas looked at Falco and frowned.

'That's not Valentina,' he began, then suddenly felt his heart wrenched from his chest. Falco simply stared back.

Thomas looked again into the car. He had been wrong. It was Valentina, but not the Valentina he knew.

'My favorite stone is a diamond. I would like to wear a necklace of the finest diamonds just to sparkle for a night, to know what it feels like to be a lady.'

It was then that he opened the car door and fell onto her body, weeping in despair and disbelief, grieving for the woman he knew and for himself, so cruelly betrayed. He clung to her, still warm and soft and smelling strongly of a perfume he didn't recognize. How could Valentina dress like this? What was she doing in this car with this strange man? The night before her wedding? Nothing made sense. He shook her, as if he could wake her. Wasn't his love enough?

He felt rough hands as they pulled him off her and dragged him away. Suddenly the car was surrounded by men in blue uniforms and hats. Police cars had drawn up, their sirens wailing. The press had arrived from Naples too and there were cameras, flashbulbs, raised voices. In the midst of all this chaos it started to rain, and detectives hurried to cover the crime scene before the deluge destroyed the evidence.

Thomas was cast aside like an extra in a movie. He watched in confusion as the police hovered about the dead man. No one seemed to take any notice of Valentina. Then he saw a couple of men gesticulate crudely at her before erupting into raucous laughter. He realized that while he was dwelling in a Hell of fire and pain, everyone else around him was celebrating. There were smiles, pats on backs, jokes. A fat detective in a long coat rubbed his hands together before lighting a cigarette beneath his hat, as if to say, *Right, all done here, case solved.*

Thomas staggered over to him. 'Do something!' he yelled, his eyes bulging with fury.

'And you are?' the detective replied, studying him with narrow, intelligent eyes.

'Valentina is my fiancée!' he stammered.

'*Was* your fiancée. That woman's not in a position to marry anybody.' Thomas's mouth opened and closed like a drowning man's, but nothing came out. 'You're a stranger here, aren't you, *signore*?' he continued. 'The woman is of no importance to us.'

'Why not? She's been murdered, for God's sake!'

The detective shrugged. 'She was simply in the wrong place at the wrong time,' he said. 'Pretty girl. *Che peccato!*'

As the rain fell, dripping down his hair and into his eyes, Thomas stumbled over to Falco and grabbed the collar of his shirt.

'You know who did this!' he hissed.

Falco's big shoulders began to shudder. The iron backbone that held him up began to melt and he hunched forward, hugging himself. Thomas was stunned to see such a powerfully built man cry and felt a surprising sense of relief as he too began to sob like a child. They clung to each other in the rain.

'I tried to tell her not to go!' Falco howled. 'She did not listen.'

Thomas was unable to speak. Desolation had winded him. The woman he was set to marry had all the time loved another and for that she had paid with her life. He withdrew from Falco's embrace and vomited onto the ground. Someone had cut through Valentina's soft, delicate throat with a knife. The brutality of the killing, in cold blood, left him crazed with anguish. Whoever had robbed Valentina of her future had stolen his too.

He tried to picture her gentle face but could only see the mask that lay slumped in the front of the Alfa Romeo. The mask of the stranger who had lived a parallel life about which he knew nothing. As he stood bent over the wet ground, the fog began to clear:

'War reduces men to animals and turns women into shameful creatures . . . I don't want her to make the mistakes that I have made in my life . . . You don't know me, Tommy.'

She was desperate to be taken away from Incantellaria. Was that all he was to her? A ticket to a new life where she could start afresh and leave her sordid, shameful ways behind her?

He felt a hand on his back and turned to see Lattarullo standing beside him in the rain. 'I never knew her, did I?' he said, looking at the carabiniere in desolation.

Lattarullo shrugged. 'You are not alone, Signor Arbuckle. None of us did.'

'Why do they behave as if she doesn't matter?' The police still buzzed around the dead man like wasps about a honeypot.

'You don't recognize him, do you?'

'Who is he?' Thomas blinked at him in innocence. 'Who the devil is he?'

'That, my friend, *is* the devil. Lupo Bianco.'

Later when Thomas returned to the trattoria like a sleepwalker, he collected together the portraits of Valentina that he had drawn. The first was an illustration of her virtue and mystery, drawn the morning after the *festa di Santa Benedetta* on the cliffs by the lookout point, more lovely than the dawn but, as he now reflected, just as transient. The second was an illustration of motherhood. He had captured to perfection the tenderness in her expression as she had watched her baby suckling her breast. Her love for their daughter was genuine, unadulterated, pure. Perhaps it had even surprised her in its intensity. He rummaged around for the third, then remembered Valentina had taken it home with her.

Immacolata's house was as still and quiet as a tomb. The old widow sat in the shadows, erecting a shrine for her daughter to accompany the two she had already made for her husband and son. Her eyes were fixed on her task with dull resignation. When Thomas approached her, she spoke in a soft voice. 'I am called a widow because I lost my husband but what am I now that I have lost two children? There is no word because it is too terrible to articulate.' She crossed herself. 'They are together with God.' Thomas wanted to ask her whether she knew about Valentina's double life but the old woman looked so fragile sitting there in her own private Hell that he couldn't bring himself to ask.

'I would like to see Valentina's room,' he said instead.

Immacolata nodded gravely. 'Up the stairs, across the landing to the left.' He left her with her candles and chanting and climbed the staircase to the room Valentina had occupied only the evening before.

When he entered her small room, the shutters were closed, the curtains drawn, her white nightdress laid out on the bed in preparation for the night. On the dressing table lay her brushes and bottles so recently used. His throat grew tight and he found it difficult to breathe as the room filled with the scent of figs. He sank onto the bed and pulled her nightdress to his face, inhaling her fragrance.

To find the missing portrait became an obsession. He pulled out every drawer, searched through the clothes in her wardrobe, looked under the bed, beneath the sheets and rug, everywhere. He did not leave a single thing in the room unturned. It was not there.

24

Italy 1971

Alba made her excuses and left Lattarullo, having barely touched her tea. The retired carabiniere watched her go, amazed that she hadn't known the terrible circumstances of her mother's death. The violence of it still touched him to this day. He often thought about it. Valentina had been the personification of beauty and grace, in spite of the secret world she had inhabited. It was only a matter of time before a grubby-nosed journalist burrowed about in her business and exposed her in *Il Mezzogiorno*. Lorenzo added another few verses to the ballad he had composed, about premonition, murder, and the underworld of a woman as lovely as a field of wild violets. He had sung it nightly, his plaintive voice resounding through the town until everyone knew it by heart and Valentina transcended normal memory to live on in legend. Her delicate footprints were stamped all over the town. Little had changed in the years since she had died. Everything reminded him of her and sometimes, in the silver glow of a full moon, he believed he had seen her slipping stealthily around a corner, the white fabric of her dress catching the light and his imagination. Valentina had been like a rainbow that appears solid from a distance but vanishes the moment one gets close. An impossible sylph, an exquisite rainbow – her murder served only to make her more mysterious.

Alba ran up the rocks toward Immacolata's house, her heart pounding. Her father had lied to her, her step-mother had colluded, even Falco and Immacolata had withheld the truth. Did they think her a simpleton? She had a right to know about her mother. She thought of Fitz and Viv; even they, in their wildest dreams, would never have envisaged this.

Her feet slipped on the rocks and she grazed her knee, drawing blood. She swore loudly but brushed herself off and continued, determined to extract the whole truth from Falco. When she arrived at the house, Beata was under the trees reading to Cosima. The little girl was curled up against her grandmother, sucking her thumb.

'Where's Falco?' Alba demanded. Beata looked up from her book. When she saw Alba's pink face and glassy eyes her own face darkened and she stiffened like an animal sensing danger. Cosima watched her cousin with a serious expression.

'He's in the lemon grove,' she said and watched as Alba hurried down the path and disappeared into the trees.

'Is Alba angry?' Cosima asked.

Beata kissed her temple. 'I think she is, *carina*. Don't worry, she'll smile again, I promise.'

Alba ran through the lemon grove until she found Falco. When he saw her, he let go of his wheelbarrow and braced himself. He had feared this from the moment she had arrived. 'Why the hell didn't you tell me that my mother was murdered?' she shouted, putting her hands on her hips. 'When were you going to tell me? Or weren't you intending to tell me at all, like my father?'

'Your father only wants to protect you, Alba,' he said brusquely, setting off through the orchard toward the cliffs. Alba followed.

'So, who murdered her?'

'It's a long story.'

'Good. I have as long as you need to tell it.'

'Let us go and sit somewhere peaceful.'

'I want the truth, Falco. I have a right to know.'

Falco put his hands in his pockets. 'You do have a right to know. But it's not pleasant. You will see. It's not simply that your mother never lived to marry your father. That her life was so brutally taken from her. That's only the tip of the iceberg. Come, let us sit here.' He sat down beneath the tree where Valentina's body lay buried. Alba sat beside him, cross-legged, and raised her eyes to him expectantly.

'So, why was she murdered?' she asked. Her tone of voice was flippant, as if she were discussing a character in a novel rather than a real person, still less her mother. The cracks where Falco's heart had never mended opened again and stung.

'She was killed with a knife to her throat.' He drew a line with his finger across his own neck and watched the colour in Alba's cheeks turn to grey. 'She had been in Naples with her lover, the infamous Mafia boss, Lupo Bianco.'

'Lupo Bianco? Who's he?' Alba interrupted. 'I can't believe she took a lover the night before she was to marry my father.'

'She had been Lupo Bianco's mistress for some time.'

'So, who was he?'

'Probably the most powerful man in the south. I knew Lupo myself as a boy. We fished together. He enjoyed watching suffering, even then. First fish, later people. He cared little for life. He was wanted by the police for terrible crimes. Slippery as an eel, no one could ever pin anything on him. He profited greatly from the war. Made millions through extortion, racketeering, even murder.

He hid it all in secret bank accounts that have never been found. Whoever killed him did the police a favour, though it ignited a terrible feud between Lupo's successor, Antonio Il Morocco, and the Camorra of Naples. A feud over tuna prices which still rumbles on today.'

'Did my father know?'

'He found out the morning of her death.'

'Poor Daddy!' she sighed. 'I never realized.'

'She lay dead in Lupo Bianco's car, dripping with furs and diamonds. It was a terrible shock for him. But it didn't surprise me. I understood Valentina better than anyone. She wasn't a bad person; she was weak, that's all. She was beautiful and she loved beautiful things. She loved attention; she loved intrigue and adventure. She wanted to leave Incantellaria. She was too intelligent for a small place like this. She was like a bird whose wing-span was never allowed to spread to its full capacity. She was diminished here. She could have shone in Rome or Milan or Paris, even America. She was far too exceptional to be understood by these simple folk. Above all, though, she loved love. She was lonely. She was like an empty honeypot, always relying on others to fill her up. But she was a survivor and as cunning as a fox. Remember, it was wartime.' He shook his head, his thick, curly hair falling over his eyes. 'Perhaps I should have tried harder to stop her, but I had my own battles to fight.'

'Didn't she love my father at all?' she asked in a small voice.

Falco touched her arm tenderly. 'I think it was only after he left that she realized she loved him. Then she discovered she was pregnant and you, Alba, were her greatest joy.' Alba lowered her gaze and fixed it on the grass in front of her. 'She made sure that she ate healthily, as healthily as one could in the wartime. Thanks to her connections with Lupo Bianco and others she obtained food on the black market and an American supplied her with the medication she needed.'

'Did she continue her affair while she was carrying me?'

He said nothing. She bit the skin around her thumbnail pensively.

'You were born at home, delivered by Mamma and a midwife. From that moment on she saved herself for your father. She had plans, you see. She was going to live in England and raise a family. She was going to be respectable – a lady. Your father had told her about this great house she was going to live in. She was excited. Once you were born, nothing else mattered but you and your father. When he returned they only had eyes for each other and for you. They'd sit under the trees in the garden and watch you sleeping. You were their obsession. He'd draw her and they'd talk. But she told him nothing of her secrets. She didn't want to spoil it. I tried to convince her to tell him the truth. I was sure that if he really loved her he would only want to take her away from here where she would be safe and looked after.'

'So why was she murdered?'

Falco paused a moment and stared out to sea. His face hardened and his eyes suddenly looked dark and haunted. 'I fought with her a lot in the last few days. I told her she had to tell him the truth. She wouldn't listen. Valentina was as stubborn as a mule when she wanted to be. There was a part of her that was strong and determined. She didn't look like she could swat a fly, but beneath the angelic veneer was a sometimes hard and selfish woman. Then she had this ridiculous idea of coming clean with her lover. As if by telling him of her plans she would somehow redeem herself in God's eyes. You see, the statue of Christ remained dry.'

'The famous *festa di Santa Benedetta*, I know all about it,' she said. 'My mother saw it as a bad omen?'

'She was very superstitious. She believed it augured badly for the wedding and for her future. She went to Naples to tell Lupo Bianco that she was leaving Italy.'

'Dressed in furs and diamonds?'

'Let's just say she dressed for the moment, Alba. She was an actress.' He pursed his lips in bitterness. 'I've sometimes wondered whether she just wanted to go out on the tiles one last time. Perhaps she loved Lupo Bianco too, in her way. Maybe that final adventure had nothing whatsoever to do with superstition.'

'Would she have risked everything just for that?' Alba was shocked.

'Valentina? Absolutely. It was just another role she played, perhaps one she relished most. She would never be that person again. She was going away to be a lady. Maybe the temptation was just too much for her to resist.'

'So she was murdered because she was in the wrong place at the wrong time?'

'That's what the police said. She was killed because she saw who killed Lupo Bianco. She knew too much. It's as simple as that.'

Alba shook her head in disbelief. 'If she hadn't gone out that night, she'd be alive today.'

'Now you know the truth, surely you understand why your father kept it all from you? He swore the day she died that he would protect you from the horrors of her past.' He squeezed her hand. 'He did the right thing.'

Alba sat in front of the mirror in Valentina's small bedroom. She stared at her reflection, the image of her mother. Since learning the truth, she realized that she was exactly like her. Not only physically but in her faults as well. And she had believed her mother to be a paragon of virtue, an angel, and herself unworthy. She had despised her empty, drifting life and her alley cat immorality. The more she had reflected on her mother's perfections, the more imperfect she had become, knowing she could never match up. Yet, all along, her father must have seen the life she led and thought how like her mother she was. He must have despaired.

And what of Margo? Alba was filled with shame. Margo knew the truth and had wanted to protect her from the sordid details of her mother's past. She had only tried to give her a good home and a solid family. Alba sank her head into her hands as she now reflected on the tactlessness of handing Valentina's portrait to her father, expecting him to sit by the fire and tell her charming stories about a woman whose secret life had held so little charm. She wept as she thought of the hurt she had caused him over the years, picking as she had so often done at the raw wound that Valentina had left in his heart.

What would Fitz think of her now? She was no better than her mother had been. Fitz deserved someone better, unselfish, not like her, not like her mother. She picked up a pair of scissors and began to hack off her hair.

She watched entranced as the feathery pieces fell onto the dressing table. A thin scattering at first and then large, thick clumps. She had a lot of hair. Once the length was cut she concentrated on evening it out around her scalp. She didn't care how she looked. She no longer wanted to be beautiful. She no longer wanted to manipulate, to beguile, to hold men in her thrall. She wanted people to judge her on herself, not on a superficial and undeserved beauty. Like Valentina, she wanted to start again. Unlike Valentina, she had the chance.

Fatman's words now resurfaced to terrorize her. '*If you suck my cock I'll pay for your flight home.*' She blushed as if he had only just said it. In the course of a few days her whole life had been turned upside down. Things she had believed in were no longer true. She looked at herself differently. She moved her head in the mirror and considered her new image. Like a snake, she had shed her old skin and felt renewed, liberated. No one could say she now looked like her mother. No one would comment on her beauty, either. She smiled at her reflection and wiped her face with a towel, then went downstairs to find Immacolata.

When Cosima saw her she squealed in amazement. 'Alba's cut off all her hair, *nonna*!' Beata came in from the garden and Immacolata bustled out of the *salotto*. Alba stood at the bottom of the stairs, her hair short and spiky and uneven, but with a poise she hadn't had before.

'What have you done to your beautiful hair, my child?' Immacolata asked, shuffling over to her.

'I think she looks beautiful,' said Cosima with a smile. 'Like a pixie.'

Immacolata walked slowly over to Valentina's shrine and took the portrait in her hands. She sat down carefully and patted the sofa for Alba to join her. 'You have been talking to Falco,' she said gravely. 'Listen, Alba, your mother was a mass of contradictions. In spite of everything, she had a big heart and she loved you and your father very much.'

'But she tricked him. She had a lover.'

Immacolata took her granddaughter's hand. 'My child,' she said softly. 'How could you possibly understand what it is like to live through a war? Things were very different then. There was starvation, death, barbarity, hopelessness, Godlessness, all manner of evils. Valentina was vulnerable. Her loveliness made her vulnerable. I could not protect her from soldiers. Nor could I hide her away. Sharing the bed of an important, powerful man was her only means of survival, you have to understand that. Think of her in the context of her time. Try.' Alba stared down at the face her father had drawn so blindly.

'Falco said she loved my father,' she said.

'She did, Alba. Not at first. I encouraged her. I told her that she could do a lot worse than marry a fine, handsome English officer. But she fell in love with him all on her own.'

'So, you knew all along?'

'Of course I knew. I knew Valentina better than I know myself. A mother's love is unconditional, Alba. Valentina loved you the same. Had she watched you grow up, she would have loved you in spite of your faults. Perhaps even more so because of them. Valentina wasn't an angel, she wasn't a saint, she was a fallible human being like the rest of us. What made her different was her ability to change. But if any one of them got close to the real woman, it was your father because he made her a mother. That stripped her of all pretense. Her love for you was pure and unpremeditated.'

'I'm no better than she was, *nonna*,' said Alba. 'That is why I have cut off my hair. I don't want to be her. I don't want to be beautiful like her. I want to be me.' Immacolata ran an unsteady hand down Alba's young cheek, gazing upon her features with watery eyes.

'You still look beautiful, Alba, because your beauty comes from in here.' She pressed a clenched fist against her own chest. 'Your mother's beauty came from there too.'

'My poor father, he was only trying to protect me.'

'We all were. Your father was right to take you to England. As much as it hurt us, he did the right thing. It would not have been healthy to grow up under so dark a shadow. Everyone knew about the murder; they talked of nothing else. The papers were full of stories of Valentina's affair. She was portrayed as a whore. Not one article mentioned her heart. How big it was. How full. Not one of them mentioned what she gave, just what she took. It would have been wrong for you to live with that. You grew up ignorant and free. Now you have come back old enough to cope with the truth. I have missed the first twenty-six years of your life, but I sacrificed them willingly, knowing you were safe.'

Now it was Alba's turn to take her grandmother's hands in hers. 'It is time to let her go,' Alba said, her eyes sparkling with emotion. 'It is time to set her free. I feel her spirit lingers here in this house, casting a dark and unhappy shadow over us all.'

Immacolata thought for a moment. 'I can't get rid of the shrine,' she protested.

'Yes, you can. You must. Let's blow out the candles, open the windows and remember her with joy. I suggest we have a service in the little chapel to commemorate her. Let's have a party. Give her a good send-off.'

Despite her tears, Immacolata grew enthusiastic. 'Falco can share his memories. The good ones. Ludovico and Paolo can come and stay with their families. We can eat in the garden, a banquet.'

'Let's give her a proper headstone and plant flowers.'

'Lilies were her favorites.'

'And violets would be nice. Wild ones. Lots of them. Let's make it beautiful.'

Immacolata's face blossomed. 'You're so wise, Alba. I

could never have predicted that your coming would change so much.'

That evening the family stood together in the *salotto*. Cosima held Alba's hand, Beata took her son's, Falco remained alone with his thoughts. Immacolata took Valentina's candle in trembling hands. The flame had burned constantly since the morning of her death, twenty-six years before. Even when the wax had melted right down to the wick, another had been lit with the same flame and put in its place. Immacolata had never once let the candle go out.

She mumbled a long prayer and crossed herself vigorously. She swept her eyes over her family, resting them on her eldest son. 'It is time to let the past go,' she said, without taking her eyes off him. 'It is time to let Valentina go.' Then she blew out the candle.

They all stood very still, staring at the smoking wick. No one spoke. Then a cool gust of wind blew open the window, lifting Valentina's portrait off the wall, carrying it into the air for a moment then dropping it on to the floor where it lay, face down. The air was filled with the heavy, unmistakable scent of figs. The women smiled. Then the scent was gone and in its place was the common smell of sea air.

'She has gone to the light,' Immacolata announced. 'She is at peace.'

That night when Alba went to bed she noticed at once that the air in the room no longer held the weight of Valentina's troubled spirit, or her perfume. The window was open and the cool night air entered with the distant roar of the sea. It felt empty, like any other room, as if the memories themselves had gone. She felt elated. She sat on the bed and rummaged about in the drawer for a piece of paper and a pen, then began a letter to her father.

She was just signing her name at the bottom of the page when the door to her room opened with a creak. Cosima was standing in her white nightdress, clasping an old rag doll in her hands. 'Are you all right?' Alba asked, noticing the child's anxious face.

'Can I sleep with you tonight?' The small ceremony they held for Valentina had frightened her, Alba thought. She helped the child into bed and then began to undress.

'I used to sneak in here and look at Valentina's clothes,' said Cosima, cheering up at the prospect of not having to sleep alone.

'You did?' Alba was amazed. She didn't imagine the child would know very much about Valentina.

'I wasn't supposed to. *Nonnina* said it was sacred. But I liked to touch her dresses; they are so pretty, aren't they?'

'They really are. She must have looked beautiful in them.'

'I like the box of letters too, but they are written in English so I can't understand them.' Alba looked at her cousin in amazement.

'What letters?' Her heart quickened at the thought of discovering her father's letters to her mother.

'There, in the cupboard.'

Alba frowned. She had been through the cupboards pretty thoroughly. 'I've looked in the cupboard.'

Cosima was pleased to divulge a secret. She opened the cupboard door, swept the shoes aside and removed one of the planks of wood that made up the floor. Alba dropped to her knees and watched, incredulous, as Cosima pulled out a small cardboard box. Eagerly the two girls threw themselves on the bed to open it.

'You are naughty, Cosima,' Alba exclaimed, kissing her. 'But I do love you for it.'

Cosima blushed with pleasure. '*Nonnina* would be very cross!' she giggled.

'That is why we're not telling her.'

Alba felt the same rush of excitement she had felt on first finding the portrait under her bed. She took the paper in her hand. It was stiff and white and when she opened it the address on the top of the page was engraved in black print. It was not an English address. Neither was the writing, neat and precise, in English. Alba felt the blood drain from her face.

'Well?' Cosima insisted.

'It's in German, Cosima,' she said steadily.

'Valentina liked German uniforms,' said Cosima brightly.

'How do you know that?'

She shrugged. 'Daddy said so.'

Alba looked down at the letter. She was intelligent enough to work out that it was a love letter. Judging by the date, it was written just before her father arrived in Incantellaria for the first time. She turned over the page. It was signed *in ewige liebe* – with everlasting love. The name engraved at the head of the page was Oberst Heinz Wiermann.

Valentina hadn't had one lover, she had had two. Perhaps more. When the Allies invaded, the Germans moved north. They lost their power. Colonel Heinz Wiermann was of no use to her anymore.

Alba put the letters back. She couldn't bear to look at them. 'I don't think we should read her private correspondence. Besides, I don't speak German.' Cosima was disappointed. 'I'm tired. Let's go to bed. Have you any more surprises?' she asked.

'No,' said Cosima. 'I painted my face with her makeup once. That's all.'

Alba slipped into her nightdress and climbed into bed beside her cousin. She closed her eyes and tried to sleep, but she suspected that she had only scratched at the surface of a far bigger mystery. Had her mother been an innocent bystander in a Mafia hit over tuna prices? Nothing would be strange in a place where statues bled and carnations were magically swept up on the beach.

But if Valentina hadn't been an innocent bystander, then who had killed her, and why?

25

London 1971

Early summer was Fitz's favorite season. The leaves on the trees were still fresh and new; the blossom had gone but the white petals of the blackthorn sparkled in the morning sunlight. The flower beds burst forth with colour but were not yet overgrown. It was warm but not too warm and the birdsong rang out across the park. The air vibrated with life after the dead cold of winter. It filled him up and infected his step so that he sprang rather than walked. But with Alba gone, he didn't spring. He strolled through Hyde Park and even the flowers and sprouting trees failed to move him. Winter lingered in his bones and in his heart.

He often thought of her among the cypress trees and laburnum, her face enflamed by the setting Italian sun, turning it a gentle shade of amber pink. He imagined her surrounded by her Italian family. Enjoying lengthy banquets of tomato and mozzarella pasta, languid afternoons among the olive trees, blending in with her dark hair and skin, only those pale, luminescent eyes betraying that she was a stranger in their midst. He knew she'd love speaking the language, tasting the food, savoring the scents of eucalyptus and pine, listening to the ringing of crickets and basking in the hot, Mediterranean sun. He hoped that after a while her spirit would hanker for home. Maybe even for him.

He tried to concentrate on work. He set up Viv's book tour in France and, while she was away for the fortnight, sat on the wall of the Thames near Alba's houseboat with Sprout, just watching and remembering and longing, thankful that Viv wasn't at home to scoff at him. Viv argued that Alba was petulant, self-indulgent, wanton, egocentric – the list went on and on as if she were showing off her knowledge of words like a human thesaurus.

Perhaps Alba was all of those things. Fitz wasn't blind to her faults; he loved her in spite of them. Her laugh was light and bubbly like foam, the look in her eyes mischievous, like a child who pushes to see how far she can go. Her confidence a shell to hide behind. When he imagined making love to her his gut twisted with longing. He remembered the wild times in the *Valentina,* the naughty time in the woods at Beechfield, the tender time she was unable to let go, when inhibition had crippled her, for Alba wasn't afraid to shout; she was afraid to whisper, in case in that moment of intimacy she heard the echo of loneliness in her heart. What Viv didn't understand was that he understood Alba.

Viv returned from her book tour revitalized and in devilish good humor. It had taken the years off her too. She shone like a descaled kettle, as good as new. Her eyes sparkled and her cheeks glowed; her obvious health was rude, shockingly rude. Fitz hadn't seen her looking that good in years. When he commented on it she just smiled at him secretively, claimed she had bought a new face cream in Paris, then disappeared. No telephone calls, no bridge nights, no dinners with cheap French wine, just a gaping silence. There was only one explanation: she had found a lover in France. Fitz was jealous, not because he wanted her for himself, but because she had found love when he had lost his. He felt more alone than ever.

Then one hot night at the end of August he was slowly drinking himself numb in a pub in Bayswater, sitting outside on a bench beneath a fountain of red geraniums, when a pretty young woman approached him.

'You don't mind if I share your table, do you?' she asked. 'I'm waiting for a friend and it's completely full.'

'Of course not. Be my guest,' he said, taking his face out of his beer glass.

'Oh, is that your dog?' she asked, spotting Sprout under the table.

'Yes, it is,' he said. 'He's called Sprout.'

Her almond-shaped eyes lit up, the colour of sherry. 'What an adorable name. Mine's Louise.'

'Fitz,' said Fitz, shaking her hand.

They both laughed at the absurdity of such formality. Louise sat down and placed her glass of wine on the table, then dived beneath to pat Sprout, who wagged his tail contentedly so that it tapped the pavement, wafting the dust into a small cloud.

'Oh, he really is sweet,' she gushed, coming back up again. She had long brown hair held back by a yellow hair-band, and when Fitz ran his eyes over her neck and shoulders he saw that she was comely, with large breasts and white, silky skin.

'He's an old man,' Fitz added with a tender smile. 'In dog years he'd be sixty.'

'Well, he's very handsome,' she replied. Sprout knew he was being discussed and lifted his ears. 'Like men, dogs mature well.'

'So do some women,' Fitz said, realizing that he was flirting. He was still capable of it, after all.

Louise blushed and smiled broadly. She looked around, presumably for her friend, then turned back to Fitz. 'Are you on your own?'

'Well, not entirely.'

'Of course, you've got Sprout.'

'I am alone; this is my local.' He didn't want her to think he was one of those sad drunks who sit on their own in pubs and stagger home to grimy, neglected flats and failed lives.

'Lovely to live around here, near the park.'

'Good for Sprout.'

'I live in Chelsea. I'm waiting for the girl I live with.' She looked at her watch. 'She's always late. Born late, I think.' She laughed and lowered her eyes.

Fitz recognized her bashfulness as a sign she fancied him 'I had a girlfriend, but she broke my heart,' he said with a sigh, conscious of the devious game he was now playing.

Her face crumpled with sympathy. 'I'm so sorry.'

'Don't be. It'll mend.'

There are some things women like Louise find irresistible: a man with a broken heart, a child, or a dog. In Fitz's case he had two of the three. Louise stopped looking around for her friend.

Fitz poured out the contents of his heart, finding comfort in the fact that she was a stranger and knew nothing of his life. She listened, intrigued, and the more she listened, the more she was drawn to him, like a person on the edge of a volcano who cannot resist the temptation to peer over and watch the red and gold bubbling of lava. He bought more drinks and then ordered dinner. Her friend failed to turn up, which was a relief, for the more beer Fitz drank, the more appealing Louise became. He felt better for having off-loaded his mind. It felt lighter now that Alba wasn't in it.

At ten o'clock it was almost dark. 'What do you do, Louise?' he asked, realizing that he hadn't asked her anything about herself all evening.

'I work for an advertising company,' she said.

'How exciting,' he replied, feigning interest.

'Not really. I'm a secretary, but I hope to be promoted to an account executive shortly. I have a brain. I'd like to use it.'

'And you should. Where do you work?'

'In Oxford Street. This pub's almost my local too!'

'Stay with me tonight?' he suggested, suddenly serious. 'You can walk to work in the morning. Much better for you than sitting on a bus in the traffic.'

'I'd love to,' she replied and Fitz was astounded at how easily she had yielded. He hadn't lost his touch, then.

'Sprout will be pleased,' he said with a smile. 'He hasn't been this close to a pretty girl for a very long time.'

They walked back to his house. The air was heavy and humid; it would rain soon. He took her hand and it felt nice to have it there, in his. She giggled nervously and toyed with the hair that fell over her shoulder.

'I don't do this often,' she said. 'Go home with strange men.'

'I'm not strange. We know each other now. Besides, you can always trust a man with a dog.'

'I just don't want you to think that I'm loose. I've slept with very few men. I'm not one of those girls who has many lovers.'

Fitz thought of Alba and his heart suddenly felt heavy again. When he'd met her she had had an army of lovers. The gangplank to her door was worn thin with all the coming and going of suitors. His footprints were now lost beneath theirs.

'I don't think you're loose and I wouldn't think less of you if you were.'

'They all say that.'

'Maybe, but I mean it.' He shrugged. 'Why shouldn't women sleep around just like men?'

'Because we're not like men. We should be paragons of virtue. Settle with one man and bear his children. Does a man really want to marry a woman who has had lots of men?'

'I don't see why not. If I loved her it wouldn't matter how many men she'd slept with.'

'You're very open-minded,' she said, looking across at him with her eyes full of admiration. 'Most men I know want to marry virgins.'

'How very selfish of them. I don't imagine they're doing much to keep girls in that state, do you?'

At his house he poured two glasses of wine and showed her upstairs to the sitting room. It was small, masculine, decorated in beige and black, with wooden floorboards and white walls. He put on a record and sat beside her on the sofa. The walk back had depressed him. He wished he had not asked her home. Even Sprout knew that this wasn't a good idea.

Still, better get on with it. He knocked back his glass and kissed her. She responded enthusiastically. The novelty of kissing someone new aroused him a little. He undid her blouse and slipped it over her shoulders. Her breasts were restrained in a large white bra. Then her hand was unzipping his trousers and sliding in and he was quickly recharged, forgetting about the oversized breasts in the pleasure of her touch.

They lay back on the sofa, which was deep and comfortable. Louise withdrew her hand, disappearing from view to take him in her mouth. He closed his eyes and let the warm, tingling sensation of arousal wash over him, emptying his mind once more of Alba. Louise might not have slept with many men but she was certainly experienced. Fitz had found an old box of condoms in his bathroom cupboard, dreadful things they were, robbing him of practically all sensation, but in this instance he knew it was right to use one. Louise opened the packet with her teeth, looking up at him flirtatiously from beneath her brown lashes, then fitted it over his penis as if she were putting on a sock.

She mounted him, lifting up her skirt and sitting astride him, her naked breasts white and doughy in the dim light of the sitting room. He closed his eyes to the brown nipples that swung in front of his face, catching every now and then on his nose or lips, and tried to concentrate on keeping his erection. *It must be the beer,* he thought as he felt the slow deflating of his member. As much as she tried, Louise was unable to stimulate him. With an embarrassed cough she let him slither out like a worm.

'It doesn't matter,' she said kindly, climbing off.

'I'm sorry, it must be the beer,' he explained, ashamed. This had never happened before.

'Of course. I don't mind. You're a lovely kisser.'

He forced a smile, watching her pile her breasts back into their slings. 'Can I call you a cab?' he asked, knowing that he should have offered to drive her back to Chelsea. To his shame he couldn't bear to remain with her a moment longer than necessary. He wanted her out of his house as soon as possible. He wanted to forget he had ever met her. *Why did I bother?* he thought miserably as she pulled on her pants and sat down to put on her shoes. *No one can compare with Alba.*

Fifteen minutes later the cab arrived and the driver rang the bell. Those fifteen minutes had been agonizingly awkward. Louise had resorted to commenting on the books in the bookcases. He hadn't even had the energy to tell her that books were his business. Why bother when the relationship had died before it had started? He accompanied her downstairs and bent to kiss her cheek; as he did so she turned her head to the door and his mouth kissed her ear instead. Then she was gone. He closed the door and locked it before climbing the stairs to turn out the lights in the sitting room and switch off the music. What a debacle.

Sprout lay sleeping on the rug, looking very dear with his eyes closed and his greying face all crumpled and warm. Fitz bent down and pressed his face to the dog's head. It smelled familiar and comforting. 'We miss Alba, don't we?' he whispered. Sprout didn't move. 'But we have to move on. We have no choice. We have to forget about her. Someone else will turn up.' Sprout's nose began to twitch in his sleep; he was chasing a rabbit across a field, no doubt. Fitz patted him tenderly, then went to bed.

When he awoke in the morning he was relieved to see his penis standing to attention, proud and majestic.

He was in his office when the telephone rang. His concentration was suffering. His in tray was piled high with documents that demanded his attention: contracts to read, manuscripts from his authors and from those hoping to be represented, letters to write, documents to sign, and a list as long as his desk of telephone calls to make. He watched the pile grow higher and higher, his mind hundreds of miles away, beneath the cypress trees on the Amalfi coast. He put down his pen and picked up the receiver.

'Fitzroy Davenport.'

'Darling, it's Viv.' Her voice was sleepy.

'Hello, stranger.'

'Don't be angry, Fitzroy. Forgive an old bird?'

'Only if I can see you.'

'That's why I'm calling. Dinner tonight, my place?'

'Good.'

'Lovely, darling. Don't bother to bring wine. I've just been given a case of the most expensive Bordeaux. Had half a bottle on my own last night, it's gorgeous. I wrote the most delightful sex scene on the strength of it; it just goes on and on and on and on. Delicious.'

Fitz frowned. Viv sounded more 'Viv' than normal. 'See you later then,' he said, winding up the conversation. When he put down the telephone he felt his spirits lift. Viv was back; he had missed her. With renewed energy he picked up the first document in his in tray and placed it on the desk in front of him.

Fitz and Sprout appeared at Viv's houseboat a little before eight o'clock. Her roof was now bright with grass and flowers. The poppies, replanted, had grown wild and crimson, and the daisies and buttercups nodded their little heads in the breeze that swept up the Thames. He recalled with amused admiration the sight of the goat munching through all her newly planted grass and plants. Alba had an ingenious mind, not even Viv could deny her that. The *Valentina* now resembled a sad and empty shell. The flowers had died, the deck needed washing, the paint was beginning to peel. She looked dry and lackluster, as if in desperate need of a drink. Alba had gone, and autumn had come early to the boat.

When Viv opened the door she saw him looking wistfully at Alba's home. 'Oh, darling,' she said with a sigh, waving her cigarette in the air. 'Still not better?'

'How are you?' he said, deflecting her question because

somehow, coming from Viv, it would be too painful to answer.

'So much to tell. Come in!' He followed her through the rooms to the deck. He sank into a deck chair and put his arms behind his head.

'Well? Where have you been and what's all this about sex?' It was good to see her. She looked as blooming as a fresh peach and shamefully pleased with herself.

'I'm in love, darling. Me of all people. Lost my heart, gone!' She flicked her hand into the air. 'I'm enraptured, Fitzroy, like one of my heroines.'

'I thought you looked rather too well. Who is he? Would I like him?'

'You'll love him, darling. He's French.'

'Hence the wine.'

'Exactly.'

'Thank God. I can tell you now that your wine was shocking.'

'I know, but I was always too mean to buy the good stuff. I thought it all tasted the same. I was wrong, of course. Will you forgive me for making you drink it?' She poured him a glass of Bordeaux and handed it to him proudly. 'Pierre has his own château in Provence. I'm going to write there. It's so peaceful. Long lunches of foie gras and brioche.'

'This is good, Viv,' said Fitz, surprised. 'Well done, you. He's got good taste in wine.'

'And women,' she interjected playfully.

'Naturally. What does he do?'

'He's a gentleman, darling. He doesn't *do* anything. He's not into *doing*.'

'How old is he?'

'My age, which for you is old. But he's young at heart like I am and he makes love like a young man with a

hundred years' experience.' Fitz smiled at her affectionately. There was something very girlish about her that
hadn't been there before. 'I'm very happy, Fitzroy,' she
said a little sheepishly. 'And I want you to be happy too.'

Fitz inhaled the warm summer air and looked away.
'I'm getting there,' he said.

'I've been thinking. Why don't you be impulsive? Go to
Incantellaria. Go and get her back.'

'But you were totally against that. You said . . .'

'It doesn't matter what I said, darling. Look at you.
You're losing your shine and I just hate to see your eyes
like that.'

'Like what?' he asked with a smile.

'Sad, desperately sad, like a bunny's.'

'Oh, for goodness' sake!'

'What have you got to lose?'

'Nothing.'

'Quite. Nothing. God only helps those who help themselves. How do you know that she's not sitting on a beach
somewhere pining after you? Regretting the breakup,
which was for a very silly reason, if I recall. If I were
writing the script, which I jolly well might do, I'd send my
hero out to Incantellaria at once. He'd arrive all anxious,
his heart in his mouth, praying that she hasn't married
some Italian prince during the summer. He'd find her
alone, sitting on the cliff top watching the sea longingly
for a sight of the man she loves and has never stopped
loving. When she sees him she's too happy to be proud.
She rushes into his arms and kisses him. They'd spend a
long time kissing, I think, because at that point words just
aren't sufficient to express what's in their hearts.' She
took a drag on her cigarette. 'Desperately romantic, don't
you think?'

'I wish it were true.'

'It might be.'

'It's worth taking the chance, though, isn't it? After all, as you said, what do I have to lose?'

She raised her glass to him. 'You know I'm very fond of Alba. She's exasperating, but there's no one as entertaining or as charming as her. Perhaps you can smooth down those rough edges. She'd be lucky to get you. There's only one Fitz too, you know. I'm in love so I'm feeling generous. I'd make sure the book had a happy ending.'

The Third Portrait

26

Italy 1971

When Valentina's spirit finally moved on, a change came over the house. More remarkable, however, was the change in Immacolata. Out of the cupboards came the dresses of her past. Pinks and blues and reds, imprinted with flowers. Although fashion had moved on since the prewar days, Immacolata hadn't. She still wore the shoes she had worn when her husband had taken her dancing in Sorrento. They were black, and buckled at the ankles. Her waist might have expanded but her feet hadn't; they remained as small and delicate as her figure had once been. The revival of her old look provoked much teasing from Ludovico and Paolo, who returned with their families from the north for Valentina's memorial service and the laying of her headstone. And Immacolata smiled the wide, open smile of a woman savoring joy for the first time in many years, as surprised as the rest of them that, like riding a bicycle, the art of smiling, once learned, is never forgotten.

Alba enjoyed her own new look too, and it was much commented upon. Cutting off her hair had been a dramatic expression of self-loathing but it became an outward display of her own emotional evolution. Now she was forced to appraise her life and its lack of purpose. She wanted to become part of the fabric of the community. She wanted to be useful.

Once the celebrations of Valentina's life had passed and the visiting families had returned to their homes, Alba asked Falco if she could help out in the trattoria. 'I want to work,' she explained over lunch beneath the awning, watching the coming and going of the little blue fishing boats.

Falco sipped his limoncello. His eyes were still solemn.

'I could do with some help, if you're serious,' he replied.

'I am serious. I want to stay here with all of you. I don't want to go back to my old self and my old life.'

He looked at her. 'Who are you running from, Alba?' His words took her by surprise.

She stiffened. 'I'm not running from anyone. I just like who I am here. I feel I belong.'

'Didn't you belong in England?'

She lowered her eyes. 'I can't face Daddy now, not after what I've discovered. I certainly can't face Margo, whom I've accused all my life of being jealous of Valentina. I can't face Fitz, either.'

'Fitz?'

'The man who loves me, or did. He doesn't deserve someone like me. I'm not a very nice person, Falco.'

'That makes two of us.'

'Three,' corrected Alba. 'Valentina wasn't nice, either.' She thought of Colonel Heinz Wiermann but said nothing.

'She was a whirlwind, Alba. A force of nature. But you're young enough to change.'

'And you?'

'This dog's too old to learn new tricks.'

'Can I draw you sometime?' she asked on impulse.

'No.'

'Why not?'

He looked uncomfortable, as if he were too large for

the small chair. 'Your father was an artist. An extremely good one too.'

'I know. I found a drawing of my mother in my house-boat. He must have hidden it there a long time ago. Then there's the one he drew of me and my mother that Immacolata has.'

'There was another one, I believe,' said Falco, casting his eyes out to sea. 'I remember your father desperately searching for it in Valentina's room after her death.'

'He never found it?'

Falco shook his head. 'I believe not. When he left with you he gave one to my mother so that she would have something to remember you by.'

'Why didn't he bring me back to see her? Surely he knew that she would miss her granddaughter?'

'I think you should ask your father that.' He drained his glass.

'One day, I will. But for now I'm staying here with you. Do I have a job, then?'

Falco smiled in spite of himself. Alba's charm was dis-arming. 'You have a job for as long as you want.'

And so began a new chapter for Alba. By day she worked in the trattoria with Toto and Falco and in her spare time she drew. Cosima, to whom she had grown deeply attached, was always happy to pose for her. They sat in the evening sun on the cliff tops by the old lookout point, or down on the pebble beach after exploring the caves.

As the months went by, Cosima began to look upon Alba as a kind of mother, slipping her hand into hers as they ambled up the path home through the rocks. In the mornings she climbed into her bed and snuggled up, nestling her curly head into the soft curve where Alba's neck met her shoulder. Alba told her stories, then wrote them down and illustrated them. She found a talent she didn't know she had. She also discovered an enormous capacity for love. 'I want to thank you for loving Cosima,' said Toto one evening.

'It is I who should thank you,' she replied, noticing that his expression was unusually serious.

'Every child needs a mother. She never says she misses her. We've never talked about it. But I know that if she does, then having you around makes it so much less painful.'

'Of course she misses her mother. She probably doesn't want to talk about it, in case she hurts your feelings. Or maybe she's too busy playing to give it much thought. One can never tell. But perhaps you should mention her from time to time. What hurt me about losing mine was that no one ever spoke of her. Cosima needs to be reassured that her mother didn't reject her. That it wasn't her fault. She needs to feel loved, that's all.'

'You're right,' he said with a sigh. 'It's hard to know how much a child that young understands.'

'A great deal more than you give her credit for.'

'So, you're going to stick around for a while, then?'

It was Alba's turn to look solemn. 'I have no intention of leaving. Not ever.'

Alba was at ease with herself. She was happy to lie alone at night, listening to the song of birds and the ringing of crickets. She was no longer frightened of the dark or of being on her own. She felt secure. But her mind often wandered to Fitz, wondering what he was doing, remembering with a bittersweet nostalgia the good times they had shared. But then she would toy with Gabriele's card, running her finger over the name and telephone number, wondering whether the time had come for her to move on and explore new pastures. He had been handsome and kind. He had made her laugh in spite of the disasters she had suffered on arriving in Italy. They had somehow clicked. Fit together nicely, as if cut from the same piece of wood. After so much time on her own, she now felt ready for love.

Then Fate made the decision for her. It was the first week of October and still warm, except for a slight chill on the wind that swept in off the sea. The trattoria was full of people: tourism was picking up; articles had been written about the secret wonders of the town so that foreigners were stopping off on their way down the Amalfi coast to more famous locations like Positano and Capri. Alba was busy taking orders and returning with trays of steaming dishes. She enjoyed chatting to the locals and the new faces who were always happy to talk to the lovely young woman with short spiky hair and strange pale eyes. As she served drinks she heard the motor of a boat and lifted her gaze. Before she could identify the passenger, her heart began to thud. She put down her tray and stepped out from under the awning. With one hand on her hip, the other shielding her eyes from the sun, she squinted to get a better look. When the boat slowed down at the quay she forgot the customers and her duties and ran along the beach, her eyes stinging with excitement. 'Fitz, Fitz!' she shouted, waving her hand in the air.

Fitz stepped out onto the quay, his suitcase in one hand, a panama hat in the other. He didn't recognize the young woman running toward him, calling his name. 'Fitz, it's me, Alba!' she exclaimed, registering the bewildered look on his face.

'You've cut your hair!' he said, frowning. 'You're very brown too.' He traced his eyes up and down her thin dress, imprinted with flowers, and the simple black espadrilles she wore on her feet. She had changed so much. He wondered whether he had been wise to come. But then her smiling face was before him, her eyes bright with happiness, and he recognized the Alba he knew.

'I missed you, Fitz,' she said, touching his arm, gazing up at him. 'I missed you so much.' He put down his suitcase and drew her into his arms.

'I missed you too, darling.' He kissed her temple.

'I'm sorry I never telephoned,' she began.

'No, I should apologize for never saying goodbye. I tried to, but I was too late. You had already gone.' He began to laugh. 'Your stupid goat was eating through all Viv's new plants!' She laughed too. It bubbled up from her belly like a delicious fountain.

'Was she furious?'

'Only for a moment. She misses you too.'

'I have so much to tell you!'

'And I you.'

'You must stay at my grandmother's house. There's a spare room upstairs. I have my mother's old room.' She linked her arm through his. He put his hat back on his head and picked up his suitcase. 'Come and have a drink. I'll tell Toto to take over. I have a job now. I work in the family business with my uncle and cousin. That,' she said, pointing proudly to the trattoria, 'is it.'

She found a table for Fitz and brought him a glass of wine and a bottle of water. 'You must taste Immacolata's delicious dishes,' she said, pulling out a chair and sitting down. 'Of course, she doesn't cook now. She's too old. But they are all her own recipes. Here, choose one. It's on the house.' She handed him a menu.

'You choose whatever you think I'll like. I don't want to waste time browsing when I can be talking to you.'

She leaned forward, her brown face beaming at him contentedly. 'You came,' she said softly.

'I worried that you weren't coming back.'

'I didn't think I could face you.'

'Me?' He frowned. 'Why on earth not?'

'I realized how selfish I had been.'

'Oh, Alba!'

'No, really. I've had a lot of time to think and so much has happened. I realized that I hadn't been very kind.'

'I shouldn't have let you go. It was my fault.'

'That's very sweet of you, Fitz, but the truth is you deserved better. I only ever thought of myself. I cringe now. There are moments in my life that I would quite happily rub out if I had the chance.' Fatman flitted through her mind, but without the habitual plummeting of the stomach. 'I'm glad you're here.'

'So am I.' He took her hand and caressed her skin with his thumb. 'I like your hair short. It suits you.'

'It suits the *new* me,' she said proudly. 'I didn't want to look like my mother anymore.'

'So, did you find out all you wanted to know?'

'I grew up with a dream, Fitz. It wasn't real. Now I know the real woman. She was complicated. I don't think she was very nice, actually. But I think I love her better now, warts and all.'

'That's good. Will you tell me about it later? Perhaps we could go for a walk. The Amalfi coast is famous for its beauty.'

'Incantellaria is lovelier than anywhere else. I'll show it to you once you've eaten. Then you must meet Immacolata, my grandmother, and Cosima, my cousin's daughter. She's just turned seven. She's adorable.'

'I thought you didn't like children.'

'Cosima's special. She's not like other children. She's blood.'

'God, you sound Italian!'

'I *am* Italian. I feel right here. I belong.'

'But Alba, I've come to take you home.'

She shook her head. 'I don't think I can face it. Not after what I've learned.'

He squeezed her hand. 'Whatever you have to face, my darling, you won't face it alone. I won't make that mistake again.'

Her eyes, a moment ago so solemn, now lit up at the dish that was being placed in front of Fitz. 'Ah, *frittelle*!'

After lunch, Alba took him up the path through the rocks to see her mother's grave beneath the olive tree. 'We held a service a month ago to remember her. Before then she hadn't been given a headstone. It's nice, isn't it, the headstone? We all chose it together.'

Fitz bent down to read it. 'What does it say?'

'"Valentina Fiorelli, the light of Incantellaria, the love of her family, now at peace with God."'

'Why didn't she have a headstone?'

Alba sat down beside him, drawing her legs underneath her. 'Because she was murdered, Fitz, the night before her wedding. She was never married to my father.'

'Good God!'

'It would make a good book, so don't tell Viv!'

'I won't. So tell *me*. From the beginning. What was she like?'

Alba was happy to tell him everything.

When Alba had finished her story, the sun was beginning to set, turning the sea to molten copper. The evening air was cool and smelled of dying foliage and leaves. Autumn was setting in. Fitz was moved by Valentina's life, but more by Thomas Arbuckle's plight. No wonder he hadn't wanted to talk about her, least of all share her with their daughter.

'So you see,' she said gravely. 'I can't go back.'

'Why not?'

'Because I can't face my father and Margo. I'm too ashamed.'

'What utter nonsense. Didn't you say that you love Valentina more now than you did before, because you know and understand her faults?'

'Yes, but that's different.'

'No, it isn't. I don't love you in spite of your faults. I love you *because* of them. They make you different from everyone else, Alba. Loving isn't about selecting only the good parts, it's about taking the whole and loving the lot.'

'I like it here because no one knows what I was like before. Here, they judge me as they see me.'

'That means your father, Margo, and I love you more, because we've loved you all along.'

'Now *you're* being silly!' she said with a light laugh.

'I'm not being silly when I say that I want you to marry me.' Fitz hadn't intended to put it quite like that. He had envisaged a romantic buildup to his proposal.

'What did you say?' The corners of her mouth curled up shyly.

He delved into his pocket and brought out a crumpled piece of tissue paper. With trembling hands he unwrapped it to reveal a simple diamond ring. He took her left hand and slipped it onto her third finger. Without letting go, he looked deep into her eyes. 'I said, Alba Arbuckle, will you take on a penniless literary agent who can offer you little more than love and an old, smelly dog?' The old Alba would have laughed at him, called him absurd, made him feel like a fool for asking. Or she might have accepted just for the fun of wearing such an exquisite ring. But now she gazed down at the diamond that glittered in the light. 'It belonged to my grandmother,' he said. 'I want it to belong to you.'

'If you'll have me,' she replied. 'I would be lucky to marry a man as good as you, Fitzroy Davenport.'

27

They decided they would spend a couple of weeks in
Incantellaria. That would give Alba time to say goodbye
to her family. Then they would return to England. To Viv,
the houseboat, Beechfield Park, her father and stepmother, and a new life together.

'We will come back, won't we?' she said, thinking of
Cosima. 'I'll miss them all so much.'

'You can come back every summer if you like.'

'What I am going to tell that little girl?'

'That it's not goodbye.'

'She's already been deserted once by her mother. Now
she'll be left again by me. I can't bear to hurt her.'

'Darling, you're not her mother.'

Alba shook her head. 'I'm the nearest thing to a mother
she's got. It'll be unbearable.'

Fitz kissed her and stroked her hair. 'We'll have children of our own, perhaps.'

'I can't imagine that.' *Can't imagine loving another child
as much as Cosima,* she thought bleakly.

'Trust me.'

She sighed in resignation. 'It's just that I've grown so
attached to her.'

'The world is getting smaller every day. It's not so far,
you know.' But Alba knew that Fitz couldn't possibly

understand her love for Cosima. It was the closest she had ever come to being a mother. Parting would break her heart.

Alba took Fitz back to Immacolata's house for dinner. To him it was a pretty building, typically Italian, cozy, vibrant, echoing with the laughter of a big family. Immacolata blessed him and smiled. To Fitz there was nothing unusual about her smile; he could not have known that once it was as rare as a rainbow. Beata and Falco welcomed him warmly in broken English, and Toto made jokes about the differences between Fitz's normal urban surroundings and the provincial quiet of Incantellaria. Toto's English was surprisingly good. Fitz immediately liked him. He had much the same easy manner as himself and a dry wit that he understood. When Cosima skipped into the room, he could see why Alba had grown to love her. She ran up and threw her thin arms around Alba's waist, her curls bouncing around her face like corkscrews.

When they sat down to dinner Alba announced their engagement. Toto made a toast; they all raised their glasses and admired the ring with enthusiasm. Yet beneath the excitement there lay an undertone of apprehension, for they all realized, except Cosima, that Alba would now be leaving them.

Alba was quick to sense their disquiet but nervous of speaking of her departure in front of the child. She watched Cosima eating her prosciutto with gusto, chattering about what she had learned at school, the games she had played, and the anticipation of going shopping again with Alba now that the weather had grown colder and her summer dresses were all too thin. Alba caught Beata's eye. The older woman smiled sympathetically. Alba was unable to communicate what lay at the forefront of her thoughts. On one hand, the prospect of marriage to Fitz made her extremely happy; on the other, leaving Incantellaria and Cosima eclipsed her happiness like a grey cloud floating in front of the sun. She sat in the shade while everyone around her sat in the light.

After dinner Cosima went to bed, leaving the adults sitting chatting in the moonlight on the terrace beneath the vine. 'So, when are you going to be leaving us?' Immacolata asked. Her voice had a hard edge. Alba understood why she felt resentful. They had only just found each other again.

'I don't know, *nonna*. Soon.'

'She'll come back to visit,' Fitz said, trying to lighten the atmosphere.

Immacolata raised her chin defiantly. 'That's what Tommy said twenty-six years ago when he took her away. He did not bring her back. Not once.'

'But I make my own decisions now. It won't be easy for me to leave you all. I can do it if I know that I will return again soon.'

Falco placed his large rough hand on his mother's small one. 'Mamma,' he said and his voice was a plea. 'She has her own life to lead. Let's be grateful for the part of her life that we have shared.'

The old woman snorted. 'What are you going to say to the child?' she said. 'You will break her heart.'

'And mine,' Alba added.

'She'll be fine,' said Toto, lighting a cigarette and throwing the match behind him. 'She has all of us.'

'It's part of growing up,' said Falco gravely. 'Things don't always remain the same; neither do people.'

'I'll tell her tomorrow,' said Alba. 'It's not goodbye.'

'Why can't Fitz stay here with us?' Immacolata asked, settling her eyes on Fitz in a silent challenge. Fitz didn't need to speak Italian to understand what she was suggesting.

He looked embarrassed. 'Because my business is in London.' Immacolata didn't much like Fitz. He lacked passion.

'You have made your choice,' she said to Alba, getting up. 'But I don't have to like it.'

'I'm going to take Fitz to that old ruined castle tomorrow,' said Alba, keen to change the subject.

Immacolata turned, her face as white as a corpse. 'Palazzo Montelimone?' she croaked, leaning on the back of her chair.

'There's nothing to see,' Falco protested. He looked shiftily at his mother. Alba's curiosity was ignited.

'I've been meaning to go since I arrived. It *is* a ruin, isn't it?' She tried to work out what silent communication passed between her grandmother and uncle.

'It's dangerous. The walls are crumbling. You mustn't go,' Immacolata insisted.

'Take him to Naples instead.'

Alba backed down. Anything to make her grandmother happy. It was the least she could do, considering she was leaving. 'Okay. We'll go to Naples,' she said in English.

'Naples it is then.' Fitz didn't care where they went so long as they left the house.

The following morning Alba borrowed Toto's small Fiat and set off in the direction of Naples. She was disappointed. She had looked forward to exploring the ruin. It had sat temptingly on the hill attracting her gaze for months. She shouldn't have told them she planned to go there. She should have just gone.

'You're very quiet,' said Fitz, watching her grim face staring at the road ahead.

'I don't want to go back to Naples,' she told him. 'I've seen enough of it.'

'We can have lunch in a nice restaurant and wander around. It won't be so bad.'

'No,' she said suddenly, the shadow passing off her features like a cloud. 'I'm turning around. There's something there, I just know it. Why else wouldn't they want me to go? They're still hiding something, I can feel it. And whatever it is, it's up there in that palazzo.'

The tires screeched on the hot road as Alba braked and steered the car back down the coast. They were both injected with enthusiasm and purpose, united on a mission, partners in crime.

After a while they turned off the road that wove down the coast and set on up the hill in the direction of the palazzo. The lane began to grow steep and narrow. After a while it forked off to the right. The forest had almost covered it with shrubs and thorns and leaves, and the cypress trees that lined it cast their shade upon it so that they now drove in near darkness. When they arrived at the black iron gates, tall and imposing though peeling with neglect, she saw that they were locked with a padlock, and the lock itself was brown with rust. They climbed out of the car and looked through the bars first at the overgrown gardens, then at the house.

An entire wall had collapsed and lay in ruins. Even the fallen stones were being gradually swallowed by ivy and other weeds. It was a compelling sight and one which drew them in. They had come this far; they weren't about to turn around now. Alba looked about her and saw that if they didn't mind suffering the odd scratch, they could squeeze through the shrubbery and climb over the wall. Fitz went first, the thorns tearing at his jeans. Then he turned to help Alba, whose short, flimsy sundress was inappropriate for such an expedition. When she jumped down on the other side she felt a surge of triumph. She brushed off her dress and licked her hand where the skin had been ripped.

'Are you all right?' he asked.

She nodded. 'I'm just a little nervous as to what we're going to find.'

'Perhaps we'll find nothing at all.'

She narrowed her eyes. 'I want to find something. I don't want to go back to England with so many questions unanswered.'

'Okay, Sherlock, let's go.'

As they walked up the drive toward the house, she was struck by the cold. It was as if the palazzo were situated at the top of a high mountain with its very own climate. It had been a humid day and she had grown hot walking up the hill. But here, in the grounds of the house, there was an icy edge to the wind and she rubbed her arms to keep warm. The sun was high in the sky but still the house was set in shadow: grey, austere, and deserted. There was little feeling of life, not even from the gardens, where she could sense the movement of the bindweed as it crept silently over the grounds like evil snakes, winding its way in possession around the foliage it had already choked to death.

One of the towers had toppled with the wall and lay across the garden like a fallen sentinel. The rooms exposed to the air were filled with leaves, and ivy climbed the floors and spread across the walls. Anything of any value had no doubt been looted. They scaled the rubble to enter the building and looked about in wonder. The paint could be seen through the leaves and moss, pale blue, like the sky at dawn. The moldings where the wall joined the ceiling were elaborate, the carving chipped in places like a row of old teeth. Alba scraped her foot over the floor to remove layers of dirt and forest, and found the marble still intact. A large oak door was still on its hinges. 'Let's go in there,' she suggested. Fitz strode over the rubble and found that the handle turned with ease. To their delight they walked through into the main body of the house where the forest had not yet trespassed.

It was quite dark and eerily silent. Alba was afraid to speak in case the sound woke demons lurking in the shadows. After a while, each room resembled the last: empty, bare, and forlorn. Just when they were on the point of turning back, Fitz opened a pair of double doors, the height of the room, into a salon that had an altogether different feel. Where the others had felt cold and damp, like a corpse, this one vibrated with the warmth of the living. It was smaller than the rest, square in shape, with a fireplace where the remains of the last fire still lay in the grate. It appeared to have been used, and recently. A large leather armchair, nibbled by mice, stood in front of it. There was nothing else in the room, just the distinct feeling that they weren't alone.

Fitz looked about suspiciously. 'Someone lives here,' he said. Alba put her finger to her lips.

'Shhhh,' she hissed. 'He might not like us trespassing!'

'I thought they said no one lived here.'

'So did I!'

Alba strained her ears for a sound, but none came, just the heavy thud of her own heartbeat. She looked over to French doors into the garden and pulled one open. It scraped along the floor. Fitz followed her outside. It was apparent that a terrace had once stood there, though the balustrade had collapsed, leaving only a small part of it.

Alba scraped her foot on the ground to expose a floor of small red tiles. Then something black in the undergrowth caught her eye. She strode over to the ruined balustrade and burrowed beneath with her hand, finding something hard and metal.

'What have you got there?' Fitz whispered.

'Looks like a telescope.' She brushed it clean, then endeavored to look through it.

'See anything interesting?'

'Just black,' she replied, tossing it back into the undergrowth.

Suddenly they felt the presence of someone behind them. They turned with a start to see a scrap of a man stepping out through the French doors.

Alba spoke. 'I hope we're not intruding. We went for a walk and got lost,' she explained, smiling charmingly.

When the man raised his bloodshot eyes to Alba he gasped as if something had knocked the wind out of him. He stood and stared at her without so much as a blink.

'*Madonna!*' he exclaimed, his voice as soft as ribbon. Then he smiled, revealing a large gap where his front teeth had been. 'I knew I walked among the dead!' He extended his hand. Alba reluctantly took it. It was clammy. 'I'm Nero Bonomi. Who are you?'

'We're from England,' she replied. 'My friend doesn't speak Italian.'

'But you, my dear, speak it like a native,' he said in English. 'With your short hair you look like a rather beautiful boy. You look like someone else too, from a long time ago. You gave me a fright, actually.' He ran his bony fingers through his blond hair. 'I was once a beautiful boy. What would Ovidio say if he could see me now?'

'Do you live here?' she asked. 'In this ruin?'

'It was a ruin when Ovidio lived here too. Or should I say Marchese Ovidio di Montelimone. He was very grand. When he died, he left it to me. Not that it was worth having. Only the memories, which are of no value to anyone else, I suppose.'

Alba noticed that the skin on his face was thick and reddened. He looked as if he were sunburnt, but on closer inspection it was clear that he was slowly drinking himself to death. A miasma of alcohol surrounded him. She could smell it. She noticed too that he wore his linen trousers very high on the waist, belted tightly, and that they were too short, revealing white socks on thin ankles. He wasn't old, but he had the fragility of an elderly man.

'What was this marchese like?' Fitz asked. Nero sat down on the balustrade and flopped one leg over the other. He didn't seem to mind that they were trespassing, wandering through his house. He seemed happy for the company. He rested his chin on his hand with a sigh. 'He was a great aesthete. He loved beautiful things.'

'Are you related?' Alba knew instinctively that he wasn't.

'No. I loved him. He loved boys, you see. I had no culture, yet he loved me. I was a simple urchin from Naples. He found me on the street and educated me. But look what I have done to my inheritance. I am good for nothing now.' He fumbled around in his pocket for a cigarette. 'If you were a boy, I could easily lose my heart to you.' He laughed, but Alba didn't think it amusing. He flicked the lighter and inhaled. 'Nothing was simple with Ovidio. He was a man of contradictions. Rich, yet he lived in a house that was decaying all about him. He loved men and yet he gave the largest slice of his heart to a woman. He went crazy for her. I nearly lost him because of her.' Alba looked at Fitz and Fitz looked at Alba. Neither spoke. But they knew. Nero continued. 'She was more beautiful than you could possibly imagine.'

'She was my mother,' said Alba. Nero stared at her

through the wafting smoke that rose up in front of his eyes. 'Valentina was my mother.'

Suddenly Nero's shoulders slumped and tears welled in his eyes. He bit his lip and his hands began to shake. 'Of course. That is why you are here. That is why I half-recognize you.'

'Was Valentina the marchese's lover?' Fitz asked.

He nodded. His head looked far too big for his emaciated body. 'She was an amazing woman. Even I admired her. It was impossible not to. She had a bewitching way about her. An allure, quite magical. I was a boy from the streets and yet I met my match with her. Forgive me.'

'Come on,' said Fitz trying to comfort him. 'What's there to forgive?'

Nero stood up. 'I let this place go. A few years ago there was a fire in one wing. It was my fault, I was drinking with friends . . . I've let it crumble about me. There's no money left. I haven't done any of the things he asked me to do. But come. There is one thing that I have kept just the way he left it.'

They followed him along a snake path that wound its way down the hill beneath an avenue of cypress trees. At the end, overlooking the sea, stood a small house made out of grey stone. Unlike the palazzo, this had not been destroyed by the forest. Only a few intrepid branches of ivy scaled the walls and wound their way around the pillars. It was a perfect little folly, like something out of a fairy tale, where goblins might have lived. Fitz and Alba's curiosity mounted. They stepped in behind Nero, peering around him in astonishment for, unlike the palazzo, this secret hideaway hadn't been disturbed; it was frozen in time.

There was only one room. It was a harmoniously proportioned square with a domed ceiling, exquisitely painted in a fresco of a cloudy blue sky filled with naked cherubs. The walls below were a warm terra-cotta, the floor covered with rugs, worn by the constant tread of feet, but not threadbare. A large four-poster bed dominated the room. The silks that draped it had discoloured to a pale green, but the quilt, made in the same fabric, retained its original rich colour. An elaborately embroidered velvet coverlet lay upon it, fraying at the edges. There was a chaise longue, an upholstered chair, a walnut-inlaid writing table where a glass ink bottle and pen were poised on the leather blotter, with paper and envelopes bearing the name Marchese Ovidio di Montelimone. Velvet curtains hung from poles; the shutters were closed; a bookshelf carried the weight of rows of leather-bound books.

On closer inspection Alba saw that all the books were either of history or erotica. She ran her fingers over the bindings, wiping away the dust to reveal shiny titles embossed in gold.

'Ovidio loved sex,' said Nero, draping himself over the chaise longue. 'This was his sanctuary. The place he came to get away from the decaying palazzo and the echoes of its glorious past that he had allowed to slip through his fingers.' He gazed up at the ceiling and took a drag of his cigarette, now so short it was in danger of burning his yellowed fingers. 'Ah, the hours of pleasure I enjoyed in this charming little grotto.' He sighed theatrically and let his eyes fall lazily on Alba, who was now looking at the paintings. They were all mythological scenes of naked young men or boys. They were beautifully framed, forming a collage on the walls. An alcove in the wall housed a statue on a black and gilt pedestal. It was a marble replica of Donatello's David. 'Isn't that exquisite? He's like a panther, isn't he? It was the languor of his pose that delighted Ovidio. He had it made especially for this grotto. He would run his hands over it. He liked to touch. He was a sensualist. As I said, he loved beautiful things.'

'Like my mother,' said Alba, imagining her mother sitting at the delicate little dressing table, brushing her hair in front of the Queen Anne mirror. There were rows of bottles and perfume flasks here too, silver brushes and a pot of face powder. Had those belonged to her mother too?

'Like Valentina,' repeated Nero and his eyes filled once again with tears.

Alba wandered around the room, past a marble fireplace that still vibrated with the heat it had provided for the marchese and his lovers, past a tallboy of drawers, all empty. Then she flopped onto the bed. She felt uneasy. She didn't want to look at Nero; she knew instinctively that he was about to divulge something terrible. She turned and caught her breath. Her eyes alighted on a picture of a beautiful young woman lying naked on grass. Her breasts were young and full, her hips round and soft, her pubic hair a shock of dark against the whiteness of her thighs. Alba recoiled. The long dark hair, laughing eyes, and mysterious smile that played about her lips were unmistakable. Indeed, inscribed at the bottom were the words *Valentina, reclining nude, Thomas Arbuckle, 1945.*

'Oh my God!'

'What is it?' Fitz hurried over.

'It's Valentina.'

'What?'

'The last portrait my father drew of my mother. The one he searched for after her death but never found. She gave it to the marchese.'

Now Alba realized why her father had been so desperate to find it. It was the most intimate of them all. A picture that should have been for their eyes only. Yet she had given it away. Alba took it down off the wall and brushed the dust off the frame. Fitz sat on the bed beside her. Neither noticed that Nero's shoulders had begun to shake. 'How dare he!' she exclaimed in fury. 'How dare *she*!' She remembered her father's grey, tormented face when she had given him the first portrait. How little she had understood him. 'It breaks my heart to think of Daddy searching for this, while all along it was here with this pig. Wherever he is, I spit on his grave.'

Nero turned, his face an open wound. 'Now you know why this house is cursed. Why it's in ruins. Why it will turn to dust. Why Ovidio was murdered.' His voice was a desperate howl, an animal in pain.

Fitz and Alba stared at him in amazement. 'The marchese was murdered too?' said Fitz.

'My Ovidio was murdered.' He sank to the floor and curled up into a ball.

'Why was he murdered?' Alba asked in confusion. 'I don't understand.'

'Because he killed Valentina,' he wailed. 'Because he killed her.'

28

Fitz and Alba found Lattarullo drinking limoncello in the trattoria with the retired mayor. When they approached, Lattarullo's face turned serious for they were both pale, as if they had just walked with the dead. The mayor excused himself so that they could be alone. He knew what they had come to talk about. It was better that they discussed such matters with the carabiniere. After all, he had known the girl's father and been the first at the murder scene. He had hoped that they wouldn't rummage around in the past. Best left alone and forgotten.

'Take a seat,' said Lattarullo, forcing a smile.

'We need to talk,' said Alba. She took Fitz's hand. 'We've just been up to the palazzo.'

Lattarullo's shoulders dropped. 'You talked to Nero,' he said. 'He's a drunk. He's got no money. Squandered it all on drink and gambling. He's as ruined as the house.'

'The marchese killed Valentina. Why?' Alba's voice was formidable.

The carabiniere sat back in his chair and bit the inside of his cheek. 'You've solved a case that the best detectives couldn't solve.'

'They didn't even try,' she snapped.

'They had Lupo Bianco, what did they care about a domestic matter?'

'Why did he kill her? He loved her.'

'Because he didn't want your father to have her.'

'He was jealous?'

'If he couldn't have her, no one else should. She drove him crazy. That's what Valentina did. She drove men crazy. The marchese was already crazier than the rest.'

'I know she had a German lover. I saw his letters.'

'Yes, she had a German protector. She had many. She drove them all crazy. Even the ones she didn't want.'

'It's so pointless.' Alba sighed heavily.

'And such a waste.' Lattarullo turned and ordered three limoncellos.

It was only later that evening, when Alba sat with Fitz and Falco on the terrace, that the full truth was finally revealed. Immacolata and Beata had retired to their rooms; Toto was in the town with friends. Cosima was tucked up in bed, hugging her rag doll and the happy memories of the day. The setting sun glowed golden in a pale, watery sky, dyeing the clouds floating upon it pink like cotton candy. It was a magnificent scene. Alba was aware of her imminent departure and her heart filled with unbearable sorrow.

When she showed her uncle the portrait he rubbed his chin. *'Madonna!'* he gasped, peering closer. 'Where did you find it?'

'At the palazzo,' Alba replied defiantly.

His rough face turned solemn. 'So you went?'

'You know me, Falco. I don't give up.'

'Nero showed us the grotto,' said Fitz. 'It was there that Alba discovered the portrait.'

'And the truth,' she added. 'That the marchese killed my mother.'

Falco poured a glass of water and took a gulp. 'So, the picture was there all along,' he muttered.

'It was not hers to give away,' grumbled Alba. 'It belonged to my father.'

'You must take it to him,' said Falco.

'I can't,' she sighed, recalling the effect of the first one.

'I think you are wrong, Alba. I think you should tell him.'

'Falco's right. I think it's time he knew the truth,' Fitz interjected wisely.

Alba sighed heavily in resignation. 'I can't believe the bastard killed my mother out of jealousy. It's so bloody futile.'

Falco raised his eyebrow. 'Who told you that?'

'Lattarullo,' said Alba.

Her uncle thought for a moment and then said gravely, 'That's not the full story.'

Alba's heart lurched. 'There's more?'

'The marchese killed Valentina because of you.'

Alba was appalled. 'Because of *me*?'

'He thought you were his.'

She clutched her throat, finding it hard to breathe. 'How do you know that I'm not? Am I?' She was horrified, suddenly doubting her own parentage.

'Valentina knew. The marchese knew too, in his heart.'

'He killed her for revenge,' said Fitz, shaking his head. 'What a coward.'

'Because he had lost her and because he was going to lose you as well. The marchese had no heir. He was old and sad. Valentina and you were his future, his life. Without you he had nothing. He wanted to rob Tommy of his future as Valentina was robbing him of his.'

'Nero said that he was murdered.' Alba's eyes met Falco's. He did not look away, his eyes as hard as hematite.

'Let's just say that here in the south families have their ways of taking revenge.'

'You, Falco?' Her voice was a whisper.

'I slashed his throat like he slashed Valentina's and I watched him die, choking in his own blood,' he said. The simple act of unburdening his secret expelled the dark shadows from his eyes. 'It was a matter of honour.'

A few days later, Alba broke the news to Cosima. She deliberately took her into town to buy new dresses at the shop owned by the dwarfs, hoping that the excitement of a few purchases would make up for the disappointment that would follow. Cosima tried them on, twirled around like a dancer, took time to make up her mind as she had the first time Alba had taken her. Because she felt guilty and because she wanted the child to remember her with affection, Alba bought her all five with tights and cardigans to match and a pale blue coat for when it got very cold. Cosima was overwhelmed, but this time she didn't cry. She thanked her cousin, pressing her small face up to Alba's to kiss her on her cheek. Alba had to bite back her tears. She hadn't even left and yet the seams of her heart were already tearing.

She led Cosima up the path through the rocks to the lookout point where she had first drawn her. It felt like another lifetime. In the space of only a few months, she had lived so many.

'Shall I give a fashion show tonight?'

'Definitely. They should see your new autumn collection,' Alba replied, making her voice jolly.

'You bought me *so* many,' Cosima said, placing enormous emphasis on the 'so.' 'Five. They're so pretty. I love pretty things.'

'That's because you're pretty too. And not only pretty, Cosima, you're sweet like honey.'

'We should have brought a picnic. I'm hungry.'

'It's all that shopping. Wears you out. Wait till you come to London and then we'll really hit the shops. When you're a little bit bigger perhaps.' Cosima nodded, unable to comprehend the idea of London. 'Darling, I have something important to tell you.' She coughed. Cosima lifted her clear gaze and smiled expectantly. 'I'm going to be leaving soon.' She blinked back tears as her voice cracked.

Cosima blanched. 'Leaving?' she repeated.

'Yes, Fitz has asked me to marry him.'

'Where are you going?'

'To England.'

'Can't I come with you?'

Alba drew her into her arms and kissed the top of her head. 'I'm afraid not. What would your papa do without you? And *nonna*? Not to mention *nonnina*. They'd all be very sad without you.'

'But I'll be sad without you,' she said.

'I'll come back and visit you.'

'Don't you love me anymore?' she asked in a small voice and Alba heard the tearing of those seams again, this time louder and more viciously split.

'Oh, Cosima. Of course I do. I love you so much it hurts. I don't want to leave you. I want to marry Fitz and live here. But his work is in London. He's not Italian like I am. It's hard enough leaving the family, but leaving you will be the hardest part of all. But let's try to look on the bright side. I'll write to you and telephone you and send you dresses from London. They're much prettier than the dresses I bought you today. Much, much prettier. And I'll come back and visit you. One day, when you're bigger, you can come and visit me.' They sat in silence, their arms tightly wrapped around each other, as the day slowly seeped away.

Alba remained another ten days with the Fiorellis. While she was still among them Cosima forgot about her impending departure. Children live in the moment and with Alba there, the moment was a happy one. She put on her fashion show and the applause was louder than it had been before, but she didn't know the grown-ups were overcompensating. Alba showed Fitz all the places that were now dear to her: the old lookout point, the lemon grove, and the stream. She showed him her paintings, all hung up in her room and around the house, where Immacolata had put the best of her great-granddaughter on display. Fitz was impressed. He picked them up, studied them carefully, complimenting her over and over again.

Immacolata sulked. Although she no longer wore the clothes of mourning, she wore the face: long and grey and fixed into a permanent scowl. Only at the harbour, when Alba was on the point of leaving, did it break its mold. 'I'm only cross because I love you,' she said, taking Alba's face in her hands and kissing her forehead.

'I'll telephone you and write and visit. I promise I'll come back soon,' Alba explained in a sudden attack of panic.

'I know you will. Go with God, my child, and may He protect you.' She crossed herself vigorously, then let her go. Alba embraced Beata and Toto but reserved her biggest hug for Falco. They held each other for a long moment before pulling away.

Cosima allowed herself to be swept into Alba's fierce embrace. They both wept. Fitz took Alba's hand and helped her into the boat. The small group stood forlornly on the quay. It was a sad parting. As the boat motored out of the harbor Cosima lifted her small hand and waved.

29

Cook had scones and homemade jams for tea. Scones were delicious any time but never more so than in winter, when the damp and cold demanded to be compensated with something warm and sweet. Verity Forthright popped one into her mouth, which had begun to water long before she had arrived at Cook's cottage on the Arbuckle estate. The scones were small, bite-sized, and they melted on the tongue. She picked up the linen napkin, part of a set of six that old Mrs. Arbuckle had given Cook one Christmas, and dabbed the corners of her mouth. 'Edith, my dear, you really are unsurpassed in the kitchen. These scones are so tasty.' Cook buttered one for herself.

'I think I'll make scones for Alba's homecoming tea,' she replied thoughtfully. 'Of course, I'll roast potatoes with the lunch. I recall Fitzroy liked my roast potatoes.' Verity's mouth watered again.

'It's all rather sudden, isn't it?' she said, narrowing her eyes and dropping a large dollop of jam onto her second scone.

'Alba's never been conventional. That's not her way. Apparently, Mrs. Arbuckle tells me, Fitzroy went all the way out to Italy to ask her to marry him.' She smiled at the romance of it.

'Fortunate for him, she accepted. Would have been a wasted journey otherwise,' she said. Cook poured them both cups of tea.

'She telephoned from Italy with the good news. I think they make a lovely couple. Lovely,' she said. 'He's calm and kind and she's fiery and volatile. They complement each other.'

'That's not what you thought six months ago,' Verity reminded her.

'It's a woman's prerogative to change her mind.'

'Maybe he's managed to calm her down a bit. She needed calming down. She needs to wear longer skirts too. He's a sensible man; perhaps he'll make her more respectable. I know Mrs. Arbuckle would like that.'

'Mrs. Arbuckle likes things just so,' said Cook, putting down her teacup. 'She's genteel. She wasn't born to it like old Mrs. Arbuckle. Mrs. Arbuckle married it and that's quite different. Such people are always affected, I think. She minds very much about class and breeding. Fortunately, so she tells me, Fitzroy is from a very good Norfolk family. She knows a cousin of his. He's, as she puts it, a 'proper' person.'

'Mrs. Arbuckle will be happy Alba's getting married at all, I imagine,' said Verity. Cook was aware that she was fishing for gossip but she was too delighted at the news to resist talking about it.

'Alba's always been a great worry to her. To both of them. Arriving at the house as she does, with a storm brewing in her eyes. It's that mother of hers, you see. Those Italians are a fiery lot. Mrs. Arbuckle likes people from her own world and Alba's never really fitted in. It'll be a burden off her shoulders. Caroline will be next, mark my words.'

Verity wasn't the slightest bit interested in Caroline.

She stuffed a third scone into her mouth, then steered the conversation back to Alba.

'Don't you think the captain will be a bit sad to give his daughter away? After all, you've often told me that out of all his children, Alba was the most special.'

'I believe so, not that he would ever say such a thing. I see it in his eyes, you know. My Ernie always said that I have the intuition of a witch. She has the power to hurt him in a way that no one else can. It breaks my heart to see him suffer on account of her malice. He gives her everything, everything. That girl has never done a day's work in her life, thanks to the generosity of the captain. However, the strangest thing happened a while back.' She hesitated. She had sworn not to tell Verity, knowing that it would be passed around the village even before the old vulture had had time to digest it. However, the weight of knowledge was too heavy to bear alone. Verity's mouth stopped midchew and she sat very straight. Cook wished she hadn't started. But then, she reasoned to herself, she'd only tell Verity the good bits. 'A letter arrived from Alba,' she stated.

'A letter?'

'Addressed to the captain. I recognized her handwriting and the Italian postmark.'

Verity washed the scone down with tea. 'And?'

'Well, he went into his study to read it. I was busy in the drinks cupboard so I could see his expression as he read it. It was long, pages and pages in her large, careless writing. I could see through the paper that she had done a lot of crossing out.'

'You were quite close then?'

'Very. The captain didn't even notice I was there, so engrossed was he in the contents of the letter.'

'What did it say?'

Cook sighed and shrugged. 'I don't know, but when he had read it he was transformed.'

Verity looked puzzled. 'How?'

'Well, he looked younger.'

'Younger?'

'Yes. And happier. Gone were those dark circles under his eyes. If you ask me, there was something in the letter that gave him back his youth.'

'Honestly, Edith, you're exaggerating.'

'I most certainly am not. It was most peculiar. It was as if he let something go. Something heavy and sad. He just let it go.'

'Then what?'

'He just sat there, rubbing his chin and staring up at the portrait of his father that hangs on the wall.'

'His father?'

'Yes, old Mr. Arbuckle. I don't know what he was thinking about, but he sat there a long time, just thinking.'

'What do you think the letter said?' asked Verity, bringing her teacup to her lips with a loud slurp.

'Well, I heard Mrs. Arbuckle and the captain talking in the sitting room some time afterward. I was in the hall, you see, laying up for dinner. When it's just the two of them they often like to eat there, on the refectory table.'

'Yes, yes, what did they say?'

'Well, they spoke in hushed voices. I think they knew I was out there; they could hear me clanking around, you see. It's hard to keep the cutlery quiet. So they spoke carefully and I didn't pick it all up. I heard the sentence, *'Alba now knows the truth.'* Then he said with some jubilation, 'She apologized.' That struck me, you see, because I don't imagine Alba's ever apologized for anything in her life.'

Verity frowned. 'Apologized for what? What truth?' Cook felt herself grow hot. *Enough,* she said to herself.

You've told Verity enough. Verity's face was uncomfortably close to her own. It was no good. It was all going to come out.

'It's all rather baffling. But if you ask me, since Alba went to Italy to find her mother's family, she must have discovered something else. I don't know what . . .' Verity was staring at her with the eyes of a snake. 'Oh, Verity,' she said suddenly. 'I can't keep it from you. I have to share it with someone. I heard the word . . .' She paused, then added in a loud whisper, 'Murder.'

When the word had been absorbed and digested, Verity gasped. 'Good God. You don't think the captain murdered his first wife, do you?'

Cook wrung her hands. 'No, I don't. But what else could it be?'

'Why would Alba apologize for that?'

'Dear Verity, Alba was apologizing for finding out.'

'Of course.'

'I'd never imagine the captain capable of murder,' said Cook.

'Remember, there was a war on. He was killing Germans left, right, and center and a jolly good thing too! And if Valentina was anything like as temperamental as Alba, I wouldn't blame him!'

'May God strike you down!' chided Cook.

'Not until I've had the last scone,' said Verity and she popped it into her mouth.

Cook felt relieved to have unburdened her secret to her friend. Verity didn't enjoy the same sensation. Her nausea had had nothing to do with Cook's revelations and everything to do with the scones. To her shame, on her way home, she had to stop the car at the end of the drive and vomit into the bushes.

★　　★　　★

When the taxi that carried Fitz and Alba into central London swung into Earls Court, Alba forgot the sorrow of leaving Incantellaria and wriggled about in her seat with excitement. It was a clear October day. The sunshine tumbled in through the window and fell on the engagement ring that twinkled on her hand.

'I can't believe we're home,' she said with a sigh, watching it sparkle and moving her fingers to catch the light. 'To think of my cupboards full of beautiful clothes. I could die of happiness.' Fitz worried about the state of her boat. Knowing Alba, she wouldn't have emptied the fridge before leaving and the place would smell horrible. 'I feel I've been away for an age.'

'I hope your boat is still there.'

The taxi drove into Cheyne Walk. Alba sat up and looked through the front window.

'There she is!' she announced, pointing. Then, 'Bloody hell!'

Fitz leaned forward, his heart sinking at the thought of her desiccated home. He paid the taxi and followed Alba down the pontoon with the suitcases.

'I barely recognize it,' she said in delight. 'It's even had a new coat of paint!'

'Viv!' he said, dropping the cases. 'She's covered the deck with plants and flowers. It almost looks as immaculate as hers, except yours is more eccentric, like you.' Alba put the key in the lock and opened the door.

'It even smells of Viv,' she said with a laugh, sniffing the incense that hung in the air. Viv had washed and ironed all the clothes she had found hanging in the bathroom and cleaned the place from top to bottom. Alba opened the fridge. 'She's bought milk!' she shouted. 'We can have a cup of tea!' Fitz carried in the suitcases, then walked up the shining corridor to the kitchen.

'How did she get in?' he asked.

'She has a key. I gave it to her eons ago, in case it caught fire or something when I wasn't around.' Fitz pulled her into his arms and kissed her.

'Forget the tea,' he said. 'I've got a much better idea.'

Alba shot him a mischievous look. 'You and I aren't so dissimilar after all,' she laughed. She led him upstairs to her bedroom beneath the skylight. The room was neat and clean; the leak had been mended. On the bed lay a note.

As this will be your first port of call, I decided to leave the note on the bed. I probably won't be there on your return as Fitzroy didn't seem to know when he would be coming home. I only hope that you have done the decent thing and agreed to marry him. Poor darling, how he has pined! I took the liberty of dusting down the boat, it was a terrible mess and putting me off my breakfast every morning I suffered the sight of it. Not to mention the smell of squirrel excrement. Why they can't do it somewhere else is beyond me. Welcome home, darling, and forgive an old bird for being bitter and twisted. The goat was a hoot and I forgive you too?! Back soon. In France with Pierre (ask Fitzroy). Love has never been so good. Kisses in abundance, Viv

Alba looked steadily at Fitz. 'Love has never been so good,' she said and caressed his bristly face with her hand. 'Did you pine?'

'Yes,' he replied. 'Viv persuaded me to go and find you.' 'Good old Viv.'

'She's a good friend, Alba.'

'And so are you. Thank you, Fitz, for sticking by me.'

'You ran off with my heart; I had to chase after it.'

'It's mine now,' she said with a smile. 'I'm going to keep it, and this time, I'm going to treat it with care.'

He wrapped his arms around her and pulled her down onto the bed. This time making love to Alba was slow, intimate and tender. He wasn't left feeling empty and dissatisfied. He gave her his soul and received hers in return. She was like a rare and beautiful butterfly that he could hold in his hands. She didn't fly away.

After they had lazed together in a warm bath, Fitz lay on the bed while Alba went through her cupboards deciding what to wear for her father and stepmother. He noticed that she didn't throw the discarded items onto the floor as before but folded them up and put them back. She laughed at the blue suede clog boots and patterned tights, the tiny skirts and brightly coloured coats. 'I forgot how much stuff I had,' she muttered, passing her eye over the rows of handbags and shoes. 'God, I was extravagant. And Cosima thought five dresses was the end of the world.' She caught her breath as she remembered the little girl waving on the quay. She turned to Fitz. 'I don't know what to wear. Nothing feels right. I don't want to look like a tart anymore. I want to look like a young woman on the brink of becoming Mrs. Fitzroy Davenport. These clothes aren't suitable for her.'

Fitz laughed. 'Oh, darling. You'll get used to them again. In the meantime, why don't you put on a pair of jeans and a sweater?'

'I don't want any of these clothes anymore!' A frown drew her eyebrows together. 'I've moved on.'

Fitz came up behind her and put his arms around her waist. 'You look gorgeous in whatever you wear.'

She shrugged him off and began to search frantically through her drawers. Finally, in exasperation, she pulled out a faded pair of denim jeans and a white shirt.

'How's this?'

'Perfect for the future Mrs. Fitzroy Davenport.' She smiled, and Fitz was filled with relief. 'What will Margo think when David and Penelope Davenport aren't on the guest list?' he said with a chuckle.

'With any luck she's forgotten.'

'Do you think I should come clean?'

'Not a good plan.'

'I should probably write out a fake address for them.'

'That's a better idea. You can always say they sent their regrets.' Alba tried to be jolly but something was making her uncomfortable. She looked about the room that held within it so many memories. Memories that now belonged to a life she had grown out of. 'Let's go,' she suggested. 'We can take a cab to your house, pick up your things, and take your car to Beechfield. I'd sooner get going.'

'Don't you want to telephone them first?'

'No,' Alba replied. 'I've always much preferred the element of surprise.'

Fitz packed while Alba lay on the sofa reading the newspapers. Sprout was still at Fitz's mother's in the country, being fed a diet of chopped liver and steak, no doubt. Fitz's mother had never quite got over her children's leaving the nest. 'He won't want to come back,' Fitz shouted to Alba from the bedroom. 'I couldn't bear that. Life without Sprout would be miserable.' But Alba wasn't listening. She wasn't reading the papers either. Her thoughts were with Cosima and Falco.

The drive down the country lanes was just what Alba needed to lift her spirits. The sight of the falling leaves, turned golden in the autumn sunlight, warmed her heart.

The wind carried them on its tail, so that they danced pretty twirls before landing on the ground as light as snowflakes, and the odd pheasant flew out from the hedgerows, his feathers spraying into the air. The plowed fields lay bare beneath the sky, and large black birds pecked at the corn left there by the combines at harvest time. Autumn was, along with spring, her favorite season, for she relished the change, before summer lost its bloom, while winter lay sleeping. She hoped that maybe they could buy a small house in the countryside somewhere. Live a quieter life. She no longer felt at home in her houseboat and London had lost its appeal. She looked across at Fitz. She would make him happy.

Her heart swelled as the car swept up the drive. The gravel was strewn with orange and brown leaves which Peter, the gardener, was doing his best to sweep away for burning. He tipped his cap at her and she waved back. She didn't feel strange coming home as she had so often felt in the past. She felt she belonged there, for memories of her childhood were attached to every corner of the estate. Memories forgotten and now remembered.

Fitz tooted the horn. The house rose up before them imperious and still, the curve in the roof betraying a secret smile, for it had watched for centuries the ups and downs of the lives within it with quiet amusement. As they drew up, the door opened and Thomas stood there at the top of the steps. Alba was struck immediately by the change in his demeanor. He stood straight with his shoulders back, his head high, his delight at the sight of them unreserved and true. Alba's legs felt weak. She opened the door and climbed out shakily. Her father was no longer in the doorframe but striding toward her with his arms outstretched. Gone were the shadows that lurked about his eyes and the tension that had vibrated in the air between them. He kissed her affectionately and a lump in her throat prevented her from speaking. 'What a tremendous surprise!' he said, shaking Fitz's hand. 'This is wonderful news, dear boy. Wonderful. Come on in and I'll open a bottle of champagne.'

They followed him through the hall to the drawing room, where the air was warm and scented with cinnamon. The fire roared in the grate. 'Where's Margo?' Alba asked, noticing the lack of dogs.

'Out in the garden. I'll give her a yell.' Thomas strode into the hall. Cook emerged from the kitchen.

'Is that Alba?' she asked, keeping her sentence short in case the word 'murder' slipped out by mistake.

'Yes, isn't it a lovely surprise!' he exclaimed, walking on through the house.

'I must get on and make some scones,' she muttered, not daring to disturb the young couple in the drawing room.

Alba perched on the club fender and looked at Fitz. 'Have you noticed too?'

He nodded. 'Has he had a face-lift?'

Alba giggled. 'He's certainly got a spring in his step. Could my letter really have made such a difference?'

'I'm sure it has. The truth about your mother has obviously tormented him for years. Now you know about it, he must feel liberated.'

'And he's pleased I'm marrying you!' She rested her head on his shoulder.

'Only until he realizes I'm not one of the distinguished Davenports.'

'Oh, he's too delighted to care!'

At that moment the scurrying of little paws could be heard scratching across the hall floor. Alba lifted her head off Fitz's shoulder and stood up. The dogs trotted in followed by Margo and Thomas, Margo dressed in brown trousers and a tweed jacket over a cashmere beige sweater.

Her cheeks were ruddy and weathered and her nose red. When she saw Alba's short hair she flinched. 'Darling girl, what a lovely surprise. You look gorgeous. You really do.' She studied her stepdaughter with ill-concealed amazement. 'How different you look. It suits you. It really does, doesn't it, darling? You look lovely!' She pressed her cold face against Alba's before hurriedly pulling away. 'I'm so sorry,' she said, clasping her cheeks. 'I must be freezing. I won't kiss you, Fitz, because I'm so cold. I've been doing things in the garden. There's so much to do. Many congratulations! Will you have a summer wedding?' Alba and Fitz sat down. 'Goodness, look at the ring. Isn't it lovely. Is it a family ring?'

'It belonged to my grandmother,' Fitz replied.

'It looks beautiful, Alba, especially on your lovely brown hands. Goodness, don't you look well.'

Thomas stared at his daughter. He had noticed the change in her face but hadn't immediately understood why. Now he saw that she had cut her hair. She looked smaller without it, more fragile and certainly less like her mother. He wanted to thank her for the letter but felt the moment was inappropriate. Instead he poured her a glass of champagne. She lifted her eyes and held his for a moment. To her bewilderment she was reminded of Falco and the silent understanding that had passed between them. He had looked at her like that too, as if they were partners in crime, set apart from everyone else by their conspiracy. But before she could dwell on it there was a rustle at the door.

'Am I missing a party? I hate to miss a party.' Lavender, bent and frail, was in the doorway, leaning heavily on a walking stick, her watery eyes scanning the room for the visitor.

30

'Ah, Alba,' said Lavender, spotting her granddaughter. 'When's the wedding? I love a good wedding.' She hobbled over in spite of Margo's attempts to direct her to the leather reading chair. Alba was surprised her grandmother recognized her with short hair. She had never recognized her before. 'It's about time we had a wedding at Beechfield.'

'Thank you, Grandma,' said Alba, kissing her face where her skin was soft and diaphanous like the skin on a mushroom. 'I'm amazed you recognize me!'

Lavender was put out. 'Of course I recognize you. Good God, I really would be over the hill if I failed to recognize my own granddaughter. I like the hair, by the way. Suits you.'

'Thank you.' She looked at her father, who shrugged back at her, as bewildered as she. Margo attempted to help her to the chair but Lavender shrugged her off with a huff.

'Now, Alba. You come with me. I have something for you.' Alba pulled a face at Fitz.

'Don't be long,' said Margo, looking disappointed. 'We have so much to talk about. You will stay, won't you? I'll show Fitz to his room.'

Alba followed her grandmother up the stairs. She knew

better than to help her, even though the old woman climbed with difficulty. They walked down a long corridor; Lavender's suite of rooms was around a corner at the very end. The door was small – Alba had to bend down but once inside, it opened into a large square sitting room with tall ceilings and sash windows and a big, open fireplace which smoldered cheerfully. Next door was her bathroom and bedroom. 'Sit down, won't you,' she said. 'When I lived here this was a rather cold guest room. We rarely used it. However, now I spend most of my time in here, I can appreciate the magnificent views of the gardens. I especially love the frost in winter and the end of the day in summertime. I wouldn't want to be anywhere else.' Alba flopped into an armchair beside the fire. 'Do put another log on, dear. I don't want you catching a chill. Not before your wedding.' She disappeared into her bedroom. Alba looked about her. The room was decorated in pretty pale greens and yellows. It was light and smelled of roses. On the surfaces were little knickknacks: imitation Fabergé eggs, Halcyon Days pots, china birds, and photographs in silver frames.

Lavender returned with a red box. It was flat and square and the gold motif that decorated it was faded. Alba knew instantly that it contained a piece of jewelry. 'I wore this on my wedding day and my mother on hers. I want you to wear it when you and Fitz marry. I think you'll find it suitable.'

'How generous, Grandma,' she said, excitedly. 'I'm sure it'll be perfect.'

'Things of such quality never date, you see,' said Lavender. Alba pressed the little gold button and lifted the lid. Inside shone a three-tier pearl choker.

'It's beautiful,' she gasped.

'It's valuable too, but the monetary value is nothing

compared to the sentimental value. My wedding day was the happiest of my life and I know my mother's brought her great joy. I like Fitz. He's kind and there's a lot to be said for that these days. When you're as old as I am one realizes that kindness is the most admirable quality a person can have.'

'I will wear it with pride, Grandma.'

'And your daughter will wear it too and hers after her. It's a family tradition. Not an Arbuckle one. It runs along the female line, otherwise I would have given it to Margo when she married Thomas. No, I kept it for you. You're the eldest girl and it's yours by right.'

Alba tried it on, standing in front of the gilt mirror that hung above the fireplace. She ran her fingers over the pearls. 'I love it,' she enthused, turning to show her grandmother.

'They're very soft against the skin. I think they're most flattering. You have a lovely long neck, you see that's important to carry them off. You must have inherited that from me. The rest of you is entirely your mother, though. Arbuckles are fair.' Alba sat down and placed the pearls back in the box.

'Did my father ever talk to you about my mother?' she asked.

'A terrible business it was,' Lavender said, shaking her head. 'I admit my short-term memory isn't good, but I remember the day he came back from Italy, carrying that small baby in his arms, as if it were yesterday.'

'I grew up thinking he had married my mother,' said Alba, wondering how much her grandmother knew. She needn't have worried, however, for Lavender knew it all.

'I thought the war had broken Tommy,' she said. Alba noticed the name. The tender sound of it. Her face softened in the orange glow of the fire and she suddenly looked younger. 'But Valentina broke him. The murder was one thing, a terrible, brutal thing to do to a woman, but I think had she survived, the woman he loved had already died, there in that car in her diamonds and furs. The shock of it cut him to the quick. She might just as well have scooped out his insides with a spoon!' She paused for a moment.

'How did he meet Margo?'

'It was raining the day your father returned. He had wired us in advance but of course we knew nothing of what had happened to Valentina. We didn't expect a small baby. He arrived on the steps, the raindrops bouncing off his hat, with you in his arms, wrapped in a dreadfully inadequate blanket. I took you and we sat by the fire. You were very tiny and vulnerable. You didn't look a bit like Tommy, except for your eyes. I loved you then as if you were my own. We talked long into the night, your grandfather, Tommy, and I. He told us everything. He showed us the picture he had drawn. She was a beautiful girl, Valentina. The secretive look in that barely perceptible smile. Tommy didn't see it, neither did Hubert, but I did. I wouldn't have trusted her as far as I could throw her, but I wasn't there to warn him. Men are so gullible when faced with such beauty. We resolved then not to tell anyone that the marriage had never happened, for your sake. There's a nasty word for children born out of wedlock and we didn't want you to live with the shame of it. Things were different in those days. Tommy bought the bloody boat he had served on, the MTB, can't remember the number. He spent a small fortune converting it into a houseboat. He would spend the weeks in London working, coming down at the weekend to be with you.' Lavender's face glowed with pride. 'I had you to myself and I looked after you as if you were mine.'

'So the *Valentina* was his MTB?' said Alba in amazement.

'He was obsessed with it. I felt I had lost him too. But I had you.' She turned to Alba and her eyes glistened with tears. 'You were *my* baby. Then Margo came along.'

'How did they meet?' she asked again.

Lavender took a breath. 'Tommy was invited hunting in Gloucestershire and she was part of the house party. I don't think he fell in love. She was capable, funny, down to earth, and genuine. He wanted to get married. He wanted a mother for you.' Her face grew taut. 'She made a good wife too. Tommy was hopeless. He couldn't even wash his own shirt. The houseboat was a mess. I went once but never again. He led a decadent life. Had more than his fair share of girlfriends. He knew he needed to settle down. Margo swept into his life and put it in order. She was terrific with you, I give her that. They moved into the Dower House and started their own family. At first she brought you over to see me every day. You almost lived here at Beechfield as a little girl and we were very, very close.' She smiled again. 'You used to like playing hunt the thimble. You'd play it for hours and I read those Alison Uttley *Grey Rabbit* books over and over again. You adored Hare. 'A saw to saw things,' do you remember? No, I don't suppose you remember much of that time. You were little. But you loved me. Then Caroline came along and Miranda, then Henry, and little by little, you were swallowed up into Margo's family. You weren't mine any longer.'

'But Grandma, you never recognized me!' said Alba.

Lavender tutted loudly. 'Of course I recognized you, dear. I was only riling Margo. I never meant to hurt you in the process. I was just bitter that I was pushed aside when you were like a daughter to me. The daughter I never had. Forgive me.'

'There is nothing to forgive, Grandma,' said Alba, reaching out to touch her. 'I haven't exactly been the easiest person to be around, either. I've been horrid to Margo too.'

'So have I,' said Lavender guiltily. 'But she's been a good mother to you and she was good to Tommy. She picked him up and put him together. Took on his child and nursed his heart. She even put up with that silly boat he refused to get rid of. She's a strong woman, Alba. She's had to put up with a lot.'

'I wondered why that picture was under the bed,' she murmured. 'It all makes sense now. No wonder Margo never visited me there. She hates the boat for good reason.'

'Well, you won't want to live there now you're marrying Fitz.'

'I want to live in the country,' she said.

Lavender's eyes lit up. 'Oh, you can live in the Dower House. It's only rented out.'

'That's a brilliant idea!'

'After Hubert died, I was very happy there.'

'I'd like to spend time with Daddy. I've been horrid to him too.'

'Well, he's had a hard time. That, combined with the fact that you looked so like your mother. There was no escaping her. Then, as you grew older, he was always debating whether or not to tell you. It was a terrible burden.'

'I wrote him a letter from Italy when I found out,' she said brightly.

'And it's done him the world of good. He can finally put it all behind him and so must you. You're about to marry Fitz and start a family of your own now.'

'Thank you for the necklace. I'll treasure it,' she said and got up to kiss her grandmother fondly.

'You're a good girl, Alba,' said Lavender, patting her arm. 'You've finally grown up. About time too!'

When Alba and Lavender returned to the drawing room, Fitz was drinking champagne with Thomas and Margo. 'Look what Grandma has given me,' said Alba, rushing up to her father and opening the box.

'Ah, the pearl necklace, how nice,' he said. 'You'll make a beautiful bride in those.'

'How lovely,' enthused Margo, standing over them. 'How jolly generous of you, Lavender.'

'We've had a nice chat,' said Alba, sitting beside Fitz. 'I had never been up to her rooms before.'

'Not as comfortable as the Dower House, I'm afraid,' said Margo. 'But at least here we're all together.'

'Lavender suggested that we have the Dower House once we're married,' Alba volunteered. 'What do you think, Daddy?'

Thomas looked pleased. 'I think it's a tremendous idea. We lived there when we were first married.'

'Thank you, Thomas,' said Fitz, a little uneasily. 'We'll think about it.' Alba frowned at him. 'Well, darling, remember I work in London.' Alba felt deflated. She didn't want to live in London.

Later, in his bedroom, she broached the subject again. 'Can't you commute?' she said, lying on the bed while he changed for dinner.

Fitz sighed. 'I'm not sure that it's feasible.'

'Think how much Sprout would love it here. All this land to run about on. We could perhaps buy him a friend.'

He buttoned up his shirt. 'I thought you loved the city.'

'I used to. I've grown disenchanted by it.'

'That's only because you've been living in Incantellaria

for five months. You'll snap out of it. You'll be trawling the shops on Bond Street again before you can blink.'

'I want a quieter life now,' she said, remembering the trattoria with a stab of regret. 'I miss it.'

'Say we compromise,' he suggested. 'We could have the Dower House at weekends.'

'What am I supposed to do all week?'

'Paint.'

'In London?'

'You can convert my spare room into a studio.'

'I need the countryside to inspire me,' she said, nearly choking on the thought of those lemon groves, the old lookout point, the wide expanse of sea, and of Cosima, her curls bouncing about her shoulders, twirling around in her new dresses.

'Darling, you've only just come back. Give yourself time to adjust.' He kissed her. 'I love you. I want you to be happy. If you want to be here, then we'll work something out.'

After dinner, during which they had discussed the wedding in great detail, Thomas asked Alba into the study. 'There's something I want you to have,' he said, exchanging a glance with his wife.

'I'll be there shortly. I just need something from my room,' she replied, running off into the hall. Thomas went into the study and took the portrait of his father down from the wall.

He reached into the safe and grabbed the scroll that lay right at the very back. He no longer felt the pull of Valentina's presence, that invisible demand to be remembered. He opened it to look at her once again. This time he felt detached; for the first time, her face seemed that of a stranger to him. At last he could relegate her to the past and leave her there.

Alba stepped into the room and closed the door behind her. She saw the scroll in his hand and looked at him questioningly. 'I think you should have this,' he said, handing it to her. 'I don't want it anymore.'

'She was beautiful, wasn't she? But very human,' she said, watching her father pour himself a whiskey and sit down in the worn leather chair he always sat in after dinner. He leaned over and opened the humidor, chose a cigar, and began slowly to cut it.

'So, how was Incantellaria?'

'Probably the same as when you were there. It's one of those places that will never change.'

'You said in your letter that Immacolata is still going strong. I'll be damned. She was old when I knew her.'

'She's very small and wizened, like a nut. But she loves me like a daughter. When I first arrived she never smiled. Then later, when I convinced her to get rid of those morbid shrines, she wore colours again and a rather beautiful smile.'

'I imagine she was once a lovely-looking young woman.' He recalled Jack warning him off Valentina because all daughters grow up to look like their mothers. Valentina did not live long enough to disprove his theory.

'I worked in the trattoria with Toto and Falco,' Alba continued.

'Toto all grown up, eh?'

'He has a daughter called Cosima.' Suddenly her face turned solemn and she took a deep breath. 'The point is, Daddy, that I understand now why you protected me from your past. I've behaved appallingly. I want to apologize.'

Thomas lit his cigar, puffing on it until the little end glowed with fire. 'It wasn't your fault. Perhaps I should have told you sooner. There was never a good moment.'

'Well, there's no better moment than the present for this,' she said, handing him the third portrait. 'Falco said I should give it to you, although I wasn't sure I should.'

'Where the devil did you find this?' He didn't know whether to be pleased or shocked. How he had searched for it. How it had tormented him.

Alba braced herself. 'I've solved it all, Daddy. I've solved the murder.'

'Go on.'

'Fitz and I went to Palazzo Montelimone.'

'You did, did you?' His expression was inscrutable.

'Falco and Immacolata told us not to go, so I knew there was something there that they didn't want me to find. An extraordinary man lives there called Nero. He said he inherited the ruin from his lover, the marchese. Anyway, he showed us this little folly. The marchese's sanctuary. He had kept it all as the marchese had left it. The portrait was hidden in there, by the bed. Nero broke down and confessed. Valentina was the marchese's lover, and it was he who murdered her. I knew she hadn't been an innocent bystander in a Mafia hit. When I heard that she had been dressed in diamonds and furs, I just knew it didn't add up.' She watched the smoke of her father's cigar form a cloud around him. 'Lattarullo said that even the best detectives in Italy hadn't worked it out. But that's not all, Daddy.'

'What else did you dig up?' he asked. His voice was steady, for he already knew. There was only one more piece left to the puzzle.

'Falco admitted that he killed the marchese.' Thomas nodded in acknowledgment. 'He said it was a matter of honour.'

'It was more than honour to me.'

Alba stared at him, her eyes wide with a mixture of

horror and admiration. The final piece to the puzzle had caused the whole picture to shift. He caught her staring and did not look away. There was something unfamiliar in his eyes. A ruthlessness she had never seen before.

'You were with him, weren't you?' she whispered. 'Falco wasn't alone, was he? You were with him. You both killed the marchese.'

Thomas answered her quietly. 'I did nothing then that I wouldn't do again.'

He handed her back the third portrait. 'You should keep this, Alba. By rights, it belongs to you.' He got up, stretched, and threw his half-smoked cigar into the fire. 'Shall we go back and join the others?'

That night when Thomas went to bed he felt light-headed with joy. 'Darling,' he said. 'It's time to get rid of the boat.' Margo was speechless. 'I don't think we should sell it. I think we should scuttle it. Sink it. Send it to the bottom of the sea along with everything it represents. It's time to let it go.'

Margo rolled over and rested her head on his chest. 'Won't Alba mind?' she asked.

'No, she's going to marry Fitz and live somewhere else. Either here or London. The *Valentina* is too small for the two of them.'

'They don't seem to agree where to live,' said Margo.

'They will. They'll just have to compromise.'

She leaned up and kissed his cheek. 'Thank you, Tommy,' she said.

'You know, you just called me Tommy,' he said in surprise.

'Did I?' she exclaimed, laughing. 'I didn't notice. Tommy! I rather like it.'

'So do I,' he said and pulled her against him. 'And I like you, darling. I like you very, very much.'

In the morning Thomas did something he should have done years ago. He walked into his study and closed the door. He sat at his desk and opened his address book. He fingered his way down to H. Then he dialed the number. After a few rings a voice he had known all his youth answered. The years fell away and he felt like a young officer again.

'Hello, Jack old boy, it's Tommy.'

31

Alba wasn't sad to see the boat scuttled. It felt like the right thing to do, after all that had happened. They dragged it out into the middle of the Channel, drilled a leak into the gas pipe, then waited as the gas built up in the bilges before dramatically catching fire with the pilot light. She stood with Margo, Fitz, and her father and watched it sink. It took longer than she expected. For a while it resisted the pull, then finally it was gone and the sea lay flat and still as before. She imagined it falling silently to the bottom, landing on sand where fish would swim in and out of the windows and coral would grow up the hull. The boat was the last link with Valentina. Now they could all get on with their lives. She noticed her father had his arm around Margo's waist and that he was gently caressing her hip. She noticed too that she called him Tommy and that he seemed to like it.

She moved into Fitz's mews house, converted the spare room into a studio, and drew endless portraits of Sprout. Sprout was only too happy to sit for her and seemed not to tire of her chat as she told him of their wedding, set to take place in the spring. He even raised his ears at the right moments and sighed in sympathy when she complained of feeling overwhelmed by it all. Margo was indefatigable. She had hired a tent and caterers. Beechfield buzzed with the coming and going of the people Margo had hired to do the flowers, the cars, the invitations, the gardens, the lighting, the music. There was much to organize and she threw herself into it with great enthusiasm. She and Alba spoke every day on the telephone and at last they had something in common that they both enjoyed discussing. To Alba's surprise, Margo listened to her ideas and was happy to go along with them. To Margo's surprise, Alba seemed not to mind taking her advice and never once threw a tantrum or sulked.

'Edith says that Mrs. Arbuckle and Alba are getting on like a house on fire,' said Verity, taking off her coat for bell-ringing practice.

'Nothing like a wedding to bring people together,' Hannah said.

'Or tear them apart,' added Verity with a snort. 'Weddings are like Christmas; all those ghastly people one hasn't seen for decades for jolly good reason. Ghastly things.'

'Oh, Verity. Don't tell me you don't like Christmas,' said Hannah, placing her scarf on the bench and patting her bun to check that it was in place.

'What's the point?' she asked, shrugging off the bitterness she felt at having no family left with whom to celebrate. Only her husband, and she thought him more tiresome than the most tedious relative.

'It's for the children, really,' said Fred, taking his rope and giving it a good pull. 'That's my girl!' he exclaimed when it rang.

'It'll be a lovely day, Alba's wedding,' said Hannah. 'Mrs. Arbuckle always does the church flowers beautifully, so the flowers will be spectacular. After all, it'll be spring and she'll have lots of choice.'

'I can see Alba with white flowers in her hair,' said Fred softly.

'Oh, Fred, you old romantic,' teased Hannah. Verity just looked cross. They stopped talking at the sound of footsteps on the stairs. Reverend Weatherbone had a distinctive spring in his stride and they all knew it was he before he reached their small attic.

'Good morning,' he said jovially. His hair was sticking out at the sides in grey wings, like on a bird that's just landed. 'I hope you've thought of a suitable rendition for Alba's wedding.'

'I've taken the liberty of composing one myself,' said Fred.

'Good,' nodded the vicar.

Verity looked put out. 'You didn't tell us about composing anything,' she said.

'He told me,' lied Hannah, then muttered a quick apology. After all, she was in God's house, in the presence of the vicar. She was getting less tolerant of Verity in her old age.

'Well, I'll let you know whether I think we should play it or not once I've heard it.'

'Isn't it delightful that Alba and Fitzroy are tying the knot in our small church? It's a great honour for me,' said Reverend Weatherbone. He couldn't help but add an afterthought, or rather, one that had occupied a great deal more of his mind than was suitable. 'I wonder what her dress will be like.'

'Short, I should imagine,' said Verity.

'Traditional,' Hannah interjected. 'Alba is a traditional girl at heart. Look where she comes from.'

'Italy?' said Verity, raising an eyebrow.

'She's only been to Italy once. That hardly makes her Italian. She's very much one of us,' said Hannah, pursing her lips.

'It's in the blood,' said Verity. 'She's not at all like the rest of the family. Arbuckles are fair and Alba is brown.'

'She's exotic,' said the vicar. 'She'll make a beautiful bride.'

'She will indeed,' Fred agreed, stroking the rope absentmindedly. 'Mrs. Arbuckle will wear something special too, I should imagine.'

'She's not the girl's mother, though, is she?' said Verity slowly.

Reverend Weatherbone noticed her snake eyes narrowing ominously. It was only a matter of time before her forked tongue would slither out with some terrible revelation heard from Edith.

He sighed. 'No, not biologically, but she's been more than a mother to Alba.' He injected authority into his voice, hoping to end the discussion there.

'A shame Alba's real mother won't see her wed. I took such pride in my daughter on her wedding day. I'll always remember it,' said Hannah.

'I knew Alba as a baby,' said Fred.

'And as a teenager, drinking in the Hen's Legs,' Hannah reminded him, winking. He grinned back mischievously. Those days had been good.

'Do you know how her mother died?' Verity asked. Reverend Weatherbone summoned his wisdom and rummaged around for compassion; there was precious little for Verity.

'She died in a car crash,' he said. 'It was a long time ago.' Just as he was about to change the subject, Verity interrupted.

'No, she didn't.'

'I don't know who you've been listening to,' said the Reverend.

'Edith overheard them talking. The captain murdered

her.' Hannah's mouth swung open and Fred looked bewildered. Reverend Weatherbone put down his Bible.

'What utter nonsense, Verity Forthright. You and Edith should be ashamed of yourselves, spreading vicious and unfounded rumours. This is God's house and I am the keeper of it. While that is so, I will not tolerate lies to be spread among the good people of Beechfield.' His voice resounded down the nave, echoing off the walls as if it were the voice of God. 'Do you understand, Verity?' His bright, shiny eyes bore into her and she shrank back beneath the weight of them.

She swallowed hard. 'That's what Edith heard.'

'Do you know what an eye for an eye, a tooth for a tooth means?'

'Of course I do.'

'It means, Verity, that as you sow, so shall you reap. I would be very careful what you sow, for you shall reap it all, tenfold. We are masters of our own fate. If I were you I would spread a little kindness about you. That too comes back tenfold. Now, wouldn't that be a surprise? I look forward to hearing your composition, Fred. Let me know when you have practiced it sufficiently. Now, let us hear less about murder and more about marriage. Alba's mother is with God and she will be present in spirit at her daughter's wedding. Don't think for a moment that she won't.' With that he turned, sending his robes flying about him, and was gone.

'That's my girl,' chuckled Fred, pulling his bell again. 'Ring out for the reverend!'

Christmas at Beechfield Park came and went with the snow, and the New Year began with a large firework display for the whole village in the field above the house. Fitz and Alba watched the bright lights explode into showers of glitter, illuminating their faces with wonder. Fitz looked ahead to the new year with optimism and joy. Alba watched the children with their sparklers and thought of Cosima. How she would love them. Time did nothing to diminish her affection or assuage her anguish. Fitz didn't notice that little by little he was losing her. That as each day passed, her mind was less on their future and more on her past.

One winter weekend, when the rain threw itself against the windowpanes, Alba sat down with Margo to write the invitations. Margo put on Mozart and lit the fire, while Fitz played a game of squash with Henry. Miranda and Caroline, who were to be bridesmaids, had gone shopping in Winchester. Margo had noticed that Alba had withdrawn into herself recently. Grown quiet and thoughtful. This was meant to be the happiest time in her life and yet she didn't seem happy. As they were alone in the cozy environment of the drawing room, she decided to do some gentle probing.

'Darling, you seem a little distracted,' she began apprehensively, taking off her reading glasses and leaving them to hang on their chain. 'You're not nervous about the wedding, are you?'

Alba didn't look at her. 'I'm fine,' she said. 'It's just all a little overwhelming.'

'I know. There's so much being organized around you, I bet you feel sometimes that you're about to sink beneath it all.'

'Yes,' Alba agreed, licking an envelope and sticking it down.

'Have you and Fitz decided where you're going to live yet?'

Alba sighed. 'Not yet. He's really got to live in London as it's not convenient to commute. But I want to be here.'

'But what about all your friends?'

'What friends, Margo? You know I don't have any. I had boyfriends, but they're hardly appropriate now. And Viv's spending all her time in France with Pierre. Fitz is my friend. I want to be where he is. It's just a shame it has to be London.'

'Maybe only for a little while. Perhaps when you have children it'll be suitable for you all to move to the country.'

'I wish Cosima could be a bridesmaid,' she said and felt a swell of emotion. 'She would so enjoy it.'

'You miss them, don't you?' said Margo, realizing the root of the problem.

'I miss them all, but I miss Cosima the most. I can't stop thinking about her. Talking to her on the telephone from time to time isn't the same. There's a delay and she's shy of it. My throat aches so much trying not to cry, I sort of dread it.' She swallowed hard. 'I feel desperate. She needs me and I'm not there.'

'Have you and Fitz talked about living in Italy?'

Alba laughed at the absurdity of the idea. 'He could never live in that sleepy place.'

Suddenly her stepmother's face turned very serious and she put down her pen. 'Darling, if you don't feel ready to get married, you can still call it off.' Alba looked at her with astonishment, like a drowning person suddenly thrown an unexpected lifeline. 'Your father and I won't mind. We just want you to be happy.'

'But you've organized everything. Gone to so much trouble. We're about to send out the invitations. I couldn't pull out now!'

Margo placed her hand on Alba's arm. Once it would have felt odd, but now it felt quite natural. Motherly.

'Darling girl,' said Margo gently. 'I would much prefer to cancel the wedding than have you sitting in London all miserable. There's no point going through with it if you're just going to divorce three years down the line. Imagine if you have children, what a ghastly business. If you want to go and live in Italy, we'll all understand and support you. If your heart is there, darling, follow it.' Alba blinked back tears and threw her arms around Margo's neck.

'I thought you'd be cross with me.'

'Oh, Alba, how you misunderstand me.' She pushed her stepdaughter away and lifted the gold locket that hung on her bosom. 'You see this?' she said. Alba nodded, wiping her face with her hand. 'I always wear it. Never take it off, ever. That's because it contains photos of my children. All four of them.' She opened it so that Alba could see. There inside neat little gold frames were small black-and-white photographs of her, Caroline, Miranda, and Henry as children. 'I love you the same as I love them. How could I not understand?'

'I'd better talk to Fitz,' said Alba finally, sniffing.

'You had better,' Margo agreed and they put all the unwritten invitations back into the box.

Alba dreaded breaking her news to Fitz. After all he had done for her, after all the time he had waited. It seemed so unfair that he was going to be hurt all over again. But as she climbed the stairs to his room she felt the quiet tingle of excitement stir within her. She pictured Cosima's little face aglow with happiness, and Immacolata and Falco smiling with joy. She saw them on the quay, welcoming her home. She knew it was the right thing to do. She knew that Fitz couldn't go with her. What would he do in such a small, provincial place?

She waited on his bed for him to return from his game of squash. The light faded and heavy dark clouds gathered in the sky. The trees were bare, their branches like hundreds of wispy fingers against the desolate backdrop. Finally, she heard voices on the stairs, the cheerful banter between him and her brother. She felt nervous. It would have been so easy to go along with it all and pretend to be happy.

Fitz registered her solemn face at once. 'What's happened?' he asked, his own good humour dispersing like bubbles.

Alba took a deep breath and plunged in. 'I want to go back to Italy.'

'I see,' he said. 'Since when?' Suddenly the air was heavy with sorrow. He sat on the bed.

'Ever since I came back, I think.'

'Have you discussed this with your parents?'

'Only Margo. I want you to come with me.'

He shook his head and stared out of the window. 'My life is here, Alba.' He felt a nasty sense of déjà vu.

'But couldn't you write a book?' she said, kneeling behind him, winding her arms around his shoulders.

'I'm an agent, not a writer.'

'You've never tried.' She pressed her cheek, damp with tears, to his.

He frowned. 'Don't you love me?' he asked and his voice cracked.

'Yes, I do,' she exclaimed, desperate to alleviate the sorrow in his soft brown eyes. 'I love you so much. We're meant to be together. Oh Fitz!' she sighed. 'What are we going to do?'

He drew her into his arms and held her tightly. 'You can't live here and I can't live there.'

The butterfly was spreading her wings, ready to fly away again. This time, he didn't know whether he'd ever get her back.

'I have to go, Fitz. Cosima needs me. I belong there.'

She nuzzled her face into his neck. 'Don't say you won't come. Don't say it's over. I couldn't bear it. Let's just see. If you change your mind, I'll be waiting for you. I'll be waiting and hoping and ready to welcome you with open arms. My love won't grow cold, not in Italy.'

Epilogue

Italy 1972

Alba's heart was full. Spring in Incantellaria was the most beautiful spring in the world. Small birds hopped on the tables and chairs outside the trattoria and the sun bathed the sea below it in the gentle, translucent light of morning. Alba wiped her hands on her apron. She wore a simple wraparound dress imprinted with blue flowers, and flip-flops. She had painted her toenails with pink varnish she and Cosima had bought at the dwarfs' shop. She had painted Cosima's too, which had taken far longer than it should have, thanks to her moving her toes and giggling. Alba ran a hand across her forehead. It was hot there in the trattoria and she worked hard, buying supplies, setting tables, serving customers. She had even learned how to cook. She had never believed herself capable of preparing delicious meals. Even Immacolata was impressed. Beata congratulated her in her quiet, dignified manner, telling her that cooking was in her blood, that she'd carry on the Fiorelli tradition and its good name long after they had all passed on.

She put a hand in the pocket of her apron and pulled out a used tissue and a white card. She turned the card over and looked at Gabriele's name engraved on it. She stared at it for a moment, there by the window, overlooking the beach. After a while she put it back. Her hair had grown a little. It was now long enough to tie into a short ponytail. It wasn't that she wanted to grow it, simply that she couldn't be bothered to cut it. She lifted her hands and drew it back into a ribbon. As she did so, she heard the distant motor of a boat. She raised her eyes to the wall, by the door.

There were three sketches in simple wooden frames. The first was of a woman's face. It was gentle, innocent, with a smile full of secrets and an indefinable sadness behind the eyes. The second was a mother and child. The expression of love on the mother's face was naked and unguarded, free of all secrets, save those of a mother's desires for her child. The third was a reclining nude. In this final portrait Valentina was flushed and sensual and wanton, embodying all the vices of earthly pleasure and always as mysterious as the sea. Yet no one but Alba noticed those portraits anymore. They blended with the walls of the trattoria like the hanging onions and garlic, ornamental plates, and religious iconography. Often she walked past them without a sideways glance.

The sound of the motorboat grew louder. It rattled into the silence of the sleepy cove, disturbing the air, sending the birds into the sky. The sense of excitement quivered in the atmosphere like a pebble thrown into a smooth pond, sending ripples far and wide. She walked outside to stand beneath the awning, a wicker basket of apples hanging on her arm. A wave of anticipation began to expand in her heart, slowly at first and then with increasing speed, until she was hurrying across the sand, carried along by the swell of it. The ribbon fell out of her hair, leaving it to fly about her face and shoulders like threads of fine silk. Then she stood breathing heavily so that her breasts rose and fell, accentuated by the low décolletage of her dress. Her face was clear and perfect, like the night sky when one is in the middle of the ocean. She smiled, not the broad, bovine smile of the townsfolk who now emerged from their homes to see who had come, but a gentle curling of the lips that reached her eyes and caused them to narrow slightly. A mere whisper of a smile. So subtle that it made her beauty almost hard to swallow. The boat drew up and a young man descended. His eyes met the strange pale eyes of the woman with the basket. She stood in the crowd yet seemed to have a space of her very own, as if she remained a little apart. Her loveliness was such that her image seemed more pronounced than the rest. It was then that he lost his heart. There on the quay-side of the small fishing town of Incantellaria he let it go willingly. He didn't know then that it was gone forever, that he would never get it back.

Reading Group Guide

Last Voyage of the Valentina

Introduction

Alba Arbuckle always feels like an outsider. She hardly
knew her Italian mother, Valentina, and her English father
acts as if Valentina never existed. Alba despises country
life almost as much as she despises her stepmother and
stepsisters. On board the London houseboat named after
her dead mother, Alba's life is little more than a selfish
search for fun and pleasure.

But the discovery of her mother's portrait sends Alba
back to Italy to find her family – and the truth about
Valentina. Amid the olive groves of the Amalfi coast, she
discovers a tale of deception and betrayal revealing a
secret web of partisans and Nazis, peasants and counts,
and ultimately a forbidden truth. What Alba finds in the
past is heartrending, but it's the gateway to her own
future.

Discussion Questions

1. The book opens with a gruesome murder in the pro-
    logue, and yet the central action of the story is of love
    and self-realization. How does this killing frame your
    reading of the story? When did you realize the identi-
    ties of the killers?

2. Chapter 1 begins with Fitz and Viv watching Alba.
    Later Cook watches Alba rummage through her
    father's desk. Discuss the point of view of the narrator
    in the story and how the author uses various vantage
    points to tell the story. What role does spying play in
    revealing secrets to the reader throughout the story?

3. Lavender Arbuckle says, 'A woman is nothing without
    a man by her side. Nothing without children.' With all
    that Alba has learned, gained, and lost by the end of
    the story, would she agree?

4. Discuss the similarities and differences between
    Lavender Arbuckle and Immacolata. What does each
    one offer Alba? Who do you think is the better
    grandmother?

5. Although Alba 'only attended church to irritate the
    Buffalo in her short skirt and to show off her "boy-
    friend,"' as the service continued Alba 'didn't think
    about sex. She didn't dwell on Fitz's kiss. For once in
    her life, Alba Arbuckle thought about God.' What role
    does religion play in the story? How does attending
    church affect Alba's decision making?

6. The story is divided into three portraits. What is the relation of the segmented form of the story to its content? What do each one of these drawings by Thomas Arbuckle reveal about Valentina? Do they also reveal something about Alba or about women in general?

7. What does Alba see in Fitz that allows her to fall so hard and so fast for him? Unlike her other boyfriends he does not send her flowers after they have a spat, so what does he add to her life that her other boyfriends did not?

8. After Alba cuts her hair Falco asks her, 'Who are you running from, Alba?' Why does Alba make such a drastic change to her appearance? What does this change in her symbolize? Does this change accomplish what she wants it to?

9. Although Alba had never been back to Italy after she left it as a baby, Immacolata says that 'Alba is home' when she is in Incantellaria. At the end of the story Alba's physical home, the *Valentina,* is scuttled. Where do you think home is for Alba?

10. Valentina says that 'War reduces men to animals and turns women into shameful creatures.' To what extent is the war to blame for the tragedy that befell Valentina? To what extent is human nature at fault?

11. Alba begins the story living on the water and ends up living on dry land, yet far away from where she spent most of her life. What do water and land each represent in the story?

12. What were your feelings about Alba's decision to leave Fitz and return to Incantellaria at the end of the story? What does Alba's choice say about the strength of family bonds versus the strength of love? Do you agree with her decision?

A Conversation with Santa Montefiore

When did you begin writing? How did you know you wanted to become a professional writer?

I started writing children's books when I was about ten. Before then I had always written as a hobby and drawn pictures to go with the mini books I made. At school from the age of about fifteen I tried many times to write a proper romantic book, but because I had no experience in love, all the books were rejected. Quite rightly! I always dreamed of being a professional writer, but never in my wildest ones did I really believe it would happen. It wasn't until I was nineteen that I lived in Argentina for a year and found my first big love story. I loved it so much that leaving was heartbreaking. I returned to Argentina a year later to find, to my horror, that I didn't fit in anymore. The young people I had hung out with on this beautiful farm on the pampa had dispersed to study in the United States and other places. I was a tourist where once I had belonged, and I couldn't bring back that magical year however hard I tried. I didn't write the story, which was an allegory of my love affair with Argentina, until I was twenty-five. It came out in 2001, when I was thirty-one.

What sparked the idea for this novel?

This is my fifth novel, so I wanted to do something different. Having done four family sagas based in Argentina and Chile, I decided to move to Italy and write a murder mystery love story with a dramatic twist. The idea came from my aunt who, during London's swinging sixties, lived on a houseboat that had been a motor torpedo boat in the Second World War. I immediately seized upon the idea of having a boat with a tragic history going back to 1945 on the Amalfi coast.

Can you tell us about your inspiration for Alba? Do you see yourself as Viv, the writer in the story? Are your friends' stories inspiration for your writing?

I am not either Alba or Viv. I wanted my heroine to have a spiritual journey – a hedonistic girl who, through her search for her mother and the various heartaches that search involves, finds herself and the true meaning of happiness. My sister is very fiery and complicated, so knowing her was a help! I always have a Viv character in my books. I love writing those cameo rolls of larger-than-life people; they also add humour to my books, which are obviously sad. They give the books balance. I take inspiration from everyone I see! I am a sum of my experience – everything goes into the melting pot out of which I draw ingredients for my characters.

Your writing gives your readers a very beautiful and clear picture of the Italian countryside. Do you have a personal relationship with the Amalfi coast that allowed you to write about it so intimately? Did you visit the coast during the course of your writing?

I studied Italian and Spanish at Exeter University and spent a year in Italy. I spent a lot of time on the Amalfi coast, and once you've been there, it never leaves you!

Last Voyage of the Valentina seems to encompass many genres and could be described as both a murder mystery and a romance. How did you accomplish this so well?

I would never describe myself as a crime writer; the book is about love and the crimes committed in its name are a minor part of it. That said, I had never written about murder so I really had to plan it out very carefully, as when you're revealing truths in the second half of the book, the seeds for those truths have to be sown in the first half and then you have to decide who reveals what and when. Timing is important and how truths are revealed. It was great fun to do, having never written a book in this way before, and an enormous challenge. I hope the mystery aspect gives the book more depth and keeps you turning those pages!

Do you think it's fair to say that there is an old-fashioned sensibility to your writing?

Definitely. I am an old-fashioned kind of girl! I'm incredibly nostalgic for the past – my own past and history. Love over the photocopier doesn't do it for me! I like a great big canvas of both past and present and characters whose lives I can draw in their entirety. I love beautiful places you can smell, heartbreaking love stories, and cuddly eccentric characters that stay with you after you've finished reading the book. I write the sort of books I love to read and I know my limitations and what I'm good at.

There is a strong element of religious superstition in your novel, as tragedy befalls Valentina after the statue does not bleed. What research did you do in writing of the religious implications of this?

I didn't have to do any research because I studied Italian literature at university; also, having lived in Argentina, which is mostly made up of Italians, and Italy, superstition is all around you. I'm also a great fan of Gabriel García Márquez and Isabel Allende. I have seen spirits since I was small and have a strong, unwavering belief in spirit life after death.

Who are your favorite writers?

I adore Fanny Flagg – *Fried Green Tomatoes* is one of my

all-time favorites – Gabriel García Márquez's *Love in the Time of Cholera*, and Isabel Allende's *The House of the Spirits*. I've just read *Shadow of the Wind* by Carlos Ruiz Zafón, which I adored; and all Mary Wesley's books are touching and funny. I'm rereading *Corelli's Mandolin* because I admire the way Louis de Bernières writes. Anita Shreve is good, and of course Jodi Picoult is amazing. I cry and cry in her books, but she writes with such a light touch there's no heaviness there, just beauty. Nicholas Sparks is a good storyteller. Robert James Waller's *The Bridges of Madison County* was so powerful – that story has never left me. I love to read the classics: *Anna Karenina* by Tolstoy and *The Count of Monte Cristo* by Dumas are two of the best books I have ever read.

What is the best piece of advice about writing you have ever received? And what advice would you give to a young writer starting out?

Write about what you know. Don't think about how other people will judge you – just write from the heart without inhibition. Be brave and extravagant with your writing. You have to find your voice, and however well you write, your voice will always be unique. Write sensually – think smell and sound to evoke a sense of place – and remember when drawing characters that we don't love people for their perfections but for their imperfections that make them different from everyone else in the world. Never give up: it will happen. However many rejections you receive, remember, you only need one agent and one publisher. Starting a book is the most difficult part; once you've invented your world, don't leave it until the book is finished. Oh and one more piece of advice my husband told me: don't get it right, get it written – that is, wait until you've finished it before you start to polish it or you'll never leave chapter 1.

CBS drama

Whether you love the glamour of Dallas, the feisty exploits of Bad Girls, the courtroom drama of Boston Legal or the forensic challenges of the world's most watched drama CSI: Crime Scene Investigation, CBS Drama is bursting with colourful characters, compelling cliff-hangers, love stories, break-ups and happy endings.

Autumn's line-up includes Patricia Arquette in supernatural series Medium, big hair and bitch fights in Dallas and new Happy Hour strand daily from 6pm with a doublemeasure from everyone's favourite Boston bar Cheers.

Also at CBS Drama you're just one 'like' closer to your on screen heroes. Regular exclusive celebrity interviews and behind the scenes news is hosted on Facebook and Twitter page. Recent contributors include Dallas' Bobby Ewing (Patrick Duffy), CSI's Catherine Willows (Marg Helgenberger) and Cheers' Sam Malone (Ted Danson).

www.cbsdrama.co.uk

f facebook.com/cbsdrama

🐦 twitter.com/cbsdrama